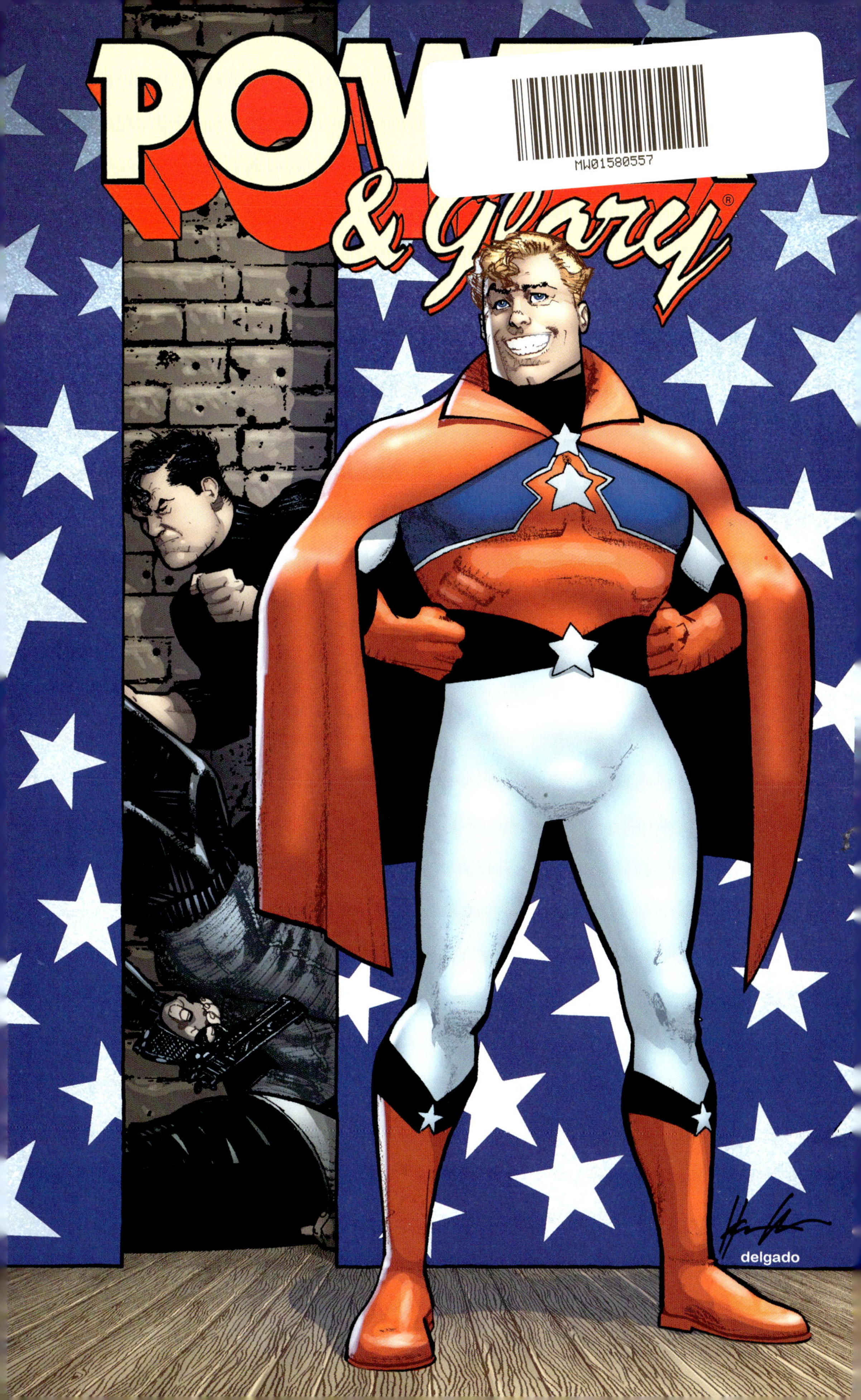
POW
& Glory
delgado

Written and Illustrated by
HOWARD CHAYKIN

Lettering
KEN BRUZENAK

Interior Coloring
RICHARD ORY
(issue #1)
'BU TONES with
LYDIA NOMURA
(issues #2-4 and Holiday Special)

Original Series Editors (Bravura)
DAN DANKO,
LARRY REYNOSA
& KARA LAMB

Digital Remastering
JERRON QUALITY COLOR
& DIGIKORE STUDIOS

Cover Colors by
EDGAR DELGADO

Characters Co-Created by
HOWARD CHAYKIN
& MIKE VOSBURG

Special Thanks to
THOMAS KINTNER

Representation
LAW OFFICES OF
HARRIS M. MILLER II, P.C.

WWW.DYNAMITEENTERTAINMENT.COM

NICK BARRUCCI • PRESIDENT
JUAN COLLADO • CHIEF OPERATING OFFICER
JOSEPH RYBANDT • EDITOR
JOSH JOHNSON • CREATIVE DIRECTOR
JASON ULLMEYER • GRAPHIC DESIGNER

First Printing   ISBN-10: 1-93330-506-1   ISBN-13: 978-1-93330-506-6

POWER AND GLORY. Published by Dynamite Entertainment, 155 Ninth Avenue, Suite B, Runnemede, NJ 08078. © 2008 Howard Chaykin, Inc. All rights reserved. Some contents originally published in Power & Glory #1-4 and Power & Glory Holiday Special. Power & Glory is a registered trademark of Howard Chaykin, Inc., and the Power & Glory logo and all characters and content herein and the likenesses thereof are also trademarks of Howard Chaykin, Inc., unless otherwise expressly noted. DYNAMITE, DYNAMITE ENTERTAINMENT, and the Dynamite Entertainment logo are ® and © 2009 DFI. No part of this publication may be reproduced or transmitted in any form or by any means (except for short excerpts for review purposes) without the express written permission of Howard Chaykin, Inc. or Dynamic Forces, Inc. All names, characters, events, and locales in this publication are entirely fictional. Any resemblance to actual persons (living or dead), events or places, without satiric intent, is coincidental. Printed in Canada.

For information regarding press, media rights, foreign rights, licensing, promotions, and advertising e-mail: marketing@dynamiteentertainment.com

10 9 8 7 6 5 4 3 2 1

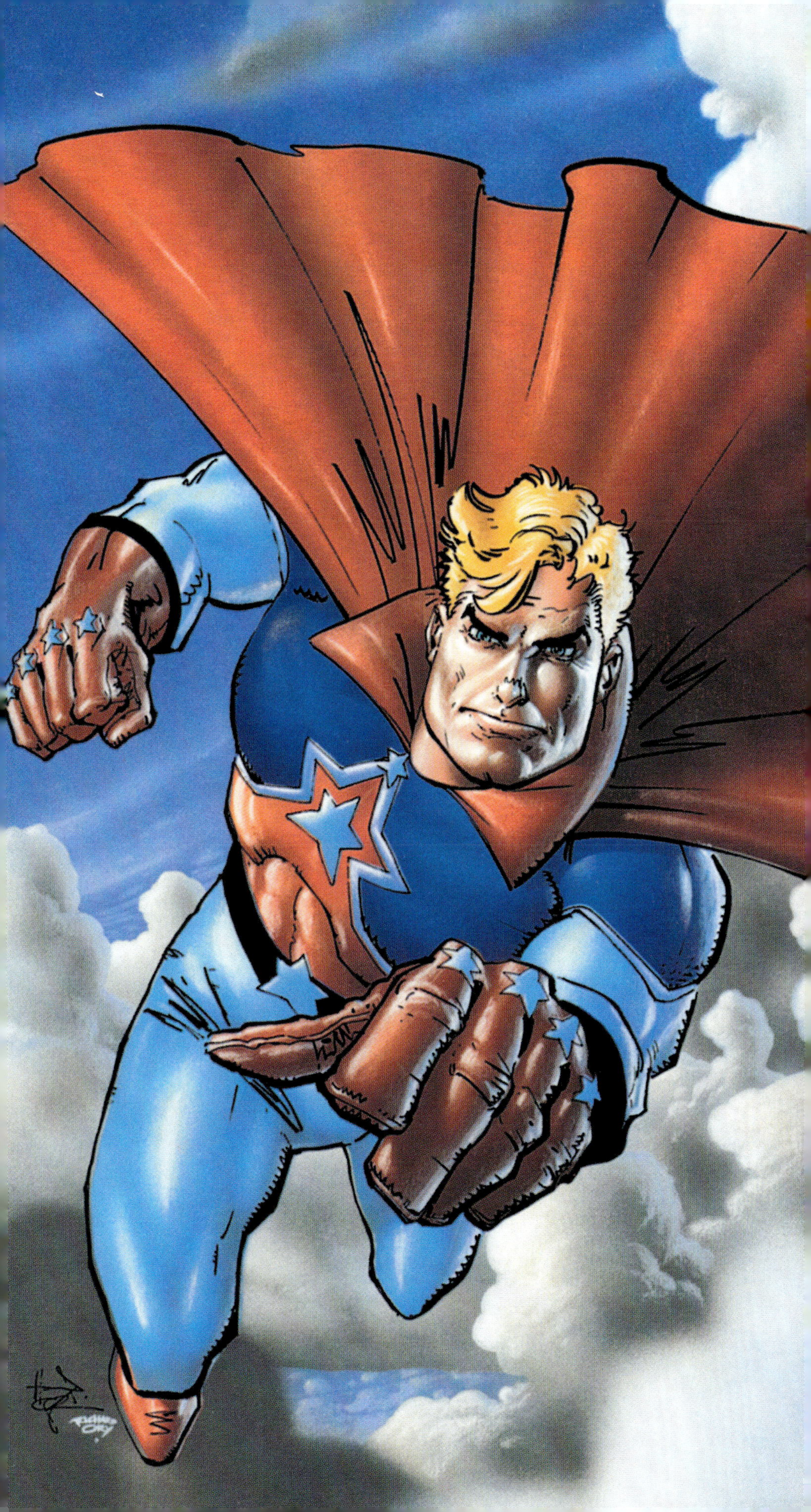

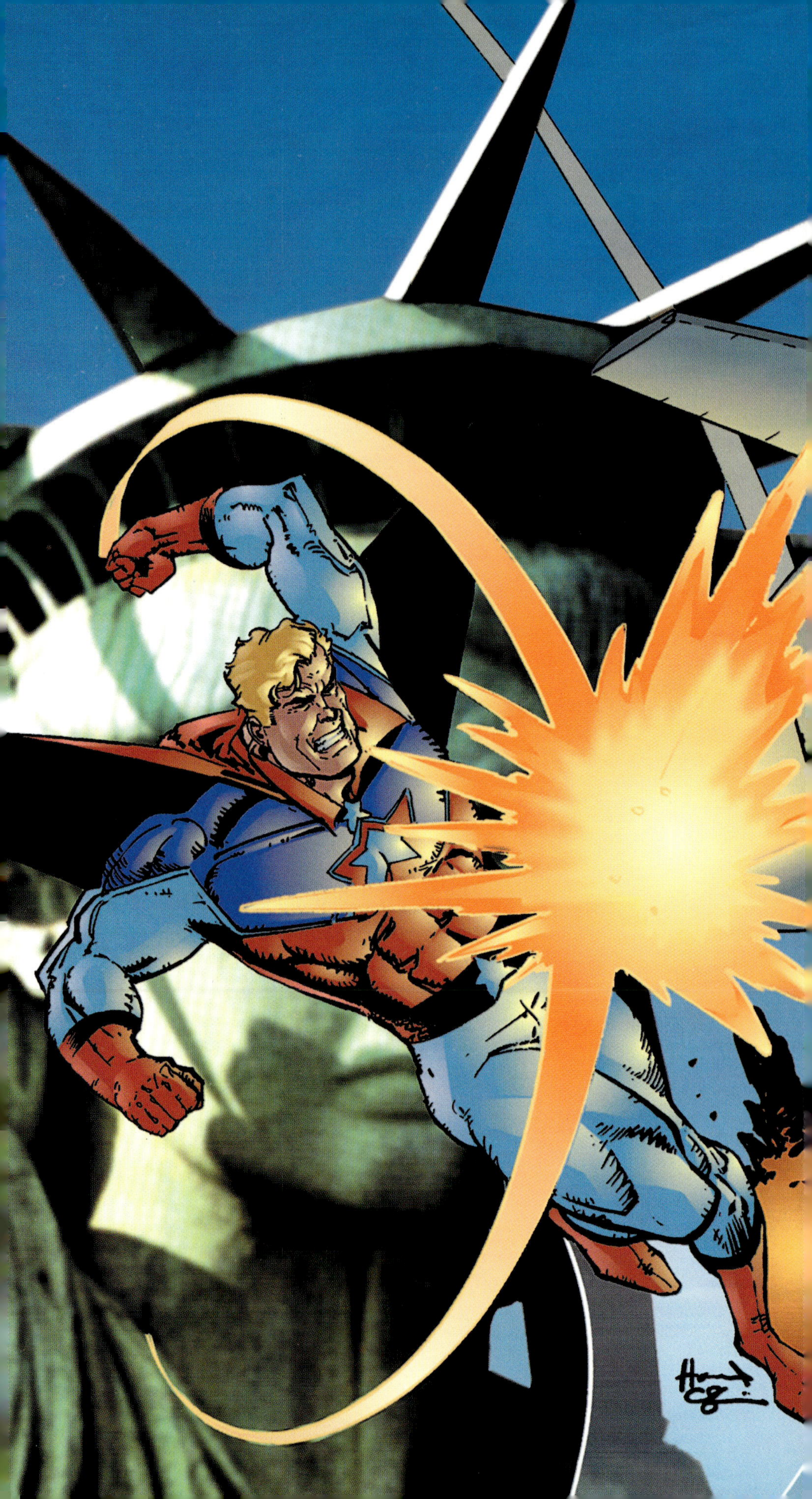

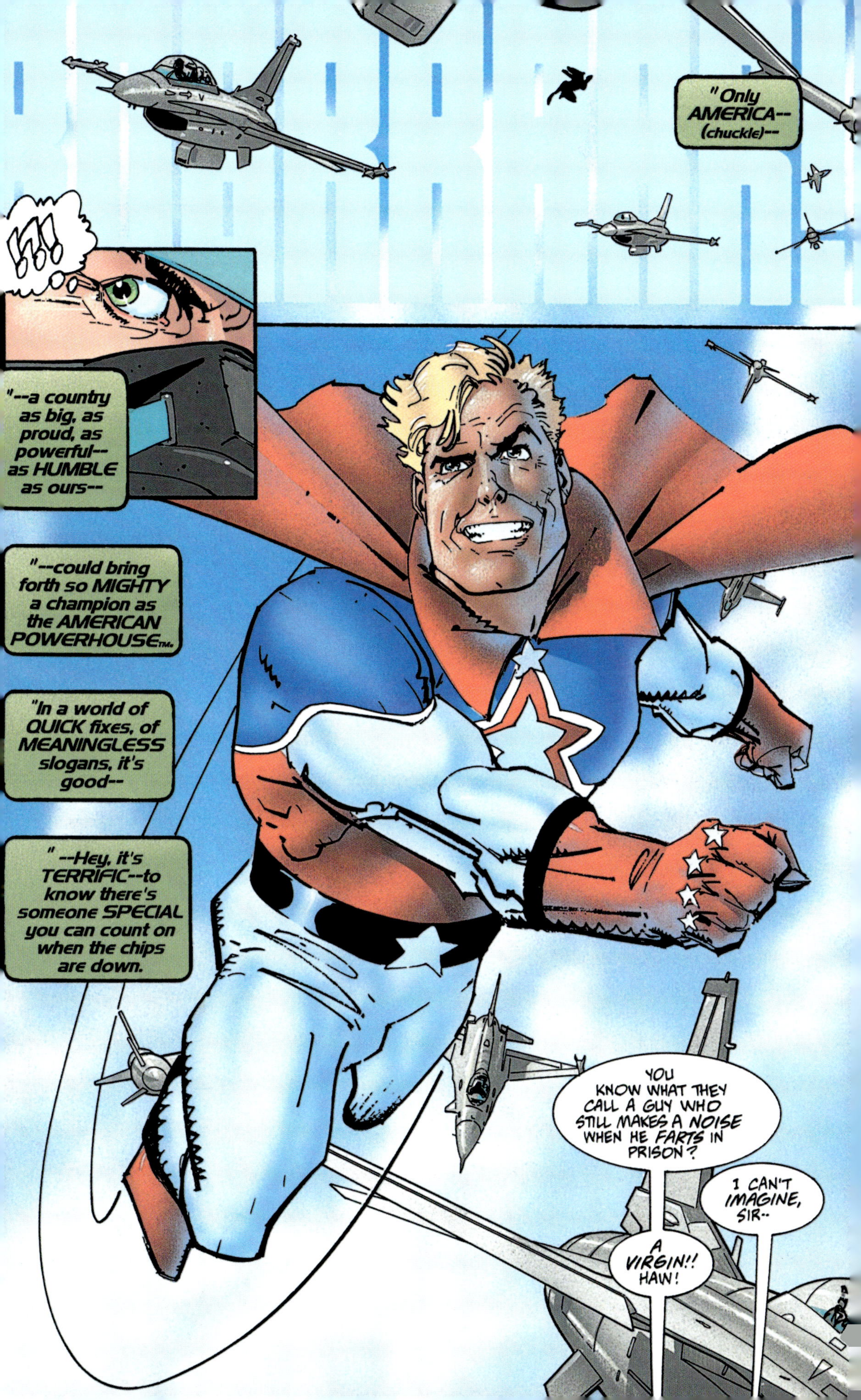
"Only AMERICA-- (chuckle)--
!?!
"--a country as big, as proud, as powerful-- as HUMBLE as ours--
"--could bring forth so MIGHTY a champion as the AMERICAN POWERHOUSE™.
"In a world of QUICK fixes, of MEANINGLESS slogans, it's good--
" --Hey, it's TERRIFIC--to know there's someone SPECIAL you can count on when the chips are down.
YOU KNOW WHAT THEY CALL A GUY WHO STILL MAKES A NOISE WHEN HE FARTS IN PRISON?
I CAN'T IMAGINE, SIR--
A VIRGIN!! HAW!

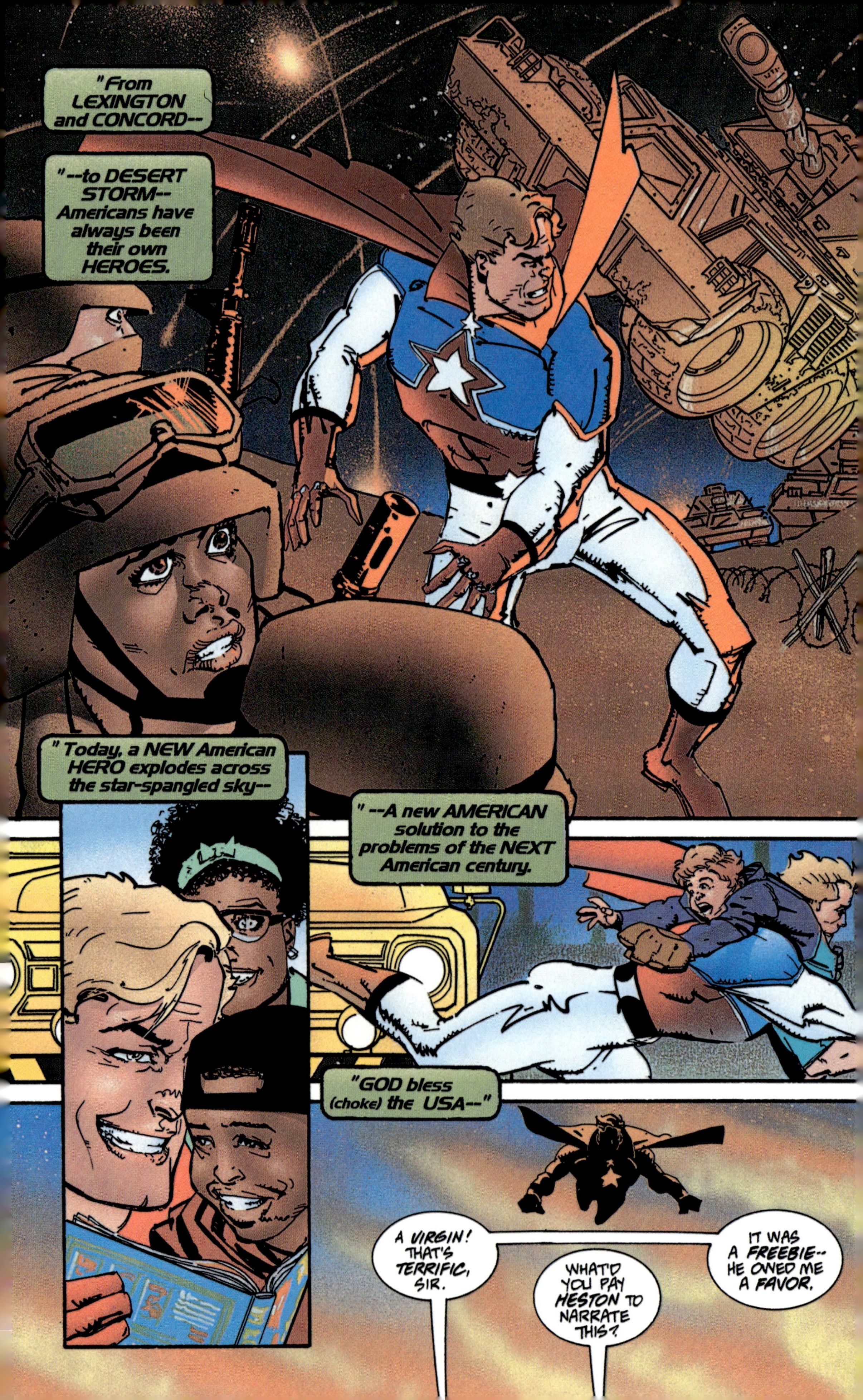
"From LEXINGTON and CONCORD--
"--to DESERT STORM-- Americans have always been their own HEROES.
"Today, a NEW American HERO explodes across the star-spangled sky--
"--A new AMERICAN solution to the problems of the NEXT American century.
"GOD bless (choke) the USA--"
A VIRGIN! THAT'S TERRIFIC, SIR.
WHAT'D YOU PAY HESTON TO NARRATE THIS?
IT WAS A FREEBIE-- HE OWED ME A FAVOR.

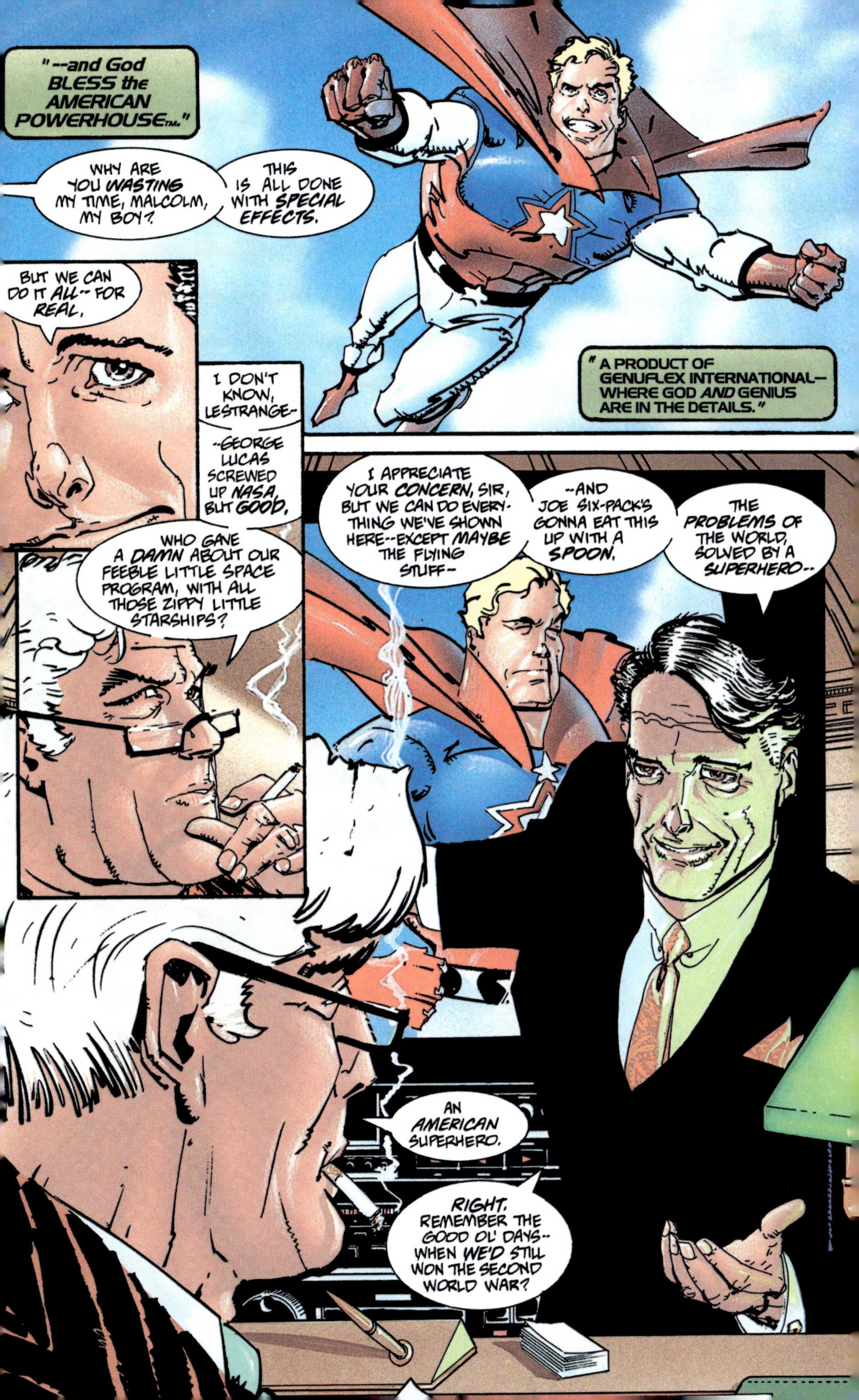
"--and God BLESS the AMERICAN POWERHOUSE™."
WHY ARE YOU WASTING MY TIME, MALCOLM, MY BOY?
THIS IS ALL DONE WITH SPECIAL EFFECTS.
BUT WE CAN DO IT ALL-- FOR REAL.
"A PRODUCT OF GENUFLEX INTERNATIONAL— WHERE GOD AND GENIUS ARE IN THE DETAILS."
I DON'T KNOW, LESTRANGE-
--GEORGE LUCAS SCREWED UP NASA, BUT GOOD.
WHO GAVE A DAMN ABOUT OUR FEEBLE LITTLE SPACE PROGRAM, WITH ALL THOSE ZIPPY LITTLE STARSHIPS?
I APPRECIATE YOUR CONCERN, SIR, BUT WE CAN DO EVERY-THING WE'VE SHOWN HERE--EXCEPT MAYBE THE FLYING STUFF--
--AND JOE SIX-PACK'S GONNA EAT THIS UP WITH A SPOON.
THE PROBLEMS OF THE WORLD, SOLVED BY A SUPERHERO--
AN AMERICAN SUPERHERO.
RIGHT. REMEMBER THE GOOD OL' DAYS-- WHEN WE'D STILL WON THE SECOND WORLD WAR?

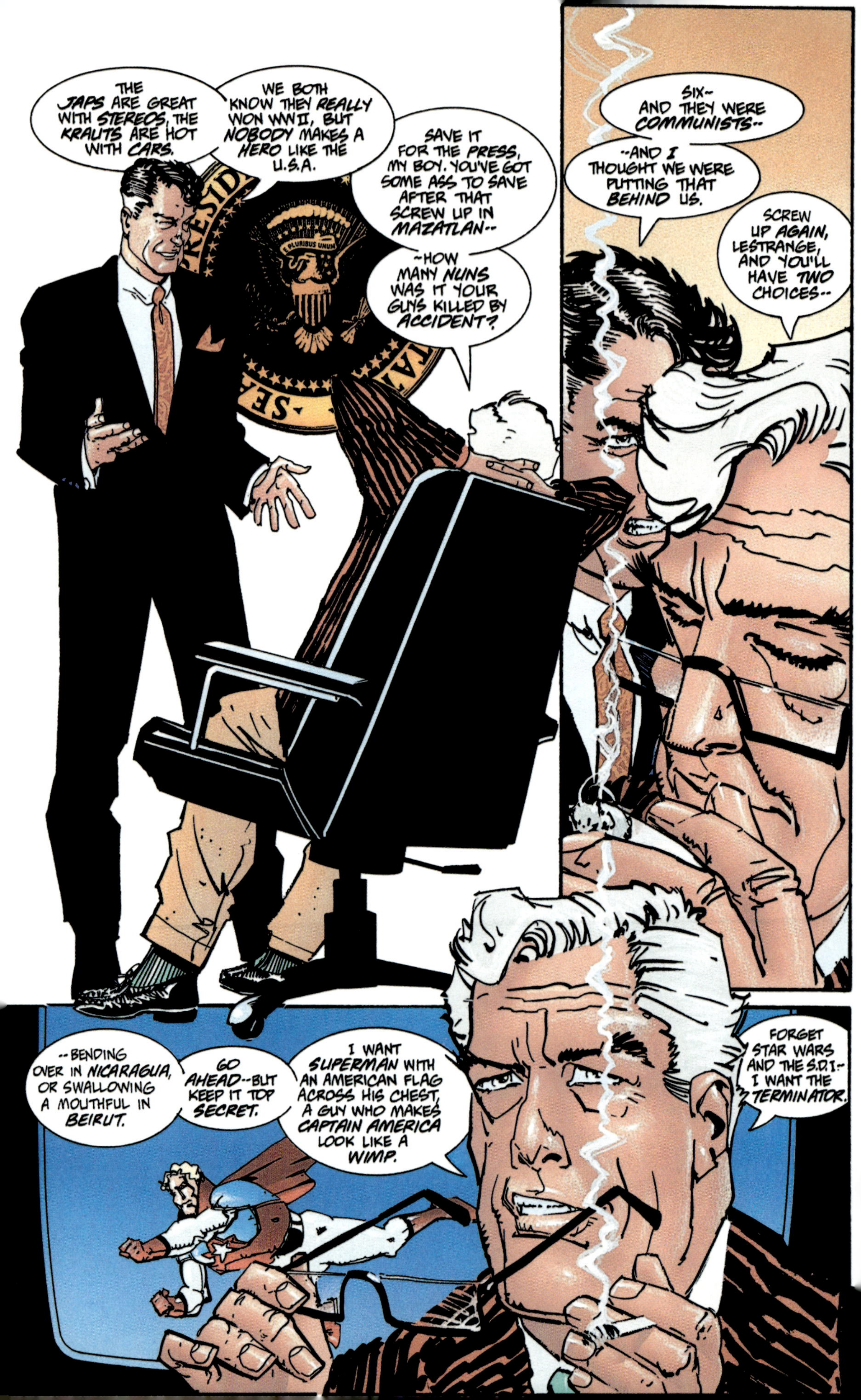

THE JAPS ARE GREAT WITH STEREOS, THE KRAUTS ARE HOT WITH CARS.
WE BOTH KNOW THEY REALLY WON WWII, BUT NOBODY MAKES A HERO LIKE THE U.S.A.
SAVE IT FOR THE PRESS, MY BOY. YOU'VE GOT SOME ASS TO SAVE AFTER THAT SCREW UP IN MAZATLAN--
--HOW MANY NUNS WAS IT YOUR GUYS KILLED BY ACCIDENT?
SIX--AND THEY WERE COMMUNISTS--
--AND I THOUGHT WE WERE PUTTING THAT BEHIND US.
SCREW UP AGAIN, LESTRANGE, AND YOU'LL HAVE TWO CHOICES--
--BENDING OVER IN NICARAGUA, OR SWALLOWING A MOUTHFUL IN BEIRUT.
GO AHEAD--BUT KEEP IT TOP SECRET.
I WANT SUPERMAN WITH AN AMERICAN FLAG ACROSS HIS CHEST, A GUY WHO MAKES CAPTAIN AMERICA LOOK LIKE A WIMP.
FORGET STAR WARS AND THE S.D.I.- I WANT THE TERMINATOR.

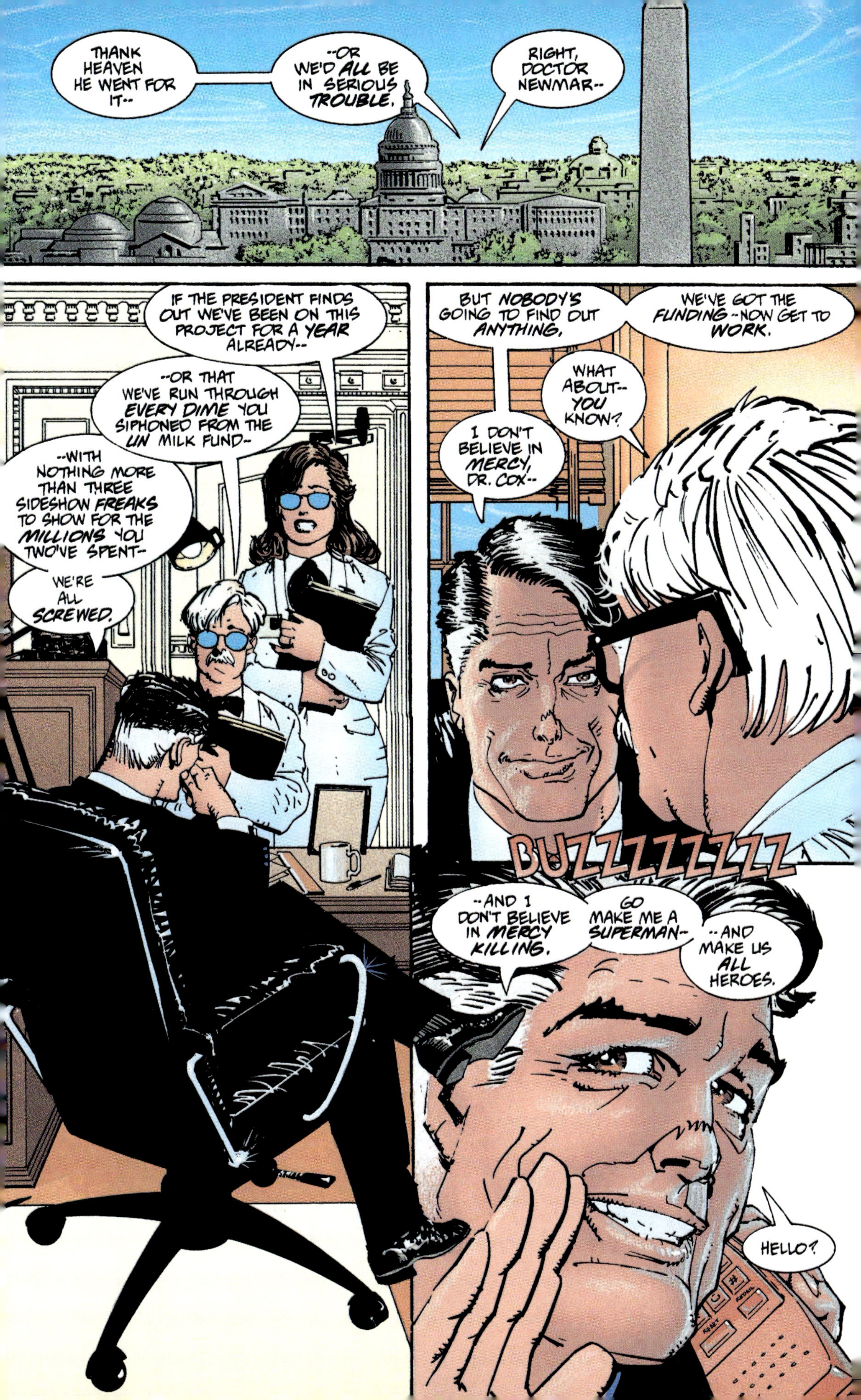
THANK HEAVEN HE WENT FOR IT--
--OR WE'D ALL BE IN SERIOUS TROUBLE.
RIGHT, DOCTOR NEWMAR--
IF THE PRESIDENT FINDS OUT WE'VE BEEN ON THIS PROJECT FOR A YEAR ALREADY--
--OR THAT WE'VE RUN THROUGH EVERY DIME YOU SIPHONED FROM THE UN MILK FUND--
--WITH NOTHING MORE THAN THREE SIDESHOW FREAKS TO SHOW FOR THE MILLIONS YOU TWO'VE SPENT--
WE'RE ALL SCREWED.
BUT NOBODY'S GOING TO FIND OUT ANYTHING.
WE'VE GOT THE FUNDING--NOW GET TO WORK.
WHAT ABOUT-- YOU KNOW?
I DON'T BELIEVE IN MERCY, DR. COX--
BUZZZZZZZZZ
--AND I DON'T BELIEVE IN MERCY KILLING.
GO MAKE ME A SUPERMAN--
--AND MAKE US ALL HEROES.
HELLO?

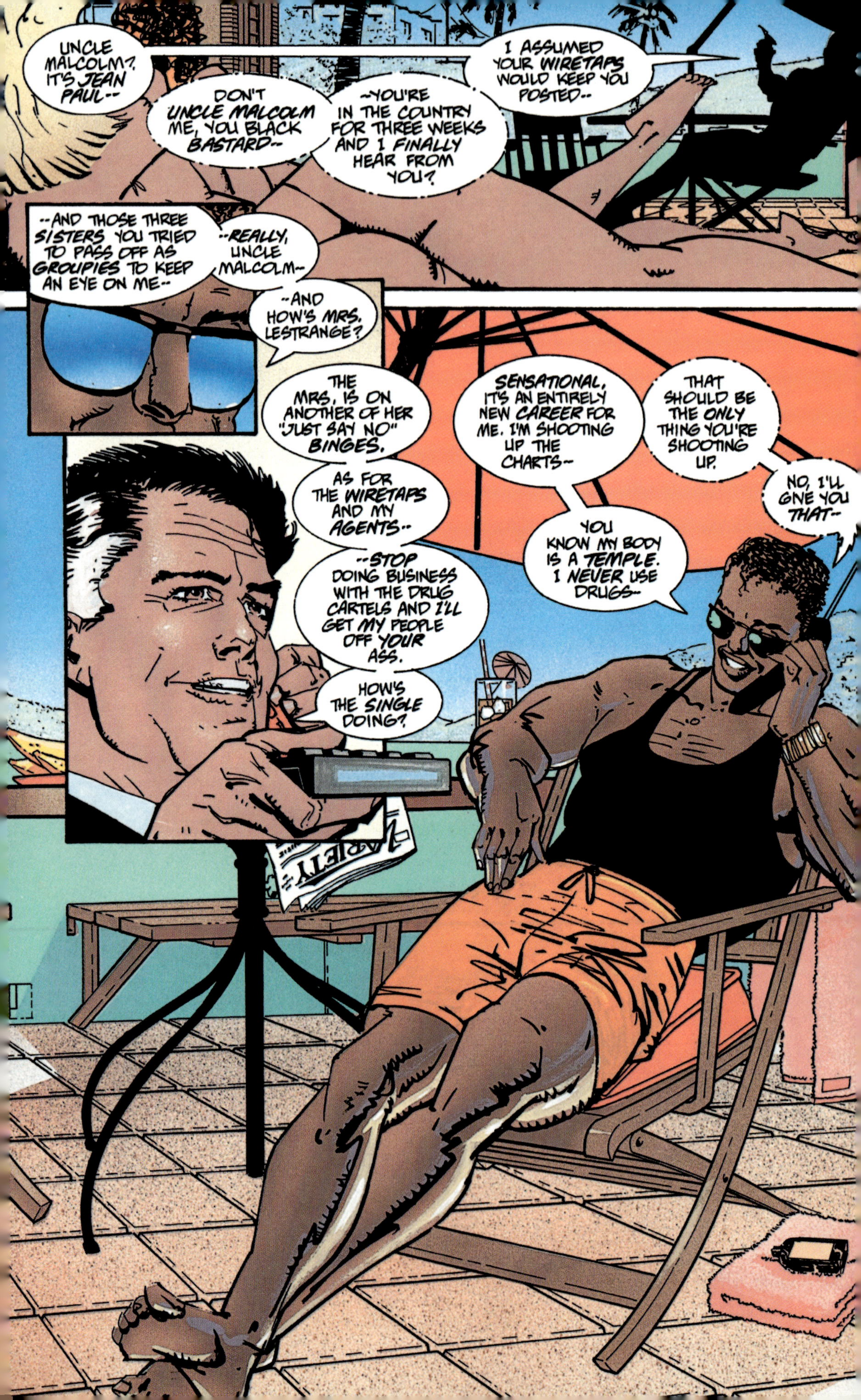
UNCLE MALCOLM? IT'S JEAN PAUL--
DON'T UNCLE MALCOLM ME, YOU BLACK BASTARD--
--YOU'RE IN THE COUNTRY FOR THREE WEEKS AND I FINALLY HEAR FROM YOU?
I ASSUMED YOUR WIRETAPS WOULD KEEP YOU POSTED--
--AND THOSE THREE SISTERS YOU TRIED TO PASS OFF AS GROUPIES TO KEEP AN EYE ON ME--
--REALLY, UNCLE MALCOLM--
--AND HOW'S MRS. LESTRANGE?
THE MRS. IS ON ANOTHER OF HER "JUST SAY NO" BINGES.
AS FOR THE WIRETAPS AND MY AGENTS--
--STOP DOING BUSINESS WITH THE DRUG CARTELS AND I'LL GET MY PEOPLE OFF YOUR ASS.
HOW'S THE SINGLE DOING?
SENSATIONAL, IT'S AN ENTIRELY NEW CAREER FOR ME. I'M SHOOTING UP THE CHARTS--
THAT SHOULD BE THE ONLY THING YOU'RE SHOOTING UP.
YOU KNOW MY BODY IS A TEMPLE. I NEVER USE DRUGS--
NO, I'LL GIVE YOU THAT--
VARIETY

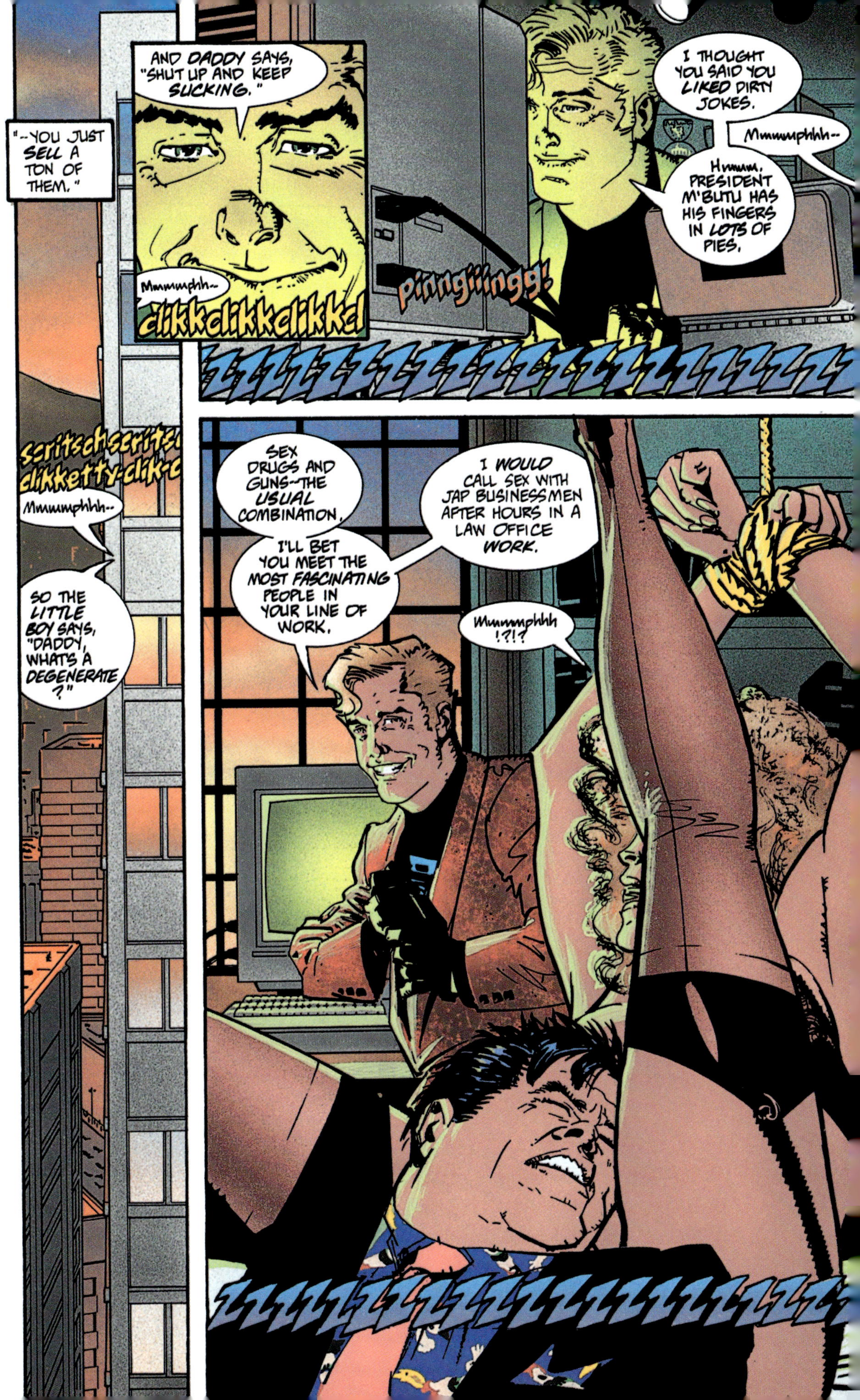

"--YOU JUST SELL A TON OF THEM."
AND DADDY SAYS, "SHUT UP AND KEEP SUCKING."
Mmmmphh--
clikkclikkclikk!
I THOUGHT YOU SAID YOU LIKED DIRTY JOKES.
Mmmmphhh--
Hmmm. PRESIDENT M'BUTU HAS HIS FINGERS IN LOTS OF PIES.
Piiingiiingg!
ZZZZZZZZZZZZZZZZZZZZZZZZZ
scritschscritsc
clikketty-clik-c
Mmmmphhh--
SO THE LITTLE BOY SAYS, "DADDY, WHAT'S A DEGENERATE?"
SEX DRUGS AND GUNS--THE USUAL COMBINATION.
I'LL BET YOU MEET THE MOST FASCINATING PEOPLE IN YOUR LINE OF WORK.
I WOULD CALL SEX WITH JAP BUSINESSMEN AFTER HOURS IN A LAW OFFICE WORK.
Mmmmphhh !?!?
ZZZZZZZZZZZZZZZZZZZZZZZZZ

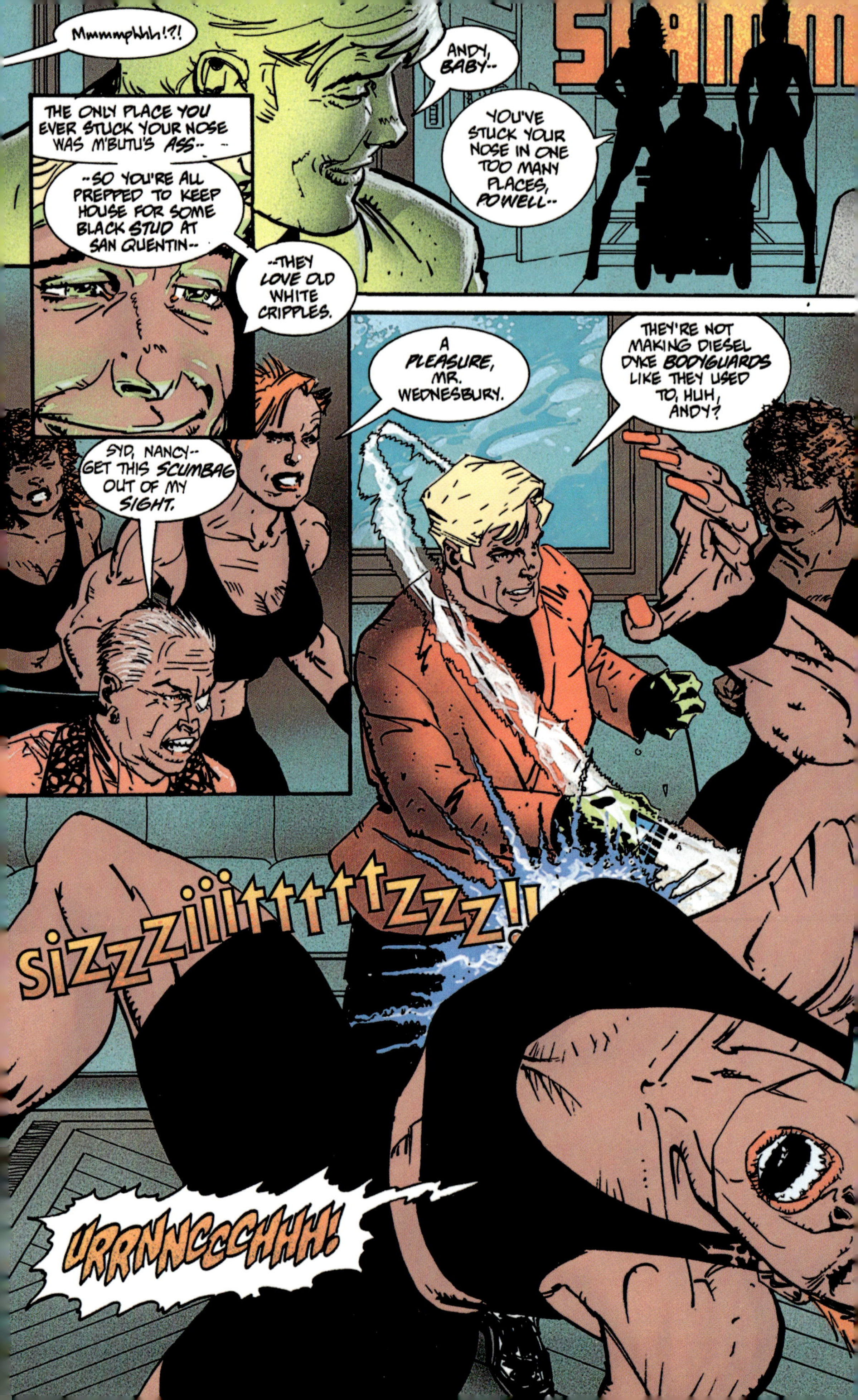
Mmmmphhh!?!
ANDY, BABY--
YOU'VE STUCK YOUR NOSE IN ONE TOO MANY PLACES, POWELL--
THE ONLY PLACE YOU EVER STUCK YOUR NOSE WAS M'BUTU'S ASS--
--SO YOU'RE ALL PREPPED TO KEEP HOUSE FOR SOME BLACK STUD AT SAN QUENTIN--
--THEY LOVE OLD WHITE CRIPPLES.
SYD, NANCY-- GET THIS SCUMBAG OUT OF MY SIGHT.
A PLEASURE, MR. WEDNESBURY.
THEY'RE NOT MAKING DIESEL DYKE BODYGUARDS LIKE THEY USED TO, HUH, ANDY?
SIZZZIIIITTTTTTZZZ!!
URRNNCCCHHH!

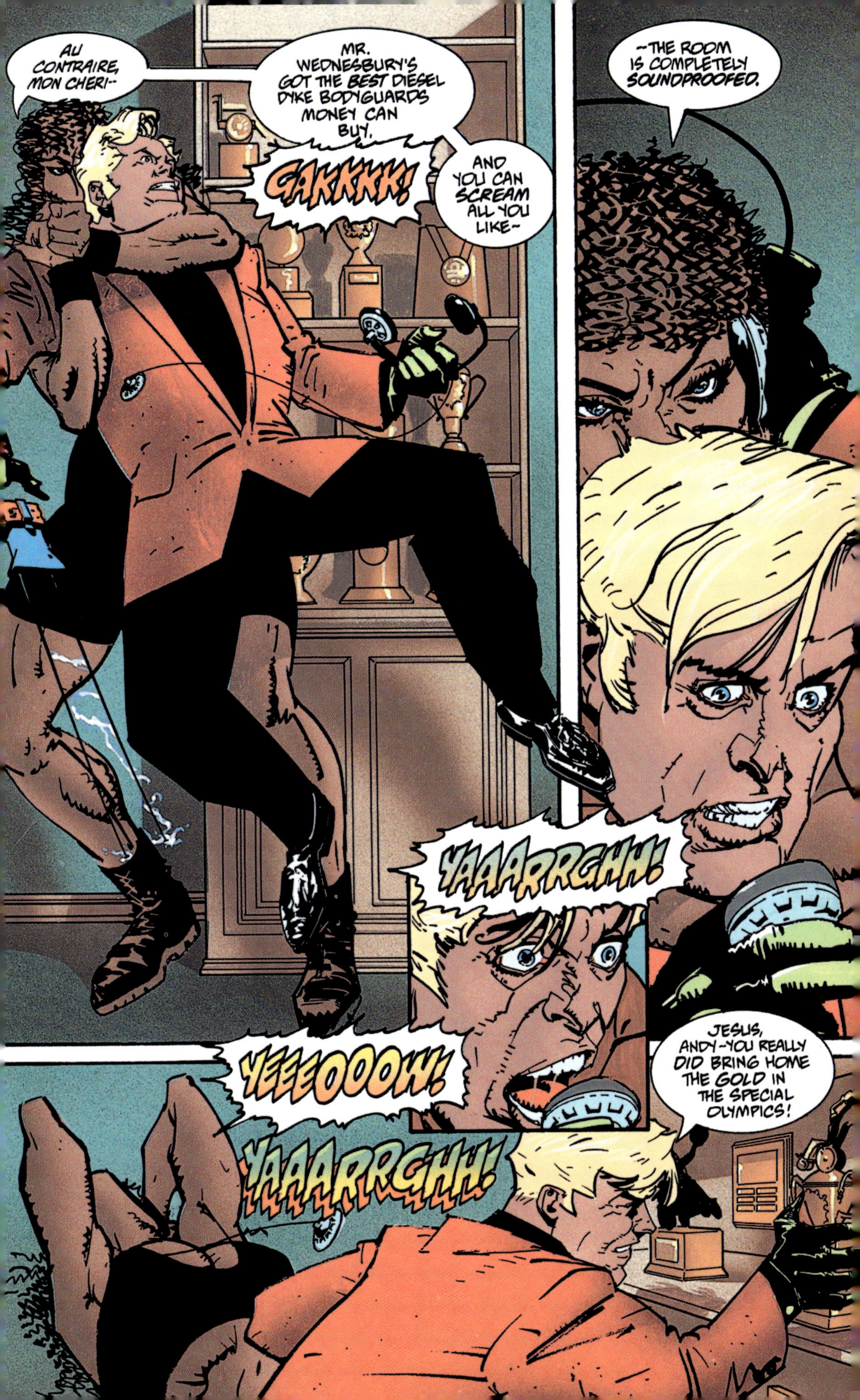
AU CONTRAIRE, MON CHERI--
MR. WEDNESBURY'S GOT THE BEST DIESEL DYKE BODYGUARDS MONEY CAN BUY.
GAKKKK!
AND YOU CAN SCREAM ALL YOU LIKE--
--THE ROOM IS COMPLETELY SOUNDPROOFED.
YAAARRGHH!
YEEEOOOW!
YAAARRGHH!
JESUS, ANDY--YOU REALLY DID BRING HOME THE GOLD IN THE SPECIAL OLYMPICS!

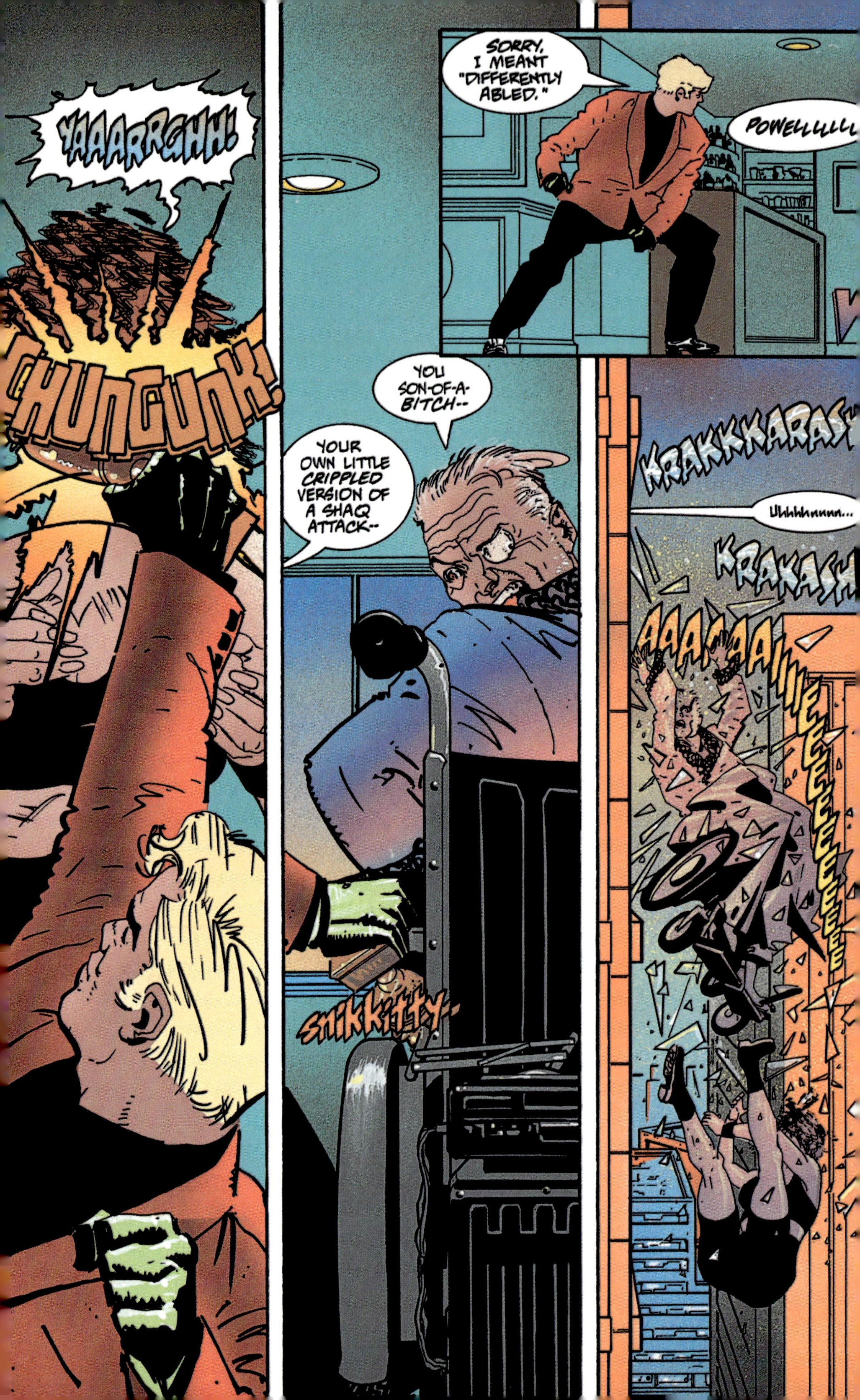
YAAARRGHH!
CHUNGUNK!
SORRY, I MEANT "DIFFERENTLY ABLED."
POWELLLLLLL
YOU SON-OF-A-BITCH--
YOUR OWN LITTLE CRIPPLED VERSION OF A SHAQ ATTACK--
SNIKKITTY-
KRAKKKARASH
Uhhhhnnnn...
KRAKASH
AAAAAAIIIEEEEEEEE

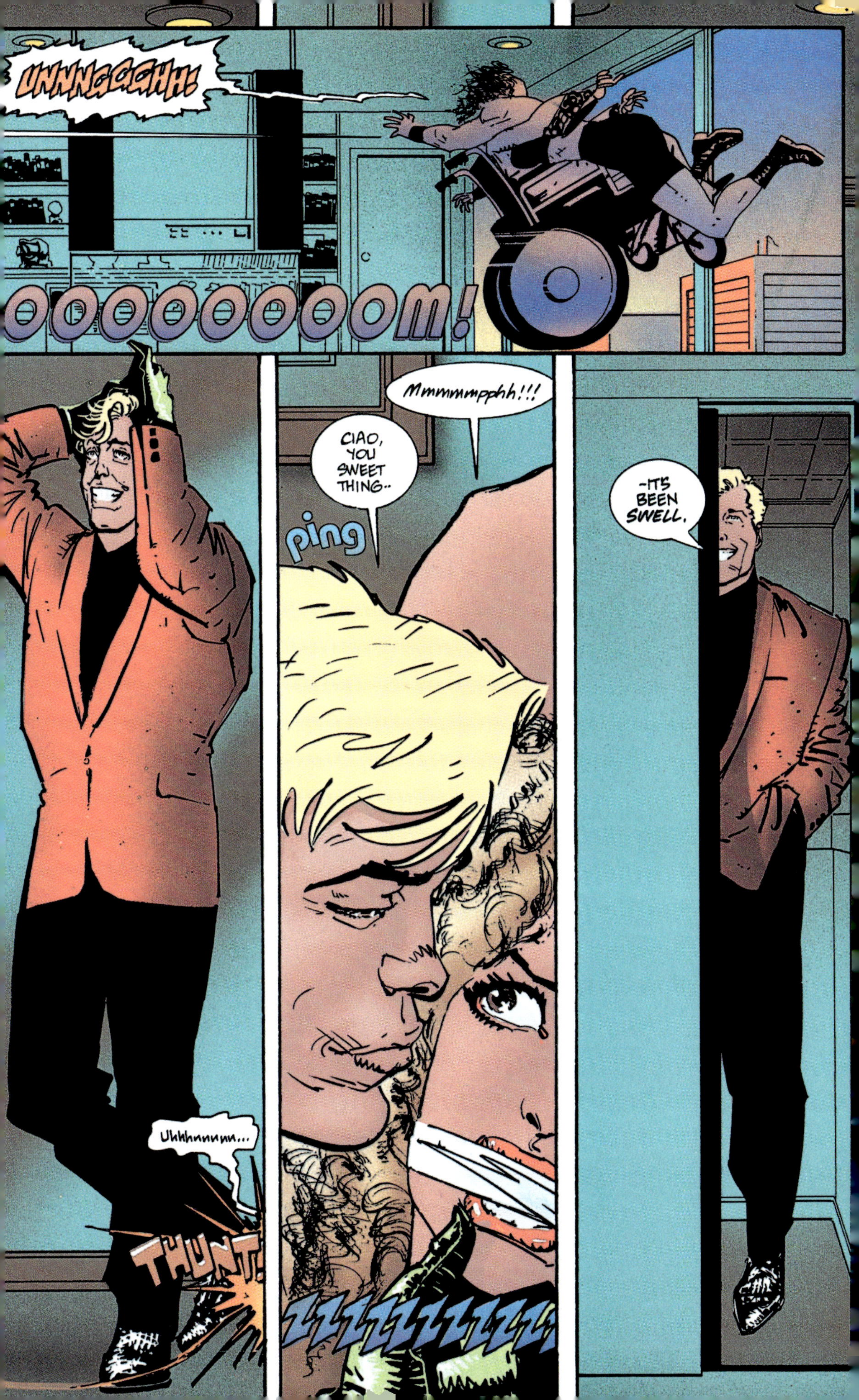
UNNNGGGHH!
OOOOOOOOOM!
Uhhhnnnnn...
THUNT!
CIAO, YOU SWEET THING..
ping
Mmmmmmpphh!!!
ZZZZZZZZZZ
-IT'S BEEN SWELL.

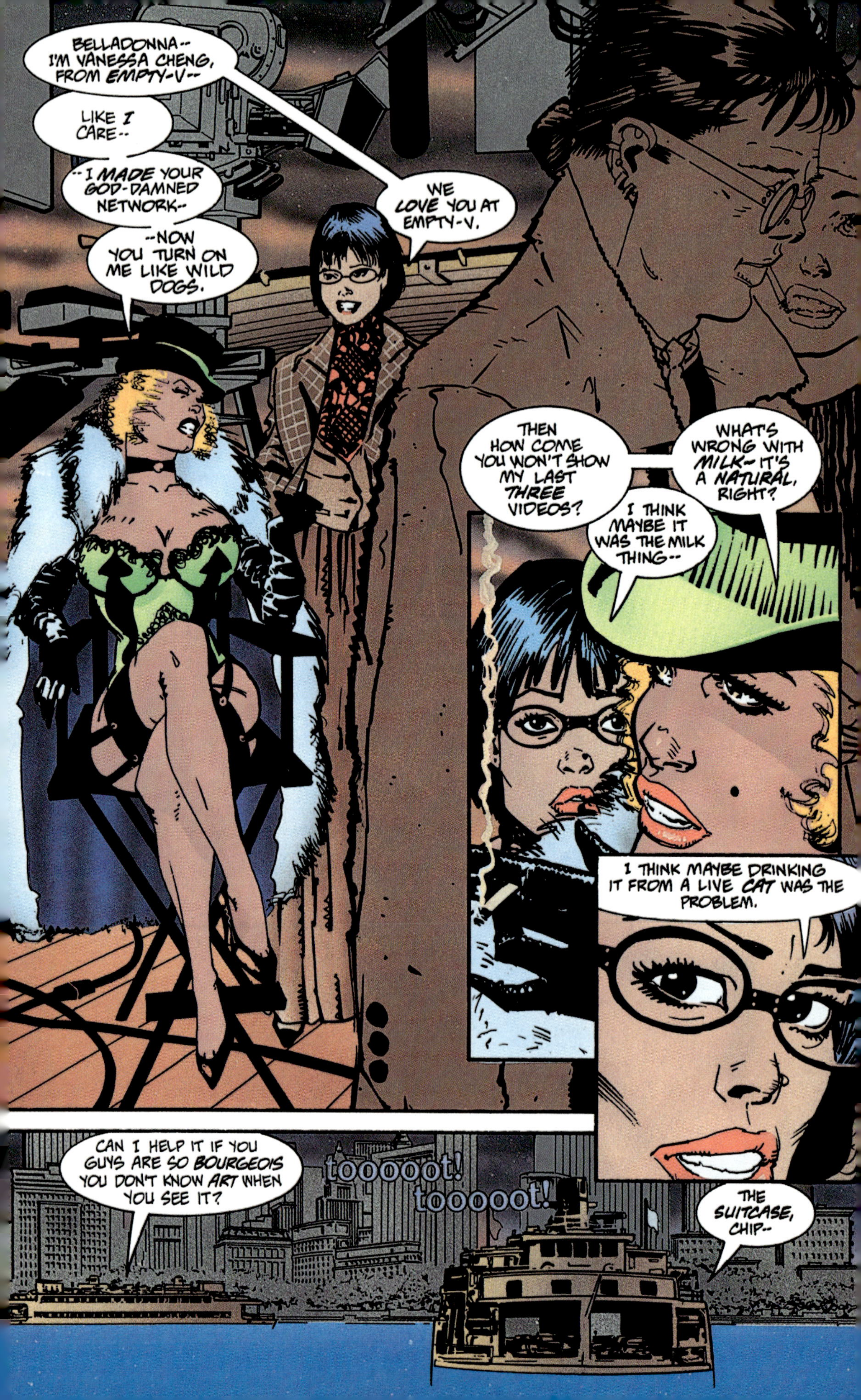
BELLADONNA-- I'M VANESSA CHENG, FROM EMPTY-V--
LIKE I CARE--
--I MADE YOUR GOD-DAMNED NETWORK--
--NOW YOU TURN ON ME LIKE WILD DOGS.
WE LOVE YOU AT EMPTY-V.
THEN HOW COME YOU WON'T SHOW MY LAST THREE VIDEOS?
I THINK MAYBE IT WAS THE MILK THING--
WHAT'S WRONG WITH MILK-- IT'S A NATURAL, RIGHT?
I THINK MAYBE DRINKING IT FROM A LIVE CAT WAS THE PROBLEM.
CAN I HELP IT IF YOU GUYS ARE SO BOURGEOIS YOU DON'T KNOW ART WHEN YOU SEE IT?
toooooot!
toooooot!
THE SUITCASE, CHIP--

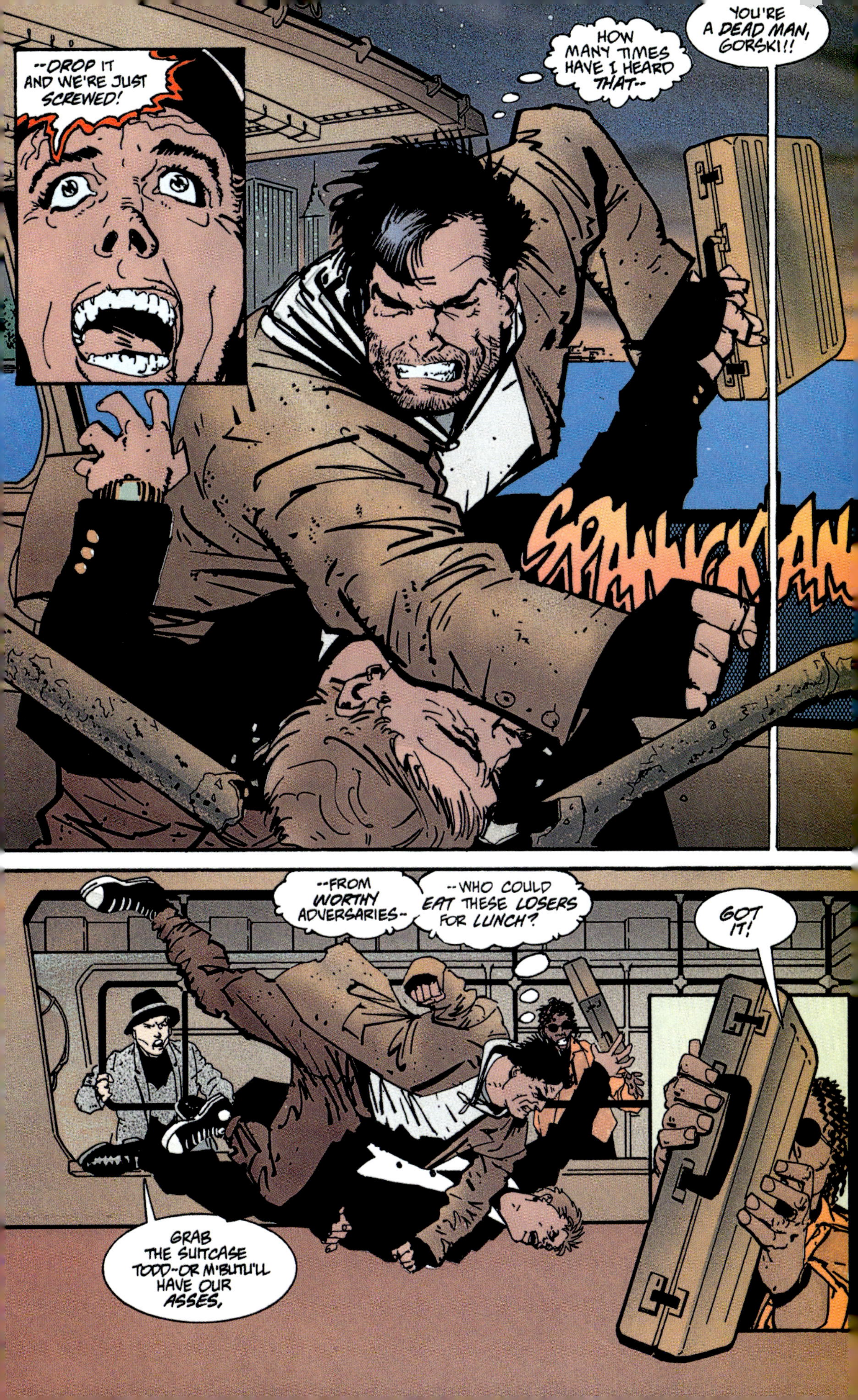
--DROP IT AND WE'RE JUST SCREWED!
HOW MANY TIMES HAVE I HEARD THAT--
YOU'RE A DEAD MAN, GORSKI!!
SPANKKAN
--FROM WORTHY ADVERSARIES--
--WHO COULD EAT THESE LOSERS FOR LUNCH?
GOT IT!
GRAB THE SUITCASE TODD--OR M'BUTU'LL HAVE OUR ASSES.

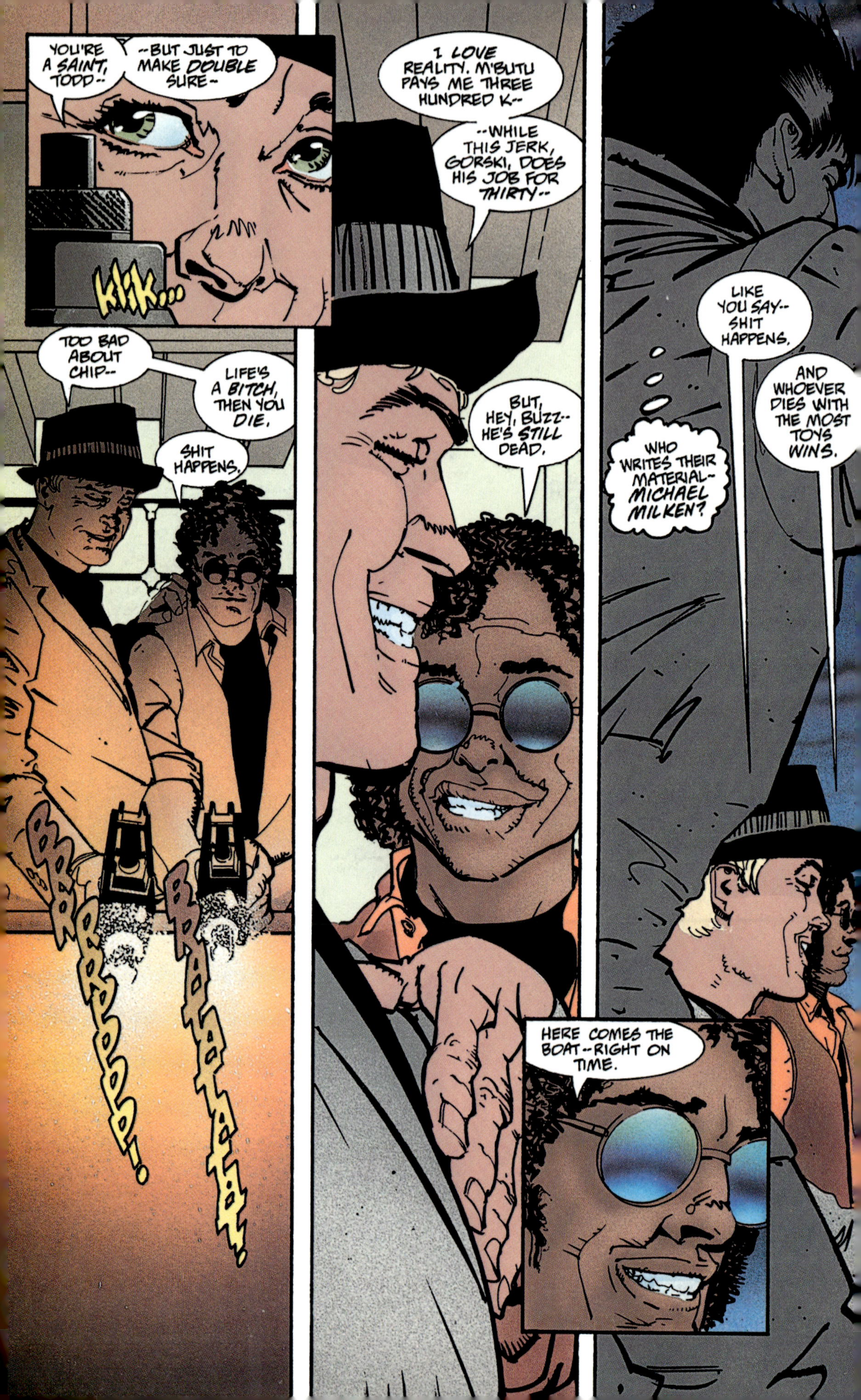

YOU'RE A SAINT, TODD--
--BUT JUST TO MAKE DOUBLE SURE--
KLIK...
TOO BAD ABOUT CHIP--
LIFE'S A BITCH, THEN YOU DIE.
SHIT HAPPENS.
BRRRRRDDD!
BRRRATATAT!
I LOVE REALITY. M'BUTU PAYS ME THREE HUNDRED K--
--WHILE THIS JERK, GORSKI, DOES HIS JOB FOR THIRTY--
BUT, HEY, BUZZ-- HE'S STILL DEAD.
LIKE YOU SAY-- SHIT HAPPENS.
AND WHOEVER DIES WITH THE MOST TOYS WINS.
WHO WRITES THEIR MATERIAL-- MICHAEL MILKEN?
HERE COMES THE BOAT--RIGHT ON TIME.

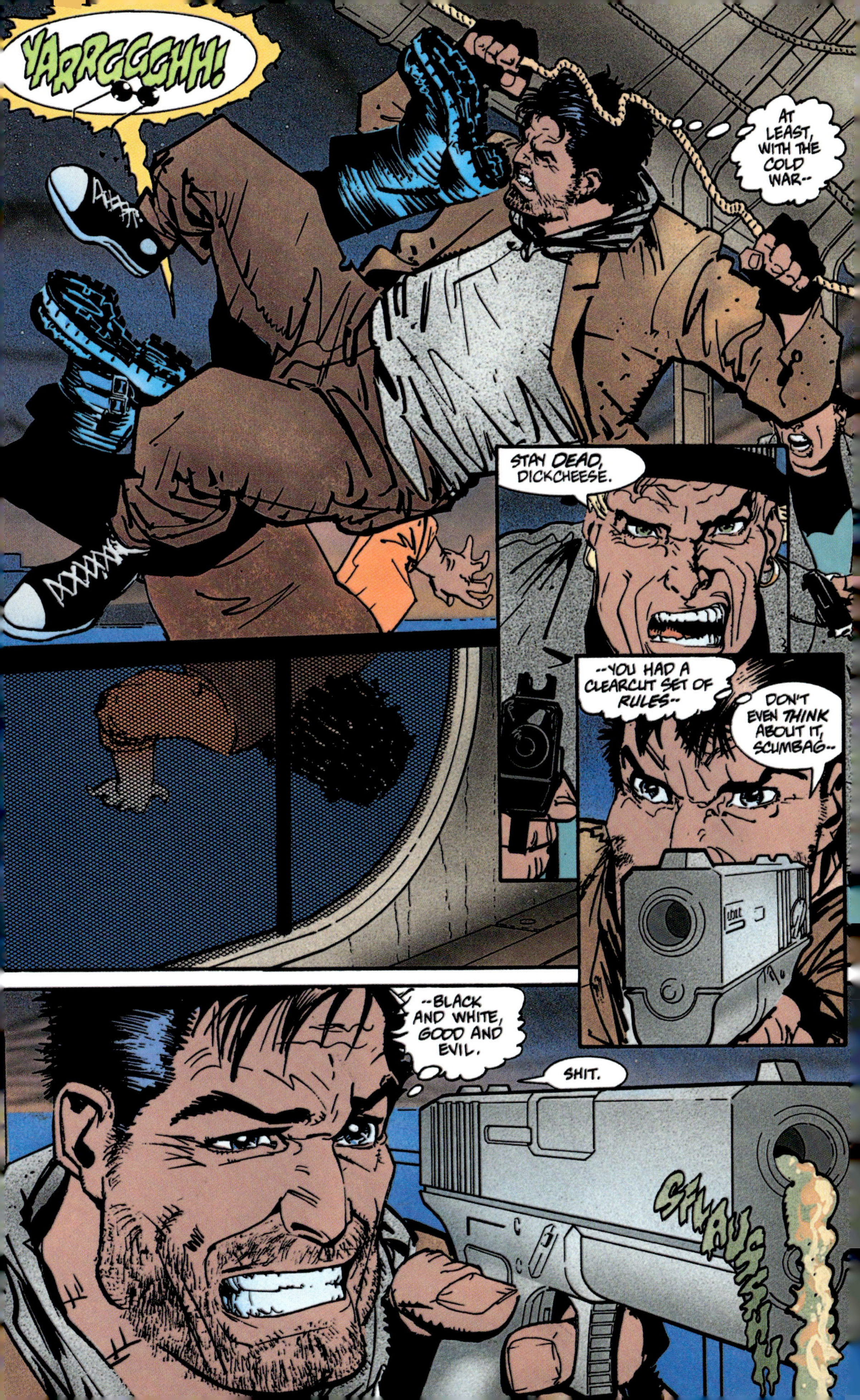
YARRGGGHH!
AT LEAST, WITH THE COLD WAR--
STAY DEAD, DICKCHEESE.
--YOU HAD A CLEARCUT SET OF RULES--
DON'T EVEN THINK ABOUT IT, SCUMBAG--
--BLACK AND WHITE, GOOD AND EVIL.
SHIT.
SPLAUSHH

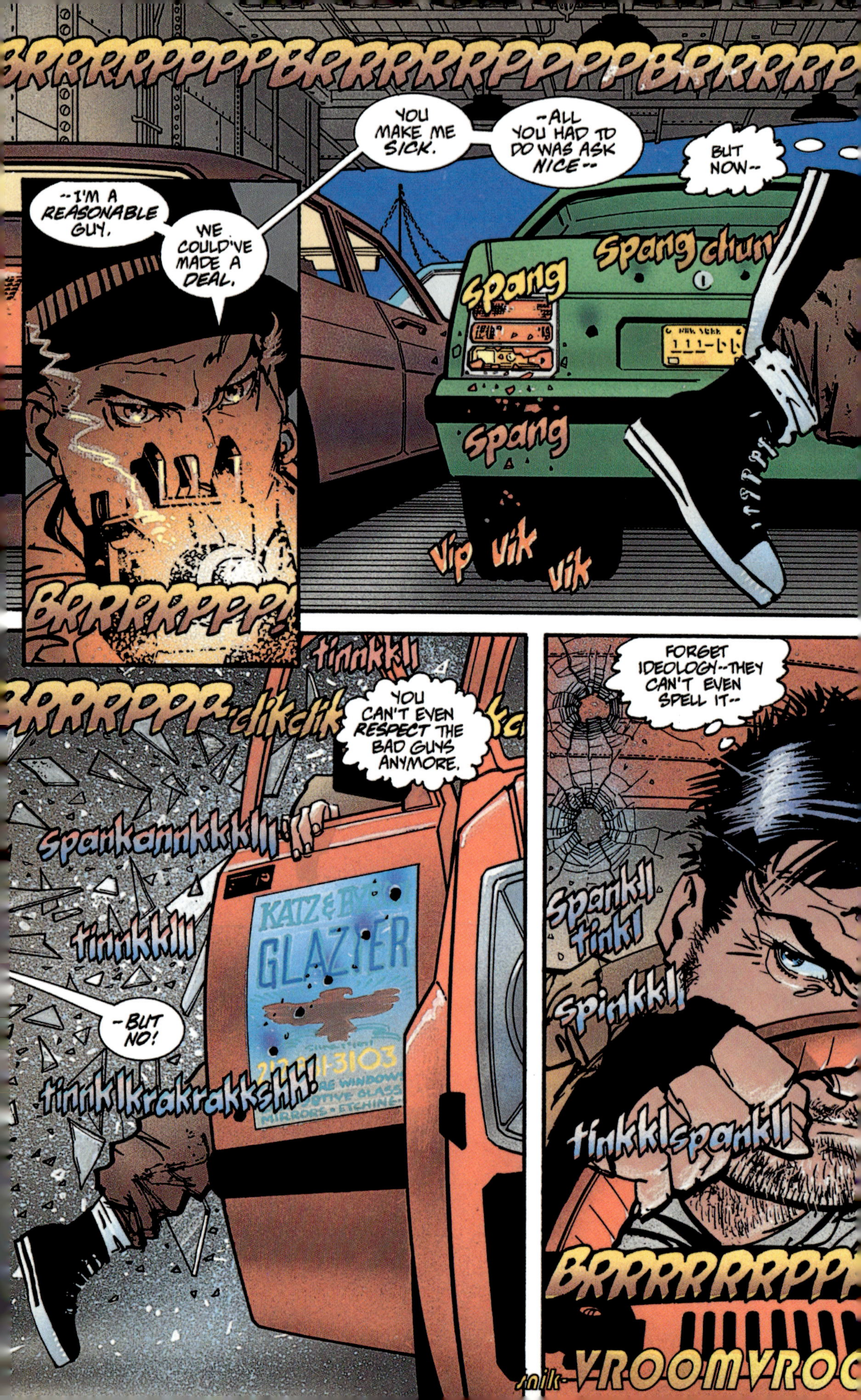
BRRRRPPPPPBRRRRRRPPPPPBRRRRRP
--I'M A REASONABLE GUY.
WE COULD'VE MADE A DEAL.
BRRRRRPPPP!
YOU MAKE ME SICK.
--ALL YOU HAD TO DO WAS ASK NICE--
BUT NOW--
Spang
Spang chun
Spang
vip vik vik
BRRRRPPPP clikclik
tinnkkll
YOU CAN'T EVEN RESPECT THE BAD GUYS ANYMORE.
Spankannkkklll
tinnkklll
-BUT NO!
tinnklkrakrakkshh!
KATZ & BYRD GLAZIER
FORGET IDEOLOGY--THEY CAN'T EVEN SPELL IT--
Spankll tinkl
Spinkkll
tinkklspankll
BRRRRRRPPP
VROOMVROO

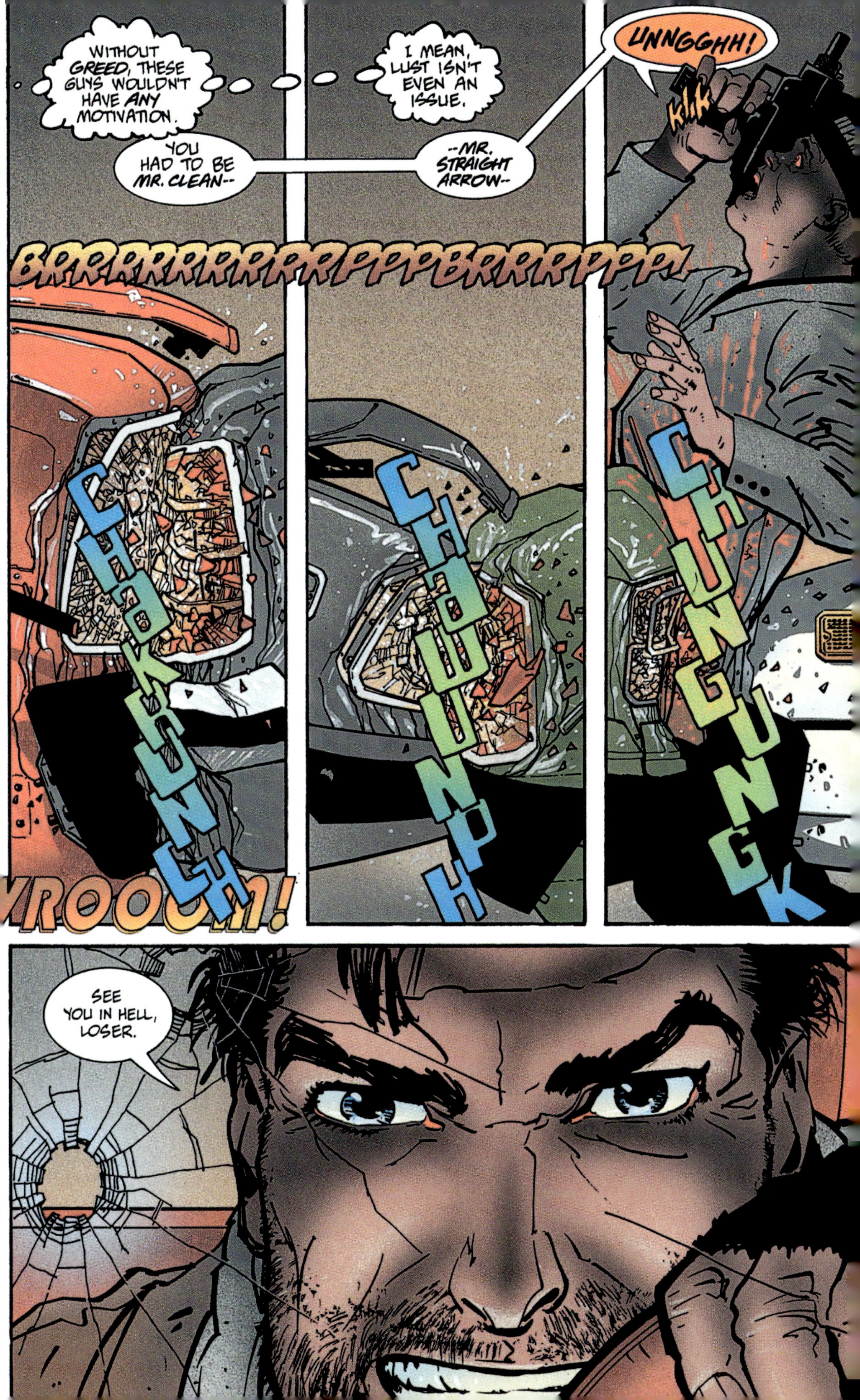
WITHOUT GREED, THESE GUYS WOULDN'T HAVE ANY MOTIVATION.
YOU HAD TO BE MR. CLEAN--
I MEAN, LUST ISN'T EVEN AN ISSUE.
--MR. STRAIGHT ARROW--
UNNGGHH!
KLIK
BRRRRRRRRRPPPBRRRRPPP!
CHAKKUNNCH
CHAWUNPH
CHUNGUNGK
VROOOM!
SEE YOU IN HELL, LOSER.

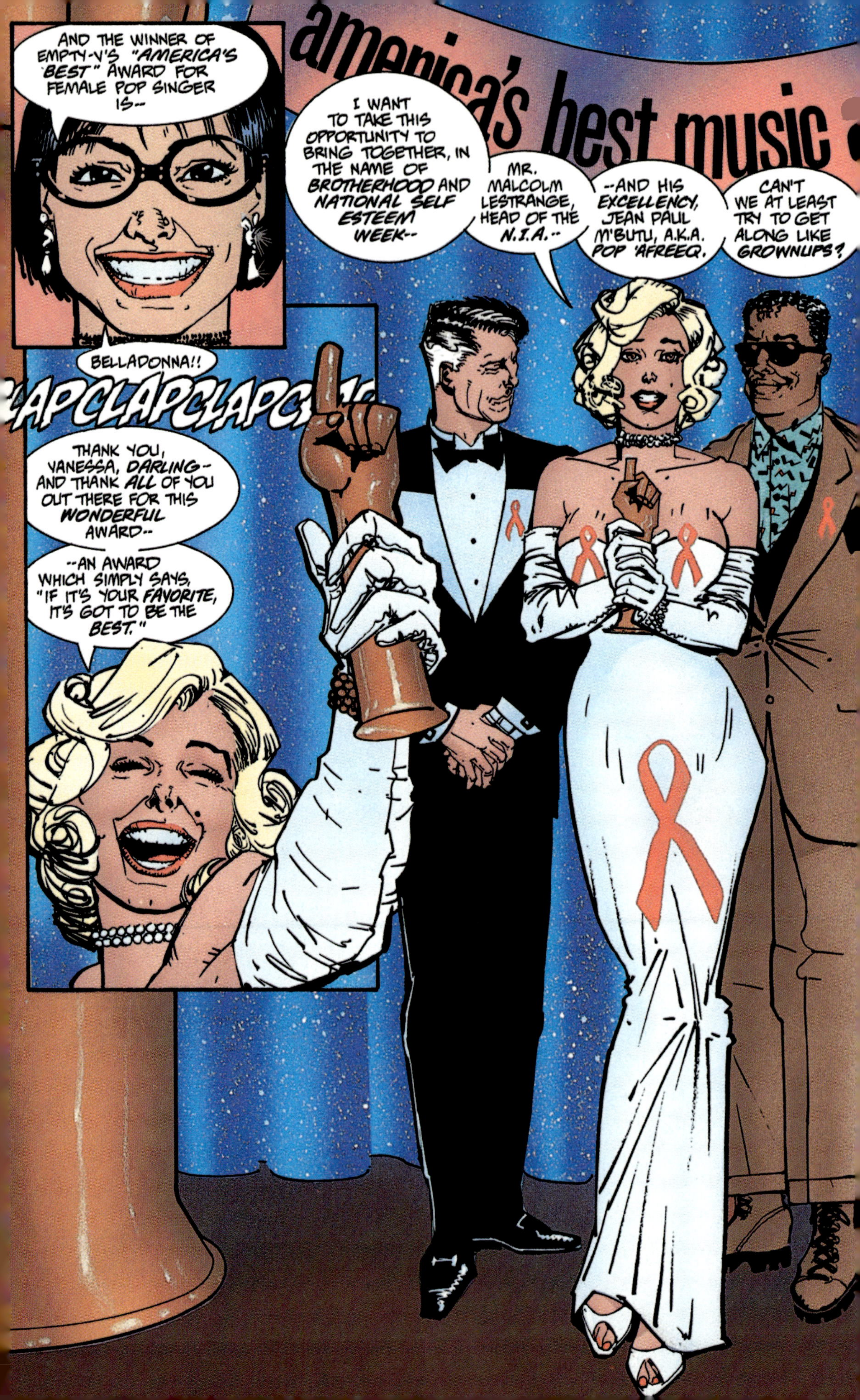
america's best music a
AND THE WINNER OF EMPTY-V'S "AMERICA'S BEST" AWARD FOR FEMALE POP SINGER IS--
BELLADONNA!!
CLAPCLAPCLAPCLAPC
THANK YOU, VANESSA, DARLING-- AND THANK ALL OF YOU OUT THERE FOR THIS WONDERFUL AWARD--
--AN AWARD WHICH SIMPLY SAYS, "IF IT'S YOUR FAVORITE, IT'S GOT TO BE THE BEST."
I WANT TO TAKE THIS OPPORTUNITY TO BRING TOGETHER, IN THE NAME OF BROTHERHOOD AND NATIONAL SELF ESTEEM WEEK--
MR. MALCOLM LESTRANGE, HEAD OF THE N.I.A.--
--AND HIS EXCELLENCY, JEAN PAUL M'BUTU, A.K.A. POP 'AFREEQ.
CAN'T WE AT LEAST TRY TO GET ALONG LIKE GROWNUPS?

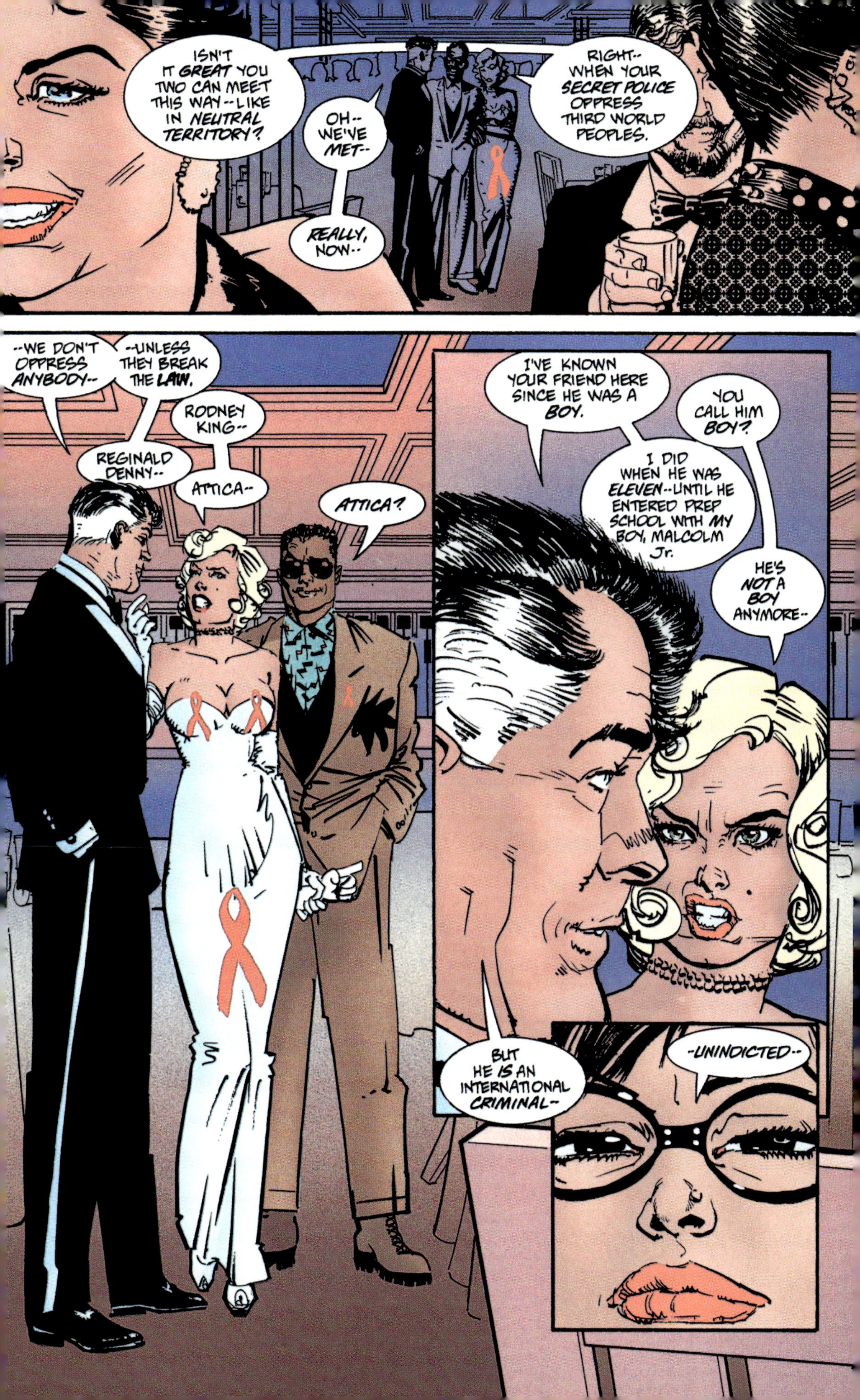
ISN'T IT GREAT YOU TWO CAN MEET THIS WAY--LIKE IN NEUTRAL TERRITORY?
OH-- WE'VE MET--
REALLY, NOW--
RIGHT-- WHEN YOUR SECRET POLICE OPPRESS THIRD WORLD PEOPLES.
--WE DON'T OPPRESS ANYBODY--
--UNLESS THEY BREAK THE LAW.
REGINALD DENNY--
RODNEY KING--
ATTICA--
ATTICA?
I'VE KNOWN YOUR FRIEND HERE SINCE HE WAS A BOY.
YOU CALL HIM BOY?
I DID WHEN HE WAS ELEVEN--UNTIL HE ENTERED PREP SCHOOL WITH MY BOY, MALCOLM Jr.
HE'S NOT A BOY ANYMORE--
BUT HE IS AN INTERNATIONAL CRIMINAL--
-UNINDICTED--

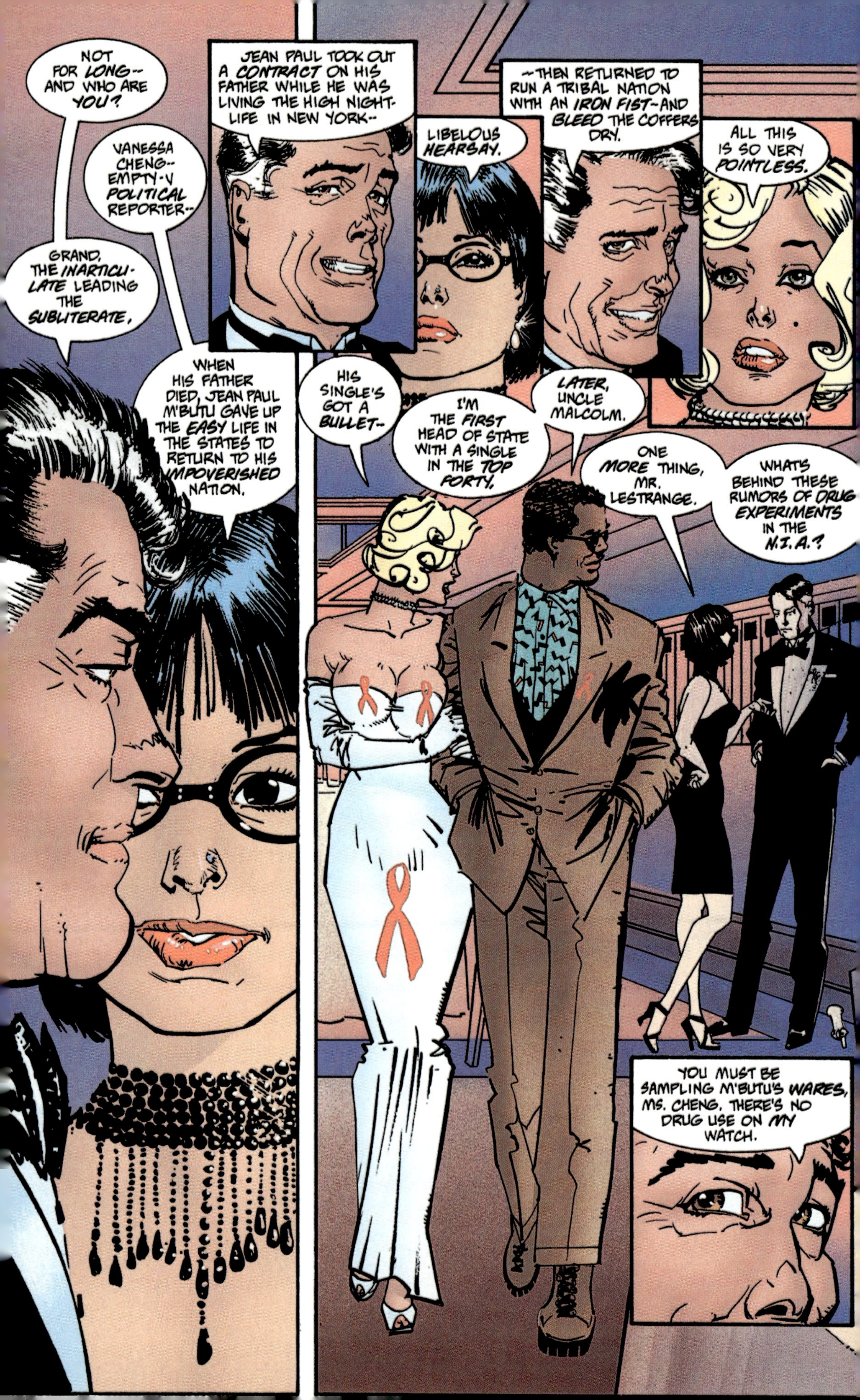
NOT FOR LONG-- AND WHO ARE YOU?
VANESSA CHENG-- EMPTY-V POLITICAL REPORTER--
GRAND, THE INARTICULATE LEADING THE SUBLITERATE.
JEAN PAUL TOOK OUT A CONTRACT ON HIS FATHER WHILE HE WAS LIVING THE HIGH NIGHT-LIFE IN NEW YORK--
LIBELOUS HEARSAY.
--THEN RETURNED TO RUN A TRIBAL NATION WITH AN IRON FIST--AND BLEED THE COFFERS DRY.
ALL THIS IS SO VERY POINTLESS.
WHEN HIS FATHER DIED, JEAN PAUL M'BUTU GAVE UP THE EASY LIFE IN THE STATES TO RETURN TO HIS IMPOVERISHED NATION.
HIS SINGLE'S GOT A BULLET--
I'M THE FIRST HEAD OF STATE WITH A SINGLE IN THE TOP FORTY.
LATER, UNCLE MALCOLM.
ONE MORE THING, MR. LESTRANGE.
WHAT'S BEHIND THESE RUMORS OF DRUG EXPERIMENTS IN THE N.I.A.?
YOU MUST BE SAMPLING M'BUTU'S WARES, MS. CHENG. THERE'S NO DRUG USE ON MY WATCH.

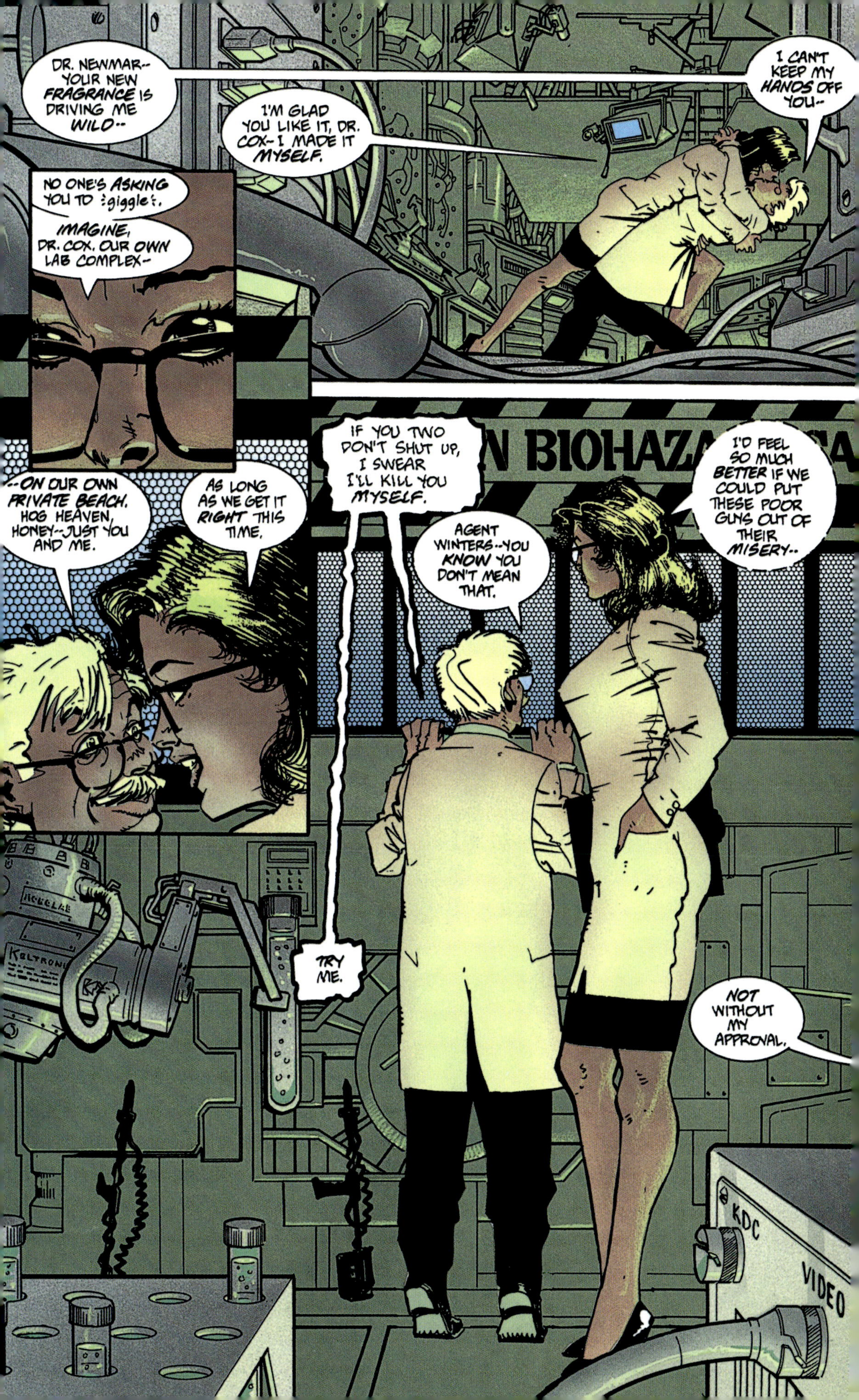
DR. NEWMAR-- YOUR NEW FRAGRANCE IS DRIVING ME WILD--
I'M GLAD YOU LIKE IT, DR. COX-- I MADE IT MYSELF.
I CAN'T KEEP MY HANDS OFF YOU--
NO ONE'S ASKING YOU TO *giggle*.
IMAGINE, DR. COX. OUR OWN LAB COMPLEX--
--ON OUR OWN PRIVATE BEACH. HOG HEAVEN, HONEY--JUST YOU AND ME.
AS LONG AS WE GET IT RIGHT THIS TIME.
BIOHAZA
IF YOU TWO DON'T SHUT UP, I SWEAR I'LL KILL YOU MYSELF.
AGENT WINTERS--YOU KNOW YOU DON'T MEAN THAT.
I'D FEEL SO MUCH BETTER IF WE COULD PUT THESE POOR GUYS OUT OF THEIR MISERY--
TRY ME.
NOT WITHOUT MY APPROVAL.
KELTRON
KDC
VIDEO

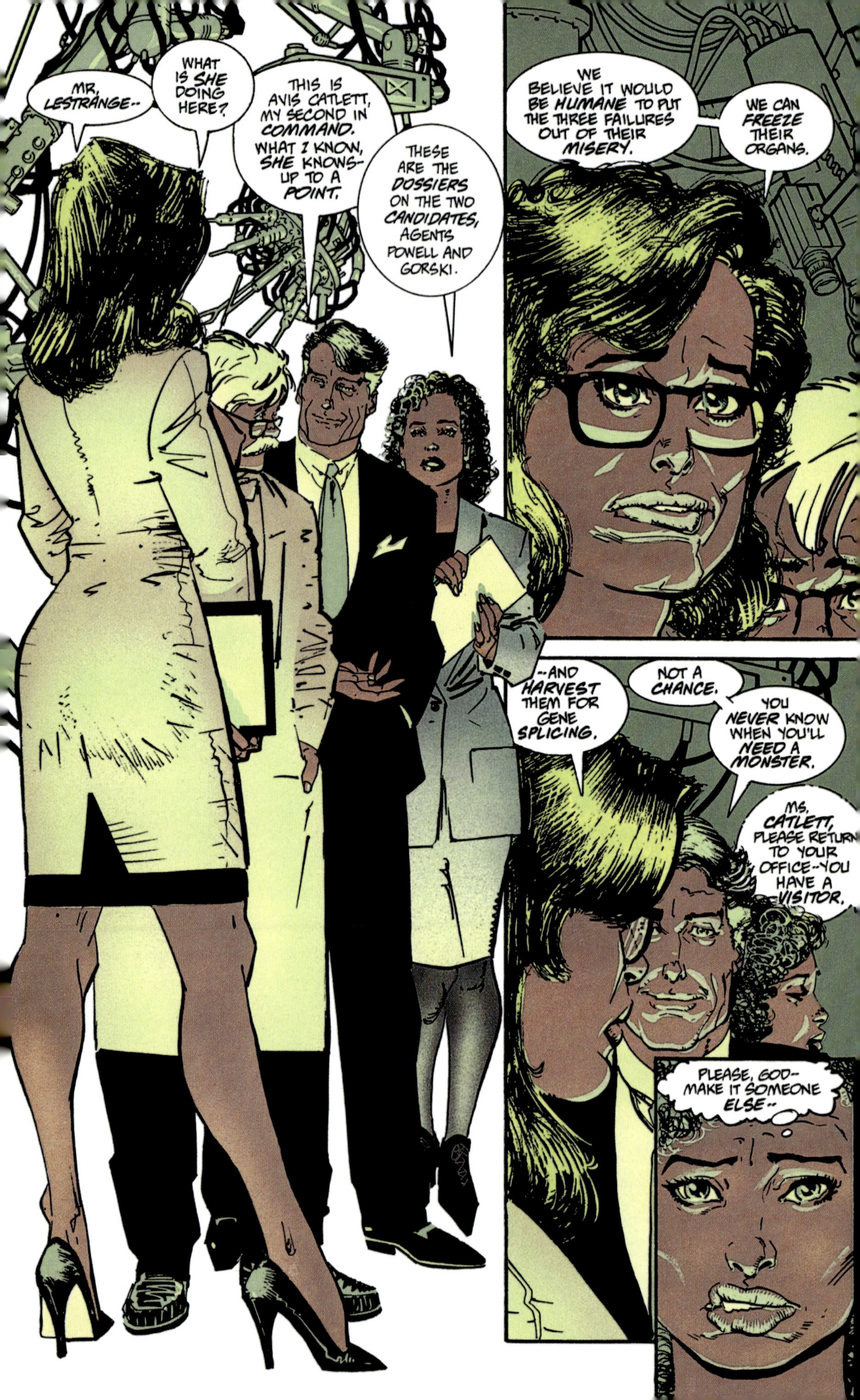
MR. LESTRANGE--
WHAT IS SHE DOING HERE?
THIS IS AVIS CATLETT, MY SECOND IN COMMAND. WHAT I KNOW, SHE KNOWS-- UP TO A POINT.
THESE ARE THE DOSSIERS ON THE TWO CANDIDATES, AGENTS POWELL AND GORSKI.
WE BELIEVE IT WOULD BE HUMANE TO PUT THE THREE FAILURES OUT OF THEIR MISERY.
WE CAN FREEZE THEIR ORGANS.
--AND HARVEST THEM FOR GENE SPLICING.
NOT A CHANCE.
YOU NEVER KNOW WHEN YOU'LL NEED A MONSTER.
MS. CATLETT, PLEASE RETURN TO YOUR OFFICE--YOU HAVE A VISITOR.
PLEASE, GOD-- MAKE IT SOMEONE ELSE--

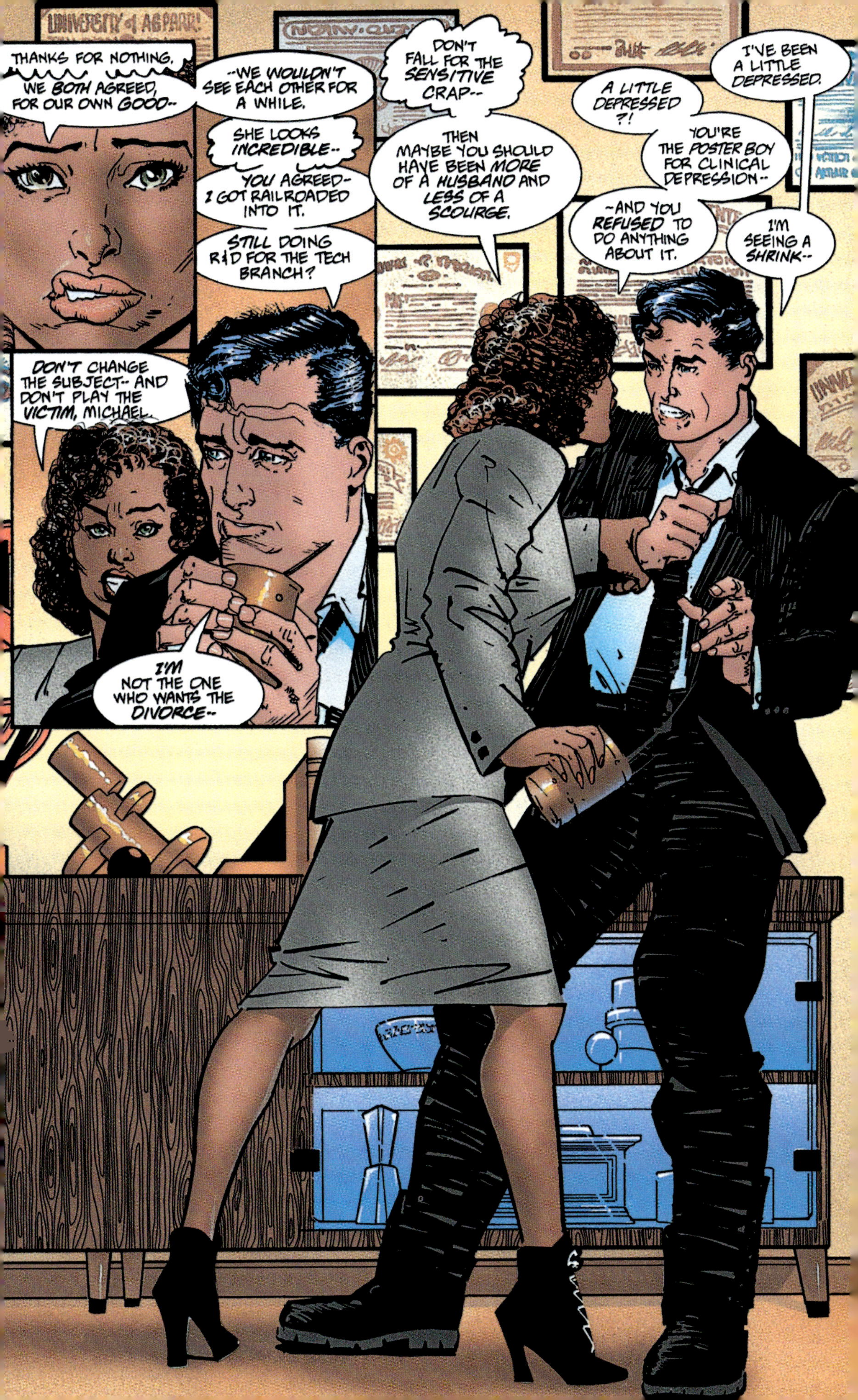
THANKS FOR NOTHING.
WE BOTH AGREED, FOR OUR OWN GOOD--
--WE WOULDN'T SEE EACH OTHER FOR A WHILE.
SHE LOOKS INCREDIBLE--
YOU AGREED-- I GOT RAILROADED INTO IT.
STILL DOING R&D FOR THE TECH BRANCH?
DON'T CHANGE THE SUBJECT-- AND DON'T PLAY THE VICTIM, MICHAEL.
I'M NOT THE ONE WHO WANTS THE DIVORCE--
DON'T FALL FOR THE SENSITIVE CRAP--
THEN MAYBE YOU SHOULD HAVE BEEN MORE OF A HUSBAND AND LESS OF A SCOURGE.
I'VE BEEN A LITTLE DEPRESSED.
A LITTLE DEPRESSED ?!
YOU'RE THE POSTER BOY FOR CLINICAL DEPRESSION--
--AND YOU REFUSED TO DO ANYTHING ABOUT IT.
I'M SEEING A SHRINK--

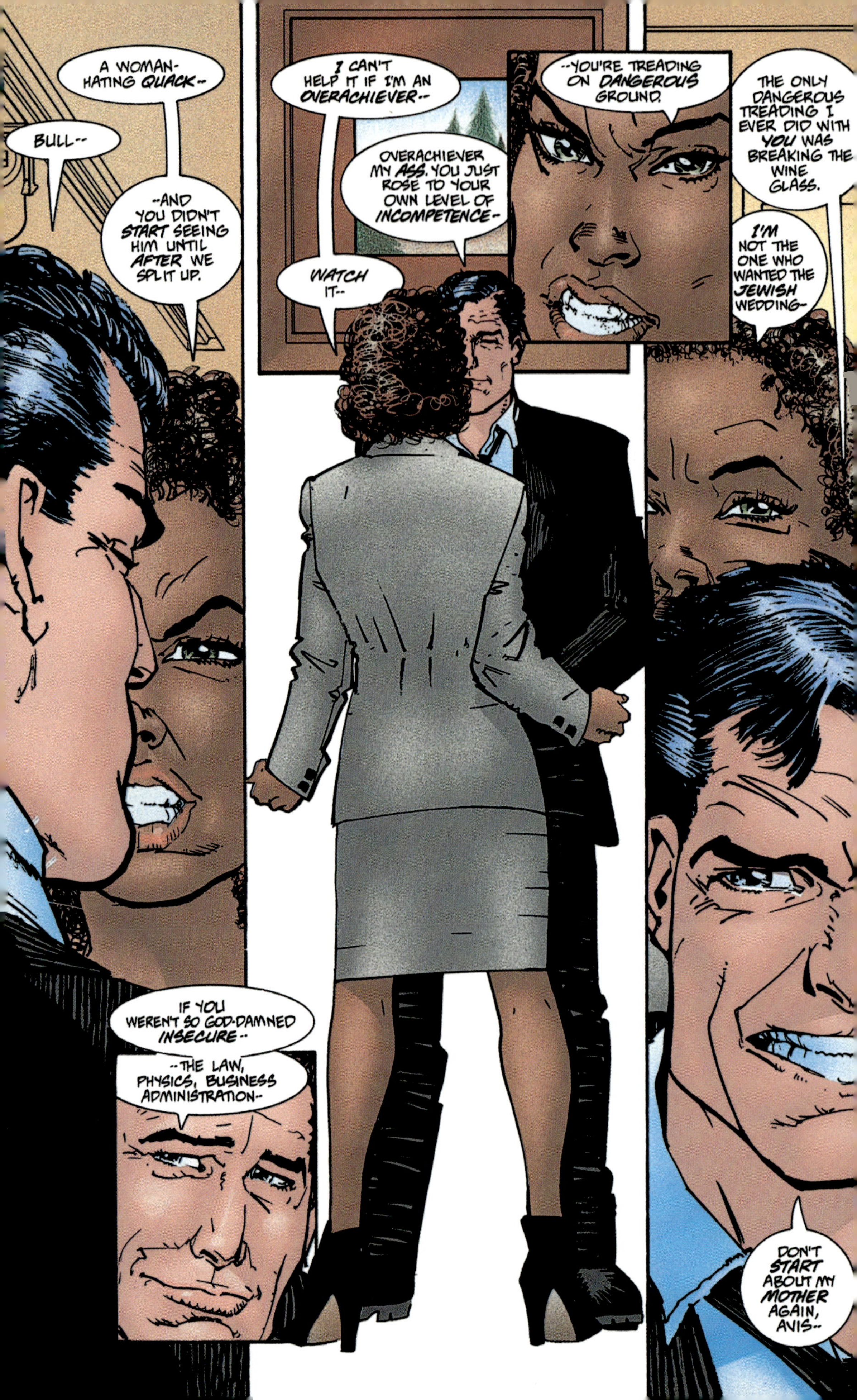
A WOMAN-HATING QUACK--
BULL--
--AND YOU DIDN'T START SEEING HIM UNTIL AFTER WE SPLIT UP.
I CAN'T HELP IT IF I'M AN OVERACHIEVER--
OVERACHIEVER MY ASS. YOU JUST ROSE TO YOUR OWN LEVEL OF INCOMPETENCE--
WATCH IT--
--YOU'RE TREADING ON DANGEROUS GROUND.
THE ONLY DANGEROUS TREADING I EVER DID WITH YOU WAS BREAKING THE WINE GLASS.
I'M NOT THE ONE WHO WANTED THE JEWISH WEDDING--
IF YOU WEREN'T SO GOD-DAMNED INSECURE--
--THE LAW, PHYSICS, BUSINESS ADMINISTRATION--
DON'T START ABOUT MY MOTHER AGAIN, AVIS--

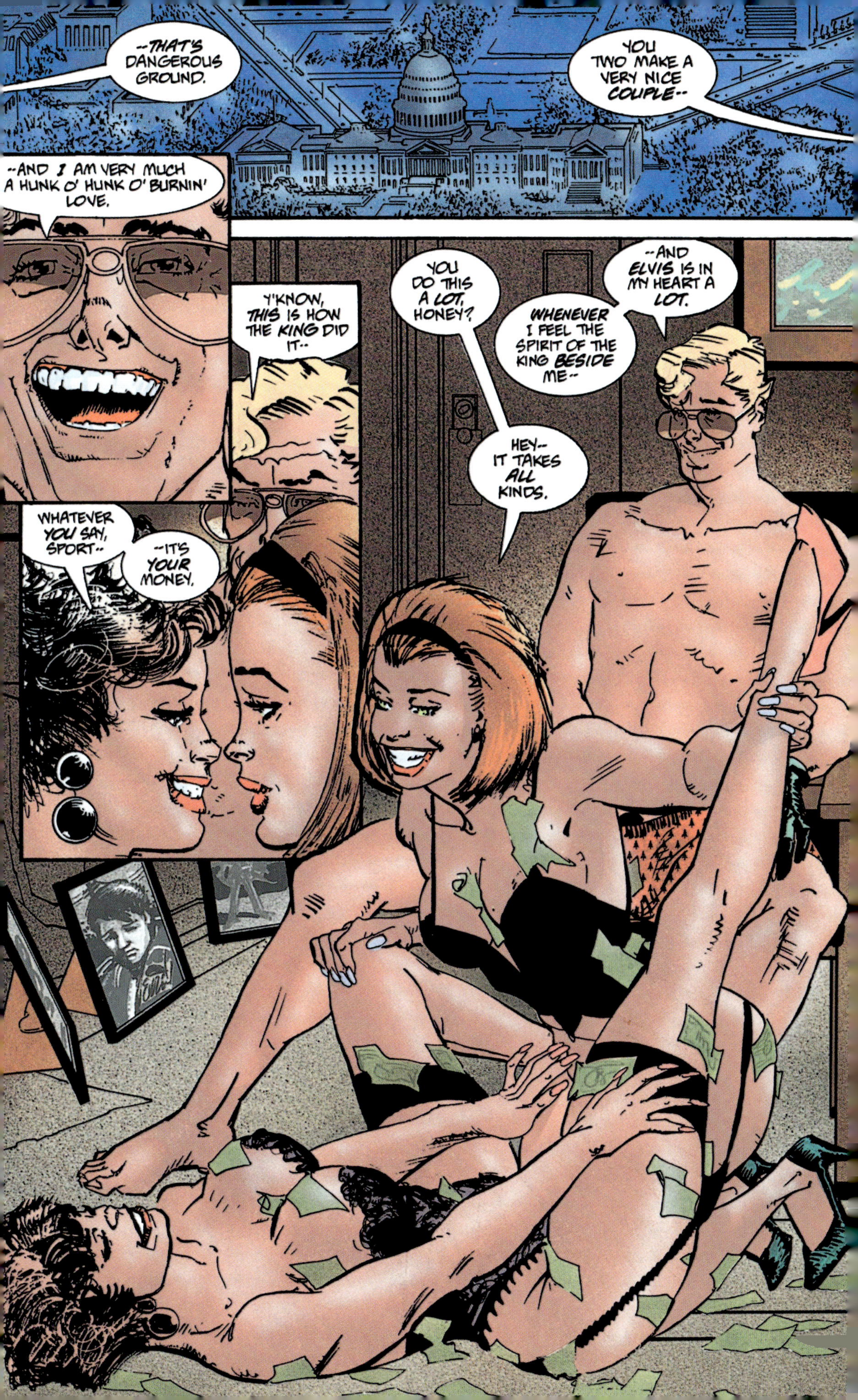
--THAT'S DANGEROUS GROUND.
YOU TWO MAKE A VERY NICE COUPLE--
--AND I AM VERY MUCH A HUNK O' HUNK O' BURNIN' LOVE.
Y'KNOW, THIS IS HOW THE KING DID IT--
YOU DO THIS A LOT, HONEY?
--AND ELVIS IS IN MY HEART A LOT.
WHENEVER I FEEL THE SPIRIT OF THE KING BESIDE ME--
HEY-- IT TAKES ALL KINDS.
WHATEVER YOU SAY, SPORT--
--IT'S YOUR MONEY.

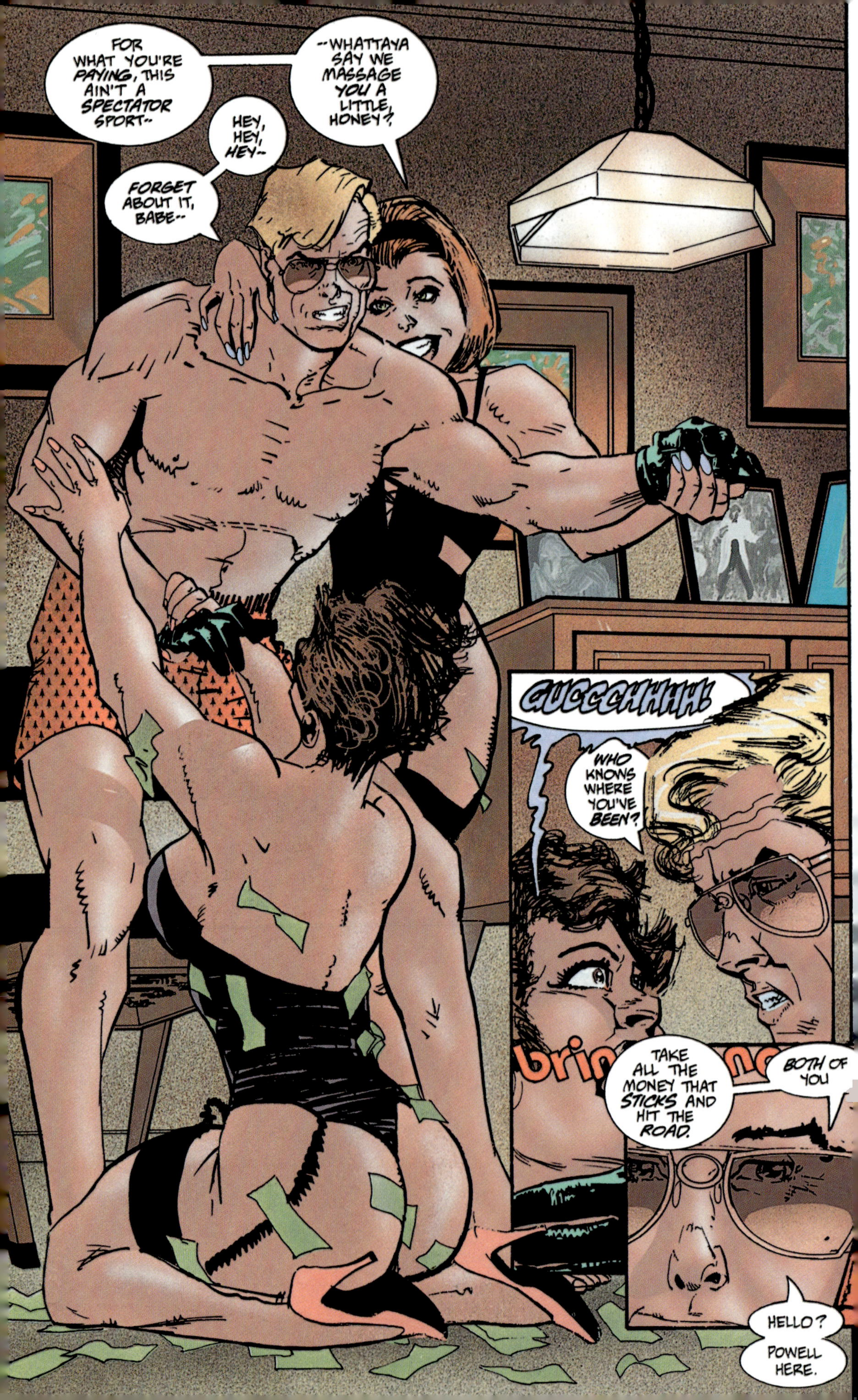
FOR WHAT YOU'RE PAYING, THIS AIN'T A SPECTATOR SPORT--
--WHATTAYA SAY WE MASSAGE YOU A LITTLE, HONEY?
HEY, HEY, HEY--
FORGET ABOUT IT, BABE--
GUCCCHHHH!
WHO KNOWS WHERE YOU'VE BEEN?
TAKE ALL THE MONEY THAT STICKS AND HIT THE ROAD.
BOTH OF YOU
HELLO? POWELL HERE.

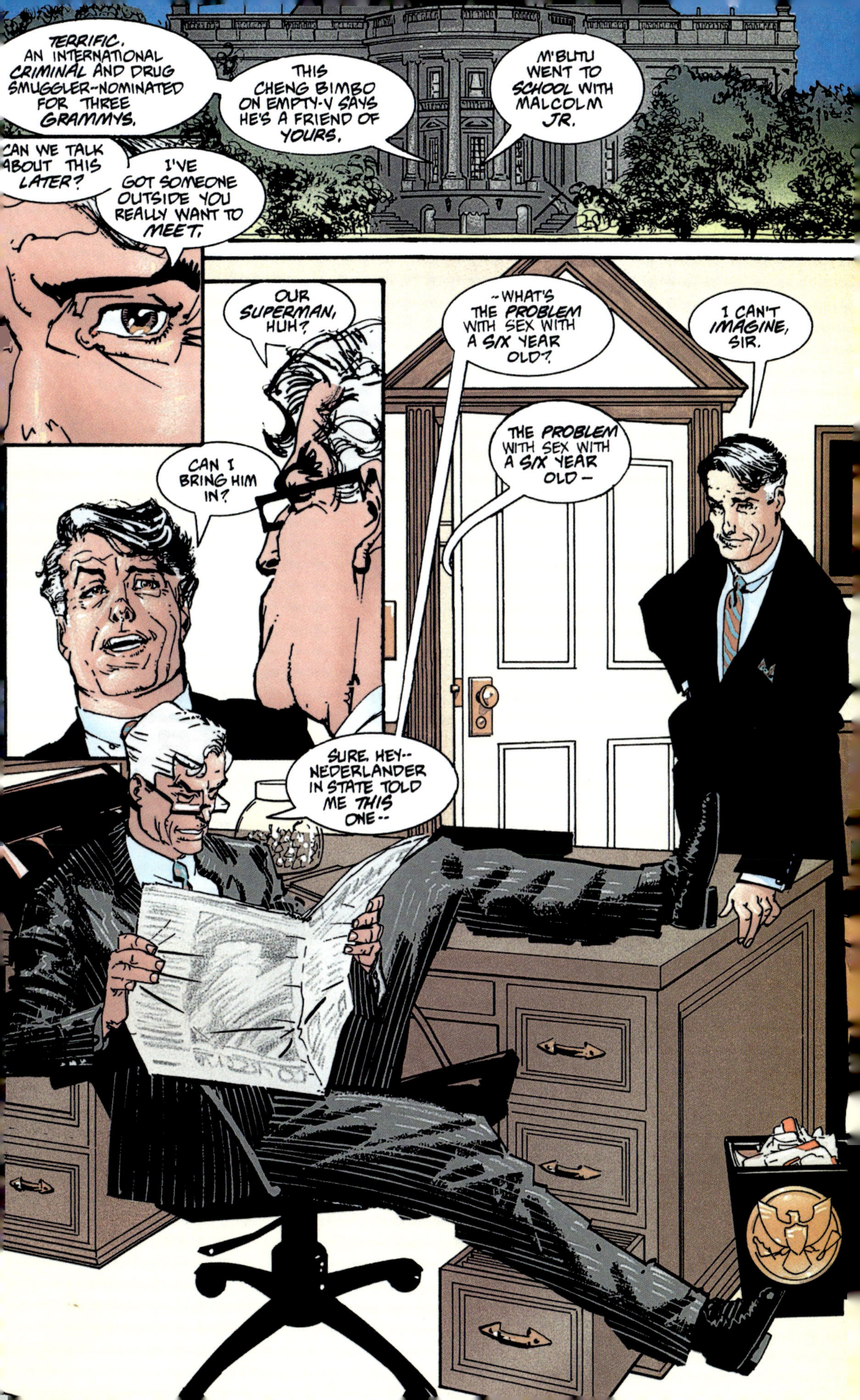
TERRIFIC. AN INTERNATIONAL CRIMINAL AND DRUG SMUGGLER--NOMINATED FOR THREE GRAMMYS.
THIS CHENG BIMBO ON EMPTY-V SAYS HE'S A FRIEND OF YOURS.
M'BUTU WENT TO SCHOOL WITH MALCOLM JR.
CAN WE TALK ABOUT THIS LATER?
I'VE GOT SOMEONE OUTSIDE YOU REALLY WANT TO MEET.
OUR SUPERMAN, HUH?
CAN I BRING HIM IN?
SURE. HEY-- NEDERLANDER IN STATE TOLD ME THIS ONE--
--WHAT'S THE PROBLEM WITH SEX WITH A SIX YEAR OLD?
THE PROBLEM WITH SEX WITH A SIX YEAR OLD--
I CAN'T IMAGINE, SIR.

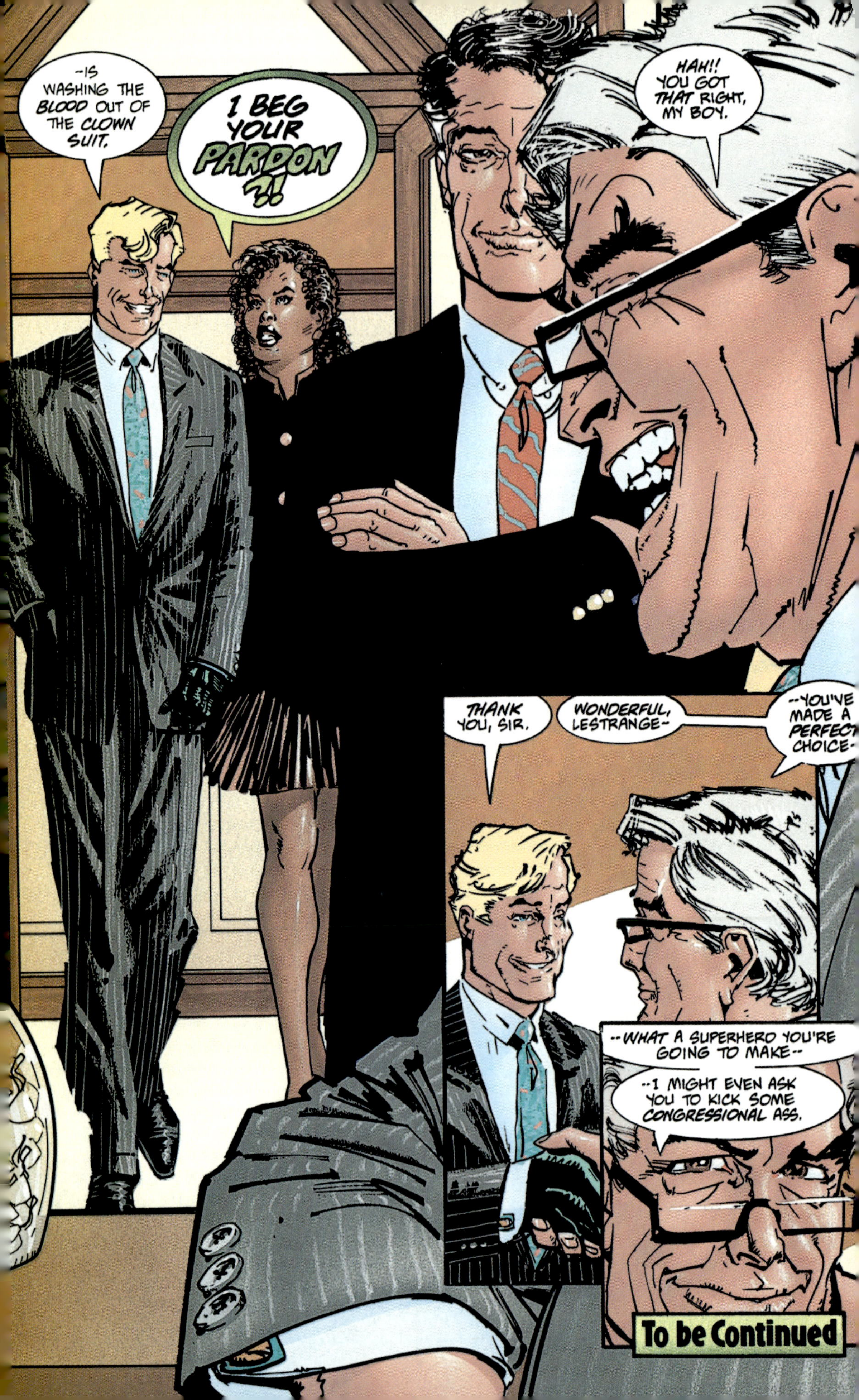
--IS WASHING THE BLOOD OUT OF THE CLOWN SUIT.
I BEG YOUR PARDON ?!
HAH!! YOU GOT THAT RIGHT, MY BOY.
THANK YOU, SIR.
WONDERFUL, LESTRANGE--
--YOU'VE MADE A PERFECT CHOICE--
--WHAT A SUPERHERO YOU'RE GOING TO MAKE--
--I MIGHT EVEN ASK YOU TO KICK SOME CONGRESSIONAL ASS.
To be Continued

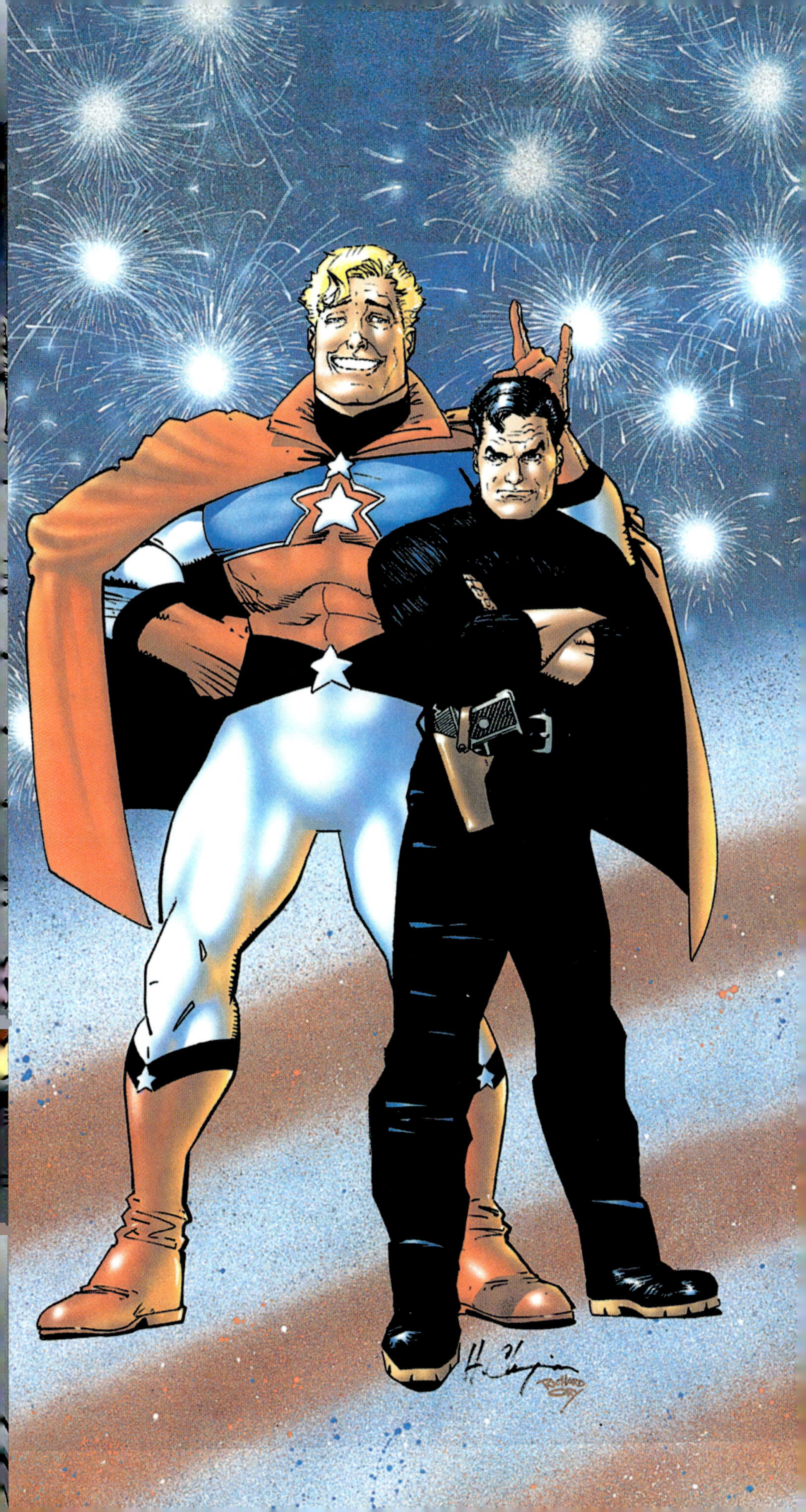

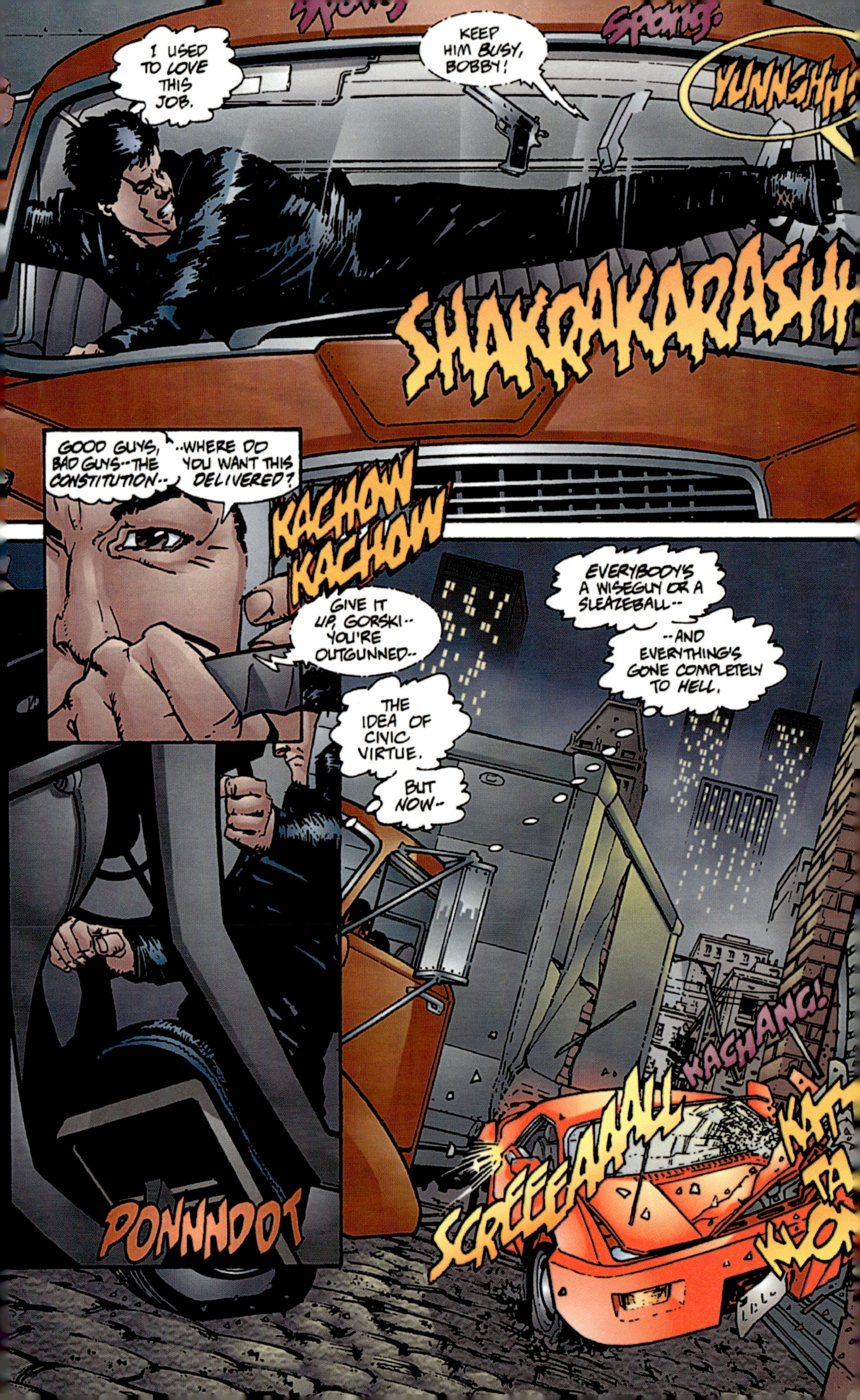
Spong
Spong
I USED TO LOVE THIS JOB.
KEEP HIM BUSY, BOBBY!
YUNNGHH!
SHAKRAKARASH!
GOOD GUYS, BAD GUYS--THE CONSTITUTION--
--WHERE DO YOU WANT THIS DELIVERED?
KACHOW KACHOW
GIVE IT UP, GORSKI-- YOU'RE OUTGUNNED--
EVERYBODY'S A WISEGUY OR A SLEAZEBALL--
--AND EVERYTHING'S GONE COMPLETELY TO HELL.
THE IDEA OF CIVIC VIRTUE.
BUT NOW--
KACHANG!
SCREEEAAALL
PONNNDOT

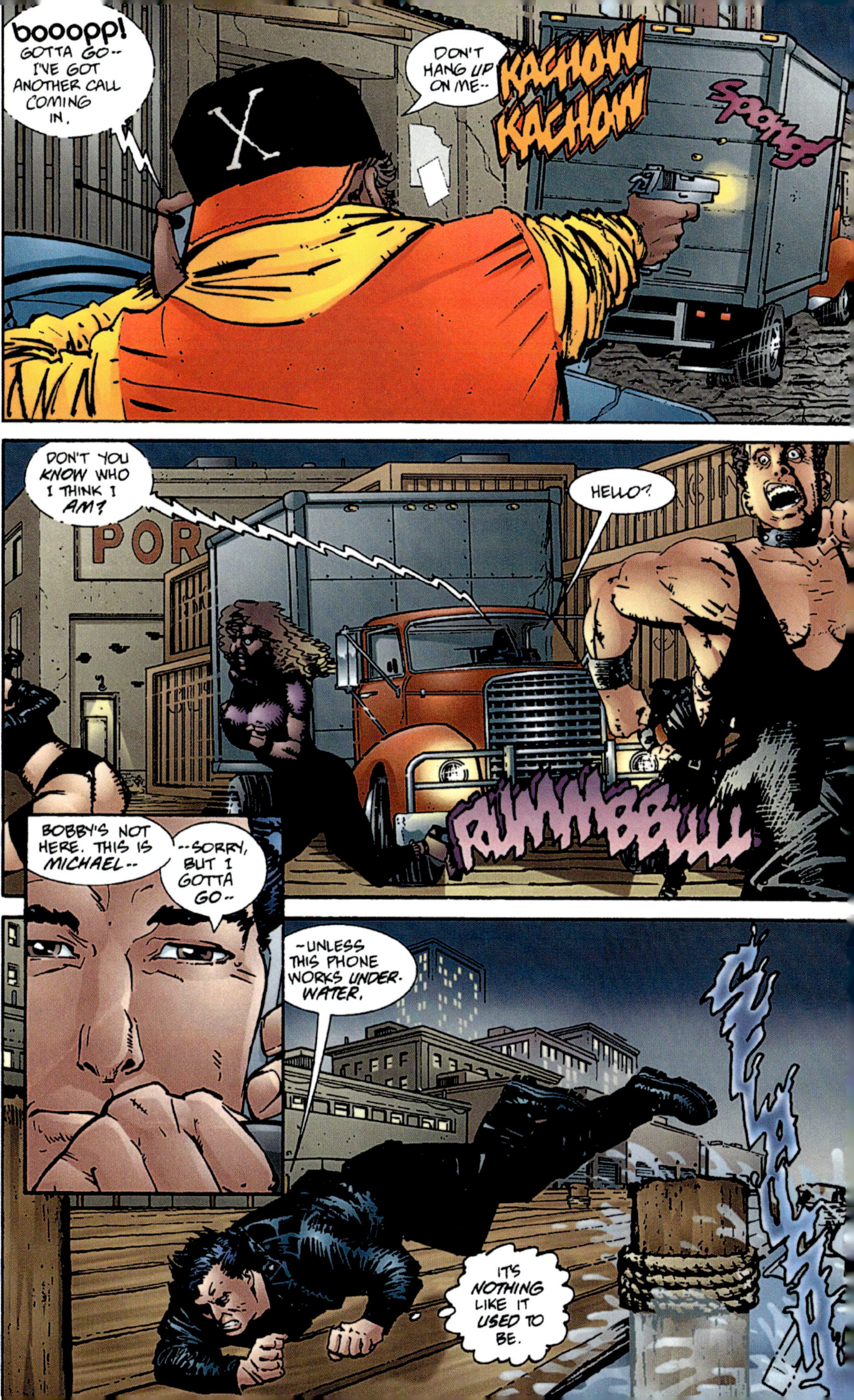
booopp! GOTTA GO-- I'VE GOT ANOTHER CALL COMING IN.
DON'T HANG UP ON ME--
KACHOW KACHOW
spong!
DON'T YOU KNOW WHO I THINK I AM?
HELLO?
POR
RUMMBBLLL
BOBBY'S NOT HERE. THIS IS MICHAEL--
--SORRY, BUT I GOTTA GO--
--UNLESS THIS PHONE WORKS UNDER-WATER.
IT'S NOTHING LIKE IT USED TO BE.

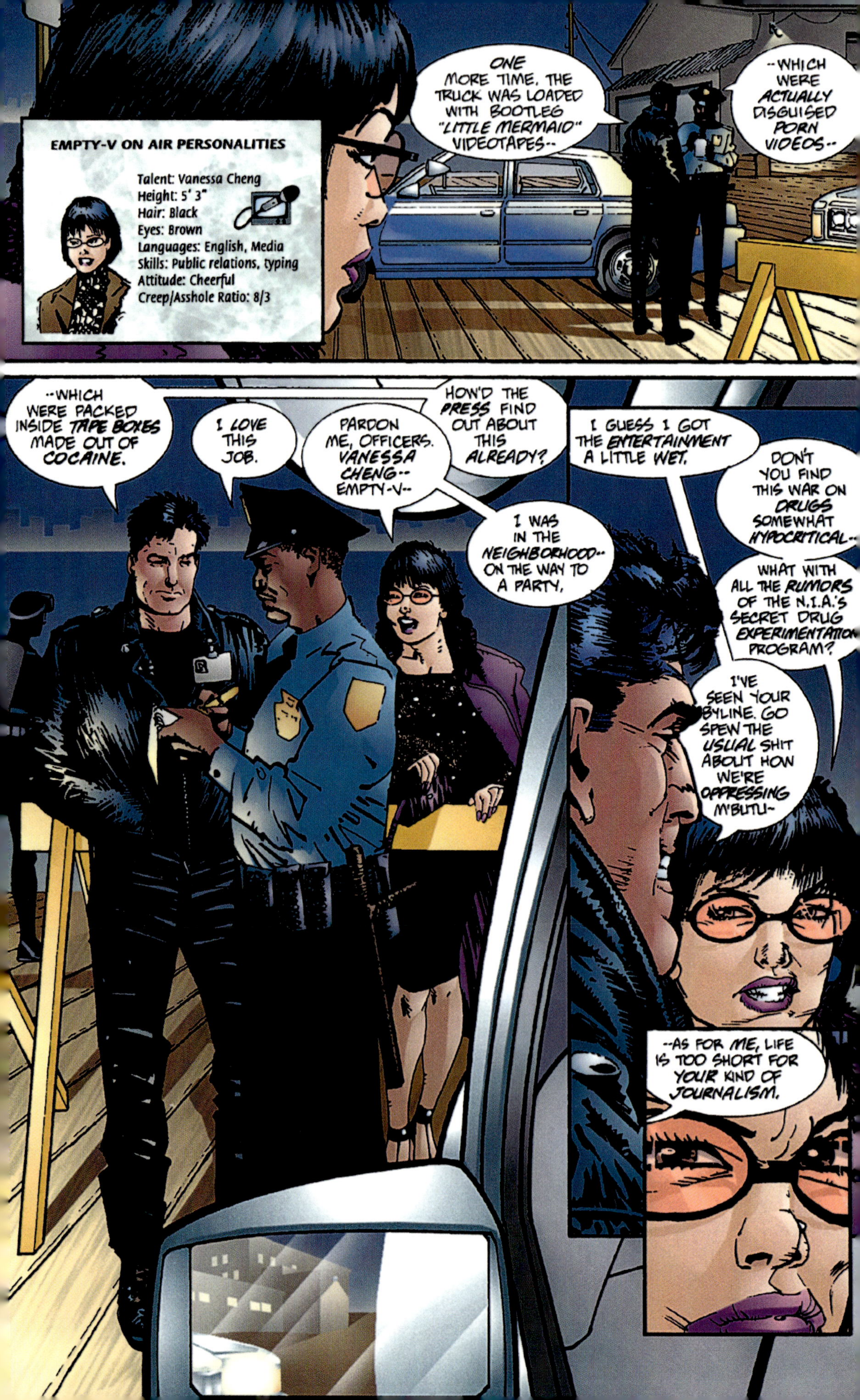
EMPTY-V ON AIR PERSONALITIES
Talent: Vanessa Cheng
Height: 5' 3"
Hair: Black
Eyes: Brown
Languages: English, Media
Skills: Public relations, typing
Attitude: Cheerful
Creep/Asshole Ratio: 8/3
ONE MORE TIME. THE TRUCK WAS LOADED WITH BOOTLEG "LITTLE MERMAID" VIDEOTAPES--
--WHICH WERE ACTUALLY DISGUISED PORN VIDEOS--
--WHICH WERE PACKED INSIDE TAPE BOXES MADE OUT OF COCAINE.
I LOVE THIS JOB.
PARDON ME, OFFICERS. VANESSA CHENG-- EMPTY-V--
HOW'D THE PRESS FIND OUT ABOUT THIS ALREADY?
I WAS IN THE NEIGHBORHOOD-- ON THE WAY TO A PARTY.
I GUESS I GOT THE ENTERTAINMENT A LITTLE WET.
DON'T YOU FIND THIS WAR ON DRUGS SOMEWHAT HYPOCRITICAL--
WHAT WITH ALL THE RUMORS OF THE N.I.A.'S SECRET DRUG EXPERIMENTATION PROGRAM?
I'VE SEEN YOUR BYLINE. GO SPEW THE USUAL SHIT ABOUT HOW WE'RE OPPRESSING M'BUTU--
--AS FOR ME, LIFE IS TOO SHORT FOR YOUR KIND OF JOURNALISM.

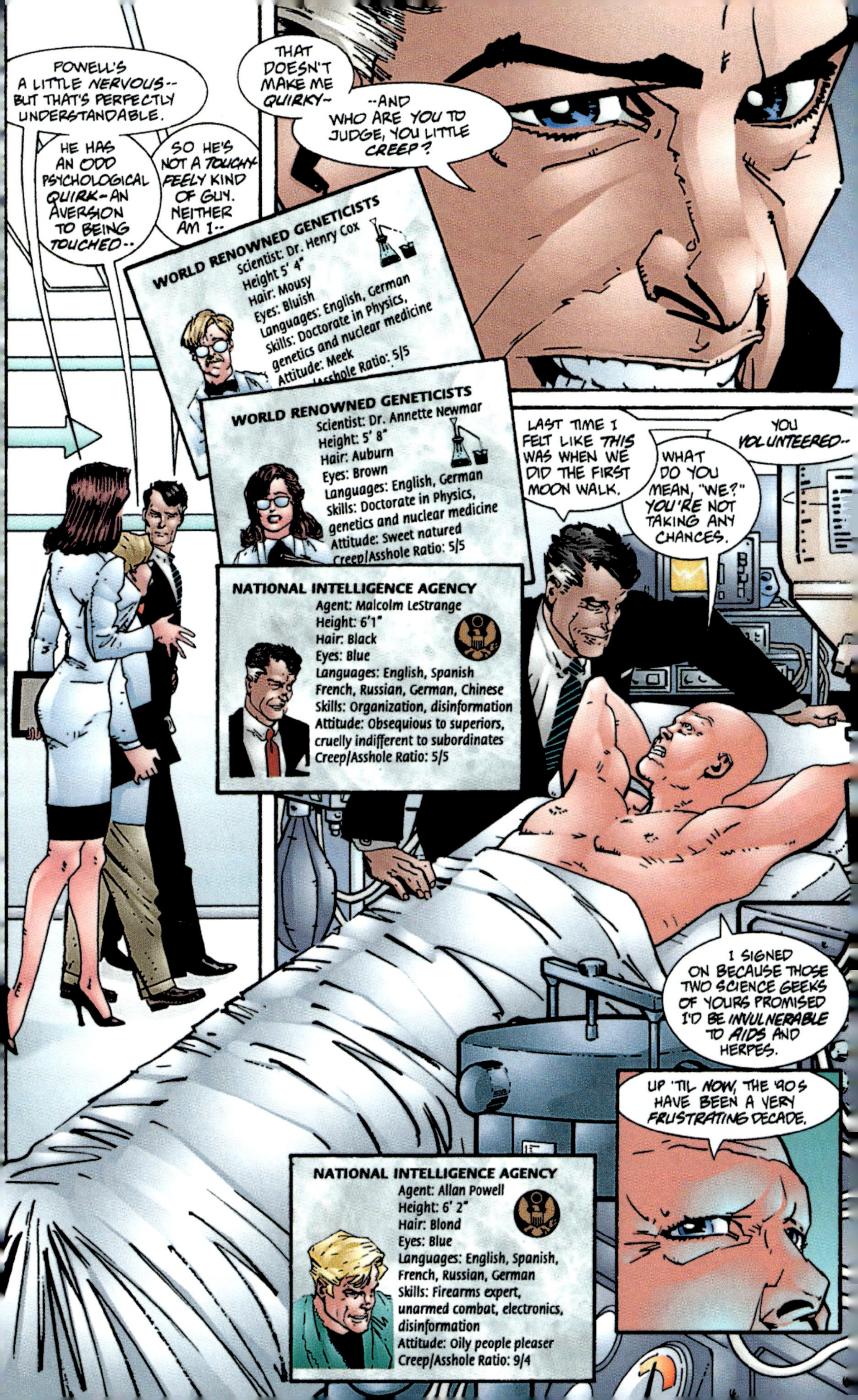
POWELL'S A LITTLE NERVOUS-- BUT THAT'S PERFECTLY UNDERSTANDABLE.
HE HAS AN ODD PSYCHOLOGICAL QUIRK--AN AVERSION TO BEING TOUCHED--
SO HE'S NOT A TOUCHY-FEELY KIND OF GUY. NEITHER AM I--
THAT DOESN'T MAKE ME QUIRKY--
--AND WHO ARE YOU TO JUDGE, YOU LITTLE CREEP?
WORLD RENOWNED GENETICISTS
Scientist: Dr. Henry Cox
Height 5' 4"
Hair: Mousy
Eyes: Bluish
Languages: English, German
Skills: Doctorate in Physics, genetics and nuclear medicine
Attitude: Meek
Creep/Asshole Ratio: 5/5
WORLD RENOWNED GENETICISTS
Scientist: Dr. Annette Newmar
Height: 5' 8"
Hair: Auburn
Eyes: Brown
Languages: English, German
Skills: Doctorate in Physics, genetics and nuclear medicine
Attitude: Sweet natured
Creep/Asshole Ratio: 5/5
NATIONAL INTELLIGENCE AGENCY
Agent: Malcolm LeStrange
Height: 6'1"
Hair: Black
Eyes: Blue
Languages: English, Spanish French, Russian, German, Chinese
Skills: Organization, disinformation
Attitude: Obsequious to superiors, cruelly indifferent to subordinates
Creep/Asshole Ratio: 5/5
LAST TIME I FELT LIKE THIS WAS WHEN WE DID THE FIRST MOON WALK.
WHAT DO YOU MEAN, "WE?" YOU'RE NOT TAKING ANY CHANCES.
YOU VOLUNTEERED--
I SIGNED ON BECAUSE THOSE TWO SCIENCE GEEKS OF YOURS PROMISED I'D BE INVULNERABLE TO AIDS AND HERPES.
UP 'TIL NOW, THE '90S HAVE BEEN A VERY FRUSTRATING DECADE.
NATIONAL INTELLIGENCE AGENCY
Agent: Allan Powell
Height: 6' 2"
Hair: Blond
Eyes: Blue
Languages: English, Spanish, French, Russian, German
Skills: Firearms expert, unarmed combat, electronics, disinformation
Attitude: Oily people pleaser
Creep/Asshole Ratio: 9/4

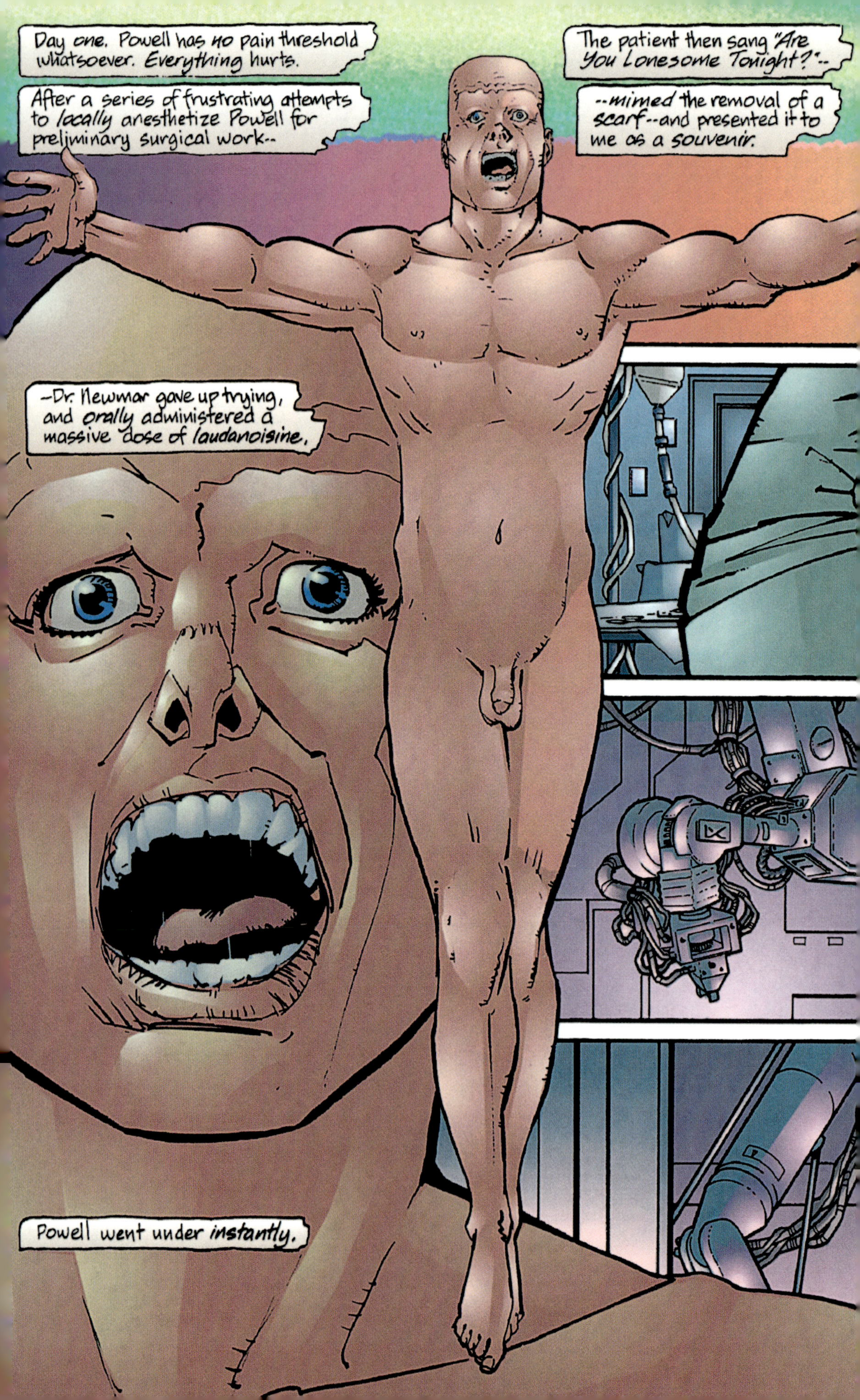
Day one. Powell has *no* pain threshold whatsoever. *Everything* hurts.
After a series of frustrating attempts to *locally* anesthetize Powell for preliminary surgical work--
--Dr. Newmar gave up trying, and *orally* administered a massive dose of *laudanoisine*.
Powell went under *instantly*.
The patient then sang *"Are You Lonesome Tonight?"*--
--*mimed* the removal of a *scarf*--and presented it to me as a *souvenir*.

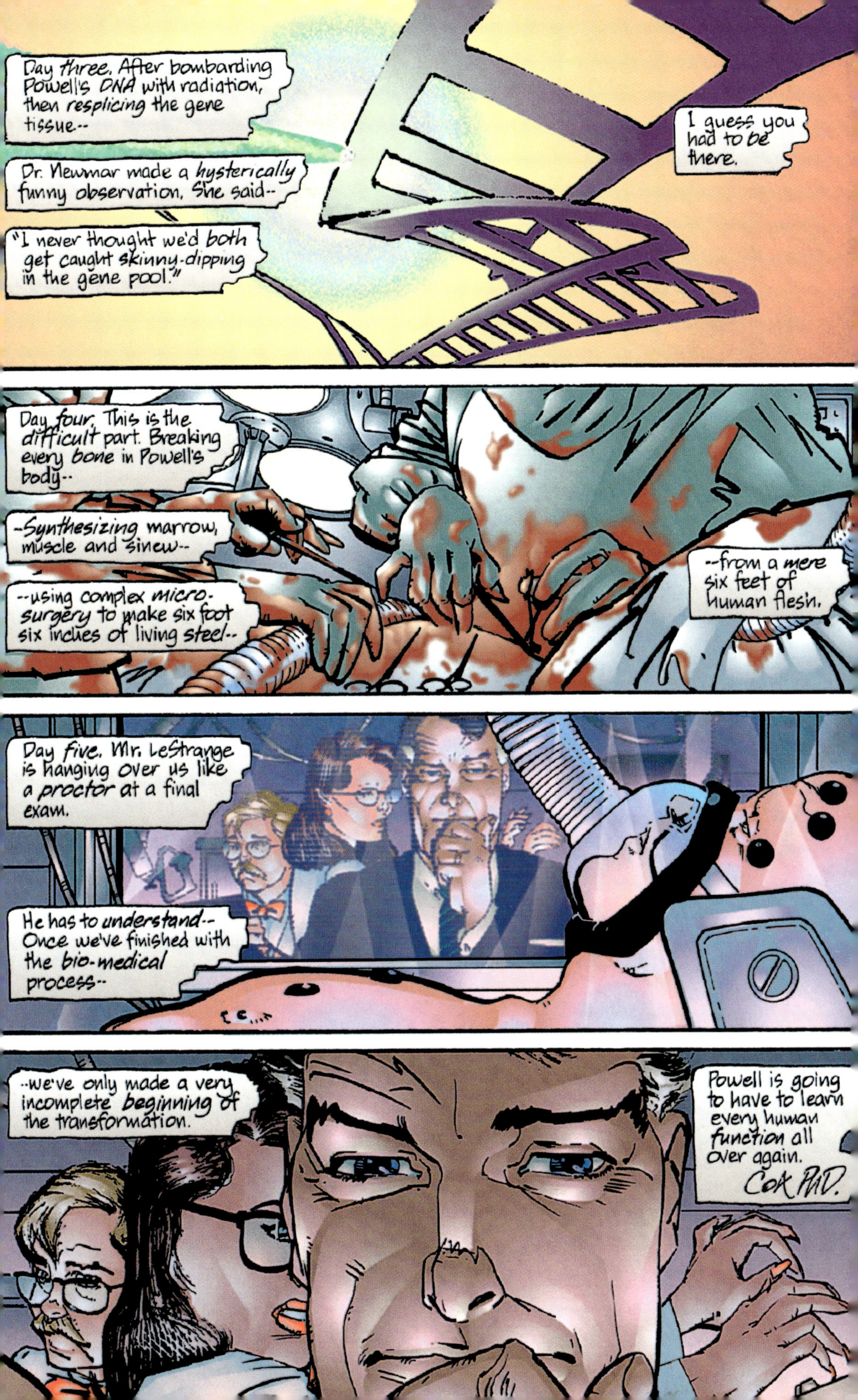
Day three. After bombarding Powell's DNA with radiation, then resplicing the gene tissue--
Dr. Newmar made a hysterically funny observation. She said--
"I never thought we'd both get caught skinny-dipping in the gene pool."
I guess you had to be there.
Day four. This is the difficult part. Breaking every bone in Powell's body--
--Synthesizing marrow, muscle and sinew--
--using complex micro-surgery to make six foot six inches of living steel--
--from a mere six feet of human flesh.
Day five. Mr. LeStrange is hanging over us like a proctor at a final exam.
He has to understand--Once we've finished with the bio-medical process--
--we've only made a very incomplete beginning of the transformation.
Powell is going to have to learn every human function all over again.
Cox PhD.

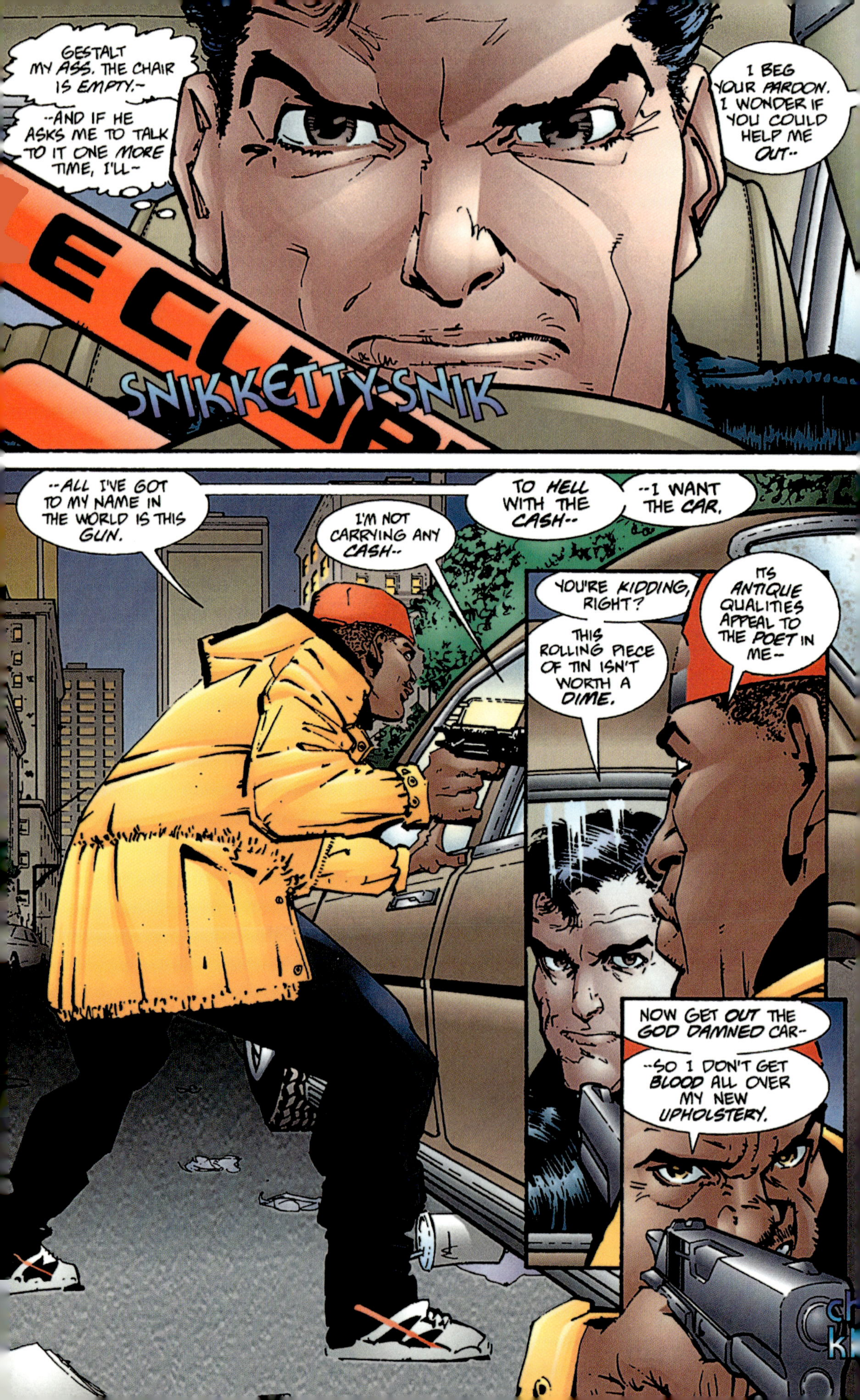
GESTALT MY ASS. THE CHAIR IS EMPTY.--
--AND IF HE ASKS ME TO TALK TO IT ONE MORE TIME, I'LL--
I BEG YOUR PARDON. I WONDER IF YOU COULD HELP ME OUT--
SNIKKETTY-SNIK
--ALL I'VE GOT TO MY NAME IN THE WORLD IS THIS GUN.
I'M NOT CARRYING ANY CASH--
TO HELL WITH THE CASH--
--I WANT THE CAR.
YOU'RE KIDDING, RIGHT?
THIS ROLLING PIECE OF TIN ISN'T WORTH A DIME.
ITS ANTIQUE QUALITIES APPEAL TO THE POET IN ME--
NOW GET OUT THE GOD DAMNED CAR--
--SO I DON'T GET BLOOD ALL OVER MY NEW UPHOLSTERY.

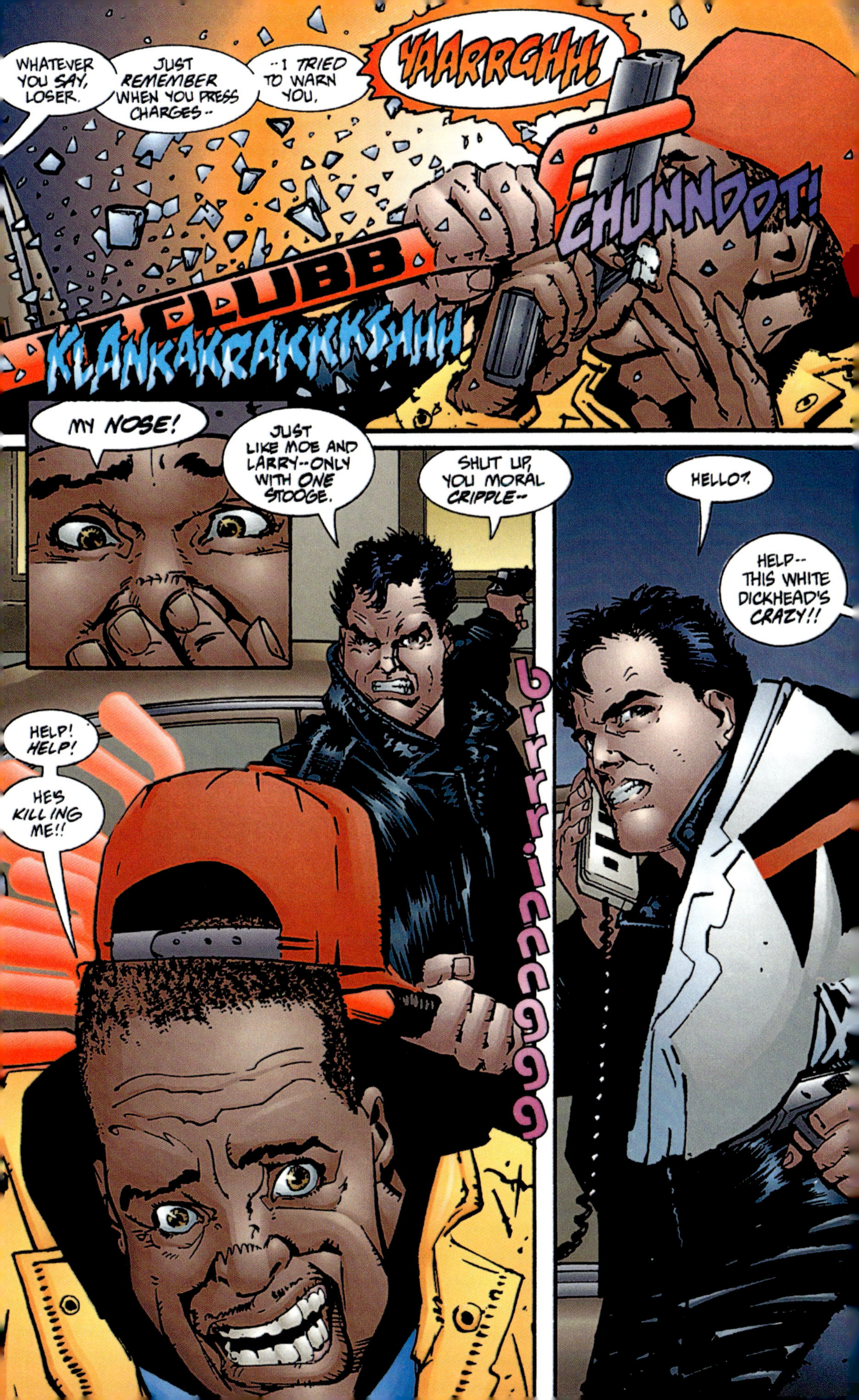

WHATEVER YOU SAY, LOSER.
JUST REMEMBER WHEN YOU PRESS CHARGES--
--I TRIED TO WARN YOU.
YAARRGHH!
CLUBB
KLANKAKRAKKKSHHH
CHUNNDOT!
MY NOSE!
JUST LIKE MOE AND LARRY--ONLY WITH ONE STOOGE.
SHUT UP, YOU MORAL CRIPPLE--
HELLO?
HELP-- THIS WHITE DICKHEAD'S CRAZY!!
brrrinnggg
HELP! HELP!
HE'S KILLING ME!!

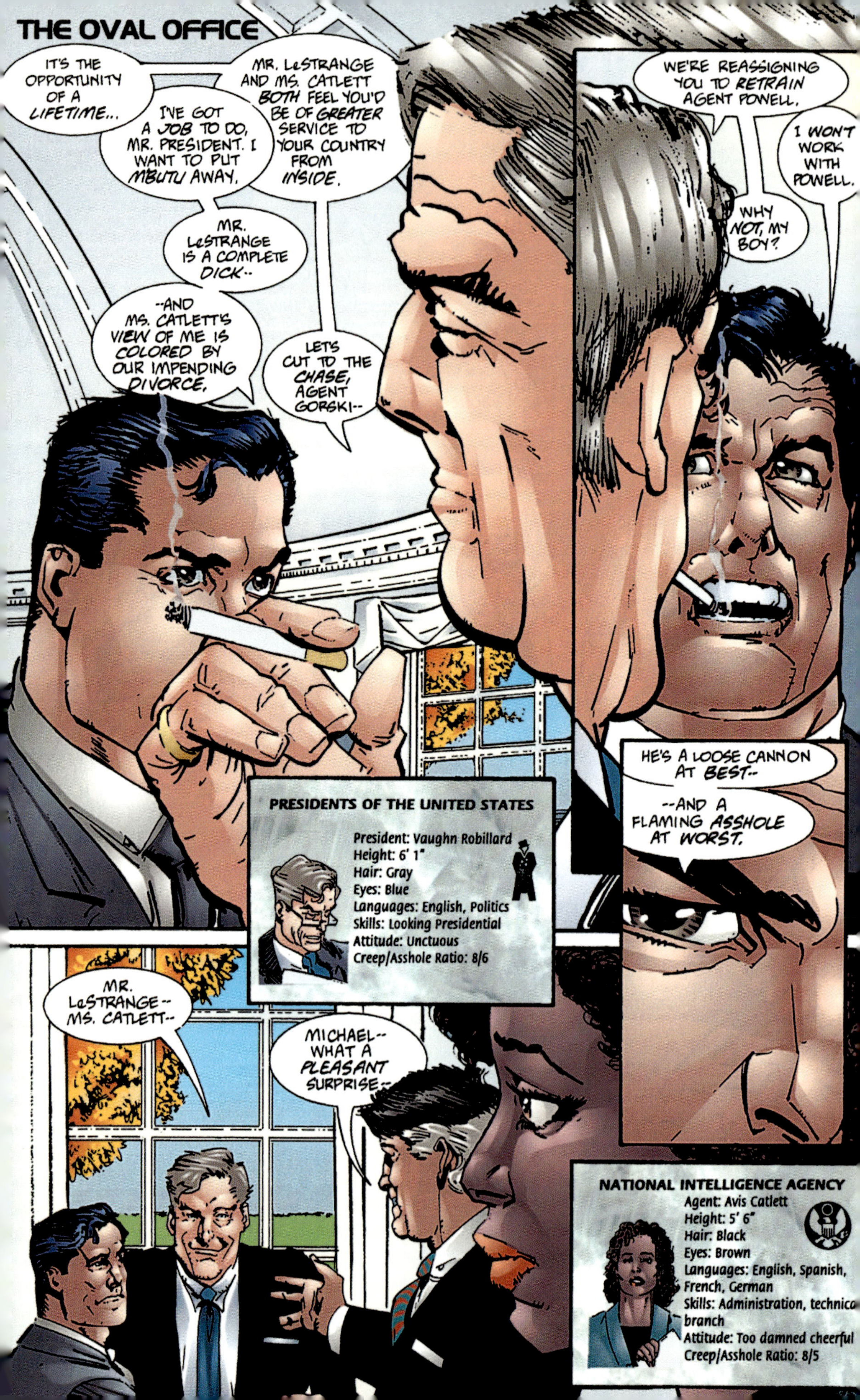
THE OVAL OFFICE
IT'S THE OPPORTUNITY OF A LIFETIME...
MR. LeSTRANGE AND MS. CATLETT BOTH FEEL YOU'D BE OF GREATER SERVICE TO YOUR COUNTRY FROM INSIDE.
I'VE GOT A JOB TO DO, MR. PRESIDENT. I WANT TO PUT MBUTU AWAY.
MR. LeSTRANGE IS A COMPLETE DICK--
--AND MS. CATLETT'S VIEW OF ME IS COLORED BY OUR IMPENDING DIVORCE.
LET'S CUT TO THE CHASE, AGENT GORSKI--
WE'RE REASSIGNING YOU TO RETRAIN AGENT POWELL.
I WON'T WORK WITH POWELL.
WHY NOT, MY BOY?
HE'S A LOOSE CANNON AT BEST--
--AND A FLAMING ASSHOLE AT WORST.
PRESIDENTS OF THE UNITED STATES
President: Vaughn Robillard
Height: 6' 1"
Hair: Gray
Eyes: Blue
Languages: English, Politics
Skills: Looking Presidential
Attitude: Unctuous
Creep/Asshole Ratio: 8/6
MR. LeSTRANGE-- MS. CATLETT--
MICHAEL-- WHAT A PLEASANT SURPRISE--
NATIONAL INTELLIGENCE AGENCY
Agent: Avis Catlett
Height: 5' 6"
Hair: Black
Eyes: Brown
Languages: English, Spanish, French, German
Skills: Administration, technica branch
Attitude: Too damned cheerful
Creep/Asshole Ratio: 8/5

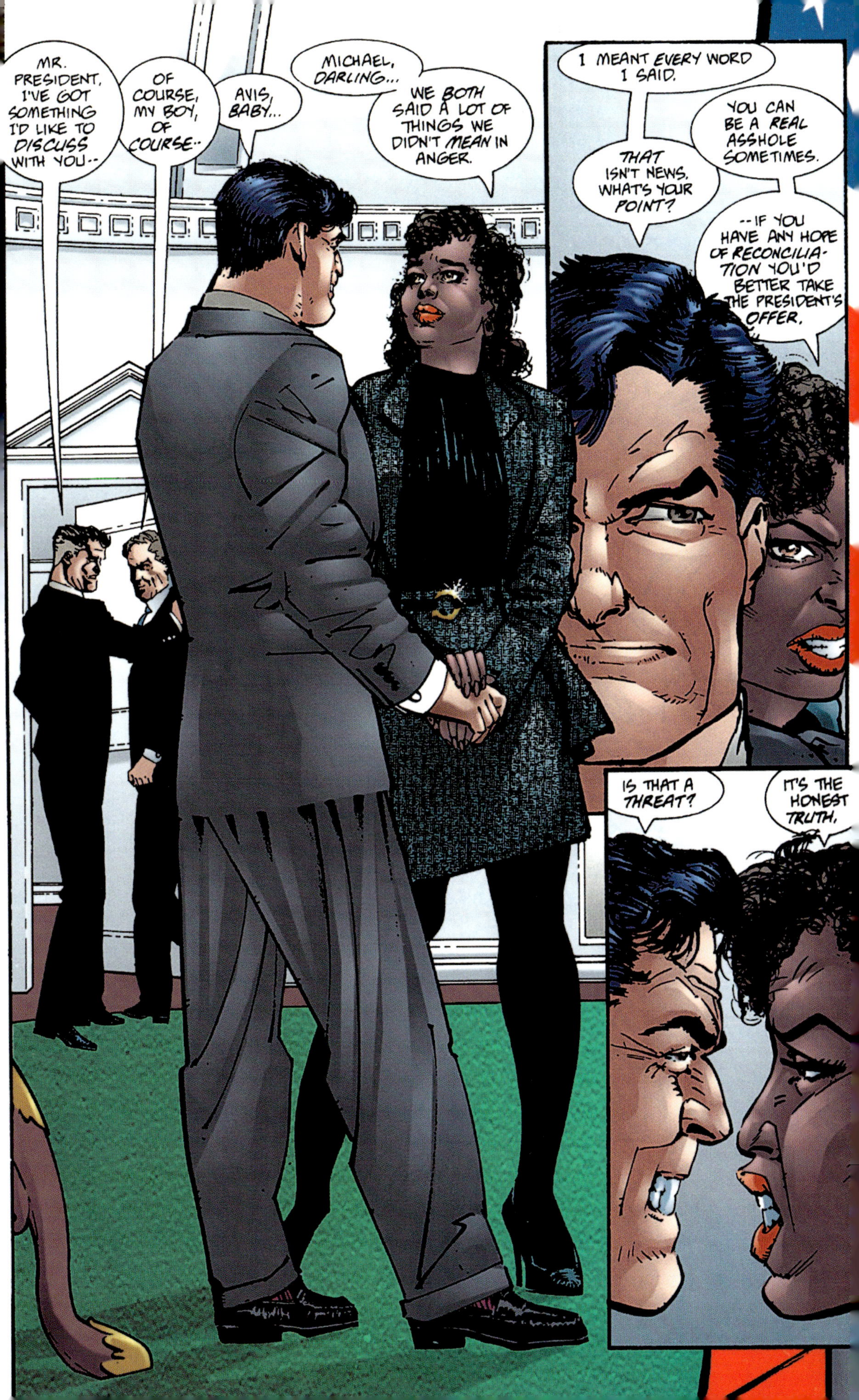
MR. PRESIDENT, I'VE GOT SOMETHING I'D LIKE TO DISCUSS WITH YOU--
OF COURSE, MY BOY, OF COURSE..
AVIS, BABY...
MICHAEL, DARLING...
WE BOTH SAID A LOT OF THINGS WE DIDN'T MEAN IN ANGER.
I MEANT EVERY WORD I SAID.
THAT ISN'T NEWS. WHAT'S YOUR POINT?
YOU CAN BE A REAL ASSHOLE SOMETIMES.
--IF YOU HAVE ANY HOPE OF RECONCILIATION YOU'D BETTER TAKE THE PRESIDENT'S OFFER.
IS THAT A THREAT?
IT'S THE HONEST TRUTH.

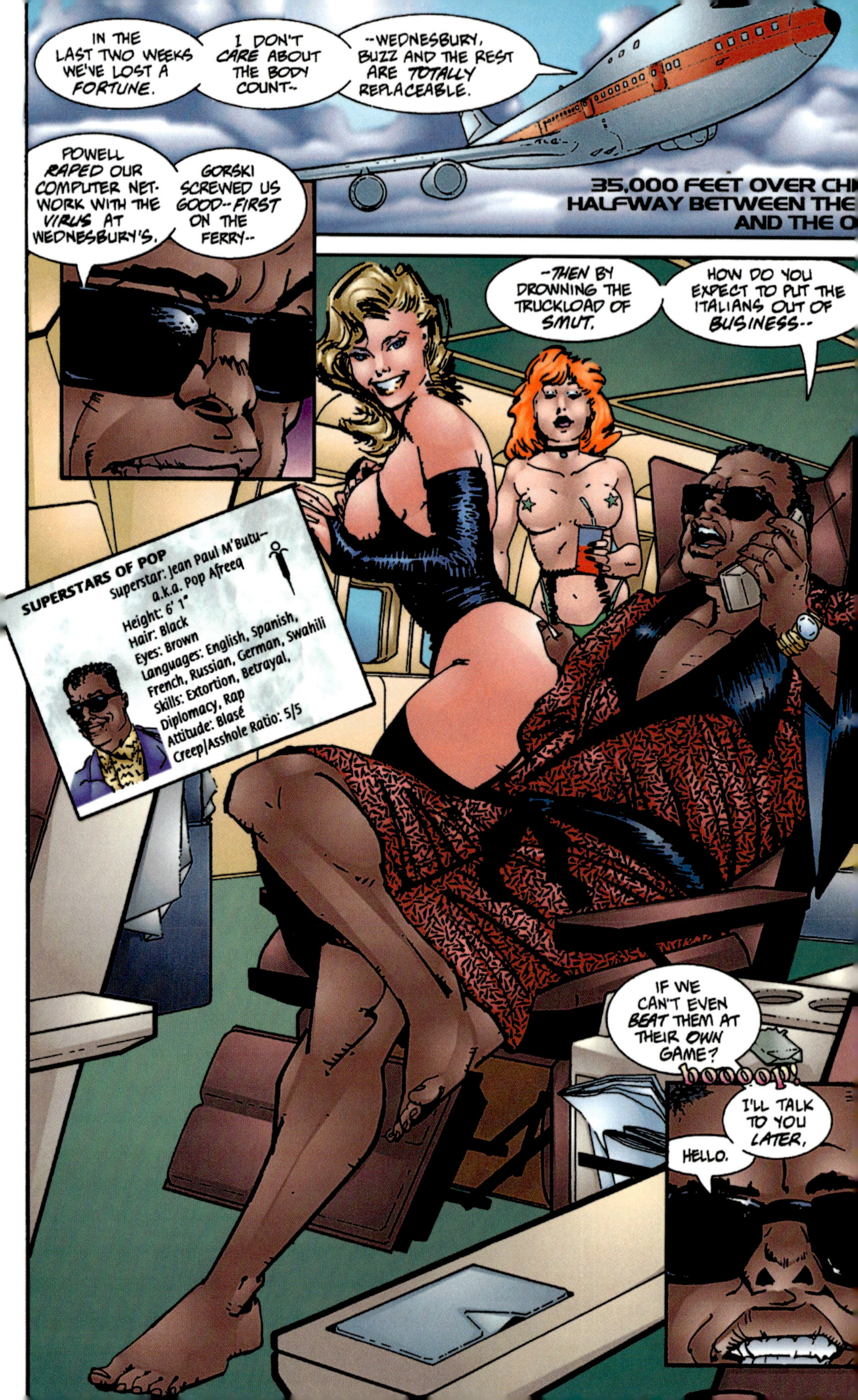
IN THE LAST TWO WEEKS WE'VE LOST A FORTUNE.
I DON'T CARE ABOUT THE BODY COUNT--
--WEDNESBURY, BUZZ AND THE REST ARE TOTALLY REPLACEABLE.
35,000 FEET OVER CH
HALFWAY BETWEEN THE
AND THE O
POWELL RAPED OUR COMPUTER NET-WORK WITH THE VIRUS AT WEDNESBURY'S.
GORSKI SCREWED US GOOD--FIRST ON THE FERRY--
--THEN BY DROWNING THE TRUCKLOAD OF SMUT.
HOW DO YOU EXPECT TO PUT THE ITALIANS OUT OF BUSINESS--
SUPERSTARS OF POP
Superstar: Jean Paul M'Butu--
a.k.a. Pop Afreeq
Height: 6' 1"
Hair: Black
Eyes: Brown
Languages: English, Spanish, French, Russian, German, Swahili
Skills: Extortion, Betrayal, Diplomacy, Rap
Attitude: Blasé
Creep/Asshole Ratio: 5/5
IF WE CAN'T EVEN BEAT THEM AT THEIR OWN GAME?
boooop!
I'LL TALK TO YOU LATER.
HELLO.

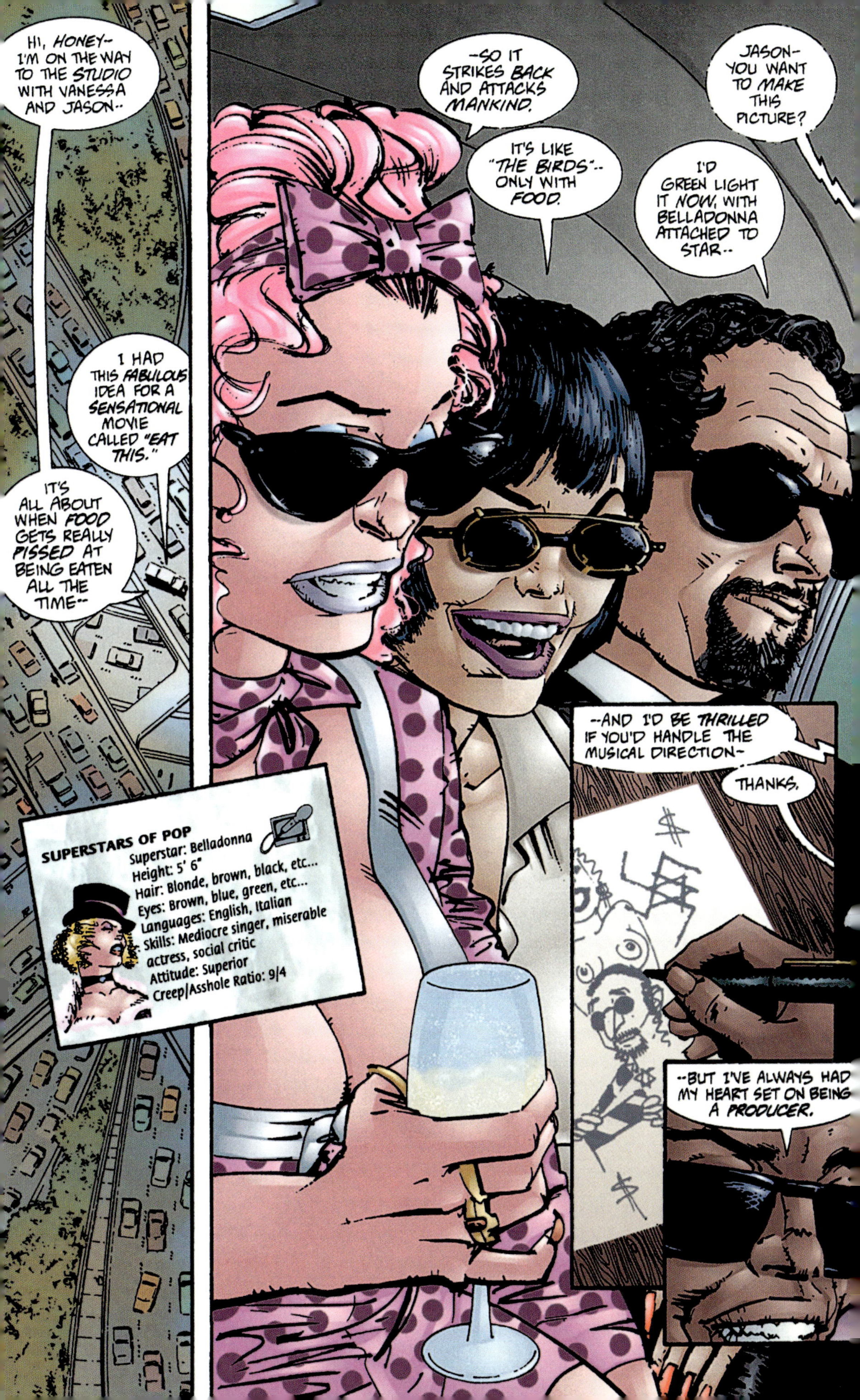
HI, HONEY-- I'M ON THE WAY TO THE STUDIO WITH VANESSA AND JASON--
I HAD THIS FABULOUS IDEA FOR A SENSATIONAL MOVIE CALLED "EAT THIS."
IT'S ALL ABOUT WHEN FOOD GETS REALLY PISSED AT BEING EATEN ALL THE TIME--
--SO IT STRIKES BACK AND ATTACKS MANKIND.
IT'S LIKE "THE BIRDS"-- ONLY WITH FOOD.
JASON-- YOU WANT TO MAKE THIS PICTURE?
I'D GREEN LIGHT IT NOW, WITH BELLADONNA ATTACHED TO STAR--
SUPERSTARS OF POP
Superstar: Belladonna
Height: 5' 6"
Hair: Blonde, brown, black, etc...
Eyes: Brown, blue, green, etc...
Languages: English, Italian
Skills: Mediocre singer, miserable actress, social critic
Attitude: Superior
Creep/Asshole Ratio: 9/4
--AND I'D BE THRILLED IF YOU'D HANDLE THE MUSICAL DIRECTION--
THANKS.
--BUT I'VE ALWAYS HAD MY HEART SET ON BEING A PRODUCER.

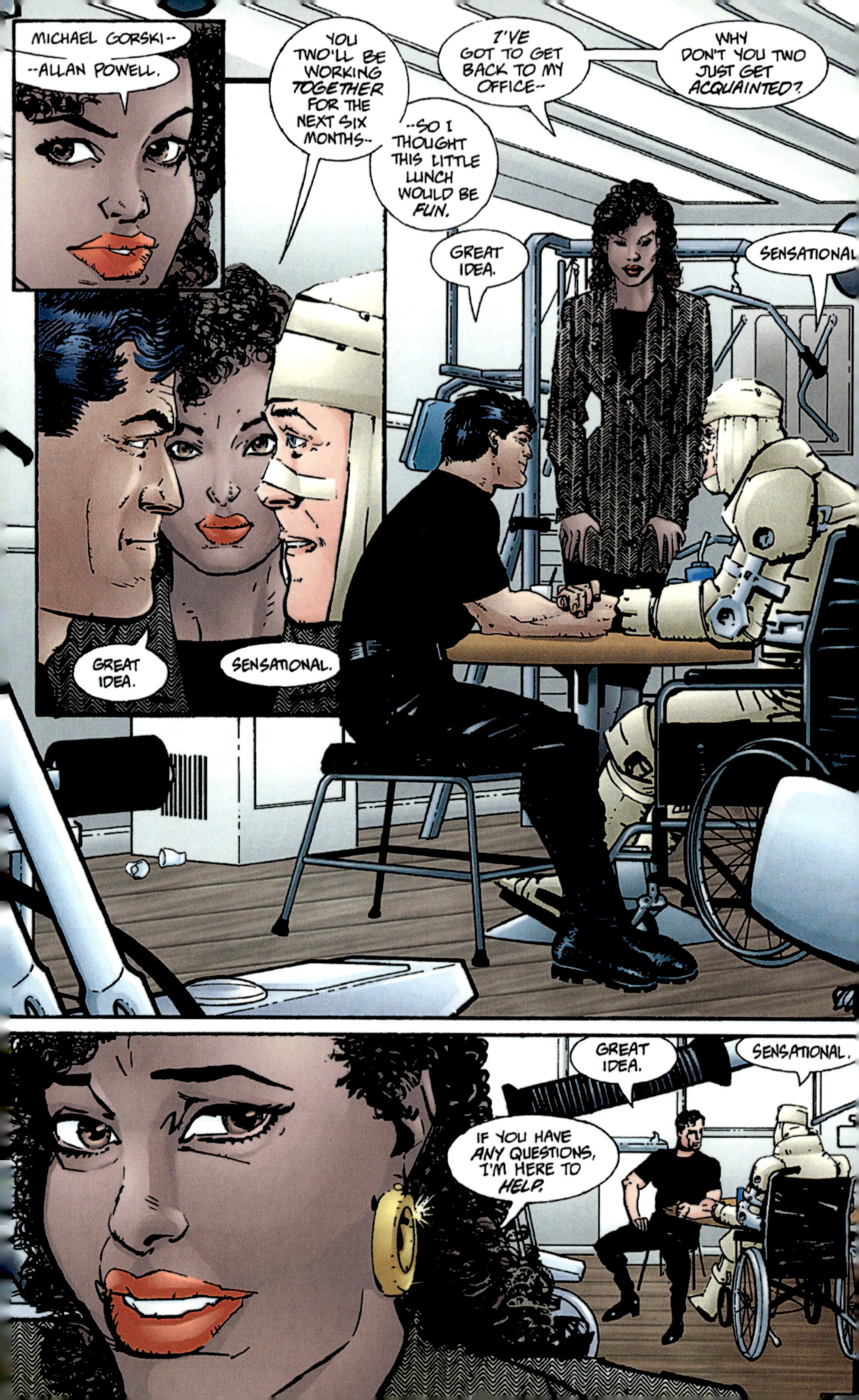
MICHAEL GORSKI--
--ALLAN POWELL.
YOU TWO'LL BE WORKING TOGETHER FOR THE NEXT SIX MONTHS--
--SO I THOUGHT THIS LITTLE LUNCH WOULD BE FUN.
I'VE GOT TO GET BACK TO MY OFFICE--
WHY DON'T YOU TWO JUST GET ACQUAINTED?
GREAT IDEA.
SENSATIONAL.
GREAT IDEA.
SENSATIONAL.
GREAT IDEA.
SENSATIONAL.
IF YOU HAVE ANY QUESTIONS, I'M HERE TO HELP.

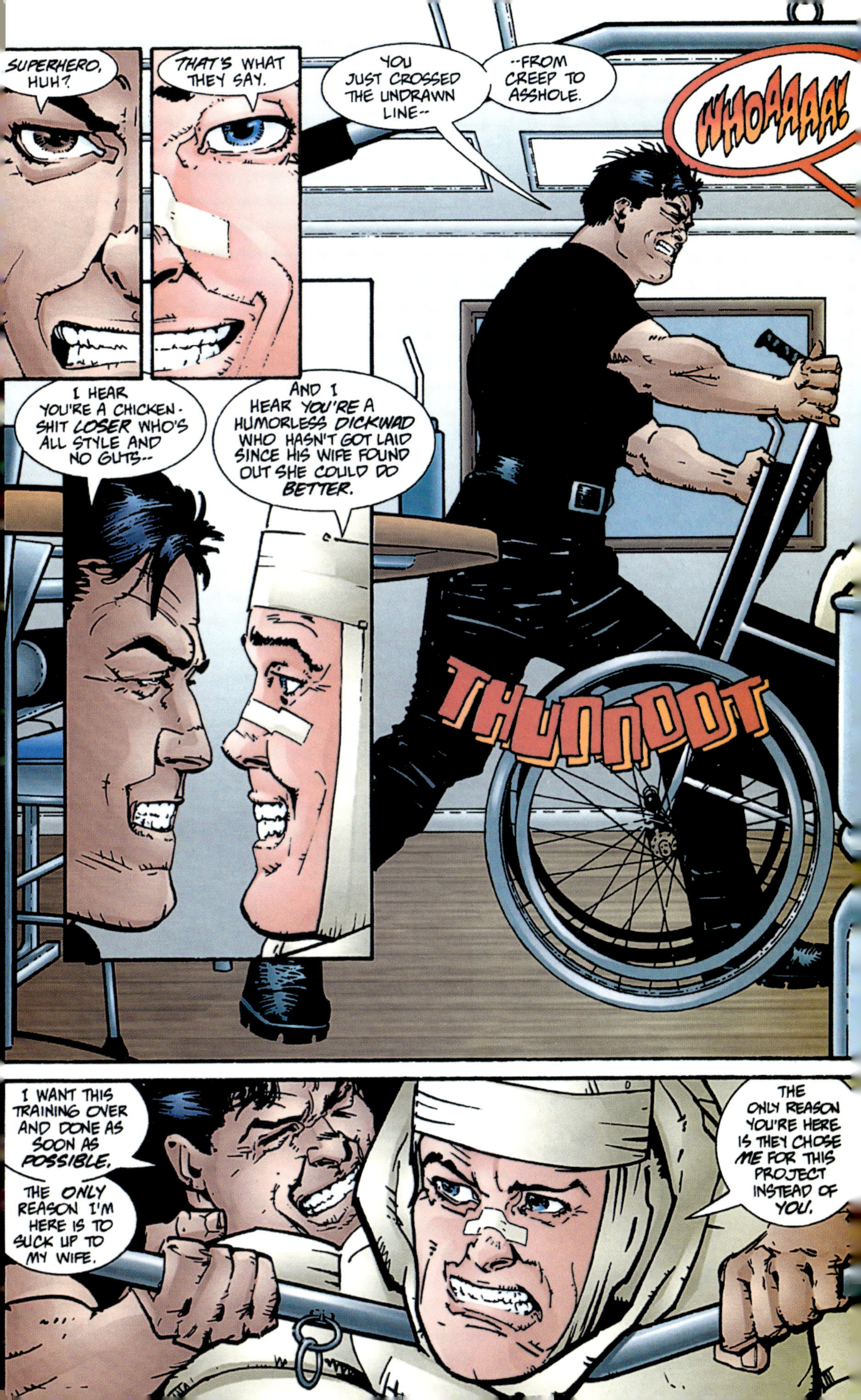
SUPERHERO, HUH?
THAT'S WHAT THEY SAY.
YOU JUST CROSSED THE UNDRAWN LINE--
--FROM CREEP TO ASSHOLE.
WHOAAAA!
I HEAR YOU'RE A CHICKEN-SHIT LOSER WHO'S ALL STYLE AND NO GUTS--
AND I HEAR YOU'RE A HUMORLESS DICKWAD WHO HASN'T GOT LAID SINCE HIS WIFE FOUND OUT SHE COULD DO BETTER.
THUNNOOT
I WANT THIS TRAINING OVER AND DONE AS SOON AS POSSIBLE.
THE ONLY REASON I'M HERE IS TO SUCK UP TO MY WIFE.
THE ONLY REASON YOU'RE HERE IS THEY CHOSE ME FOR THIS PROJECT INSTEAD OF YOU.

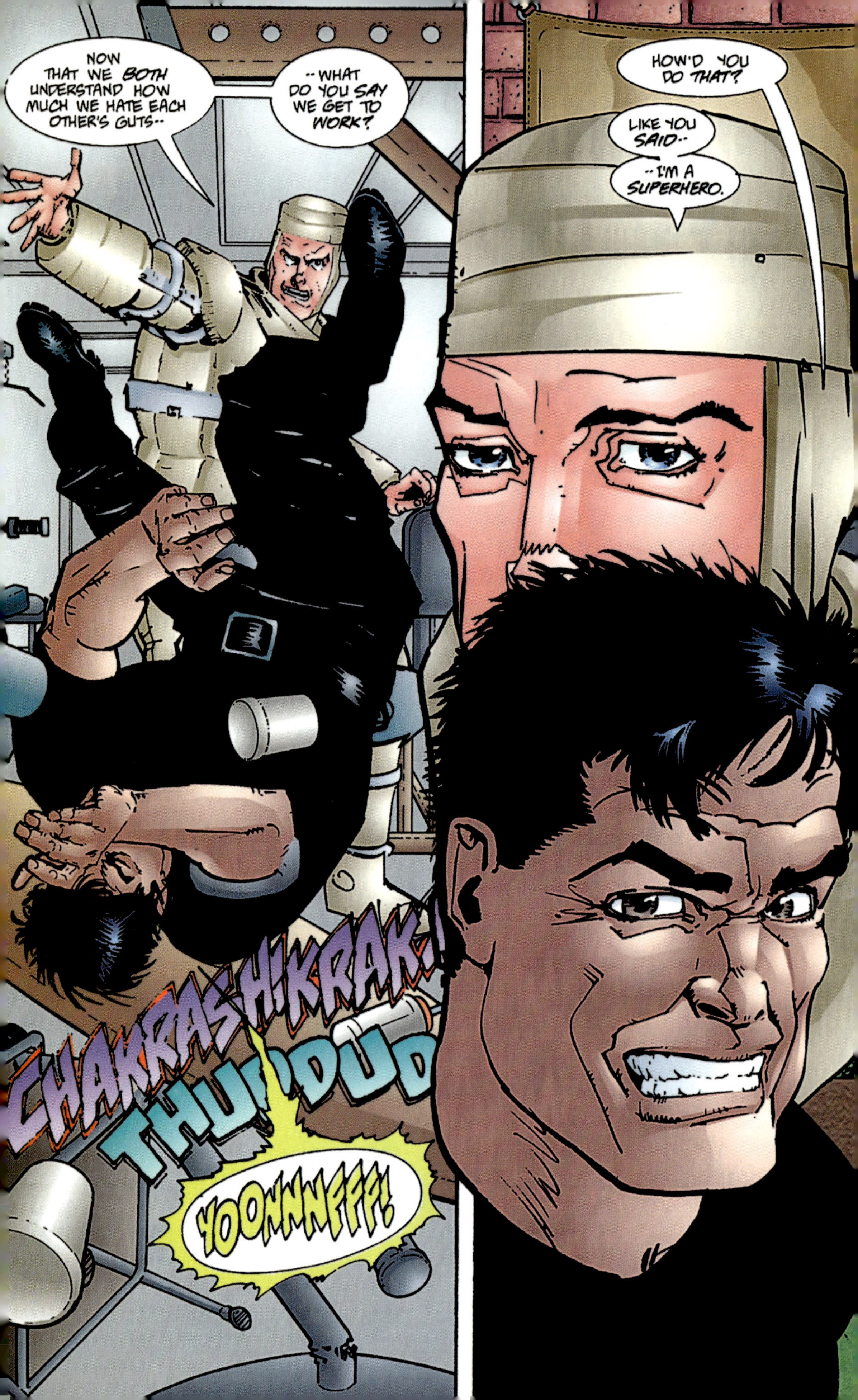
NOW THAT WE *BOTH* UNDERSTAND HOW MUCH WE HATE EACH OTHER'S GUTS--
--WHAT DO YOU SAY WE GET TO *WORK*?
CHAKRASH!-KRAK!!
THUDDUD
YOONNNFFF!
HOW'D YOU DO *THAT*?
LIKE YOU SAID--
--I'M A SUPERHERO.

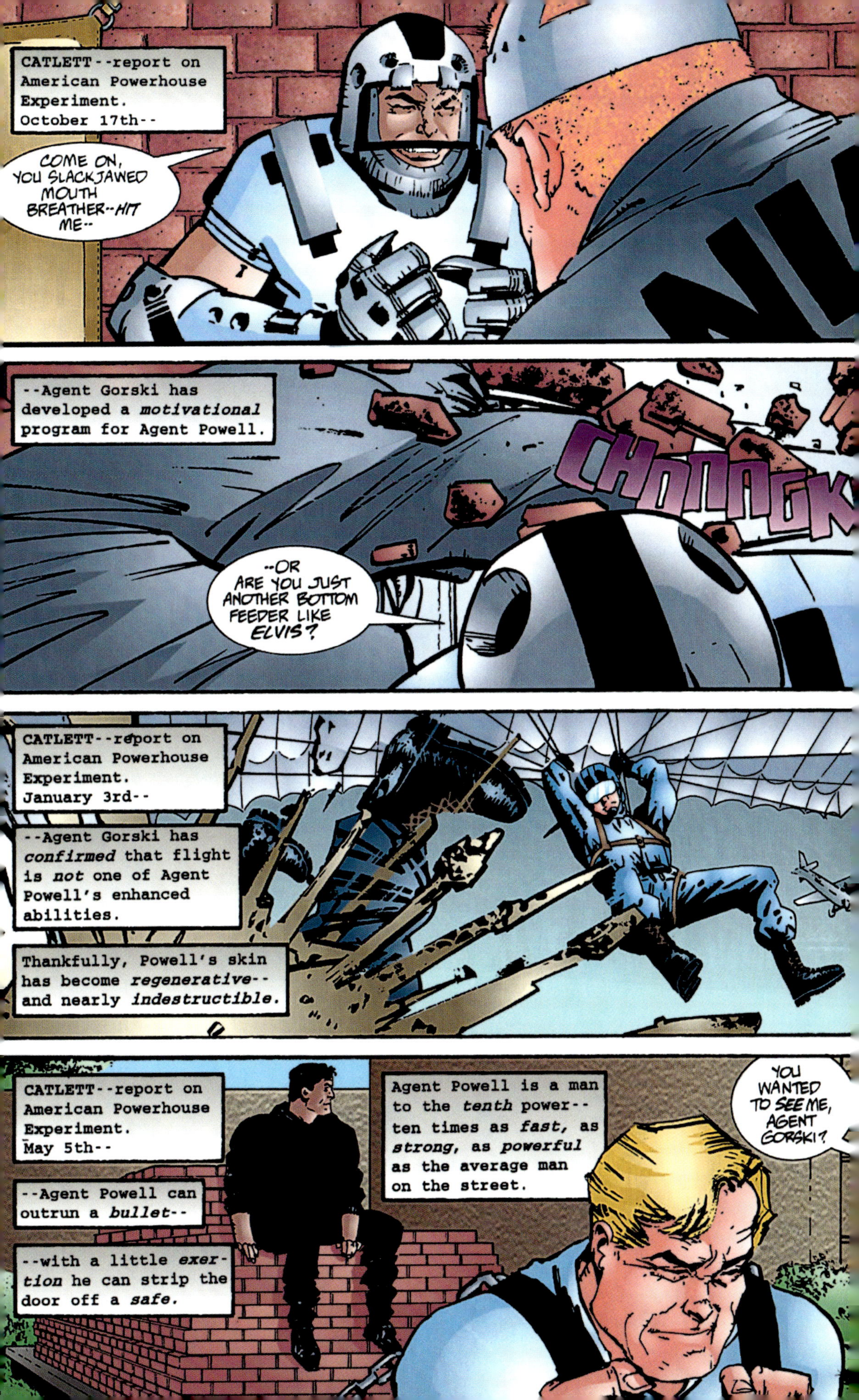
CATLETT--report on American Powerhouse Experiment. October 17th--
COME ON, YOU SLACKJAWED MOUTH BREATHER--HIT ME--
--Agent Gorski has developed a motivational program for Agent Powell.
CHONNGK
--OR ARE YOU JUST ANOTHER BOTTOM FEEDER LIKE ELVIS?
CATLETT--report on American Powerhouse Experiment. January 3rd--
--Agent Gorski has confirmed that flight is not one of Agent Powell's enhanced abilities.
Thankfully, Powell's skin has become regenerative--and nearly indestructible.
CATLETT--report on American Powerhouse Experiment. May 5th--
--Agent Powell can outrun a bullet--
--with a little exertion he can strip the door off a safe.
Agent Powell is a man to the tenth power--ten times as fast, as strong, as powerful as the average man on the street.
YOU WANTED TO SEE ME, AGENT GORSKI?

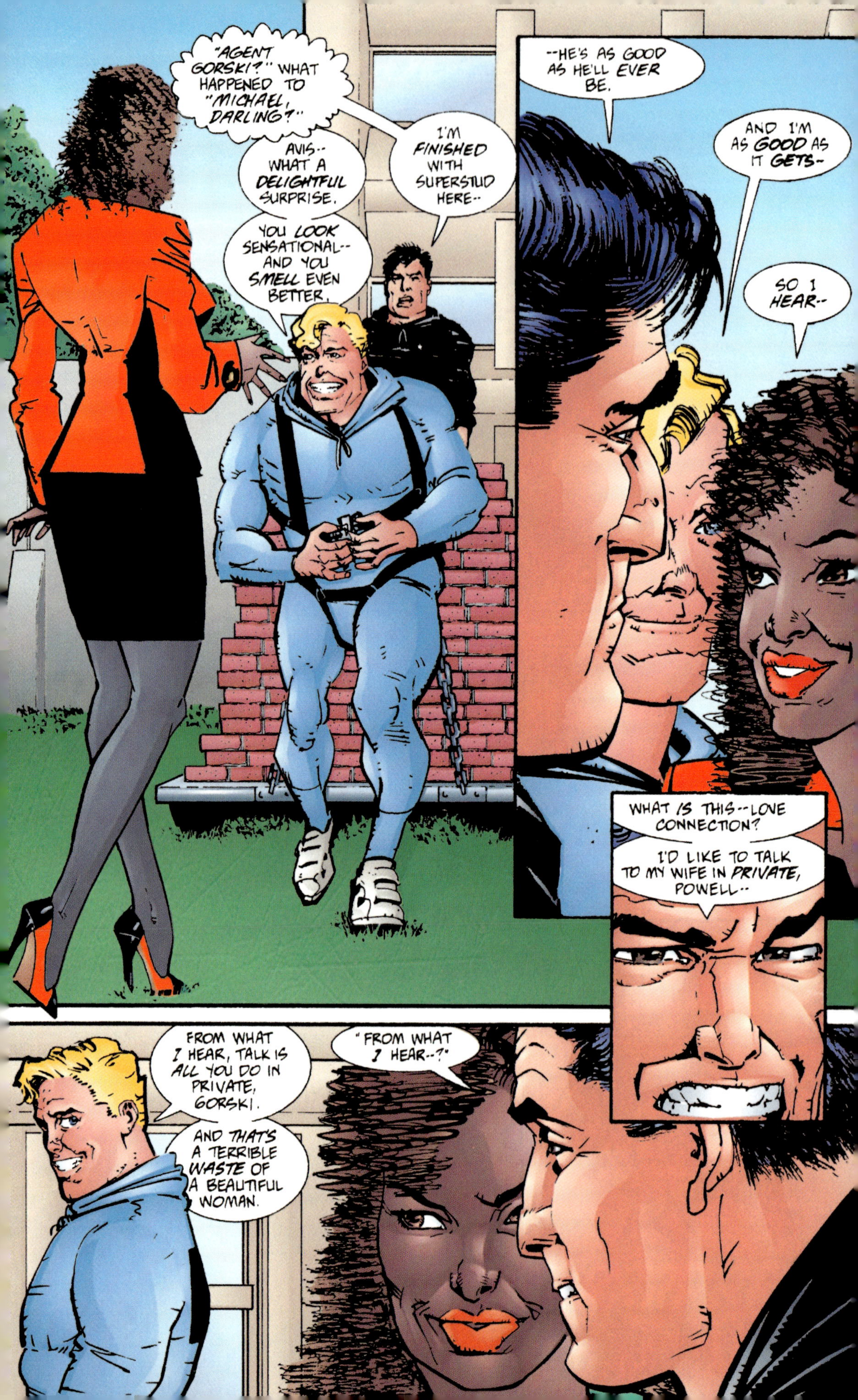
"AGENT GORSKI?" WHAT HAPPENED TO "MICHAEL, DARLING?"
I'M FINISHED WITH SUPERSTUD HERE--
AVIS-- WHAT A DELIGHTFUL SURPRISE.
YOU LOOK SENSATIONAL-- AND YOU SMELL EVEN BETTER.
--HE'S AS GOOD AS HE'LL EVER BE.
AND I'M AS GOOD AS IT GETS--
SO I HEAR--
WHAT IS THIS--LOVE CONNECTION?
I'D LIKE TO TALK TO MY WIFE IN PRIVATE, POWELL--
FROM WHAT I HEAR, TALK IS ALL YOU DO IN PRIVATE, GORSKI.
AND THAT'S A TERRIBLE WASTE OF A BEAUTIFUL WOMAN.
"FROM WHAT I HEAR--?"

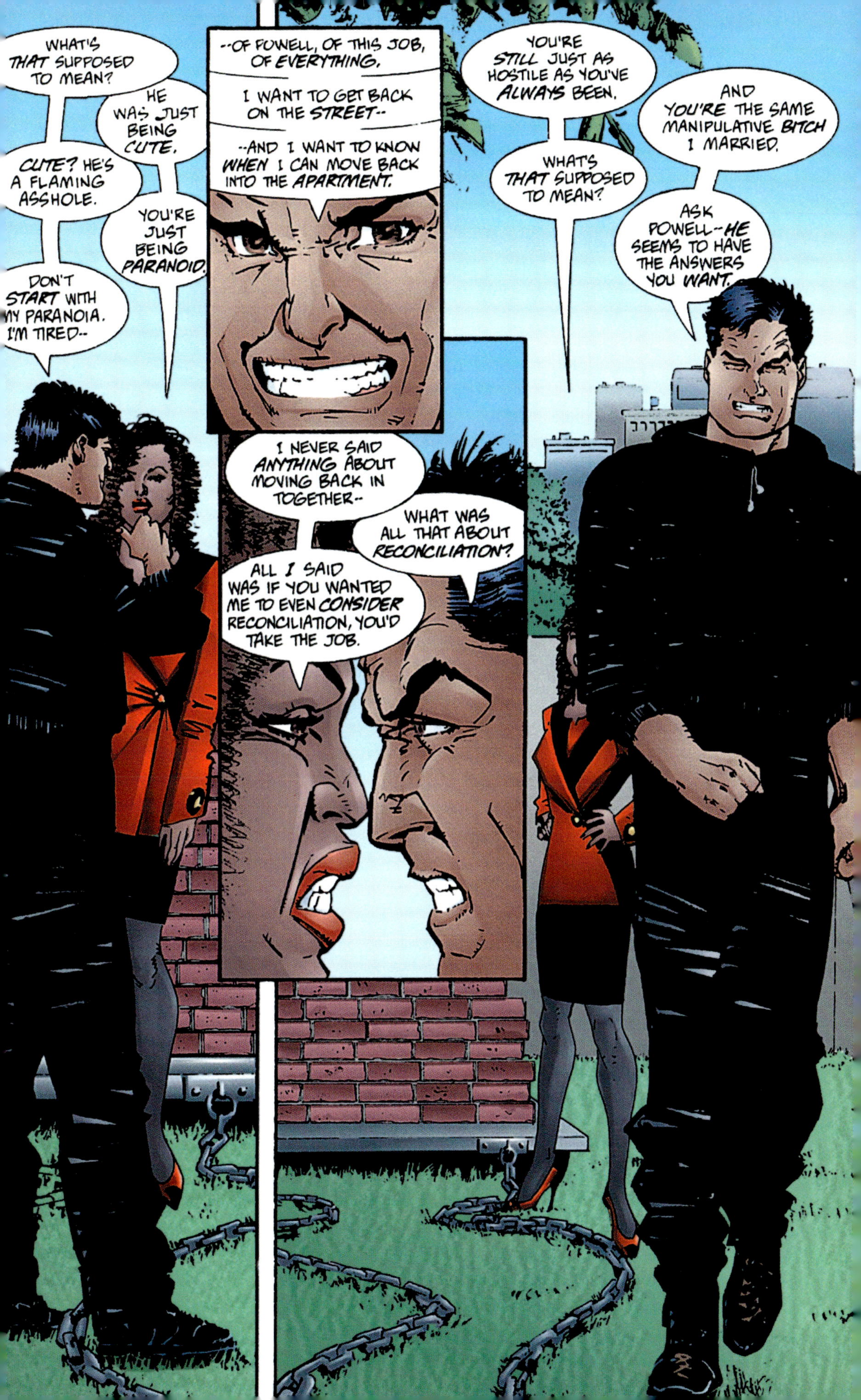
WHAT'S THAT SUPPOSED TO MEAN?
HE WAS JUST BEING CUTE.
CUTE? HE'S A FLAMING ASSHOLE.
YOU'RE JUST BEING PARANOID.
DON'T START WITH MY PARANOIA. I'M TIRED--
--OF POWELL, OF THIS JOB, OF EVERYTHING.
I WANT TO GET BACK ON THE STREET--
--AND I WANT TO KNOW WHEN I CAN MOVE BACK INTO THE APARTMENT.
I NEVER SAID ANYTHING ABOUT MOVING BACK IN TOGETHER--
WHAT WAS ALL THAT ABOUT RECONCILIATION?
ALL I SAID WAS IF YOU WANTED ME TO EVEN CONSIDER RECONCILIATION, YOU'D TAKE THE JOB.
YOU'RE STILL JUST AS HOSTILE AS YOU'VE ALWAYS BEEN.
AND YOU'RE THE SAME MANIPULATIVE BITCH I MARRIED.
WHAT'S THAT SUPPOSED TO MEAN?
ASK POWELL--HE SEEMS TO HAVE THE ANSWERS YOU WANT.

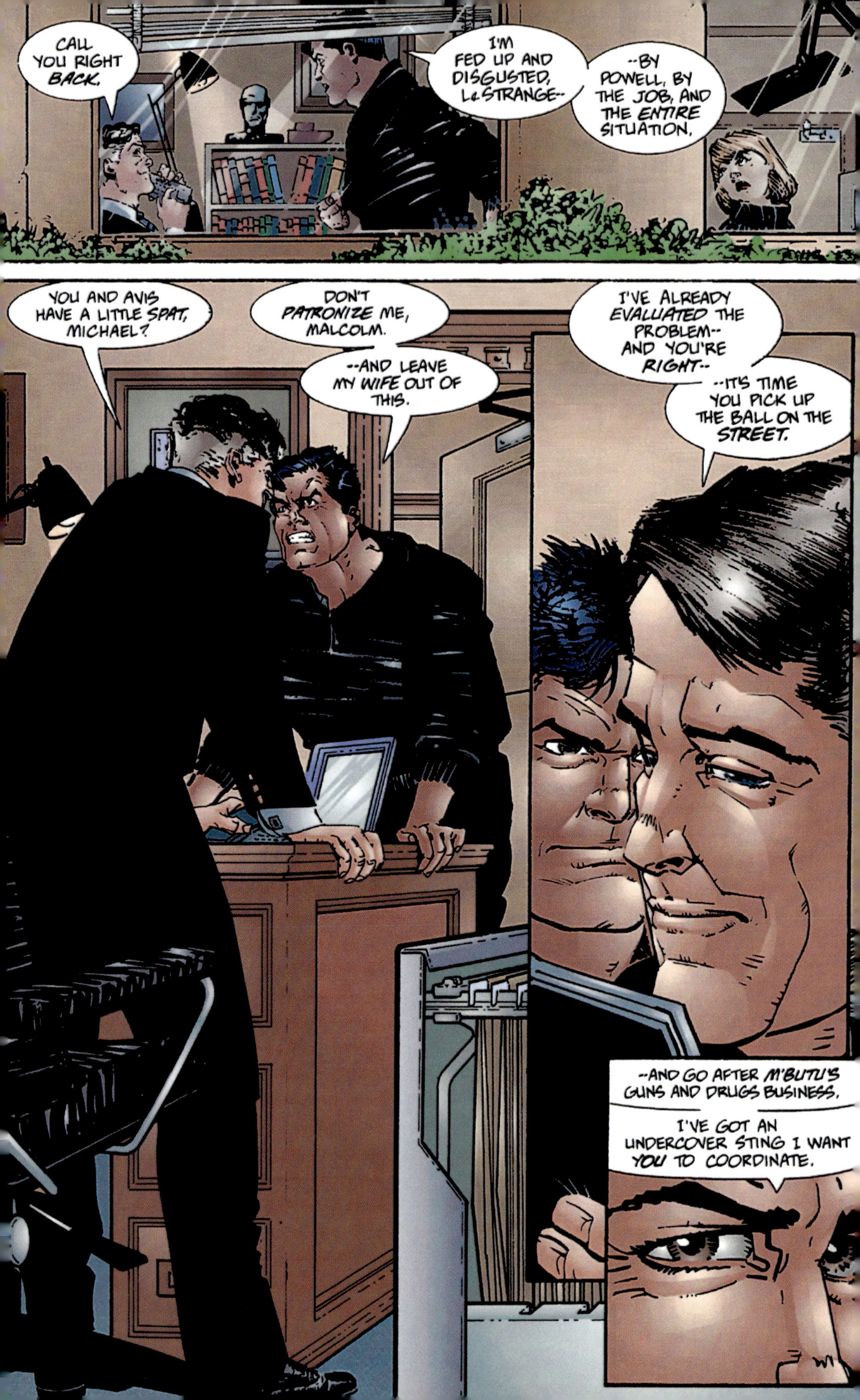
CALL YOU RIGHT BACK.
I'M FED UP AND DISGUSTED, LeSTRANGE--
--BY POWELL, BY THE JOB, AND THE ENTIRE SITUATION.
YOU AND AVIS HAVE A LITTLE SPAT, MICHAEL?
DON'T PATRONIZE ME, MALCOLM.
--AND LEAVE MY WIFE OUT OF THIS.
I'VE ALREADY EVALUATED THE PROBLEM-- AND YOU'RE RIGHT--
--IT'S TIME YOU PICK UP THE BALL ON THE STREET.
--AND GO AFTER M'BUTU'S GUNS AND DRUGS BUSINESS.
I'VE GOT AN UNDERCOVER STING I WANT YOU TO COORDINATE.

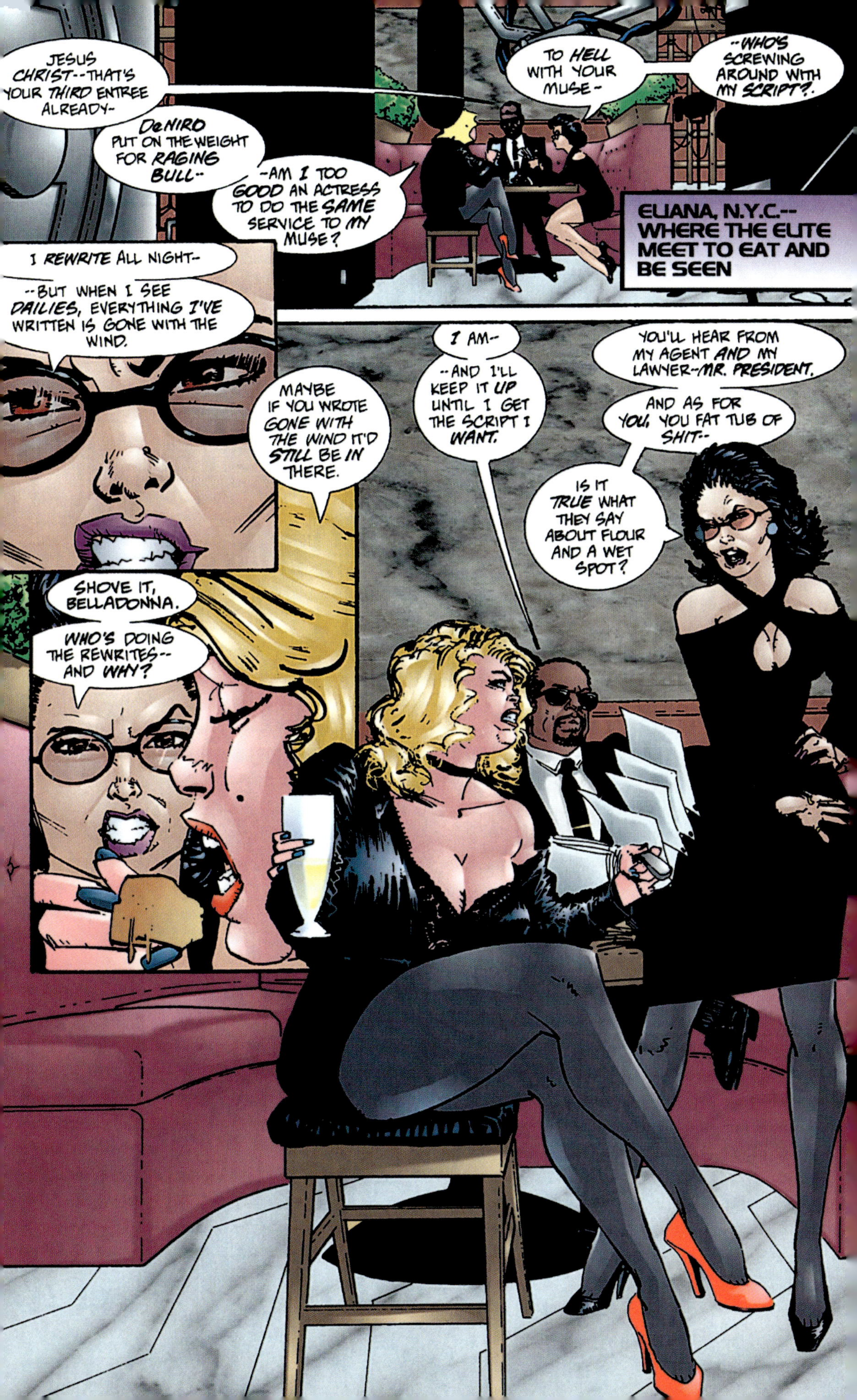
JESUS CHRIST--THAT'S YOUR THIRD ENTREE ALREADY-
DeNIRO PUT ON THE WEIGHT FOR RAGING BULL--
-AM I TOO GOOD AN ACTRESS TO DO THE SAME SERVICE TO MY MUSE?
TO HELL WITH YOUR MUSE-
-WHO'S SCREWING AROUND WITH MY SCRIPT?.
ELIANA, N.Y.C.-- WHERE THE ELITE MEET TO EAT AND BE SEEN
I REWRITE ALL NIGHT-
--BUT WHEN I SEE DAILIES, EVERYTHING I'VE WRITTEN IS GONE WITH THE WIND.
MAYBE IF YOU WROTE GONE WITH THE WIND IT'D STILL BE IN THERE.
I AM--
--AND I'LL KEEP IT UP UNTIL I GET THE SCRIPT I WANT.
YOU'LL HEAR FROM MY AGENT AND MY LAWYER--MR. PRESIDENT.
AND AS FOR YOU, YOU FAT TUB OF SHIT--
IS IT TRUE WHAT THEY SAY ABOUT FLOUR AND A WET SPOT?
SHOVE IT, BELLADONNA.
WHO'S DOING THE REWRITES-- AND WHY?

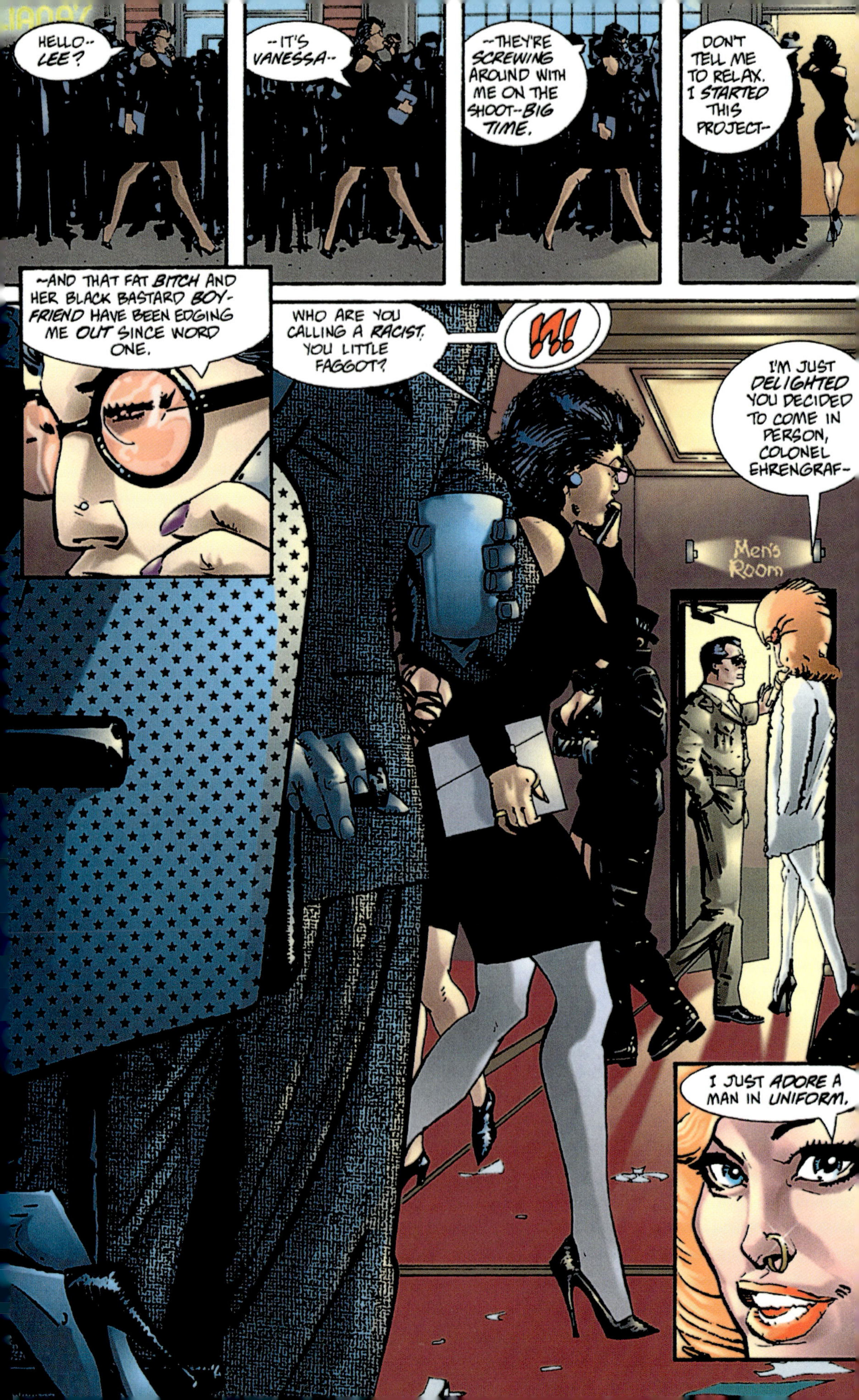
HELLO-- LEE?
--IT'S VANESSA--
--THEY'RE SCREWING AROUND WITH ME ON THE SHOOT--BIG TIME.
DON'T TELL ME TO RELAX. I STARTED THIS PROJECT-
--AND THAT FAT BITCH AND HER BLACK BASTARD BOY-FRIEND HAVE BEEN EDGING ME OUT SINCE WORD ONE.
WHO ARE YOU CALLING A RACIST, YOU LITTLE FAGGOT?
!?!
I'M JUST DELIGHTED YOU DECIDED TO COME IN PERSON, COLONEL EHRENGRAF-
Men's Room
I JUST ADORE A MAN IN UNIFORM.

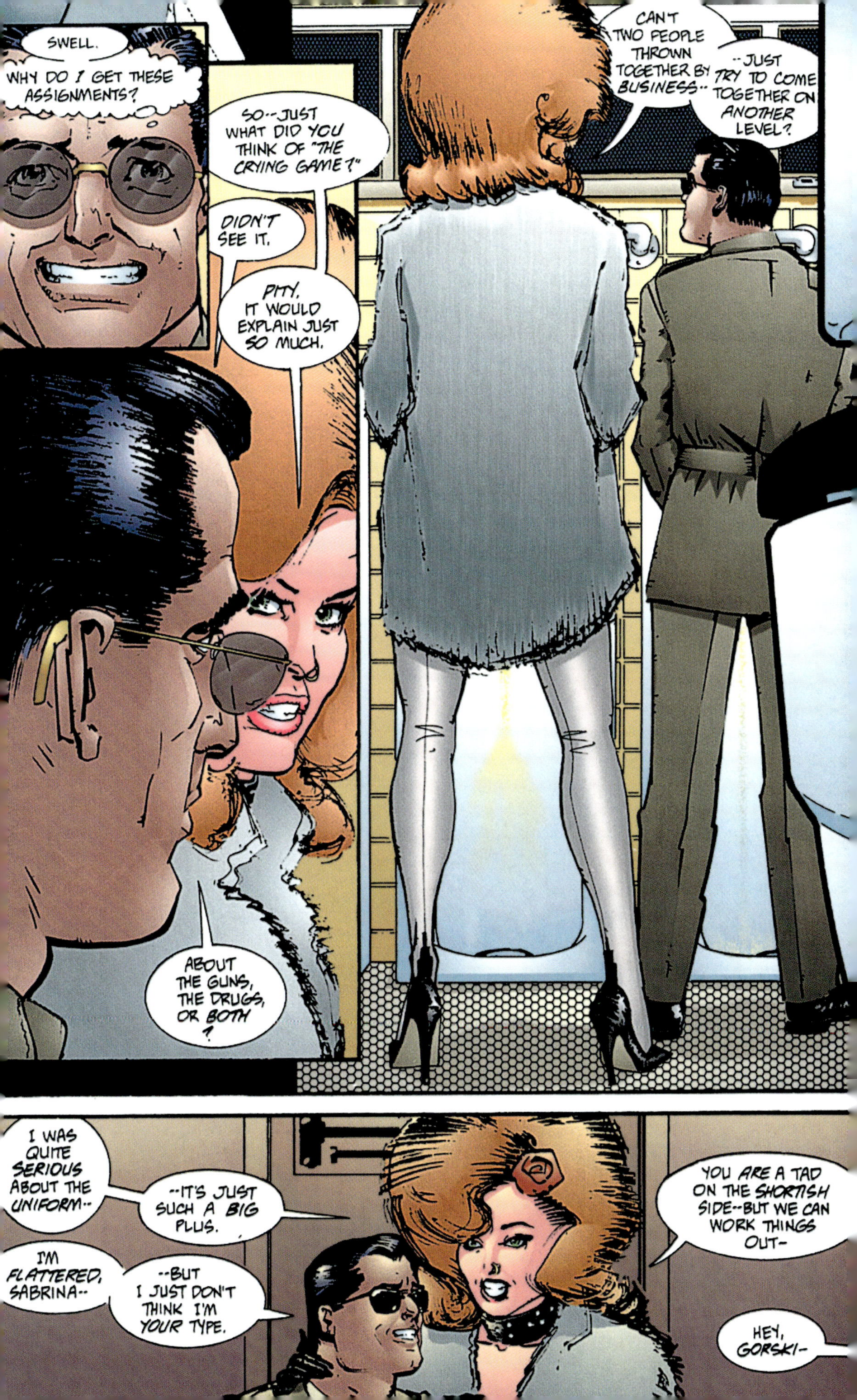
SWELL.
WHY DO I GET THESE ASSIGNMENTS?
SO--JUST WHAT DID YOU THINK OF "THE CRYING GAME?"
DIDN'T SEE IT.
PITY. IT WOULD EXPLAIN JUST SO MUCH.
ABOUT THE GUNS, THE DRUGS, OR BOTH?
CAN'T TWO PEOPLE THROWN TOGETHER BY BUSINESS--
--JUST TRY TO COME TOGETHER ON ANOTHER LEVEL?
I WAS QUITE SERIOUS ABOUT THE UNIFORM--
--IT'S JUST SUCH A BIG PLUS.
I'M FLATTERED, SABRINA--
--BUT I JUST DON'T THINK I'M YOUR TYPE.
YOU ARE A TAD ON THE SHORTISH SIDE--BUT WE CAN WORK THINGS OUT-
HEY, GORSKI-

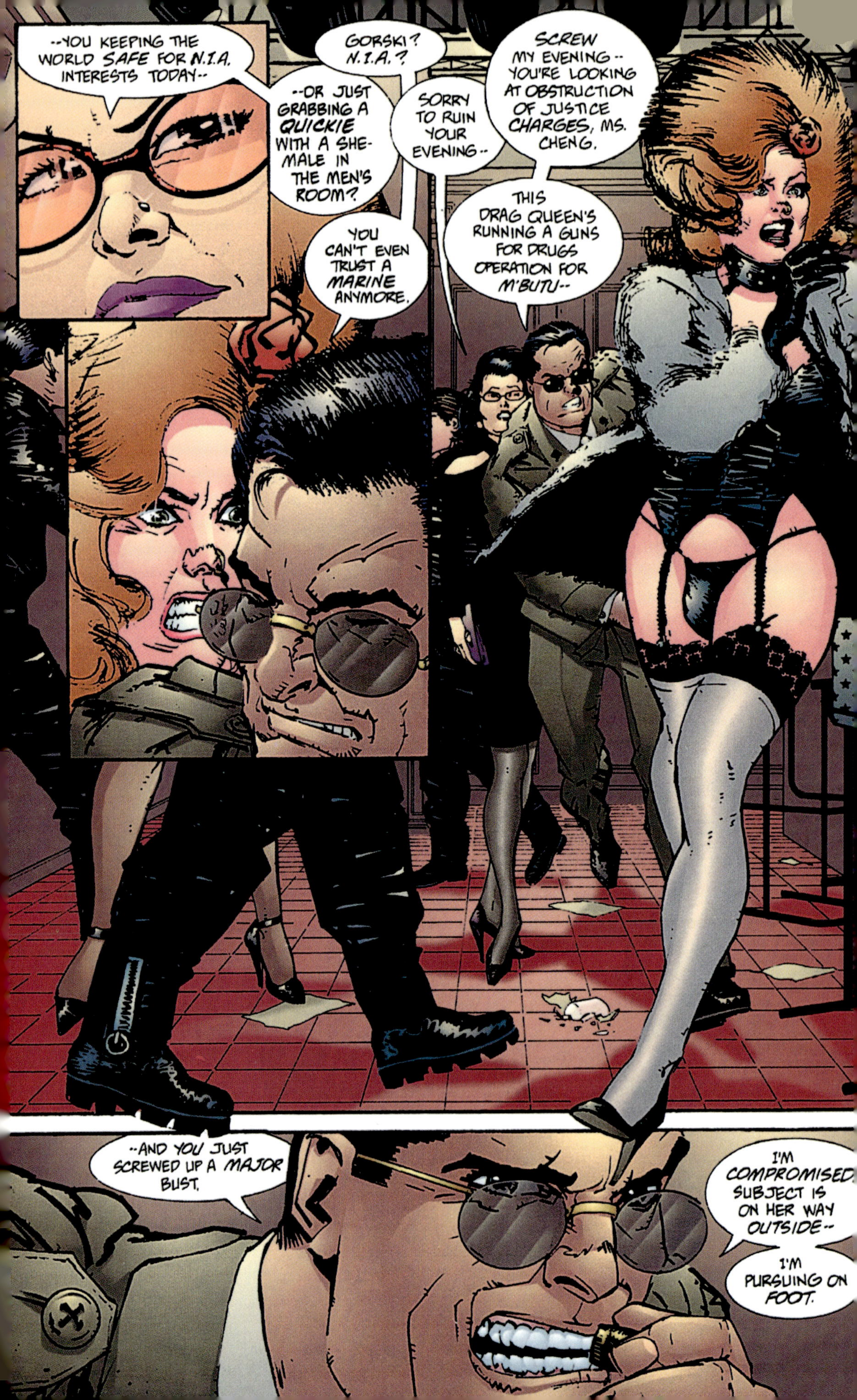
--YOU KEEPING THE WORLD SAFE FOR N.I.A. INTERESTS TODAY--
GORSKI? N.I.A.?
--OR JUST GRABBING A QUICKIE WITH A SHE-MALE IN THE MEN'S ROOM?
YOU CAN'T EVEN TRUST A MARINE ANYMORE.
SORRY TO RUIN YOUR EVENING--
SCREW MY EVENING-- YOU'RE LOOKING AT OBSTRUCTION OF JUSTICE CHARGES, MS. CHENG.
THIS DRAG QUEEN'S RUNNING A GUNS FOR DRUGS OPERATION FOR M'BUTU--
--AND YOU JUST SCREWED UP A MAJOR BUST.
I'M COMPROMISED. SUBJECT IS ON HER WAY OUTSIDE--
I'M PURSUING ON FOOT.

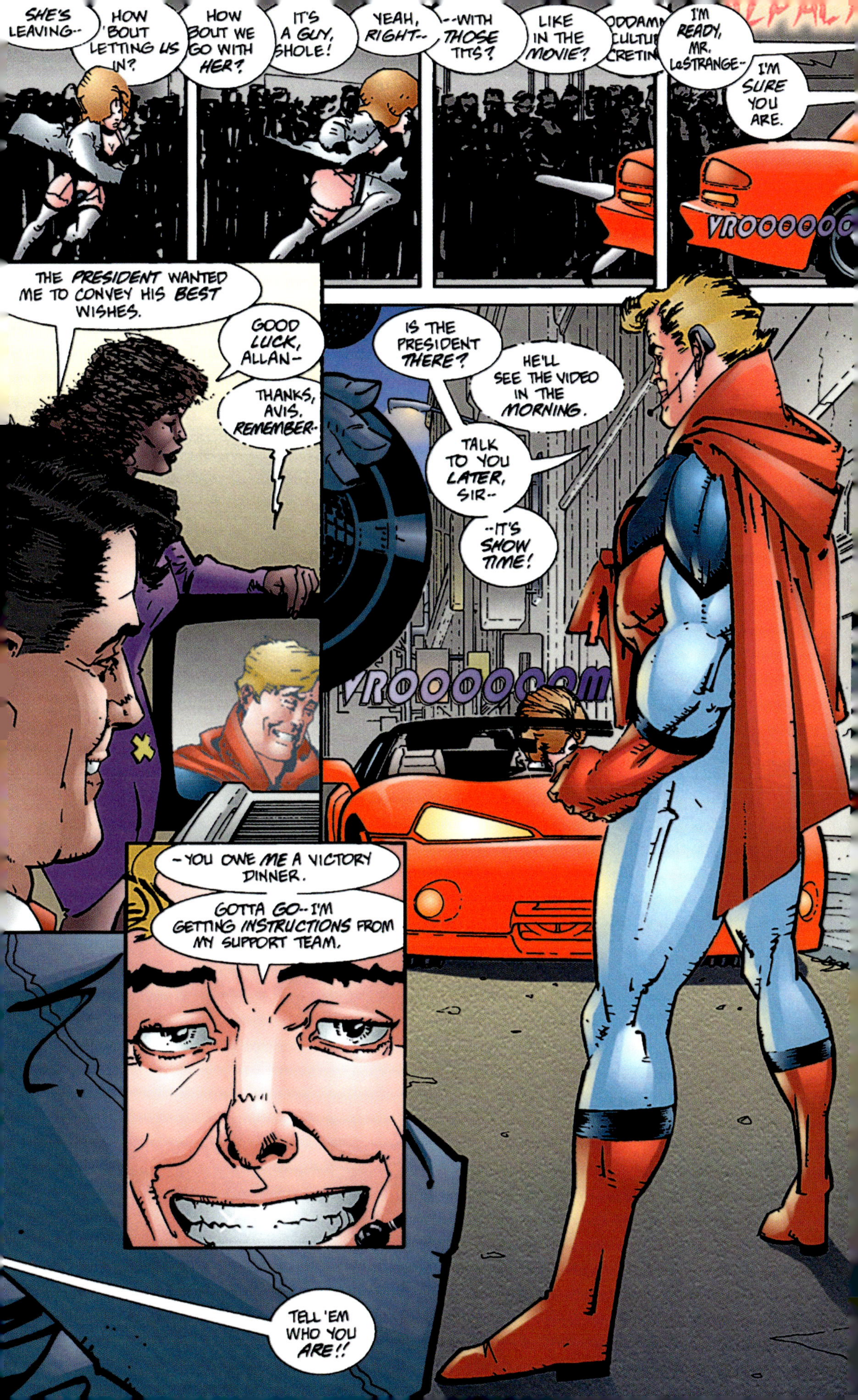
SHE'S LEAVING--
HOW 'BOUT LETTING US IN?
HOW 'BOUT WE GO WITH HER?
IT'S A GUY, SHOLE!
YEAH, RIGHT--
--WITH THOSE TITS?
LIKE IN THE MOVIE?
ODDAMN CULTU CRETIN
I'M READY, MR. LeSTRANGE--
I'M SURE YOU ARE.
VROOOOOOO
THE PRESIDENT WANTED ME TO CONVEY HIS BEST WISHES.
GOOD LUCK, ALLAN--
THANKS, AVIS. REMEMBER--
IS THE PRESIDENT THERE?
HE'LL SEE THE VIDEO IN THE MORNING.
TALK TO YOU LATER, SIR--
--IT'S SHOW TIME!
VROOOOOOOM
--YOU OWE ME A VICTORY DINNER.
GOTTA GO--I'M GETTING INSTRUCTIONS FROM MY SUPPORT TEAM.
TELL 'EM WHO YOU ARE!!

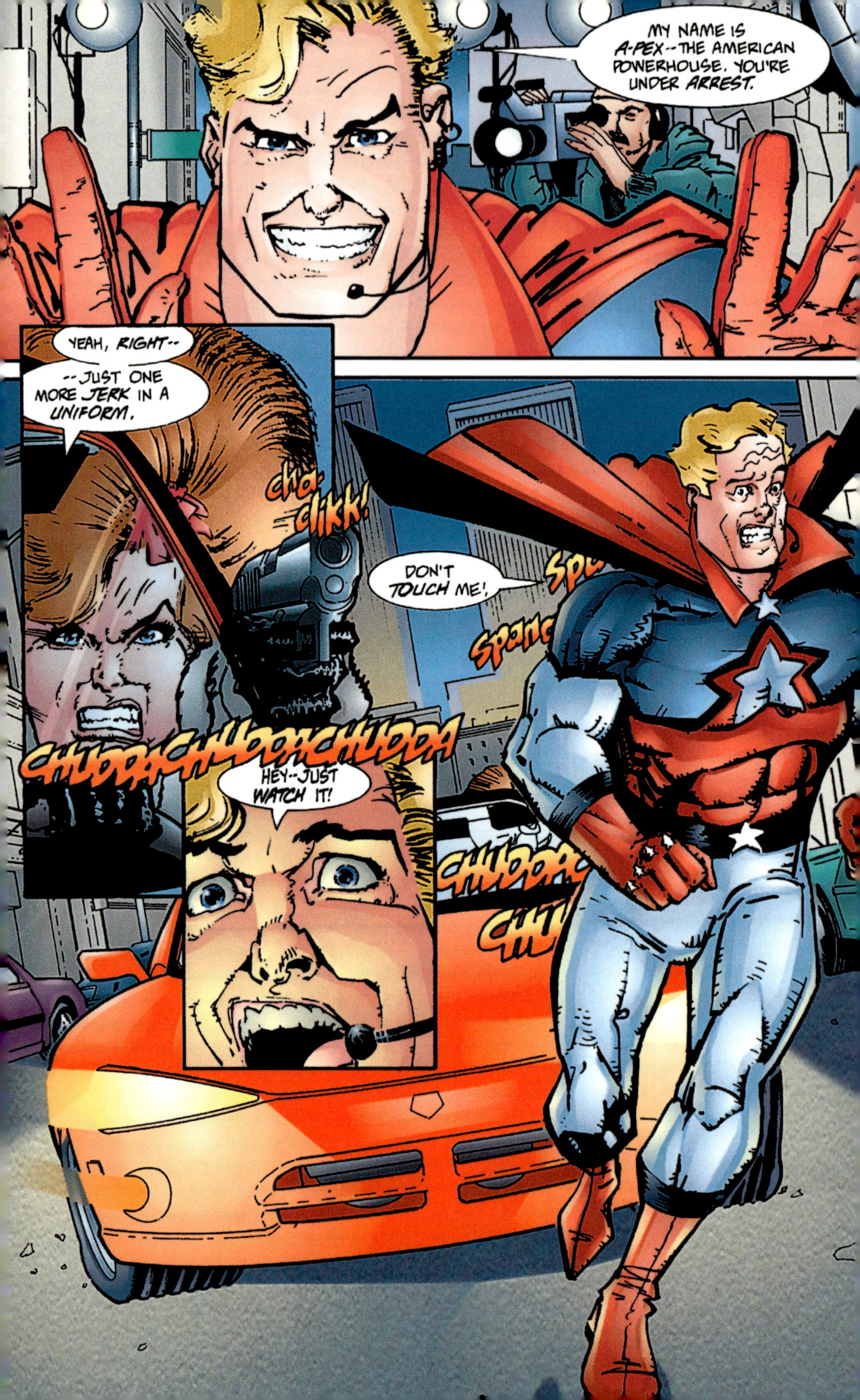

MY NAME IS A-PEX--THE AMERICAN POWERHOUSE. YOU'RE UNDER ARREST.
YEAH, RIGHT--
--JUST ONE MORE JERK IN A UNIFORM.
cha clikk!
DON'T TOUCH ME!
CHUDDACHUDDACHUDDA
HEY--JUST WATCH IT!

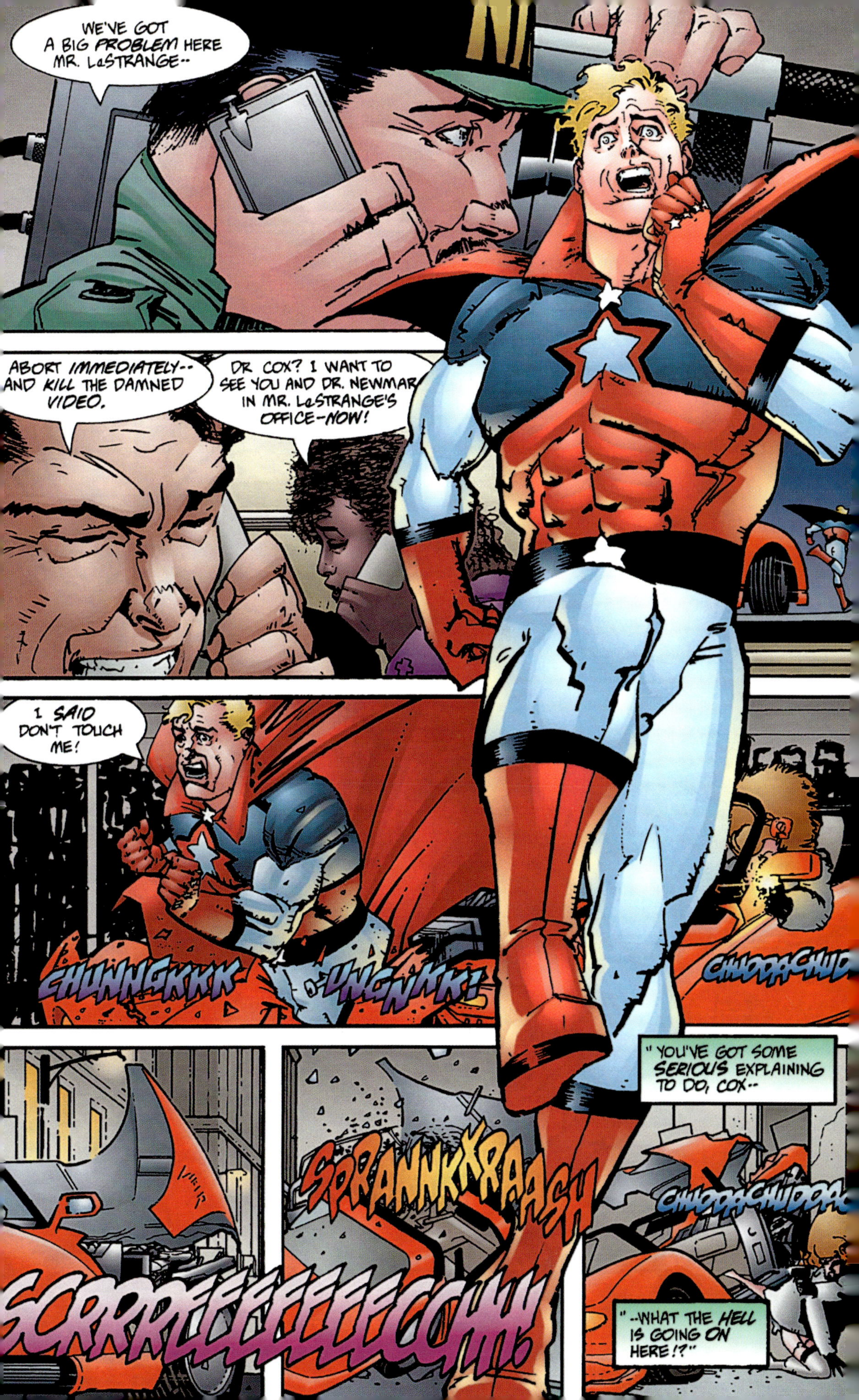
WE'VE GOT A BIG PROBLEM HERE MR. LeSTRANGE--
ABORT IMMEDIATELY-- AND KILL THE DAMNED VIDEO.
DR. COX? I WANT TO SEE YOU AND DR. NEWMAN IN MR. LeSTRANGE'S OFFICE--NOW!
I SAID DON'T TOUCH ME!
CHUNNGKKK
UNGNKK!
CHUDDACHUD
"YOU'VE GOT SOME SERIOUS EXPLAINING TO DO, COX--
SCRRREEEEEEEEECCHH!
SPRANNKKRAASH
CHUDDACHUDDA
"--WHAT THE HELL IS GOING ON HERE!?"

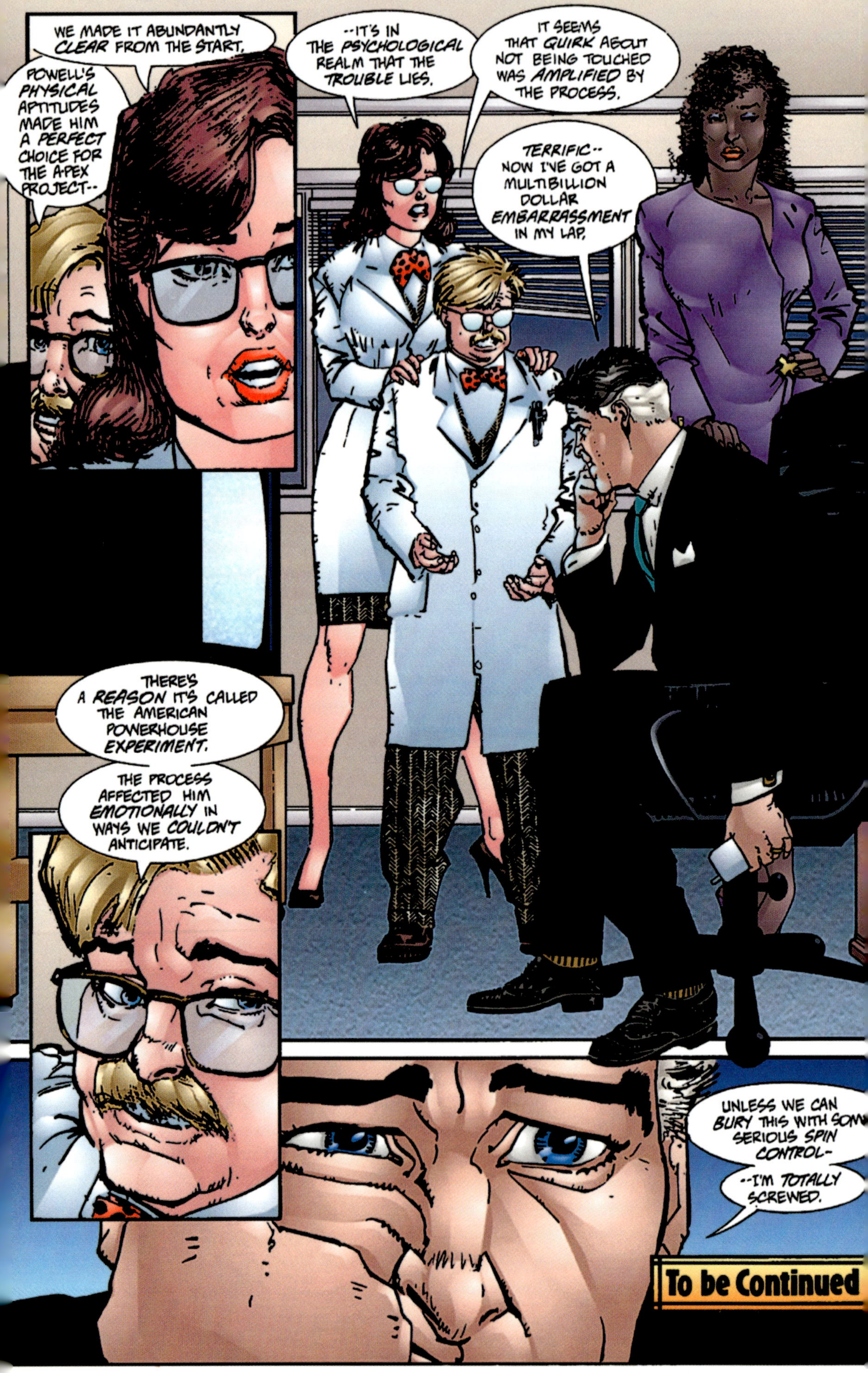
WE MADE IT ABUNDANTLY CLEAR FROM THE START.
POWELL'S PHYSICAL APTITUDES MADE HIM A PERFECT CHOICE FOR THE A-PEX PROJECT--
--IT'S IN THE PSYCHOLOGICAL REALM THAT THE TROUBLE LIES.
IT SEEMS THAT QUIRK ABOUT NOT BEING TOUCHED WAS AMPLIFIED BY THE PROCESS.
TERRIFIC-- NOW I'VE GOT A MULTIBILLION DOLLAR EMBARRASSMENT IN MY LAP.
THERE'S A REASON IT'S CALLED THE AMERICAN POWERHOUSE EXPERIMENT.
THE PROCESS AFFECTED HIM EMOTIONALLY IN WAYS WE COULDN'T ANTICIPATE.
UNLESS WE CAN BURY THIS WITH SOME SERIOUS SPIN CONTROL-
--I'M TOTALLY SCREWED.
To be Continued

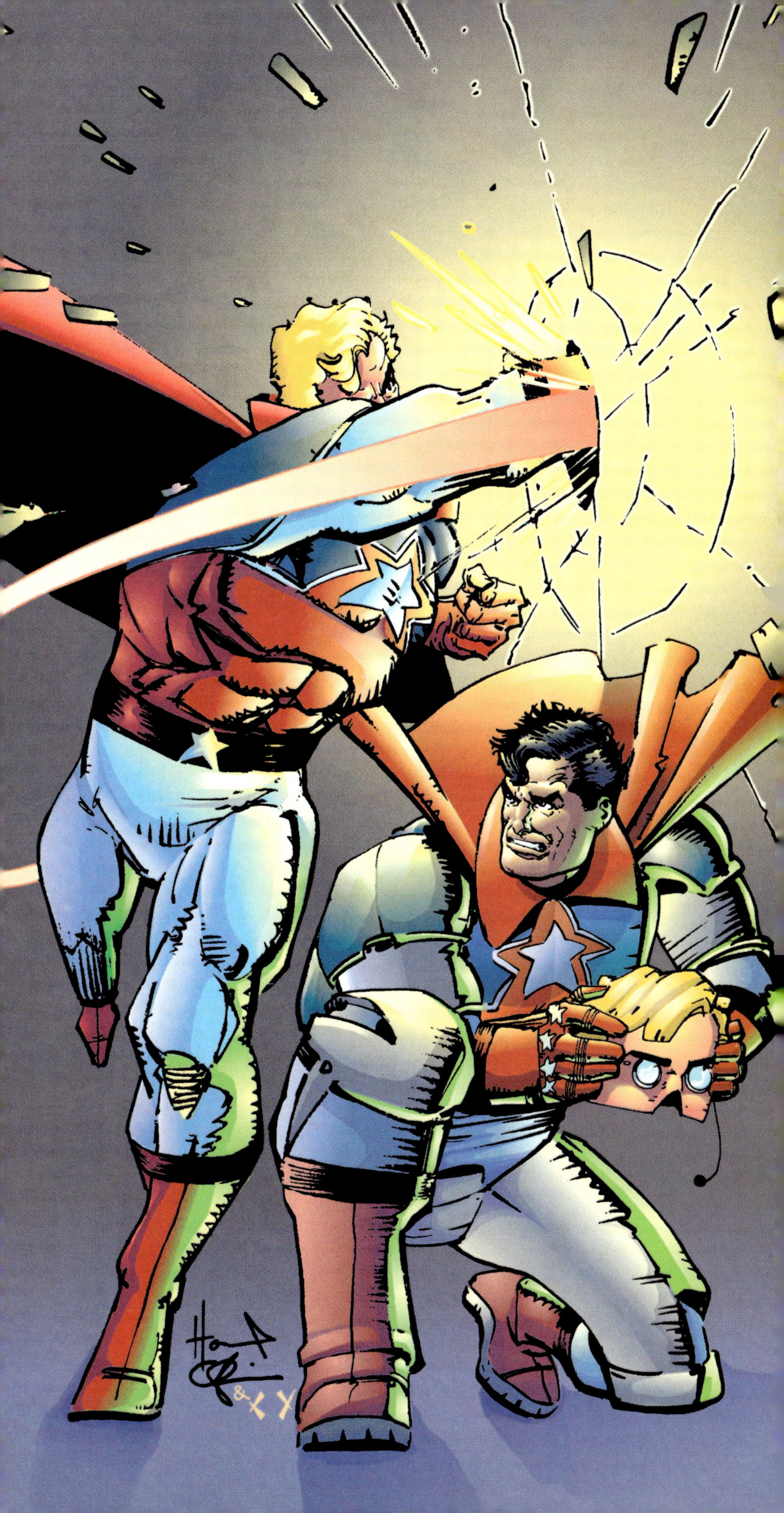

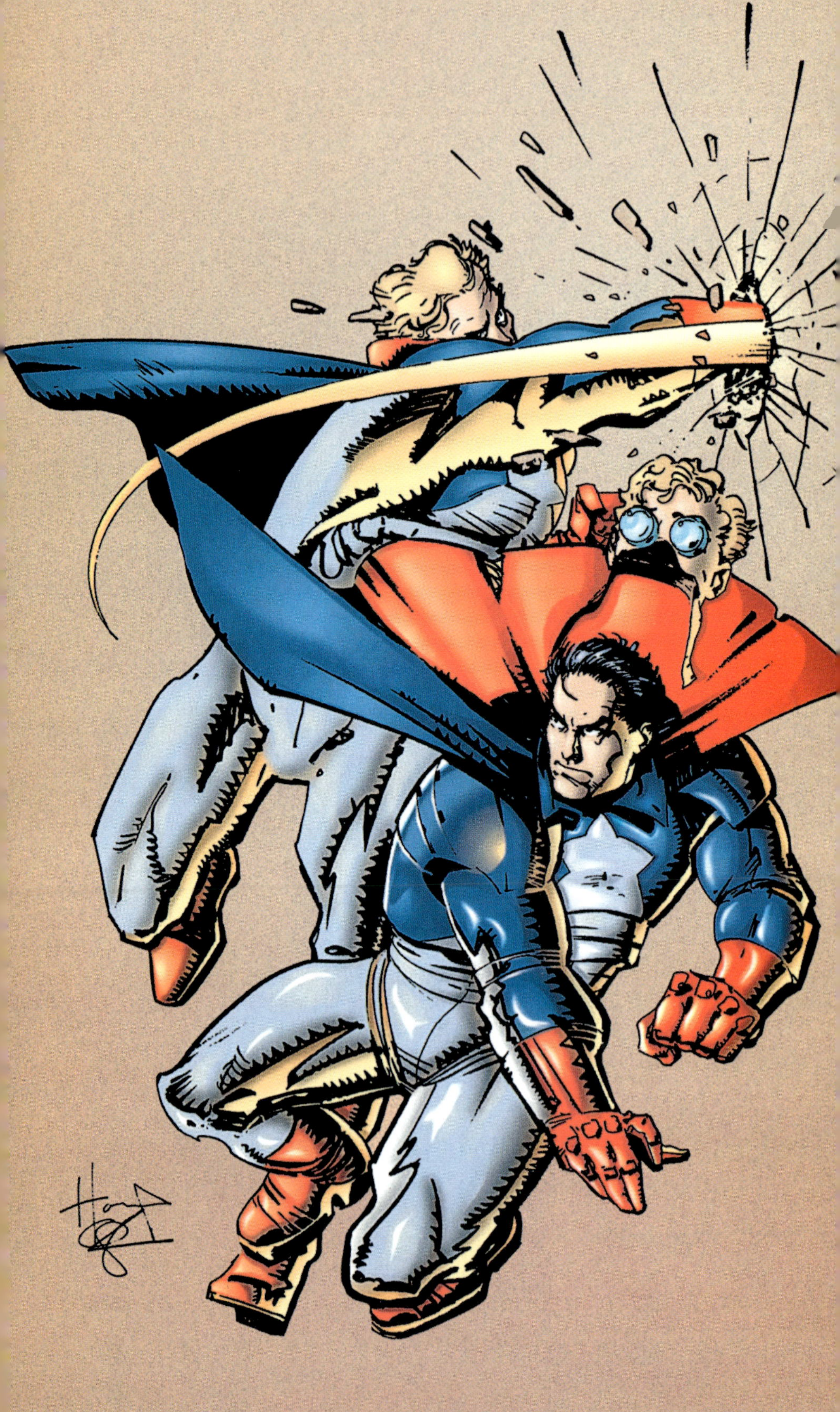

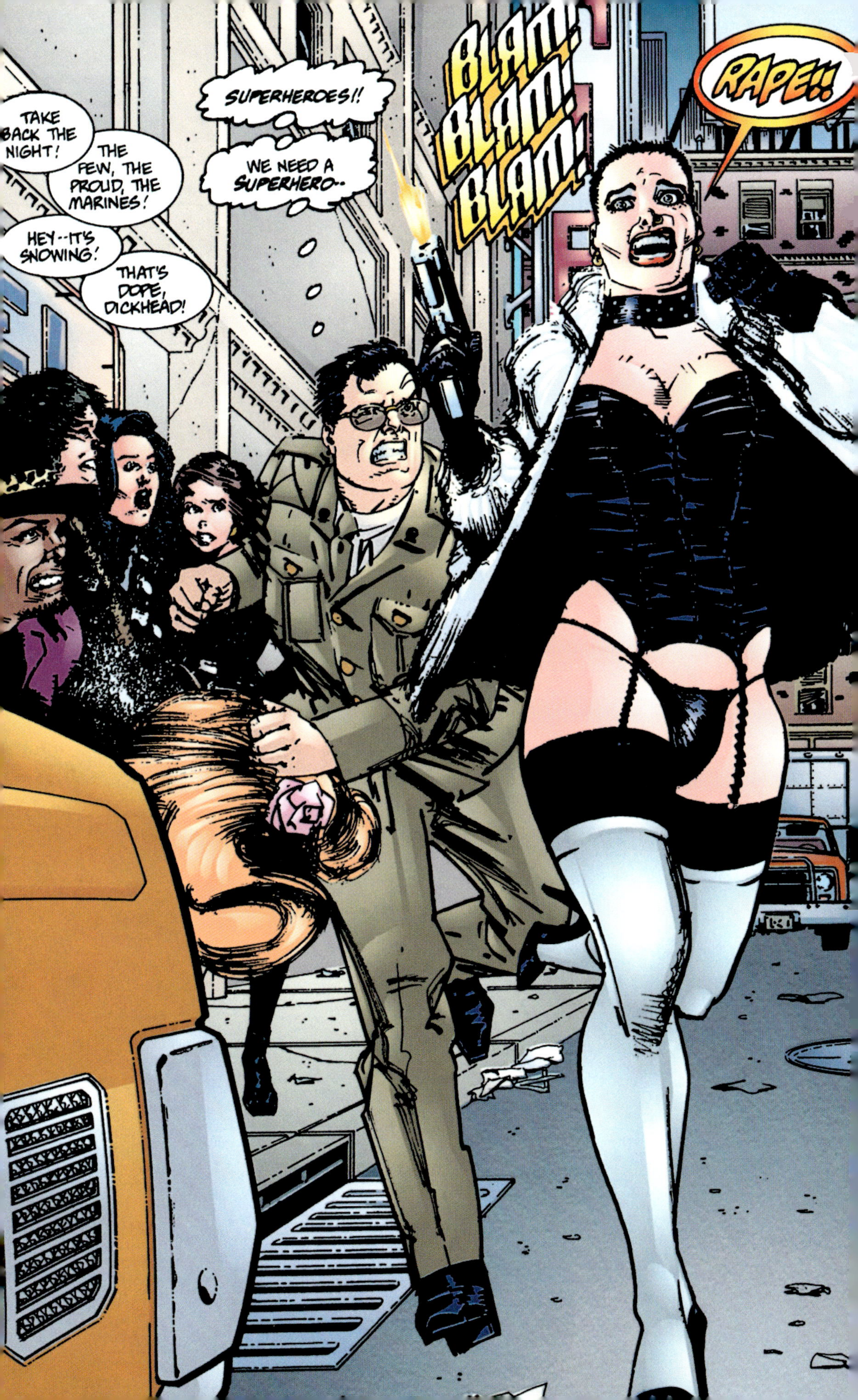
TAKE BACK THE NIGHT!
THE FEW, THE PROUD, THE MARINES!
HEY--IT'S SNOWING!
THAT'S DOPE, DICKHEAD!
SUPERHEROES!!
WE NEED A SUPERHERO..
BLAM! BLAM! BLAM!
RAPE!!

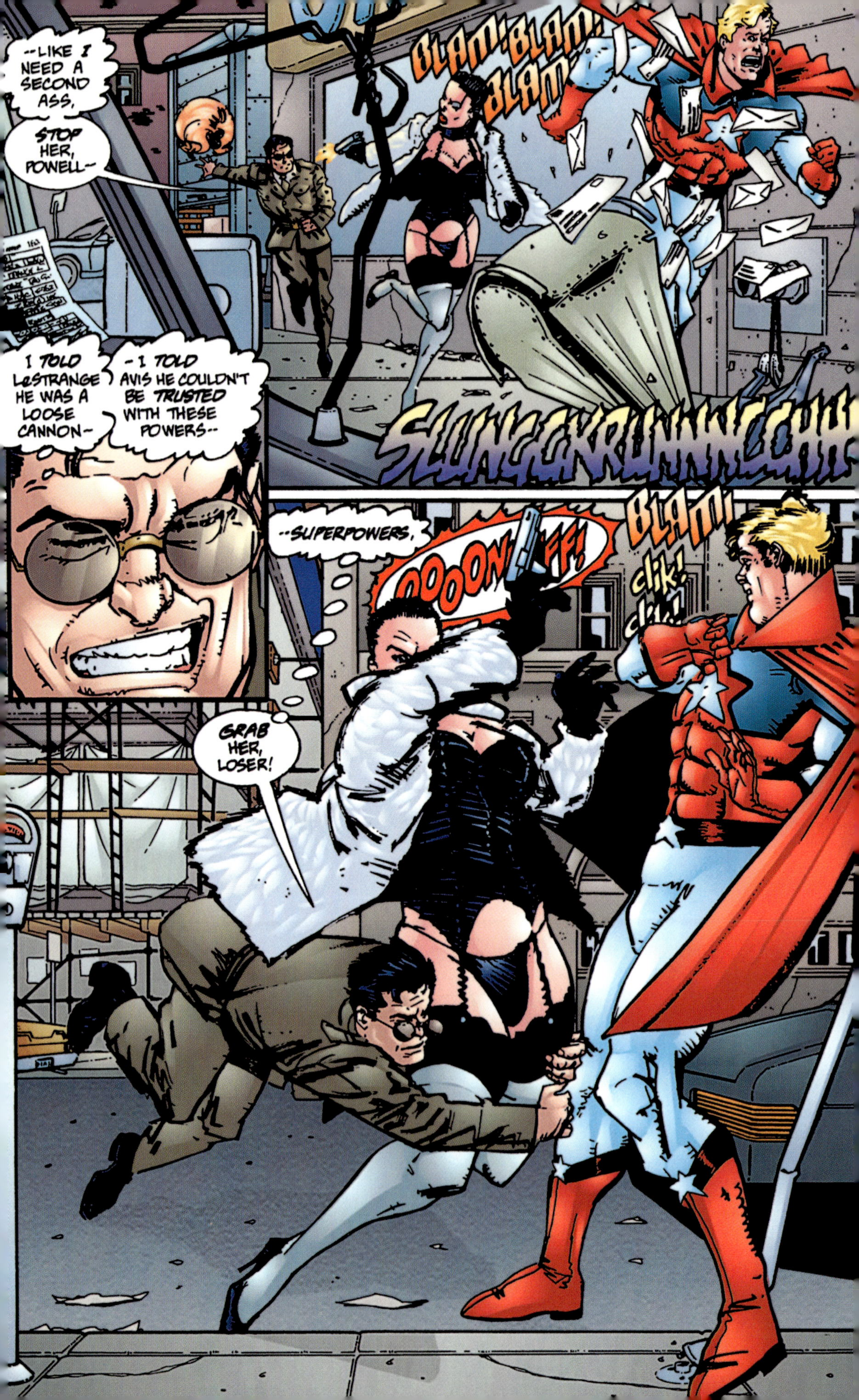

--LIKE I NEED A SECOND ASS,
STOP HER, POWELL--
BLAM! BLAM! BLAM!
SLUNGGKRUNNNCHH
I TOLD LeSTRANGE HE WAS A LOOSE CANNON-
-I TOLD AVIS HE COULDN'T BE TRUSTED WITH THESE POWERS--
--SUPERPOWERS,
BLAM!
clik!
GRAB HER, LOSER!

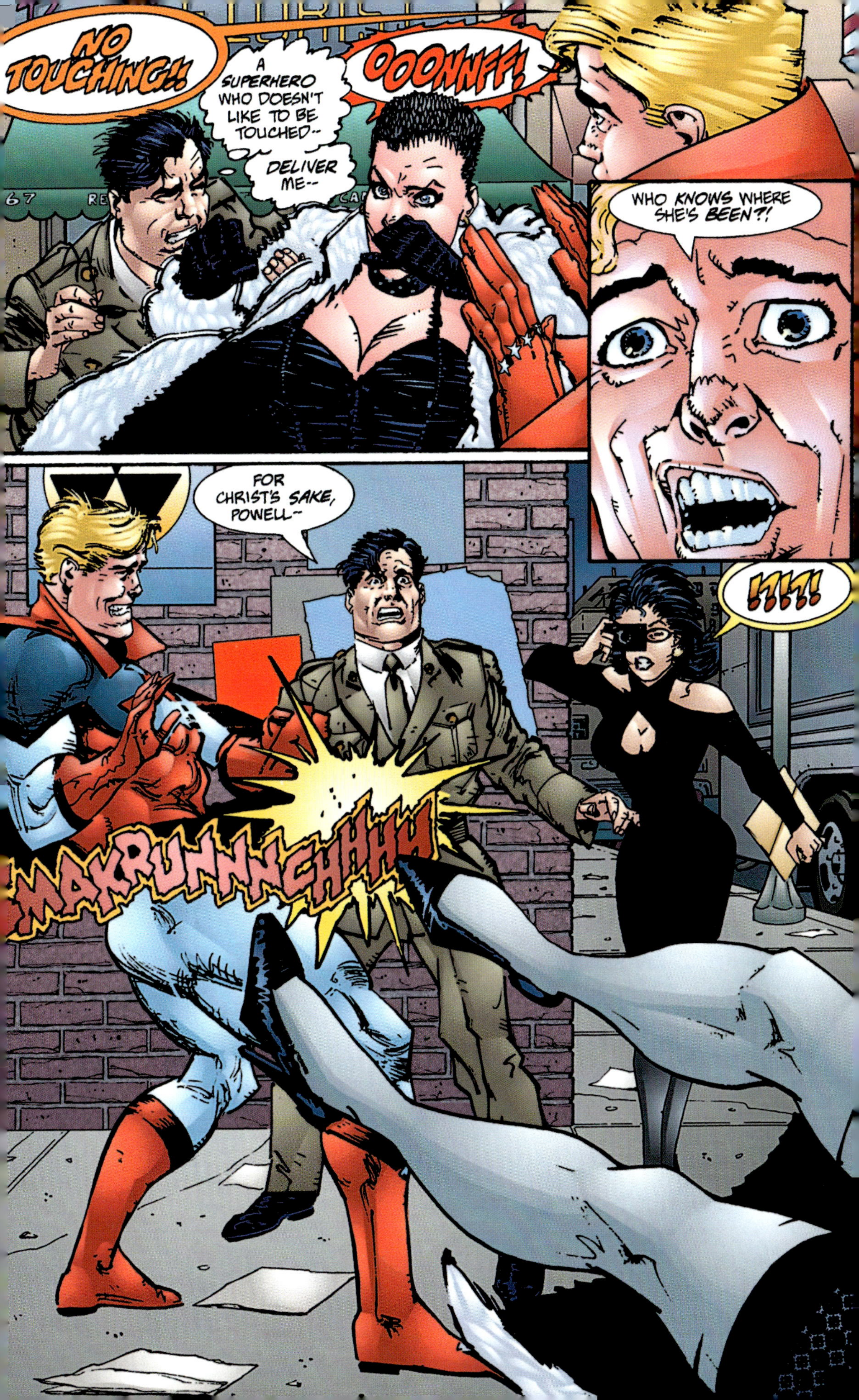
NO TOUCHING!!
A SUPERHERO WHO DOESN'T LIKE TO BE TOUCHED--
DELIVER ME--
OOOONNFF!
WHO KNOWS WHERE SHE'S BEEN?!
FOR CHRIST'S SAKE, POWELL--
!?!?!
MAKRUNNCHHHH

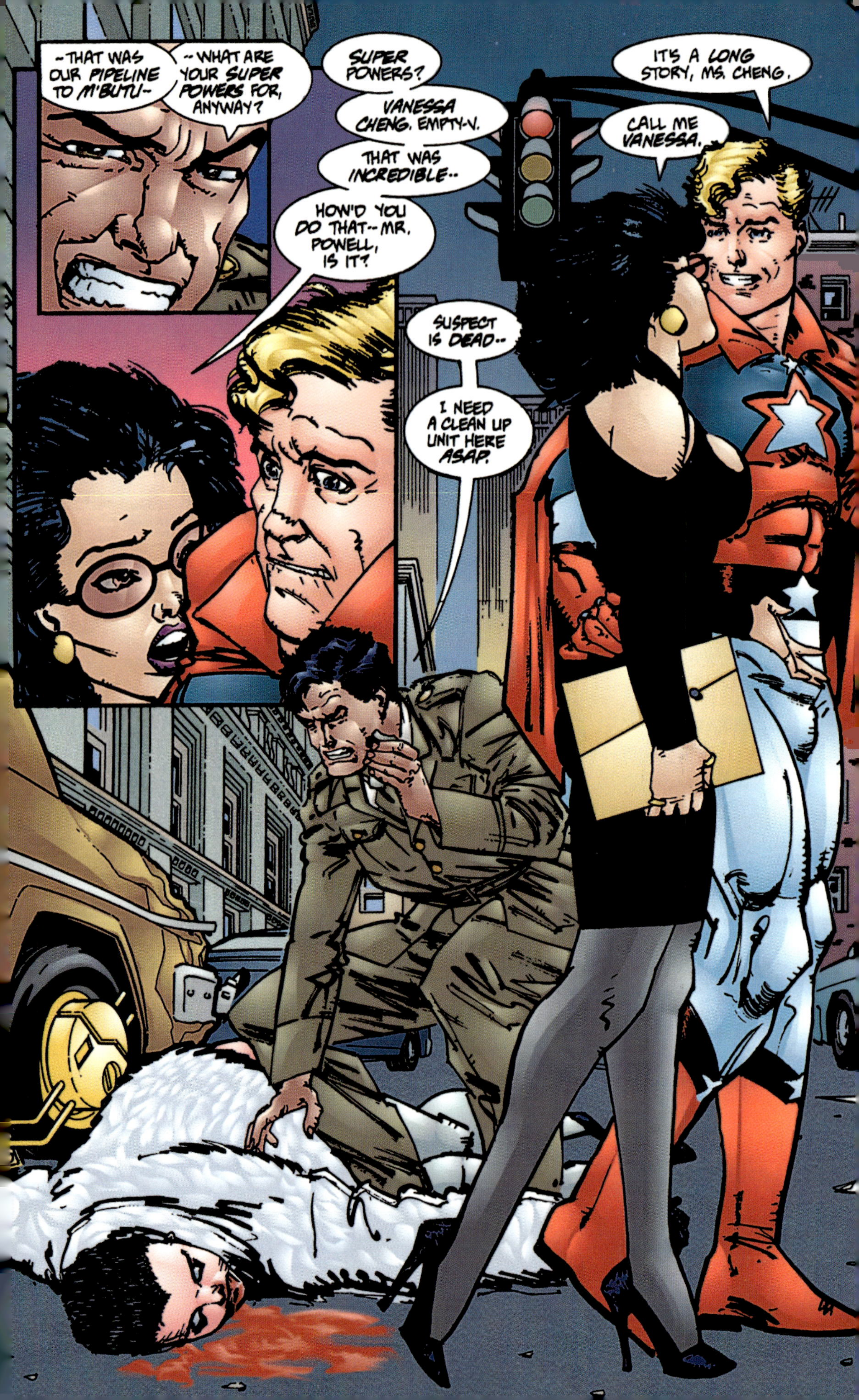

--THAT WAS OUR PIPELINE TO M'BUTU--
--WHAT ARE YOUR SUPER POWERS FOR, ANYWAY?
SUPER POWERS?
VANESSA CHENG, EMPTY-V.
THAT WAS INCREDIBLE--
HOW'D YOU DO THAT--MR. POWELL, IS IT?
SUSPECT IS DEAD--
I NEED A CLEAN UP UNIT HERE ASAP.
IT'S A LONG STORY, MS. CHENG.
CALL ME VANESSA.

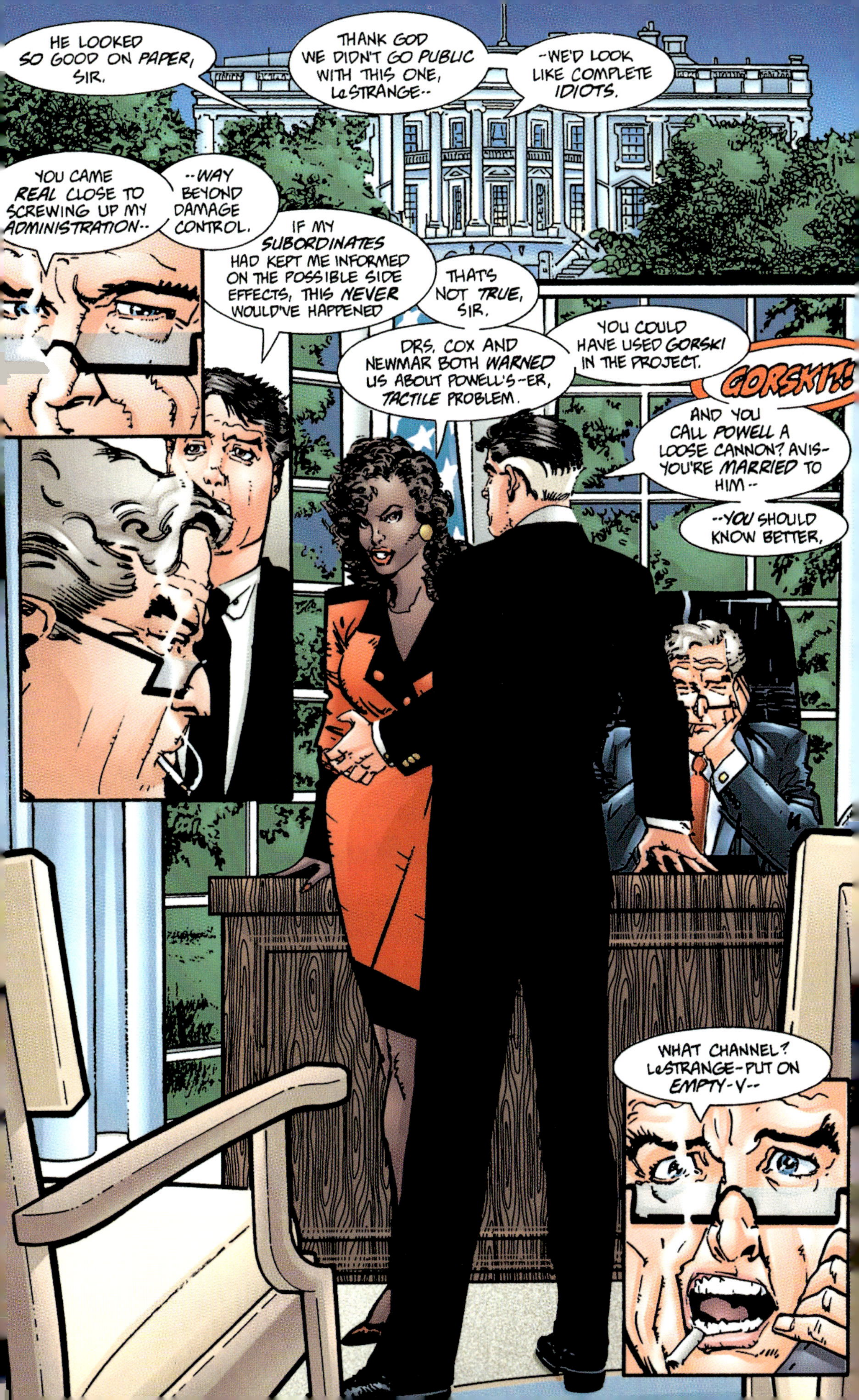
HE LOOKED SO GOOD ON PAPER, SIR.
THANK GOD WE DIDN'T GO PUBLIC WITH THIS ONE, LeSTRANGE--
--WE'D LOOK LIKE COMPLETE IDIOTS.
YOU CAME REAL CLOSE TO SCREWING UP MY ADMINISTRATION--
--WAY BEYOND DAMAGE CONTROL.
IF MY SUBORDINATES HAD KEPT ME INFORMED ON THE POSSIBLE SIDE EFFECTS, THIS NEVER WOULD'VE HAPPENED
THAT'S NOT TRUE, SIR.
DRS. COX AND NEWMAR BOTH WARNED US ABOUT POWELL'S--ER, TACTILE PROBLEM.
YOU COULD HAVE USED GORSKI IN THE PROJECT.
GORSKI!?!
AND YOU CALL POWELL A LOOSE CANNON? AVIS-YOU'RE MARRIED TO HIM--
--YOU SHOULD KNOW BETTER.
WHAT CHANNEL? LeSTRANGE--PUT ON EMPTY-V--

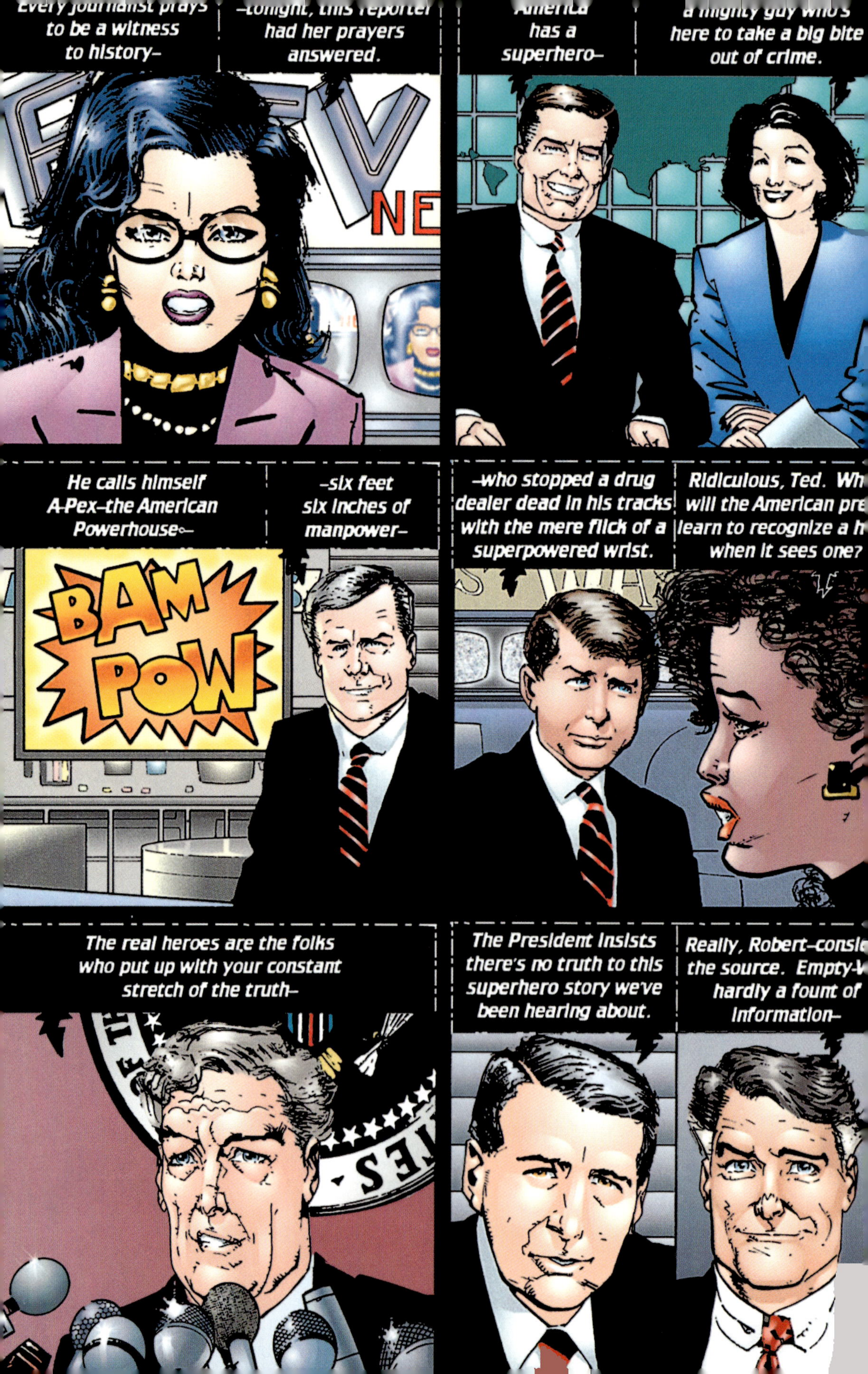

Every journalist prays
to be a witness
to history–
–tonight, this reporter
had her prayers
answered.
America
has a
superhero–
a mighty guy who's
here to take a big bite
out of crime.
He calls himself
A-Pex–the American
Powerhouse–
–six feet
six inches of
manpower–
BAM
POW
–who stopped a drug
dealer dead in his tracks
with the mere flick of a
superpowered wrist.
Ridiculous, Ted. Wh
will the American pre
learn to recognize a h
when it sees one?
The real heroes are the folks
who put up with your constant
stretch of the truth–
The President insists
there's no truth to this
superhero story we've
been hearing about.
Really, Robert–consi
the source. Empty-V
hardly a fount of
information–

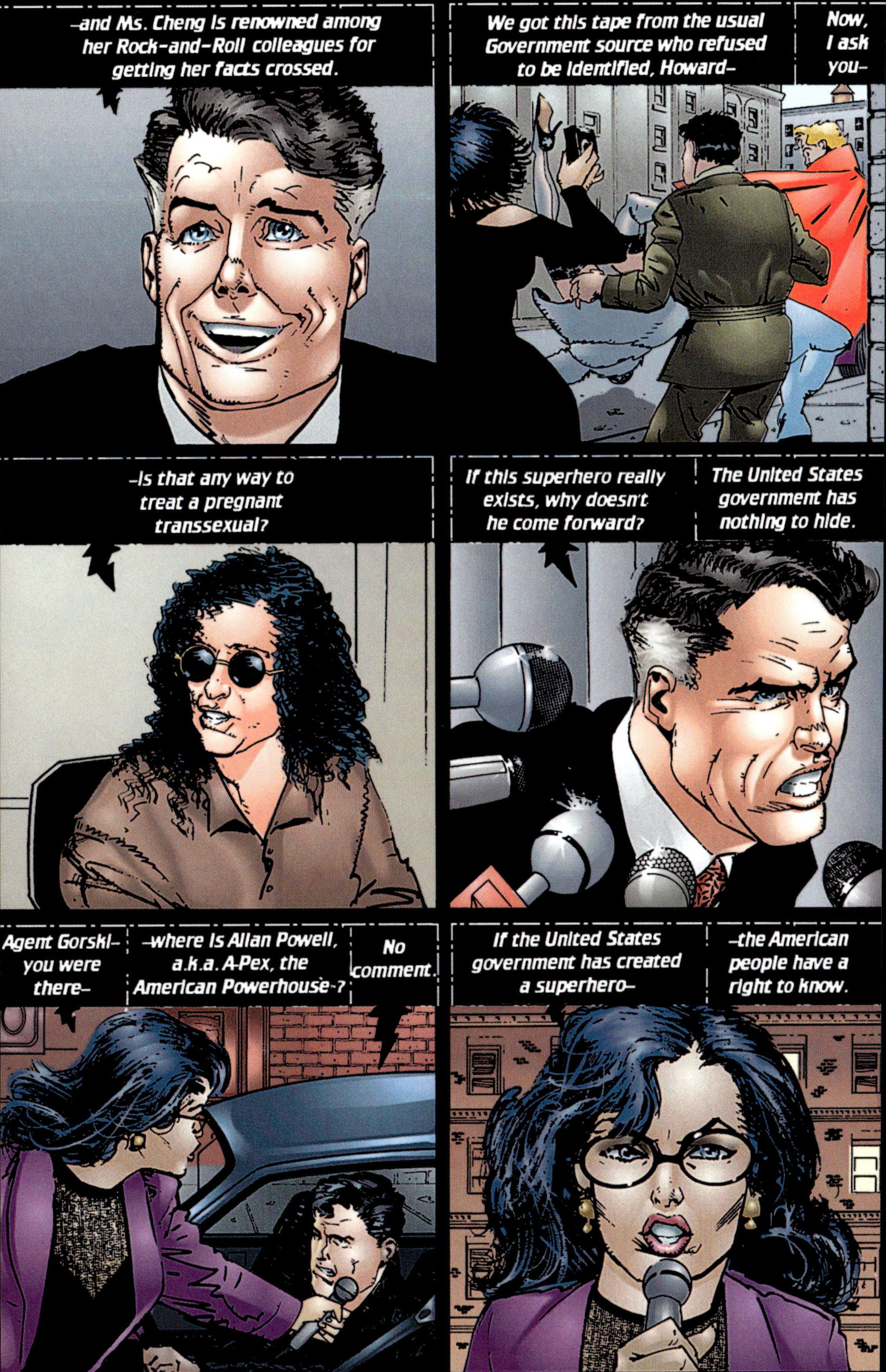
–and Ms. Cheng is renowned among her Rock–and–Roll colleagues for getting her facts crossed.
We got this tape from the usual Government source who refused to be identified, Howard–
Now, I ask you–
–Is that any way to treat a pregnant transsexual?
If this superhero really exists, why doesn't he come forward?
The United States government has nothing to hide.
Agent Gorski– you were there–
–where is Allan Powell, a.k.a. A-Pex, the American Powerhouse–?
No comment.
If the United States government has created a superhero–
–the American people have a right to know.

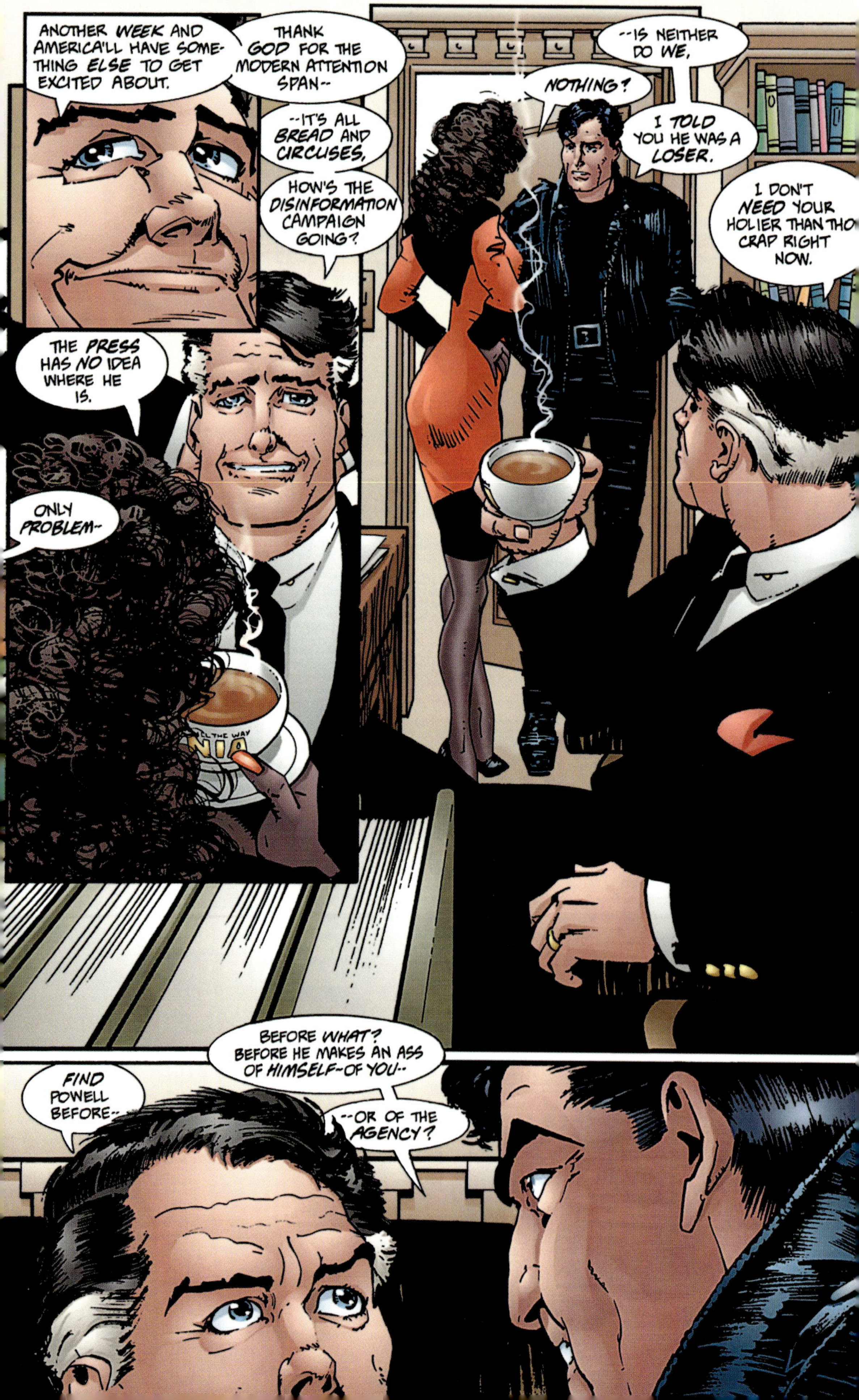
ANOTHER WEEK AND AMERICA'LL HAVE SOMETHING ELSE TO GET EXCITED ABOUT.
THANK GOD FOR THE MODERN ATTENTION SPAN--
--IT'S ALL BREAD AND CIRCUSES.
HOW'S THE DISINFORMATION CAMPAIGN GOING?
THE PRESS HAS NO IDEA WHERE HE IS.
ONLY PROBLEM--
NOTHING?
--IS NEITHER DO WE.
I TOLD YOU HE WAS A LOSER.
I DON'T NEED YOUR HOLIER THAN THO CRAP RIGHT NOW.
FIND POWELL BEFORE--
BEFORE WHAT? BEFORE HE MAKES AN ASS OF HIMSELF--OF YOU--
--OR OF THE AGENCY?

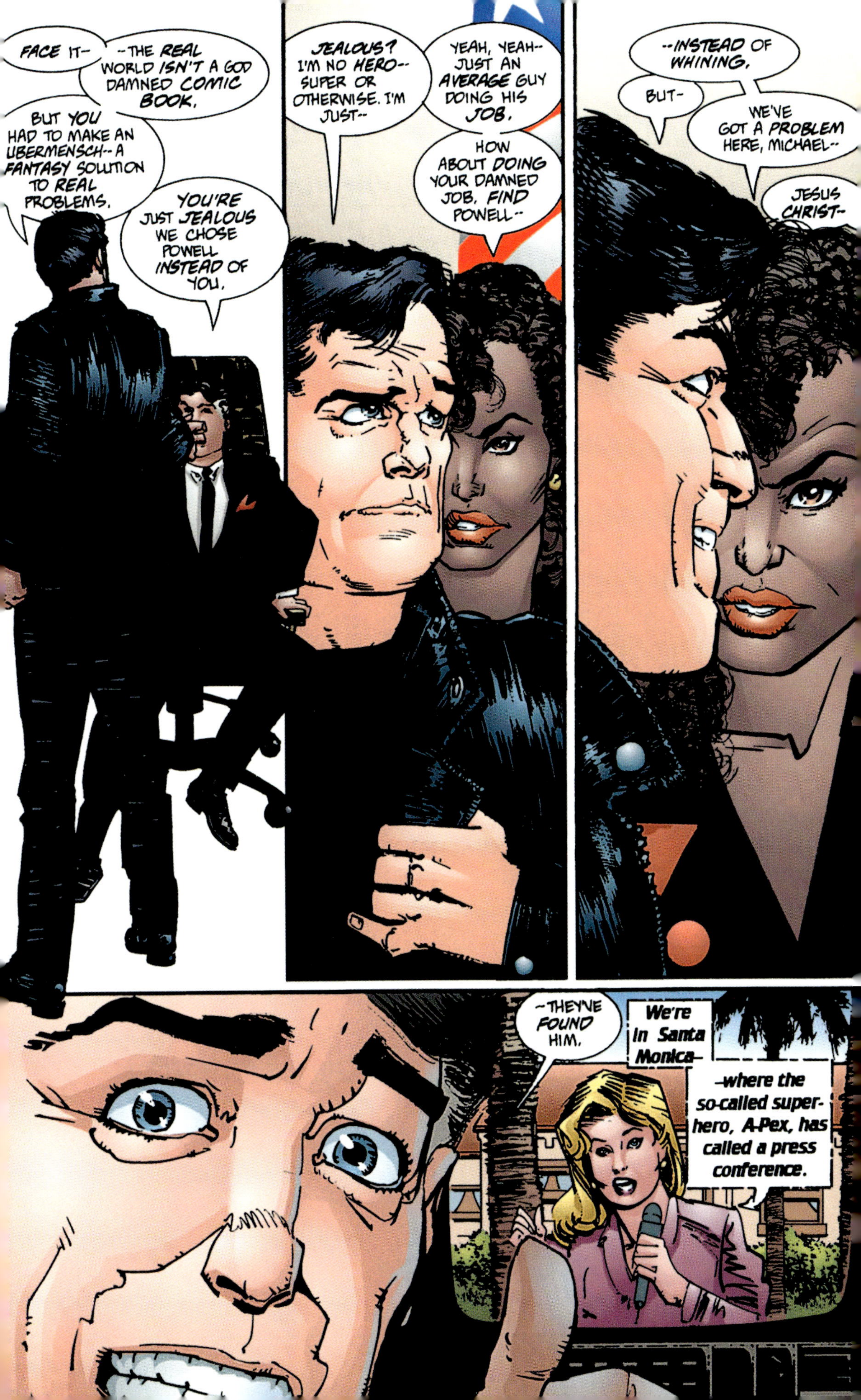
FACE IT--
--THE REAL WORLD ISN'T A GOD DAMNED COMIC BOOK.
BUT YOU HAD TO MAKE AN UBERMENSCH--A FANTASY SOLUTION TO REAL PROBLEMS.
YOU'RE JUST JEALOUS WE CHOSE POWELL INSTEAD OF YOU.
JEALOUS? I'M NO HERO-- SUPER OR OTHERWISE. I'M JUST--
YEAH, YEAH-- JUST AN AVERAGE GUY DOING HIS JOB.
HOW ABOUT DOING YOUR DAMNED JOB. FIND POWELL--
--INSTEAD OF WHINING.
BUT-
WE'VE GOT A PROBLEM HERE, MICHAEL--
JESUS CHRIST--
--THEY'VE FOUND HIM.
We're in Santa Monica--
--where the so-called super-hero, A-Pex, has called a press conference.

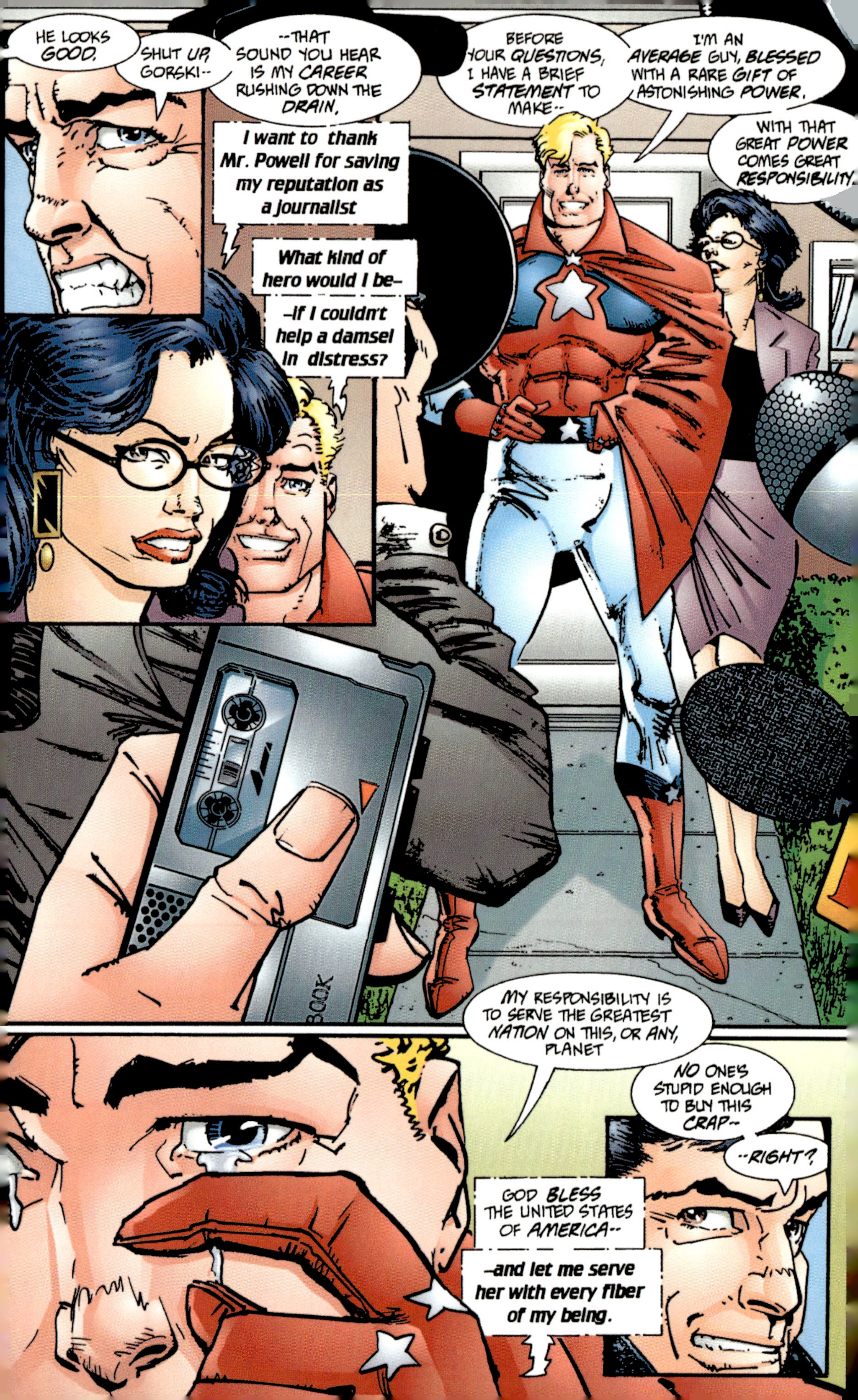
HE LOOKS GOOD.
SHUT UP, GORSKI--
--THAT SOUND YOU HEAR IS MY CAREER RUSHING DOWN THE DRAIN.
I want to thank Mr. Powell for saving my reputation as a journalist
What kind of hero would I be–
–if I couldn't help a damsel in distress?
BEFORE YOUR QUESTIONS, I HAVE A BRIEF STATEMENT TO MAKE--
I'M AN AVERAGE GUY, BLESSED WITH A RARE GIFT OF ASTONISHING POWER.
WITH THAT GREAT POWER COMES GREAT RESPONSIBILITY.
MY RESPONSIBILITY IS TO SERVE THE GREATEST NATION ON THIS, OR ANY, PLANET
NO ONE'S STUPID ENOUGH TO BUY THIS CRAP--
--RIGHT?
GOD BLESS THE UNITED STATES OF AMERICA--
–and let me serve her with every fiber of my being.

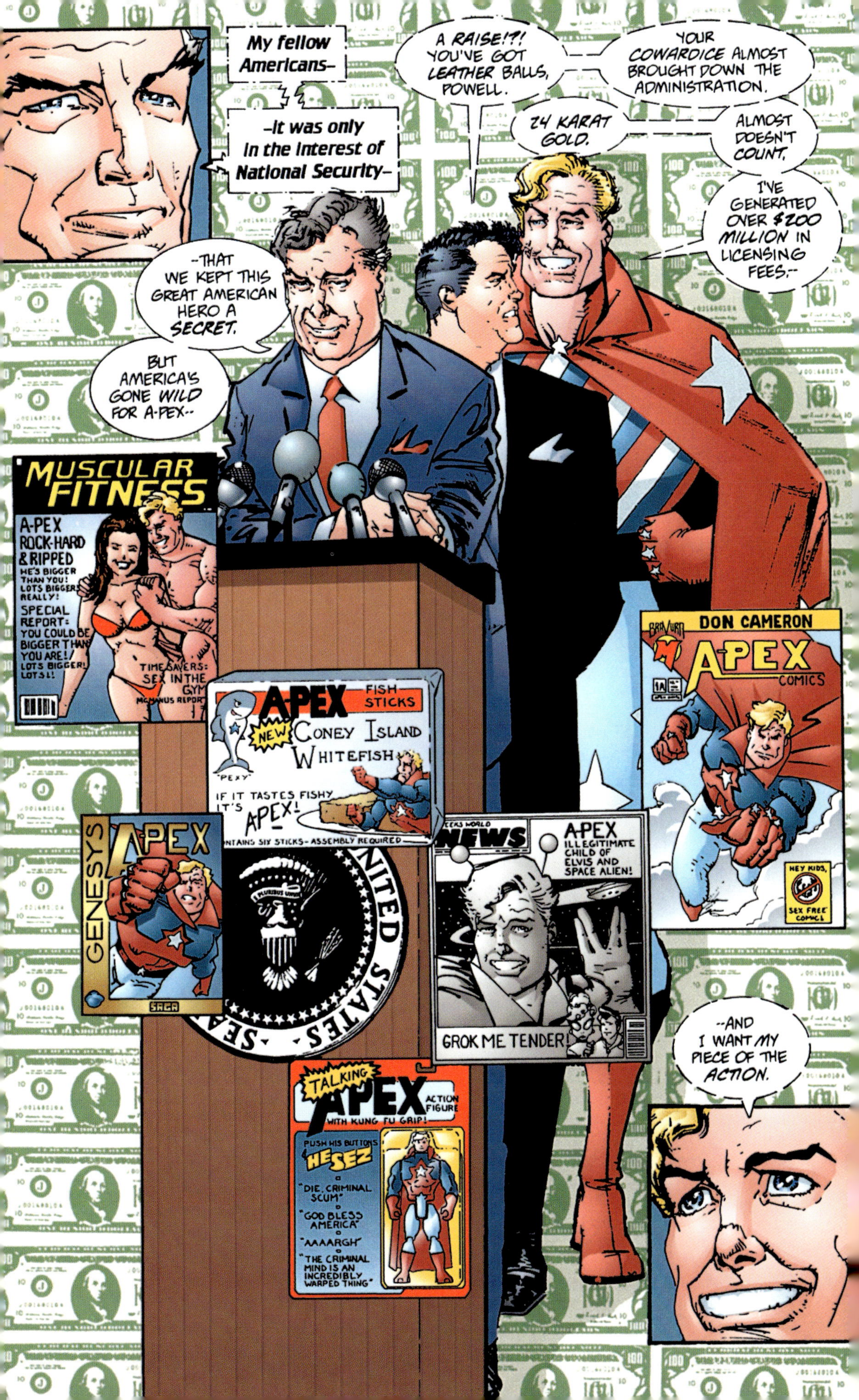
My fellow Americans-
-It was only in the interest of National Security-
A RAISE!?! YOU'VE GOT LEATHER BALLS, POWELL.
YOUR COWARDICE ALMOST BROUGHT DOWN THE ADMINISTRATION.
24 KARAT GOLD.
ALMOST DOESN'T COUNT.
I'VE GENERATED OVER $200 MILLION IN LICENSING FEES,-
-THAT WE KEPT THIS GREAT AMERICAN HERO A SECRET.
BUT AMERICA'S GONE WILD FOR A-PEX--
MUSCULAR FITNESS
A-PEX ROCK-HARD & RIPPED
HE'S BIGGER THAN YOU! LOTS BIGGER! REALLY!
SPECIAL REPORT: YOU COULD BE BIGGER THAN YOU ARE!/ LOTS BIGGER! LOTS!
TIME SAVERS: SEX IN THE GYM
A-PEX FISH STICKS
NEW CONEY ISLAND WHITEFISH
"PEXY"
IF IT TASTES FISHY IT'S APEX!
CONTAINS SIX STICKS - ASSEMBLY REQUIRED
DON CAMERON
BRAVURA
A-PEX COMICS
HEY KIDS, SEX FREE COMICS
GENESYS A-PEX
SAGA
E PLURIBUS UNUM
SEAL ... UNITED STATES
NEWS
A-PEX ILLEGITIMATE CHILD OF ELVIS AND SPACE ALIEN!
GROK ME TENDER!
--AND I WANT MY PIECE OF THE ACTION.
TALKING APEX ACTION FIGURE WITH KUNG FU GRIP!
PUSH HIS BUTTONS HE SEZ
"DIE, CRIMINAL SCUM"
"GOD BLESS AMERICA"
"AAAARGH"
"THE CRIMINAL MIND IS AN INCREDIBLY WARPED THING"

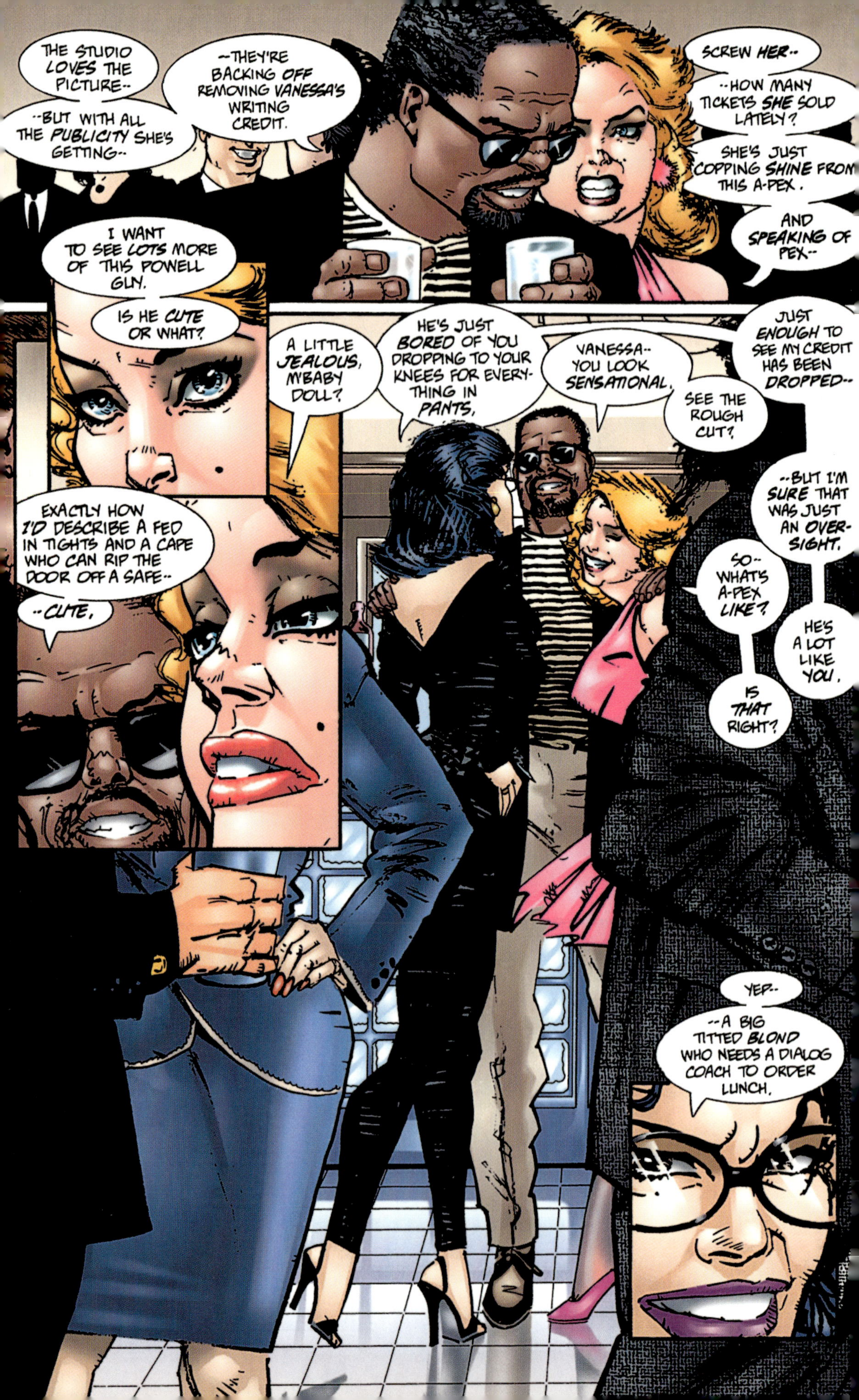
THE STUDIO LOVES THE PICTURE--
--BUT WITH ALL THE PUBLICITY SHE'S GETTING--
--THEY'RE BACKING OFF REMOVING VANESSA'S WRITING CREDIT.
SCREW HER--
--HOW MANY TICKETS SHE SOLD LATELY?
SHE'S JUST COPPING SHINE FROM THIS A-PEX.
AND SPEAKING OF PEX--
I WANT TO SEE LOTS MORE OF THIS POWELL GUY.
IS HE CUTE OR WHAT?
A LITTLE JEALOUS, MY BABY DOLL?
HE'S JUST BORED OF YOU DROPPING TO YOUR KNEES FOR EVERY-THING IN PANTS.
VANESSA-- YOU LOOK SENSATIONAL.
SEE THE ROUGH CUT?
JUST ENOUGH TO SEE MY CREDIT HAS BEEN DROPPED--
--BUT I'M SURE THAT WAS JUST AN OVER-SIGHT.
EXACTLY HOW I'D DESCRIBE A FED IN TIGHTS AND A CAPE WHO CAN RIP THE DOOR OFF A SAFE--
--CUTE.
SO-- WHAT'S A-PEX LIKE?
HE'S A LOT LIKE YOU.
IS THAT RIGHT?
YEP--
--A BIG TITTED BLOND WHO NEEDS A DIALOG COACH TO ORDER LUNCH.

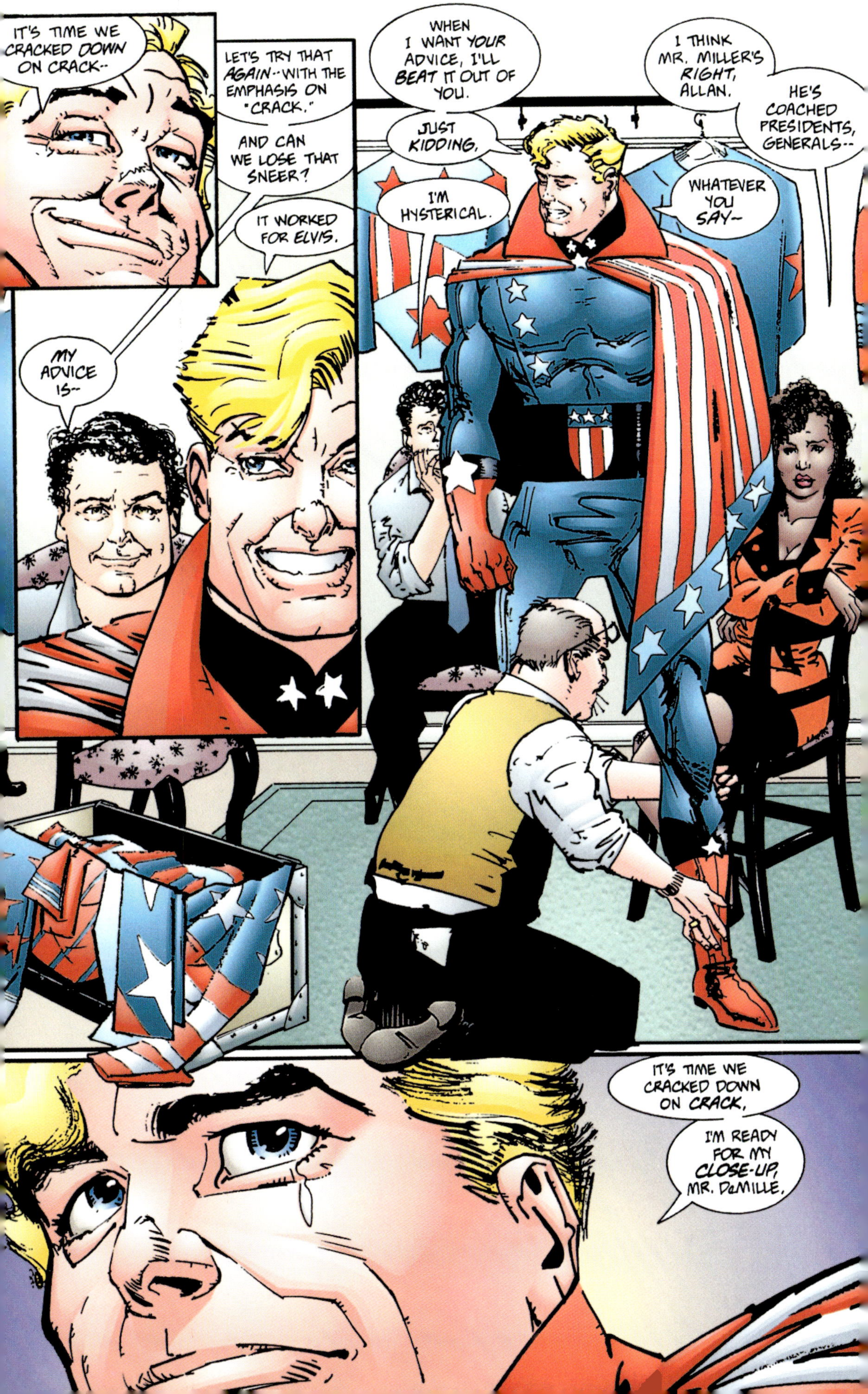

IT'S TIME WE CRACKED DOWN ON CRACK--
LET'S TRY THAT AGAIN--WITH THE EMPHASIS ON "CRACK."
AND CAN WE LOSE THAT SNEER?
IT WORKED FOR ELVIS.
MY ADVICE IS--
WHEN I WANT YOUR ADVICE, I'LL BEAT IT OUT OF YOU.
JUST KIDDING.
I'M HYSTERICAL.
I THINK MR. MILLER'S RIGHT, ALLAN.
HE'S COACHED PRESIDENTS, GENERALS--
WHATEVER YOU SAY--
IT'S TIME WE CRACKED DOWN ON CRACK.
I'M READY FOR MY CLOSE-UP, MR. DeMILLE.

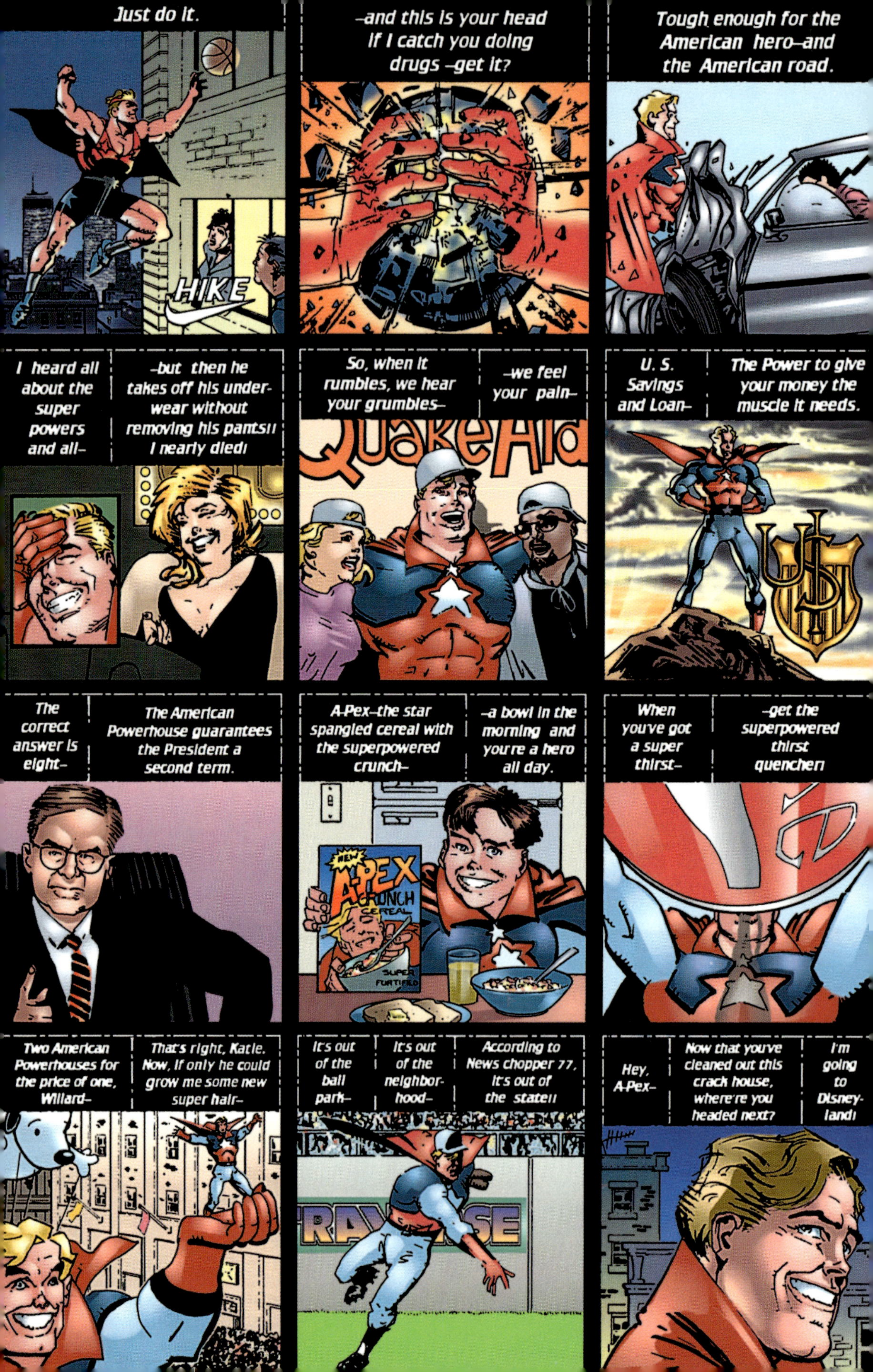

Just do it.
HIKE
–and this is your head if I catch you doing drugs –get it?
Tough enough for the American hero–and the American road.
I heard all about the super powers and all–
–but then he takes off his under-wear without removing his pants!! I nearly died!
So, when it rumbles, we hear your grumbles–
–we feel your pain–
QuakeAid
U. S. Savings and Loan–
The Power to give your money the muscle it needs.
The correct answer is eight–
The American Powerhouse guarantees the President a second term.
A-Pex–the star spangled cereal with the superpowered crunch–
–a bowl in the morning and you're a hero all day.
NEW A-PEX CRUNCH CEREAL
SUPER FORTIFIED
When you've got a super thirst–
–get the superpowered thirst quencher!
Two American Powerhouses for the price of one, Willard–
That's right, Katie. Now, if only he could grow me some new super hair–
It's out of the ball park–
It's out of the neighbor-hood–
According to News chopper 77, it's out of the state!!
Hey, A-Pex–
Now that you've cleaned out this crack house, where're you headed next?
I'm going to Disney-land!

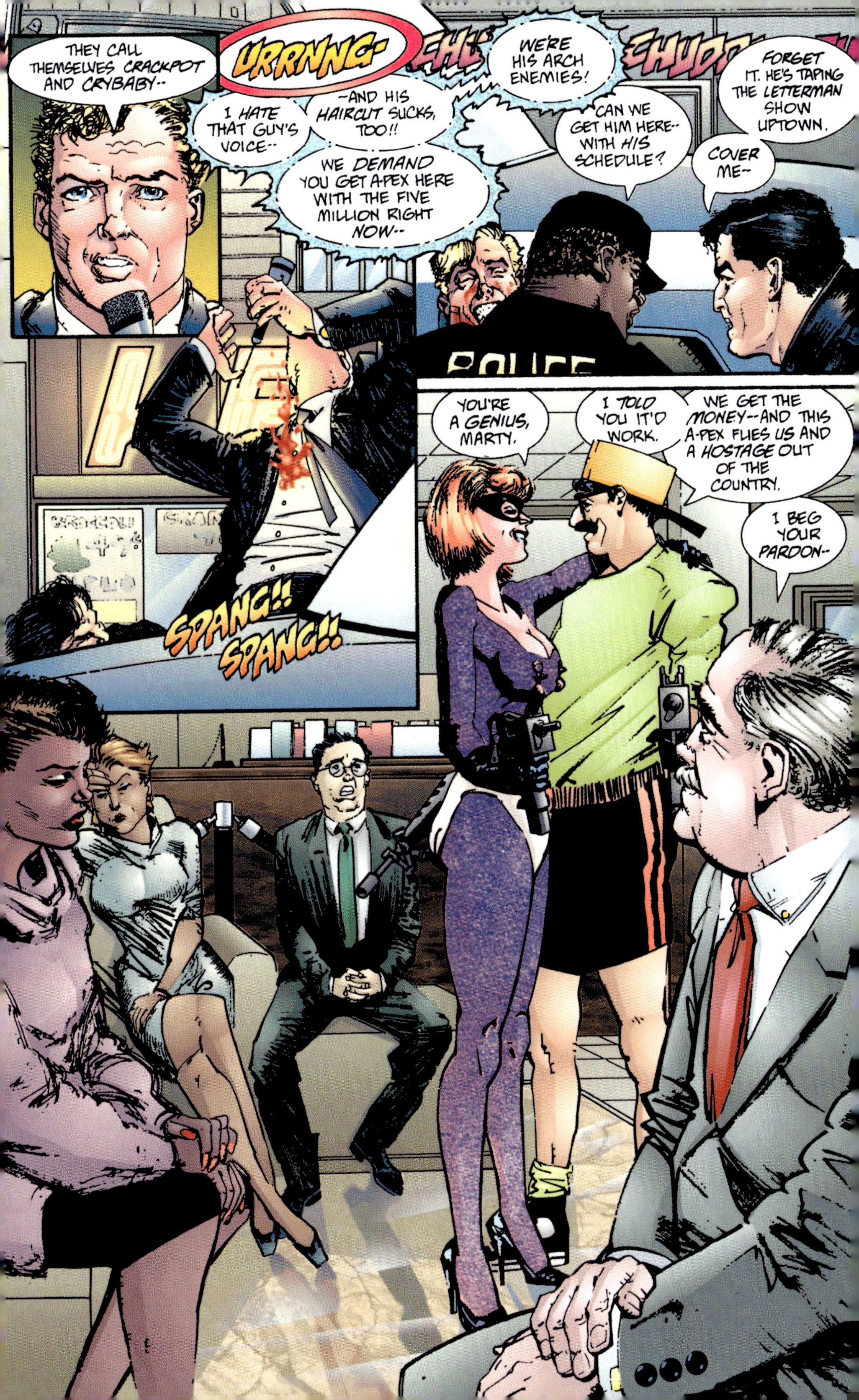

THEY CALL THEMSELVES CRACKPOT AND CRYBABY--
URRNNG-
I HATE THAT GUY'S VOICE--
--AND HIS HAIRCUT SUCKS, TOO!!
WE DEMAND YOU GET A-PEX HERE WITH THE FIVE MILLION RIGHT NOW--
WE'RE HIS ARCH ENEMIES!
CAN WE GET HIM HERE-- WITH HIS SCHEDULE?
FORGET IT. HE'S TAPING THE LETTERMAN SHOW UPTOWN.
COVER ME--
POLICE
SPANG!! SPANG!!
YOU'RE A GENIUS, MARTY.
I TOLD YOU IT'D WORK.
WE GET THE MONEY--AND THIS A-PEX FLIES US AND A HOSTAGE OUT OF THE COUNTRY.
I BEG YOUR PARDON--

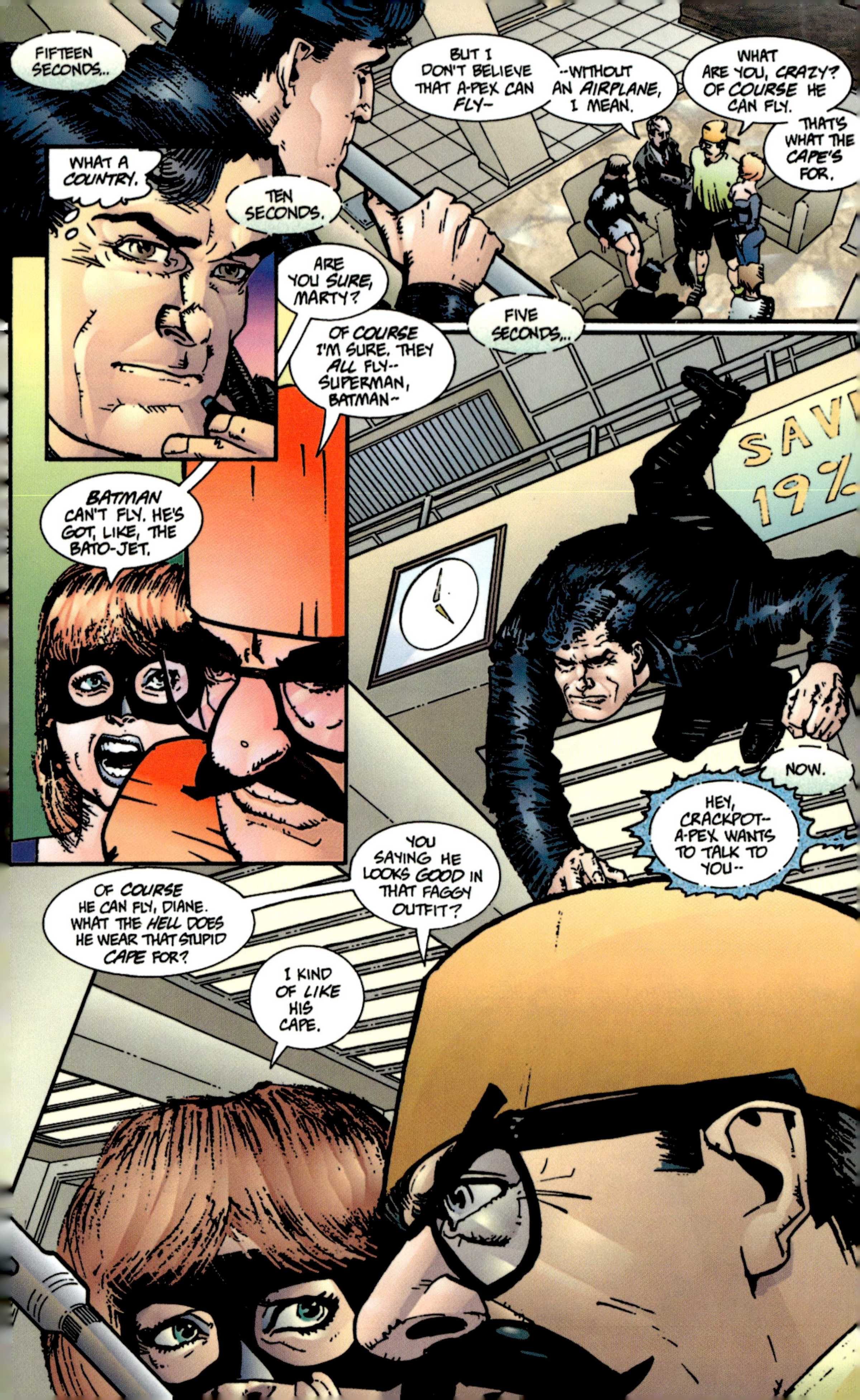
FIFTEEN SECONDS...
BUT I DON'T BELIEVE THAT A-PEX CAN FLY--
--WITHOUT AN AIRPLANE, I MEAN.
WHAT ARE YOU, CRAZY? OF COURSE HE CAN FLY.
THAT'S WHAT THE CAPE'S FOR.
WHAT A COUNTRY.
TEN SECONDS.
ARE YOU SURE, MARTY?
OF COURSE I'M SURE. THEY ALL FLY-- SUPERMAN, BATMAN--
FIVE SECONDS...
BATMAN CAN'T FLY. HE'S GOT, LIKE, THE BATO-JET.
SAV
19%
NOW.
HEY, CRACKPOT-- A-PEX WANTS TO TALK TO YOU--
OF COURSE HE CAN FLY, DIANE. WHAT THE HELL DOES HE WEAR THAT STUPID CAPE FOR?
YOU SAYING HE LOOKS GOOD IN THAT FAGGY OUTFIT?
I KIND OF LIKE HIS CAPE.

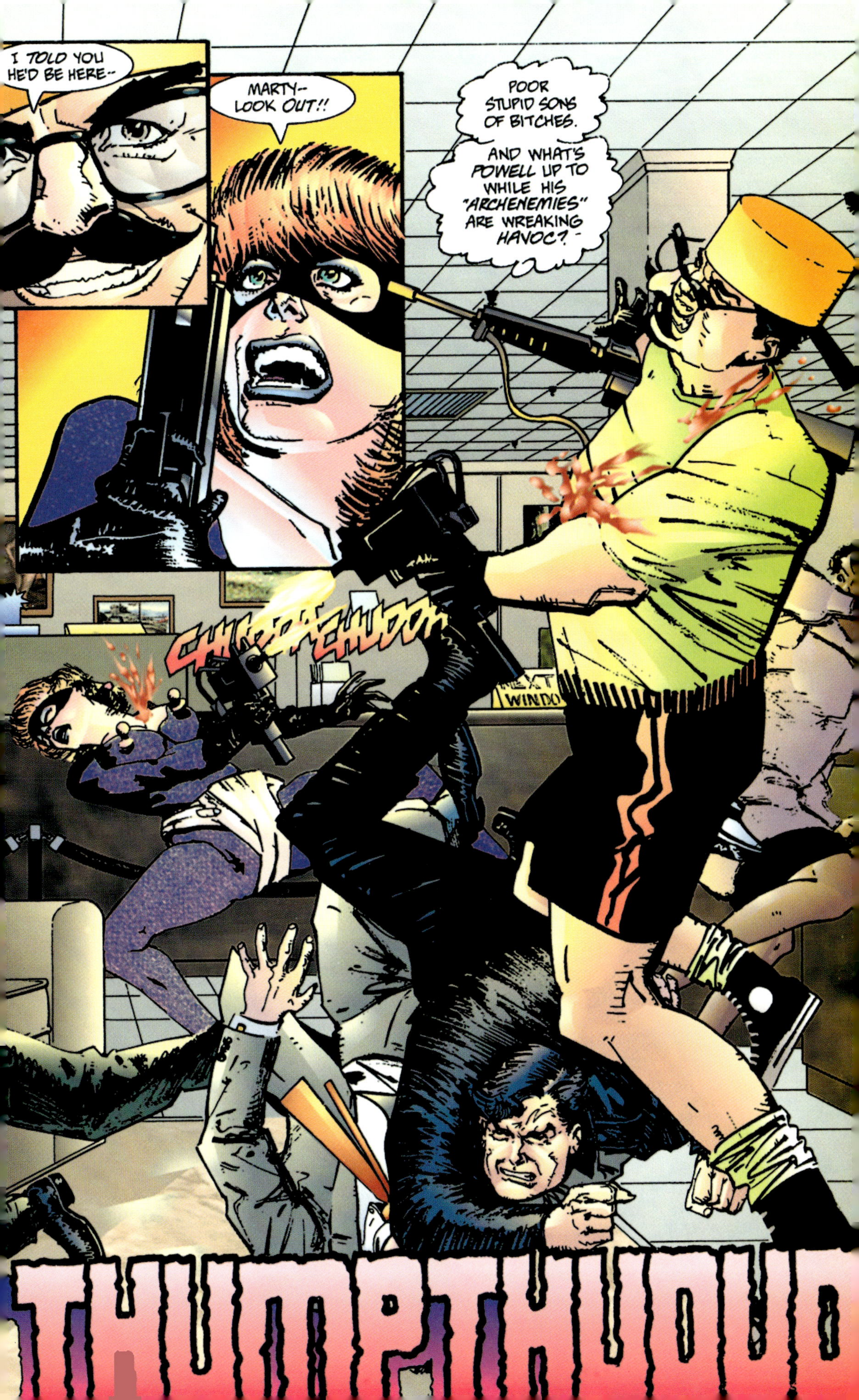
I TOLD YOU HE'D BE HERE--
MARTY-- LOOK OUT!!
POOR STUPID SONS OF BITCHES.
AND WHAT'S POWELL UP TO WHILE HIS "ARCHENEMIES" ARE WREAKING HAVOC?
THUMPTHUDD

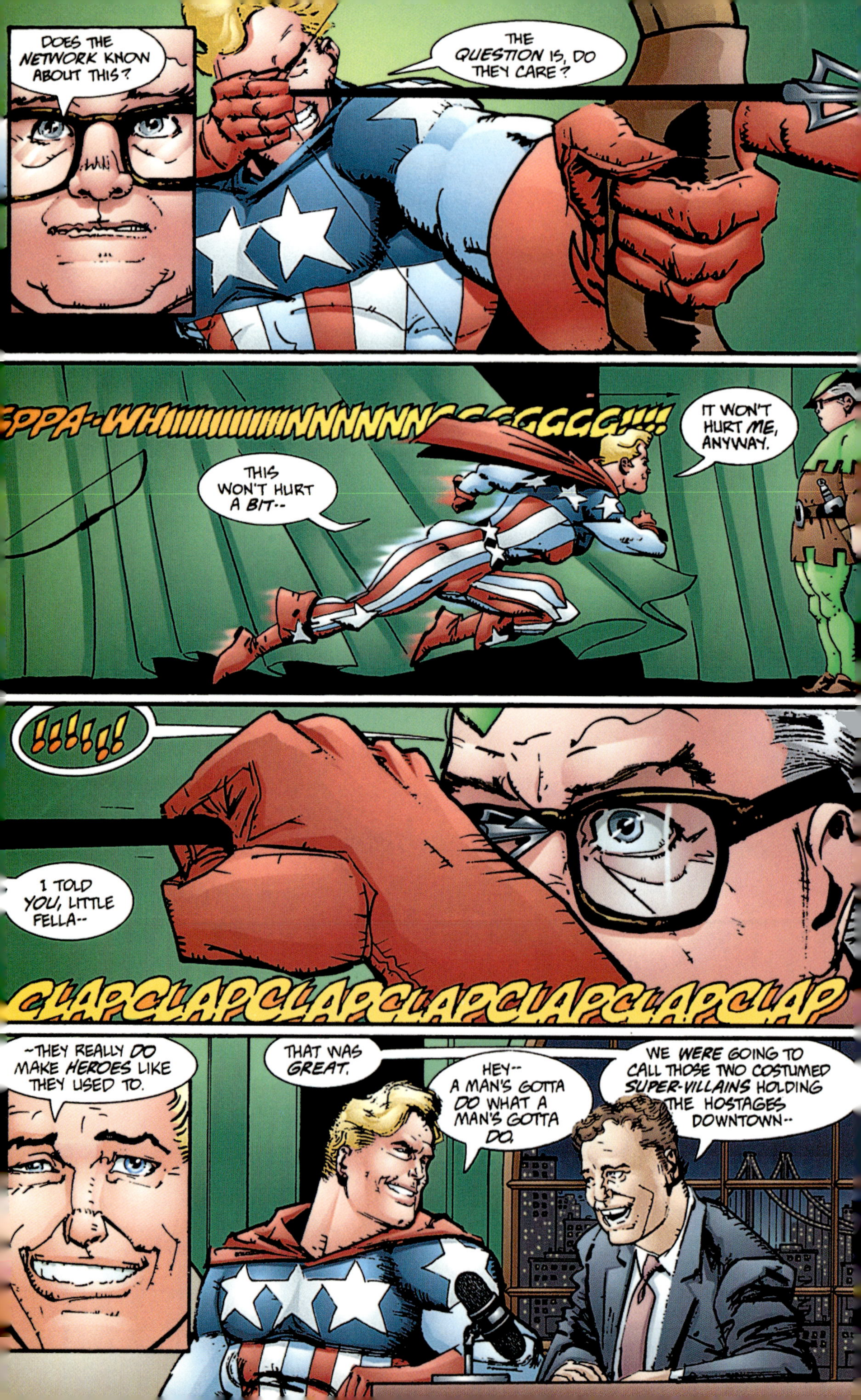
DOES THE NETWORK KNOW ABOUT THIS?
THE QUESTION IS, DO THEY CARE?
EPPA-WHIIIIIIIIIIIIINNNNNNGGGGGGG!!!!
THIS WON'T HURT A BIT--
IT WON'T HURT ME, ANYWAY.
!!!!!!
I TOLD YOU, LITTLE FELLA--
CLAPCLAPCLAPCLAPCLAPCLAPCLAP
--THEY REALLY DO MAKE HEROES LIKE THEY USED TO.
THAT WAS GREAT.
HEY-- A MAN'S GOTTA DO WHAT A MAN'S GOTTA DO.
WE WERE GOING TO CALL THOSE TWO COSTUMED SUPER-VILLAINS HOLDING THE HOSTAGES DOWNTOWN--

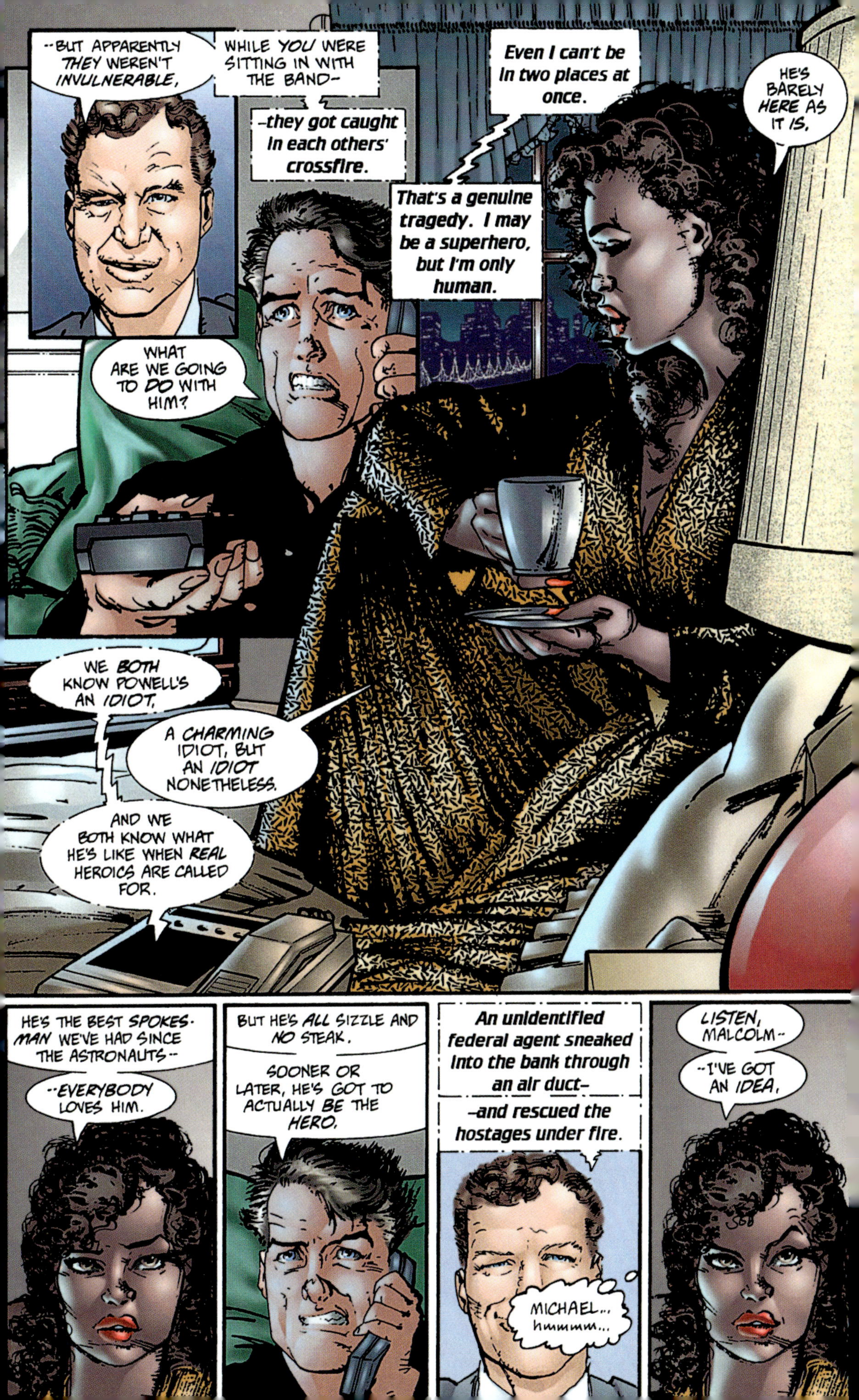
--BUT APPARENTLY THEY WEREN'T INVULNERABLE.
WHILE YOU WERE SITTING IN WITH THE BAND--
--they got caught in each others' crossfire.
Even I can't be in two places at once.
HE'S BARELY HERE AS IT IS.
That's a genuine tragedy. I may be a superhero, but I'm only human.
WHAT ARE WE GOING TO DO WITH HIM?
WE BOTH KNOW POWELL'S AN IDIOT.
A CHARMING IDIOT, BUT AN IDIOT NONETHELESS.
AND WE BOTH KNOW WHAT HE'S LIKE WHEN REAL HEROICS ARE CALLED FOR.
HE'S THE BEST SPOKESMAN WE'VE HAD SINCE THE ASTRONAUTS--
--EVERYBODY LOVES HIM.
BUT HE'S ALL SIZZLE AND NO STEAK.
SOONER OR LATER, HE'S GOT TO ACTUALLY BE THE HERO.
An unidentified federal agent sneaked into the bank through an air duct--
--and rescued the hostages under fire.
MICHAEL... hmmmm...
LISTEN, MALCOLM--
--I'VE GOT AN IDEA.

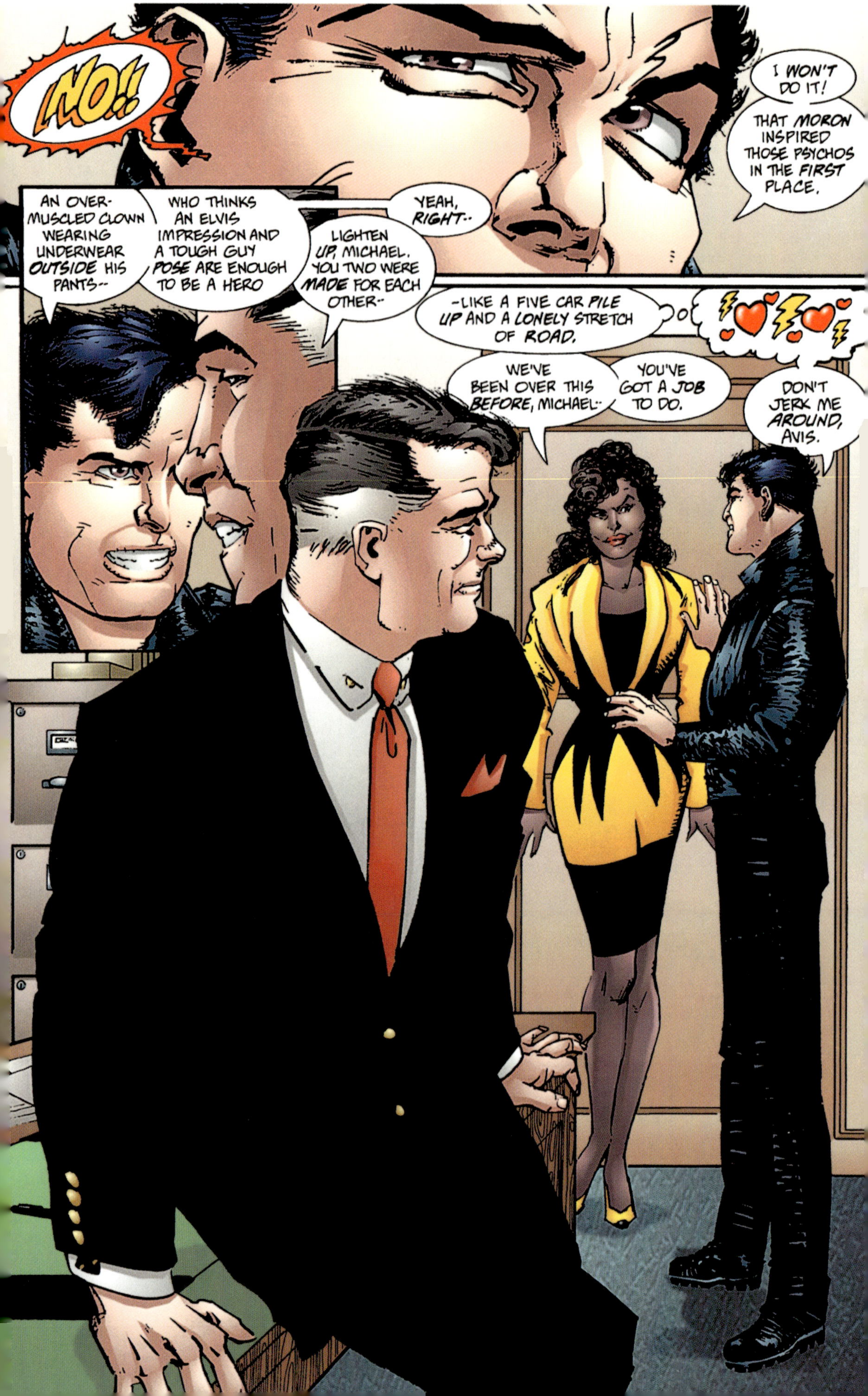
NO!!
I WON'T DO IT!
THAT MORON INSPIRED THOSE PSYCHOS IN THE FIRST PLACE.
AN OVER-MUSCLED CLOWN WEARING UNDERWEAR OUTSIDE HIS PANTS--
WHO THINKS AN ELVIS IMPRESSION AND A TOUGH GUY POSE ARE ENOUGH TO BE A HERO
YEAH, RIGHT..
LIGHTEN UP, MICHAEL. YOU TWO WERE MADE FOR EACH OTHER--
--LIKE A FIVE CAR PILE UP AND A LONELY STRETCH OF ROAD.
WE'VE BEEN OVER THIS BEFORE, MICHAEL--
YOU'VE GOT A JOB TO DO.
DON'T JERK ME AROUND, AVIS.

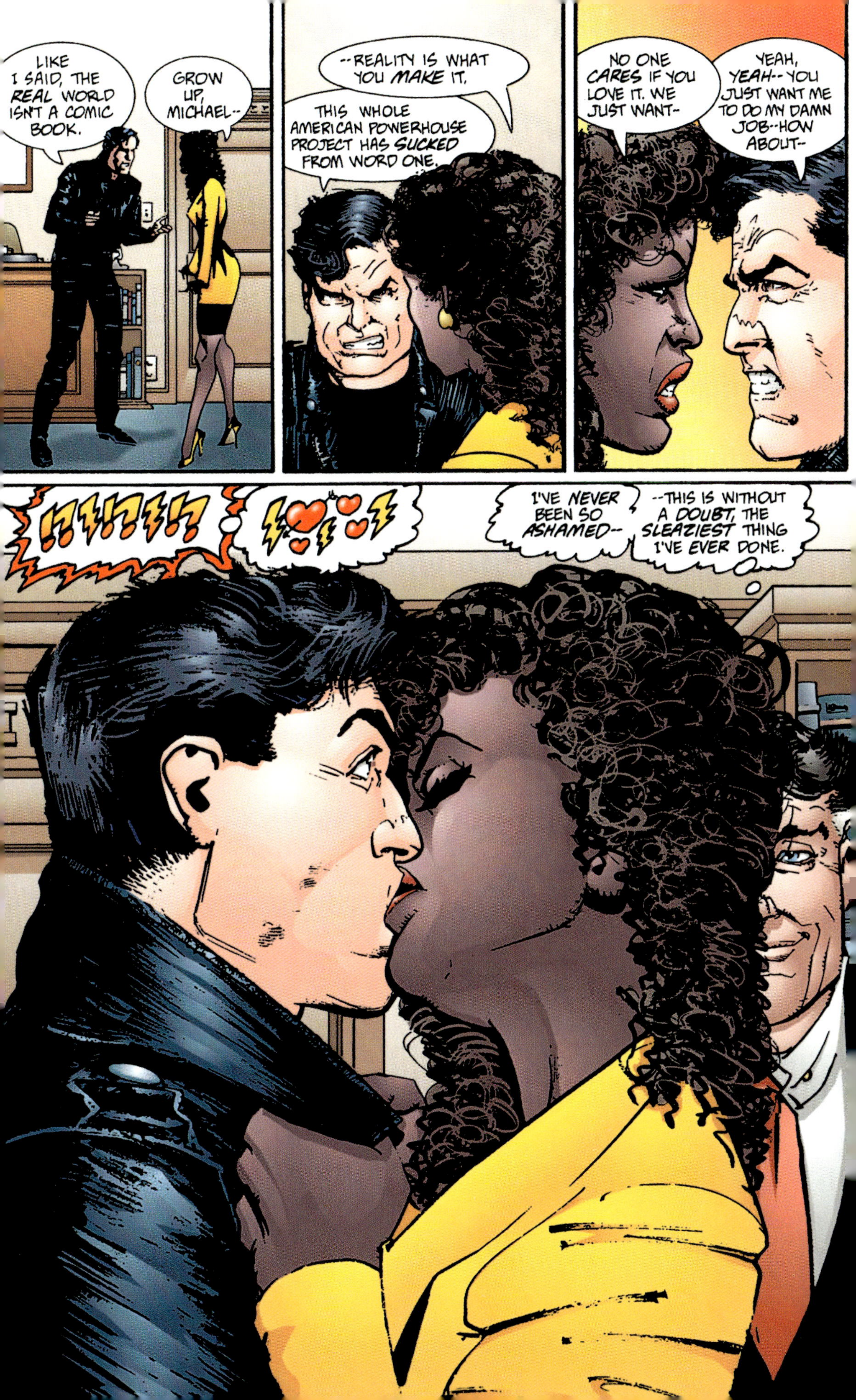
LIKE I SAID, THE REAL WORLD ISN'T A COMIC BOOK.
GROW UP, MICHAEL--
THIS WHOLE AMERICAN POWERHOUSE PROJECT HAS SUCKED FROM WORD ONE.
--REALITY IS WHAT YOU MAKE IT.
NO ONE CARES IF YOU LOVE IT. WE JUST WANT-
YEAH, YEAH--YOU JUST WANT ME TO DO MY DAMN JOB--HOW ABOUT-
!?!?!?!?
I'VE NEVER BEEN SO ASHAMED--
--THIS IS WITHOUT A DOUBT, THE SLEAZIEST THING I'VE EVER DONE.

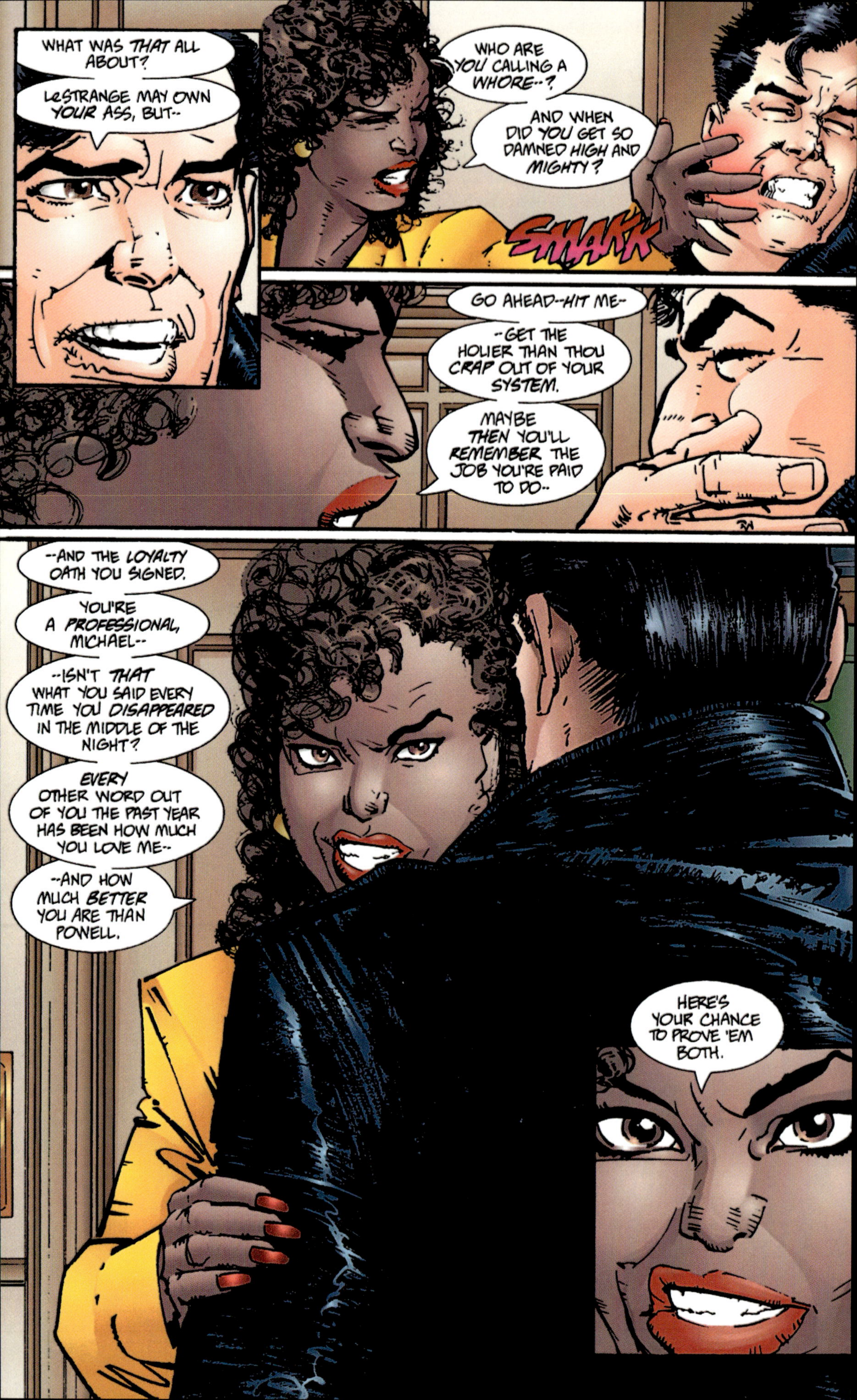
WHAT WAS THAT ALL ABOUT?
LeSTRANGE MAY OWN YOUR ASS, BUT--
WHO ARE YOU CALLING A WHORE--?
AND WHEN DID YOU GET SO DAMNED HIGH AND MIGHTY?
SMAKK
GO AHEAD--HIT ME--
--GET THE HOLIER THAN THOU CRAP OUT OF YOUR SYSTEM.
MAYBE THEN YOU'LL REMEMBER THE JOB YOU'RE PAID TO DO--
--AND THE LOYALTY OATH YOU SIGNED.
YOU'RE A PROFESSIONAL, MICHAEL--
--ISN'T THAT WHAT YOU SAID EVERY TIME YOU DISAPPEARED IN THE MIDDLE OF THE NIGHT?
EVERY OTHER WORD OUT OF YOU THE PAST YEAR HAS BEEN HOW MUCH YOU LOVE ME--
--AND HOW MUCH BETTER YOU ARE THAN POWELL.
HERE'S YOUR CHANCE TO PROVE 'EM BOTH.

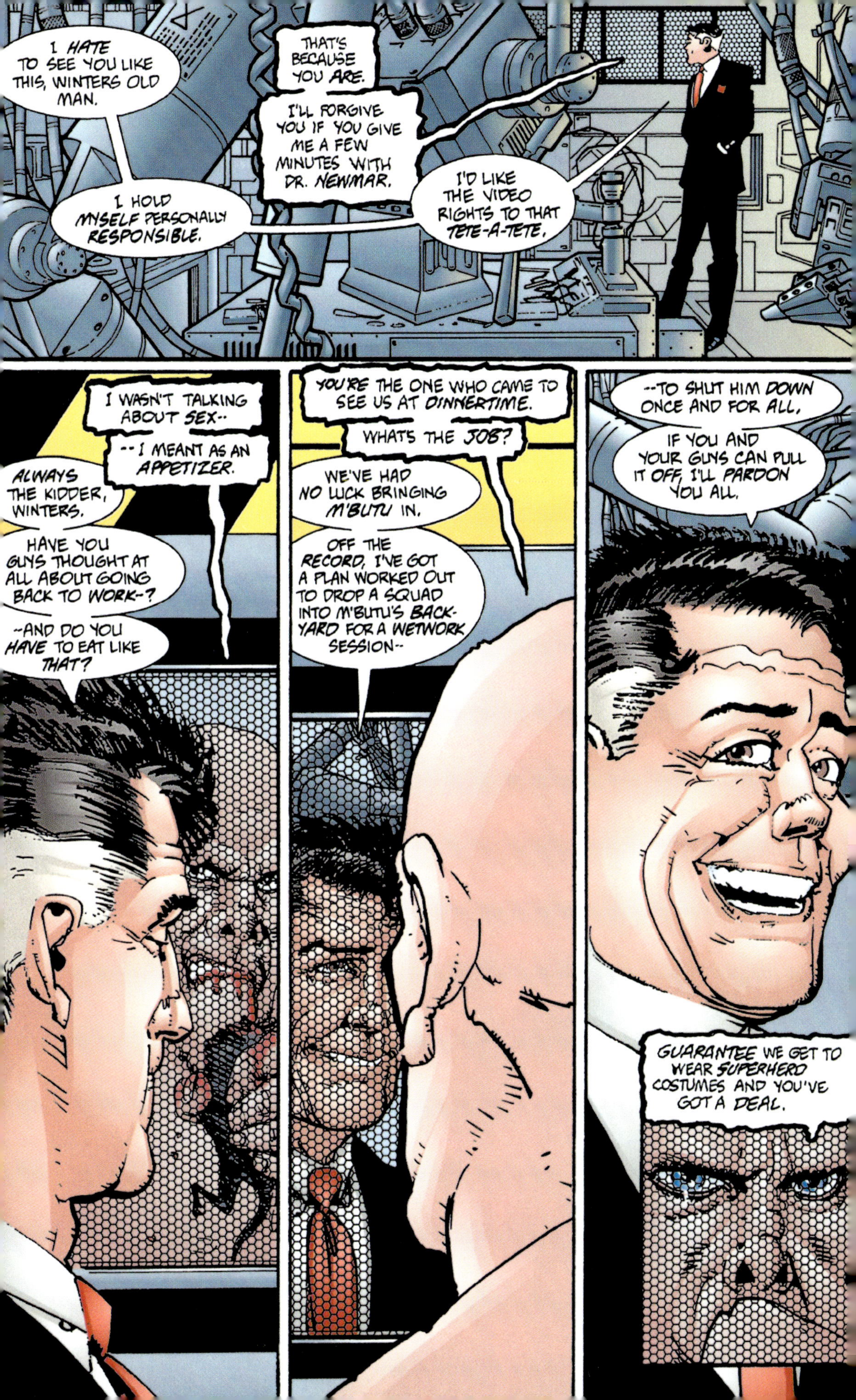

I HATE TO SEE YOU LIKE THIS, WINTERS OLD MAN.
THAT'S BECAUSE YOU ARE.
I'LL FORGIVE YOU IF YOU GIVE ME A FEW MINUTES WITH DR. NEWMAR.
I HOLD MYSELF PERSONALLY RESPONSIBLE.
I'D LIKE THE VIDEO RIGHTS TO THAT TETE-A-TETE.
I WASN'T TALKING ABOUT SEX--
--I MEANT AS AN APPETIZER.
ALWAYS THE KIDDER, WINTERS.
HAVE YOU GUYS THOUGHT AT ALL ABOUT GOING BACK TO WORK--?
--AND DO YOU HAVE TO EAT LIKE THAT?
YOU'RE THE ONE WHO CAME TO SEE US AT DINNERTIME.
WHAT'S THE JOB?
WE'VE HAD NO LUCK BRINGING M'BUTU IN.
OFF THE RECORD, I'VE GOT A PLAN WORKED OUT TO DROP A SQUAD INTO M'BUTU'S BACK-YARD FOR A NETWORK SESSION--
--TO SHUT HIM DOWN ONCE AND FOR ALL.
IF YOU AND YOUR GUYS CAN PULL IT OFF, I'LL PARDON YOU ALL.
GUARANTEE WE GET TO WEAR SUPERHERO COSTUMES AND YOU'VE GOT A DEAL.

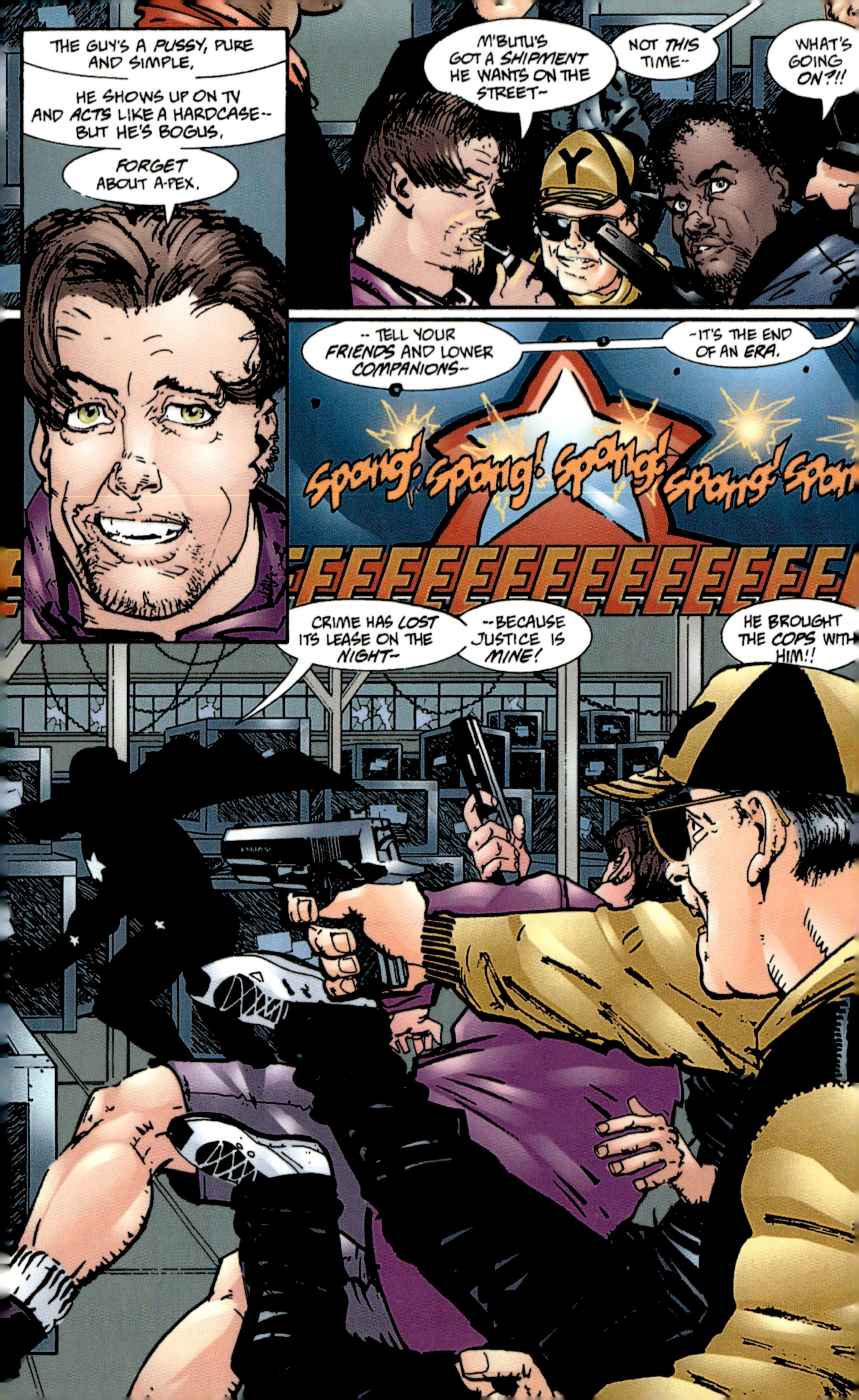
THE GUY'S A PUSSY, PURE AND SIMPLE.
HE SHOWS UP ON TV AND ACTS LIKE A HARDCASE-- BUT HE'S BOGUS.
FORGET ABOUT A-PEX.
M'BUTU'S GOT A SHIPMENT HE WANTS ON THE STREET--
NOT THIS TIME--
WHAT'S GOING ON?!!
-- TELL YOUR FRIENDS AND LOWER COMPANIONS--
--IT'S THE END OF AN ERA.
SPANG! SPANG! SPANG! SPANG! SPAN
EEEEEEEEEEEEEEEEE
CRIME HAS LOST ITS LEASE ON THE NIGHT--
--BECAUSE JUSTICE IS MINE!
HE BROUGHT THE COPS WITH HIM!!

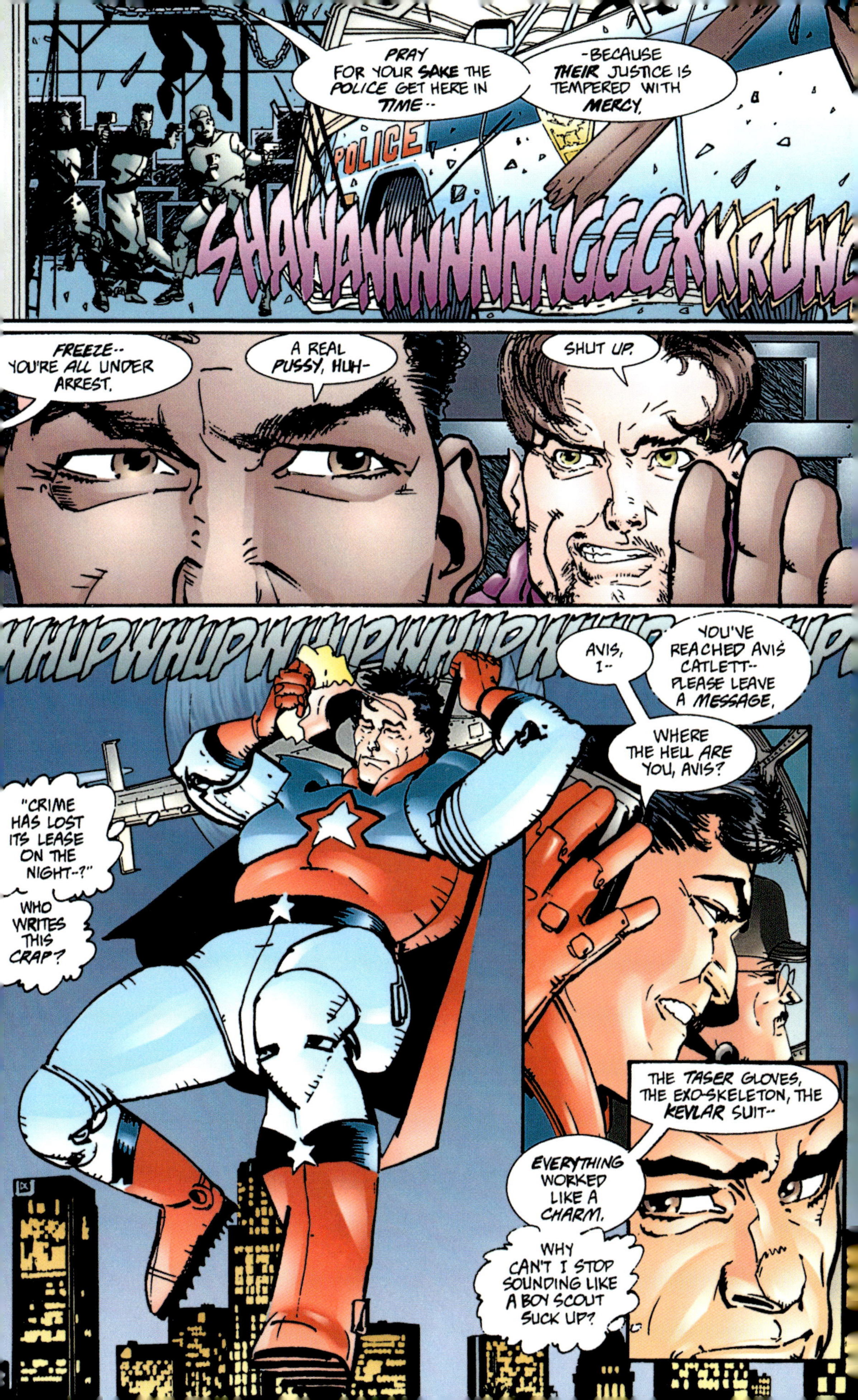
PRAY FOR YOUR SAKE THE POLICE GET HERE IN TIME--
-BECAUSE THEIR JUSTICE IS TEMPERED WITH MERCY.
POLICE
SHAWANNNNNNNGGGCKKRUNC
FREEZE-- YOU'RE ALL UNDER ARREST.
A REAL PUSSY, HUH-
SHUT UP.
AVIS, I--
YOU'VE REACHED AVIS CATLETT-- PLEASE LEAVE A MESSAGE.
WHERE THE HELL ARE YOU, AVIS?
"CRIME HAS LOST ITS LEASE ON THE NIGHT--?"
WHO WRITES THIS CRAP?
THE TASER GLOVES, THE EXO-SKELETON, THE KEVLAR SUIT--
EVERYTHING WORKED LIKE A CHARM.
WHY CAN'T I STOP SOUNDING LIKE A BOY SCOUT SUCK UP?

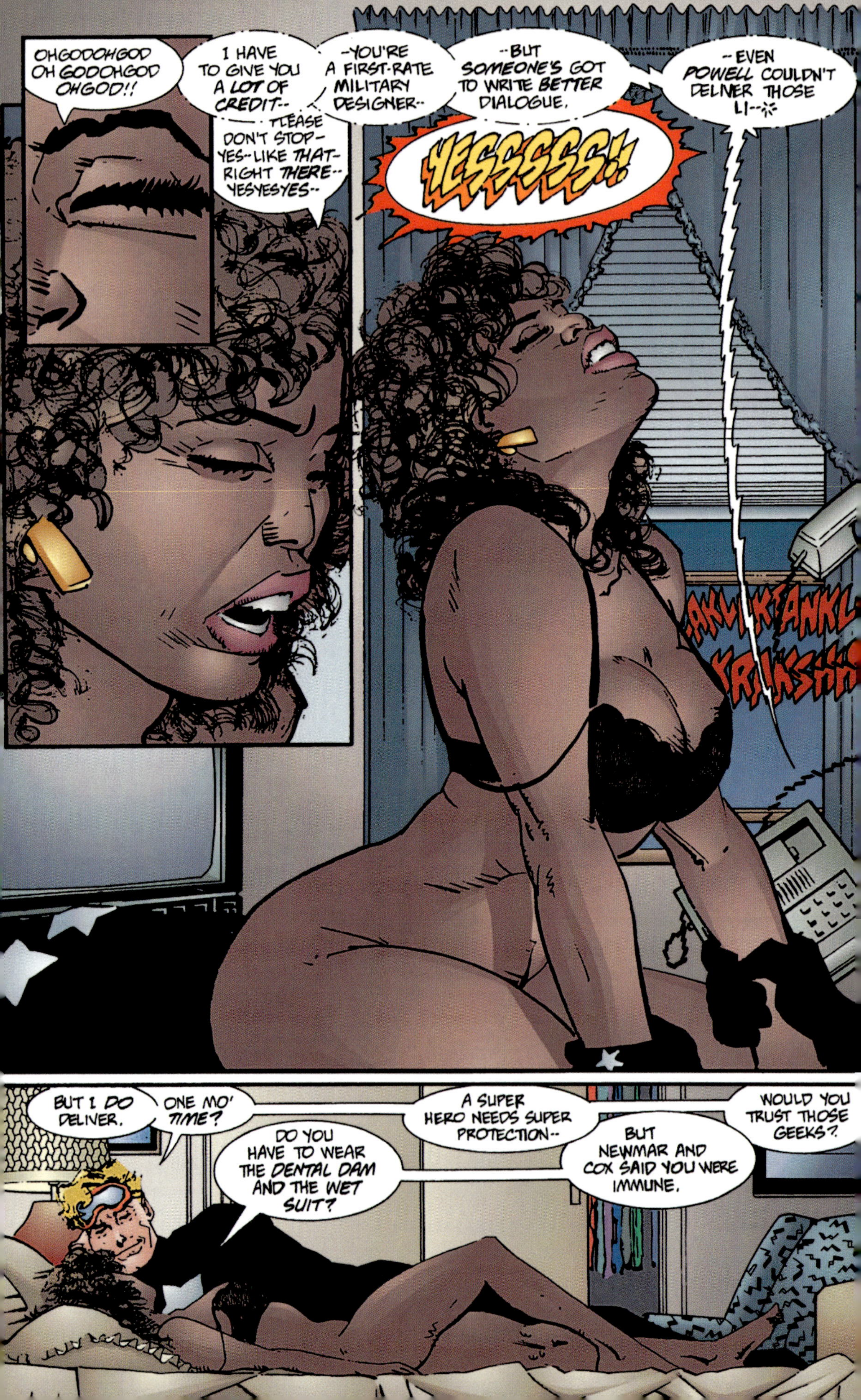
OHGODOHGOD OH GODOHGOD OHGOD!!
I HAVE TO GIVE YOU A LOT OF CREDIT--
--YOU'RE A FIRST-RATE MILITARY DESIGNER--
--BUT SOMEONE'S GOT TO WRITE BETTER DIALOGUE.
--EVEN POWELL COULDN'T DELIVER THOSE LI--
PLEASE DON'T STOP-- YES--LIKE THAT-- RIGHT THERE-- YESYESYES--
YESSSSS!!
BUT I DO DELIVER.
ONE MO' TIME?
DO YOU HAVE TO WEAR THE DENTAL DAM AND THE WET SUIT?
A SUPER HERO NEEDS SUPER PROTECTION--
BUT NEWMAR AND COX SAID YOU WERE IMMUNE.
WOULD YOU TRUST THOSE GEEKS?

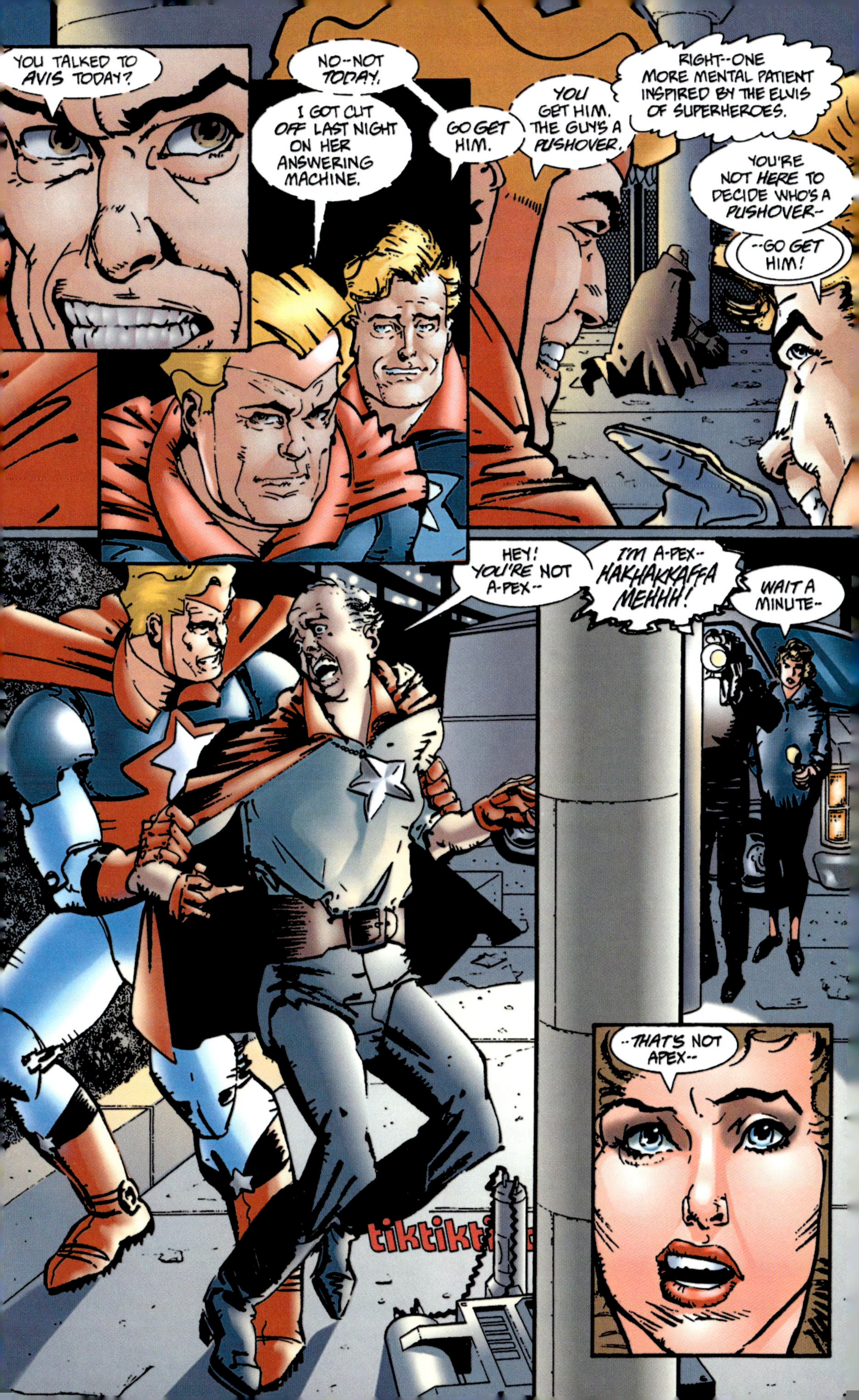
YOU TALKED TO AVIS TODAY?
NO--NOT TODAY.
I GOT CUT OFF LAST NIGHT ON HER ANSWERING MACHINE.
GO GET HIM.
YOU GET HIM. THE GUY'S A PUSHOVER.
RIGHT--ONE MORE MENTAL PATIENT INSPIRED BY THE ELVIS OF SUPERHEROES.
YOU'RE NOT HERE TO DECIDE WHO'S A PUSHOVER--
--GO GET HIM!
HEY! YOU'RE NOT A-PEX--
I'M A-PEX-- HAKHAKKAFFA MEHHH!
WAIT A MINUTE--
tiktikti
--THAT'S NOT APEX--

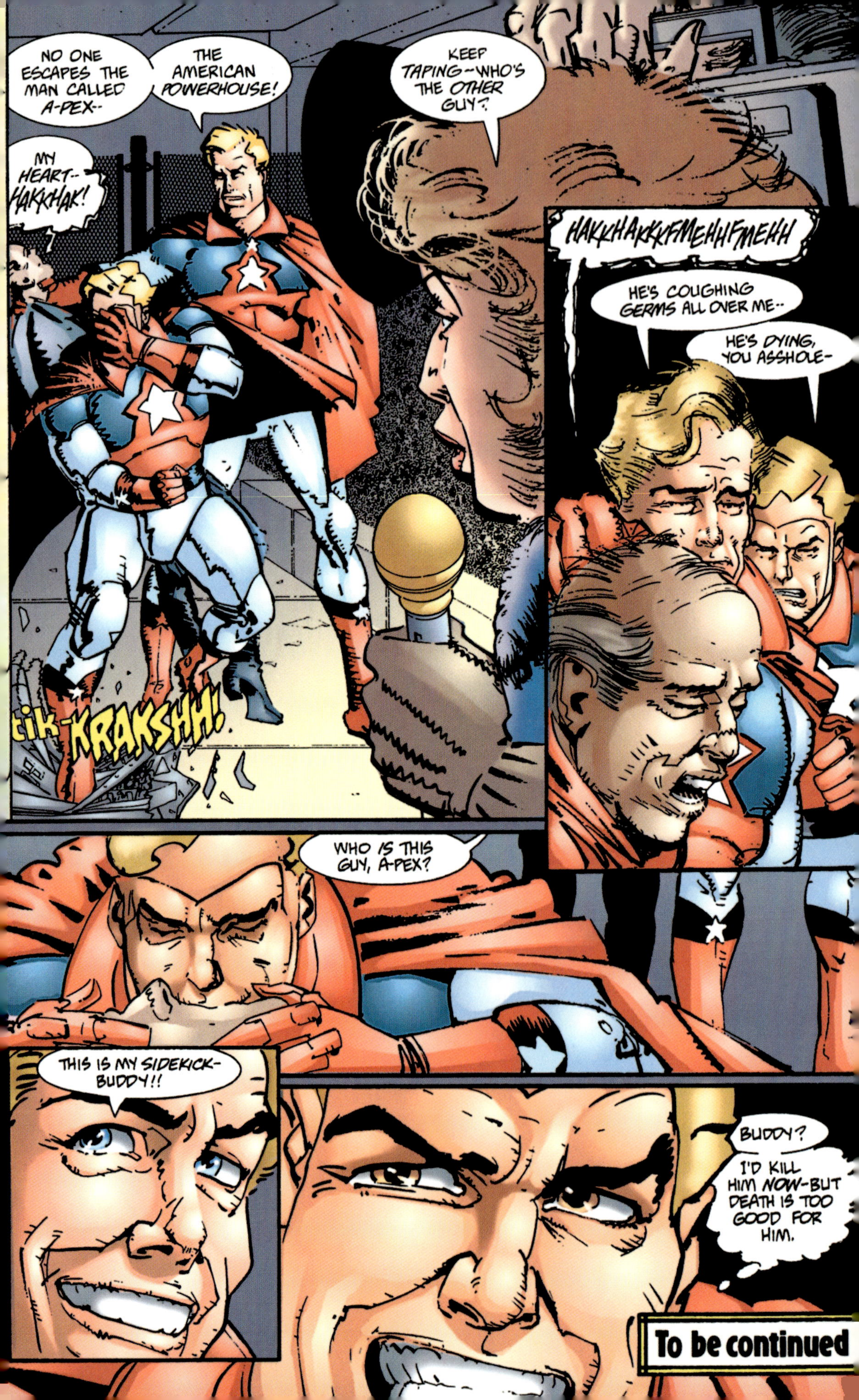
NO ONE ESCAPES THE MAN CALLED A-PEX--
THE AMERICAN POWERHOUSE!
MY HEART-- HAKKHAK!
KEEP TAPING--WHO'S THE OTHER GUY?
tik-KRAKSHH!
HAKKHAKKKFMEHHFMEHH
HE'S COUGHING GERMS ALL OVER ME--
HE'S DYING, YOU ASSHOLE-
WHO IS THIS GUY, A-PEX?
THIS IS MY SIDEKICK-BUDDY!!
BUDDY?
I'D KILL HIM NOW-BUT DEATH IS TOO GOOD FOR HIM.
To be continued

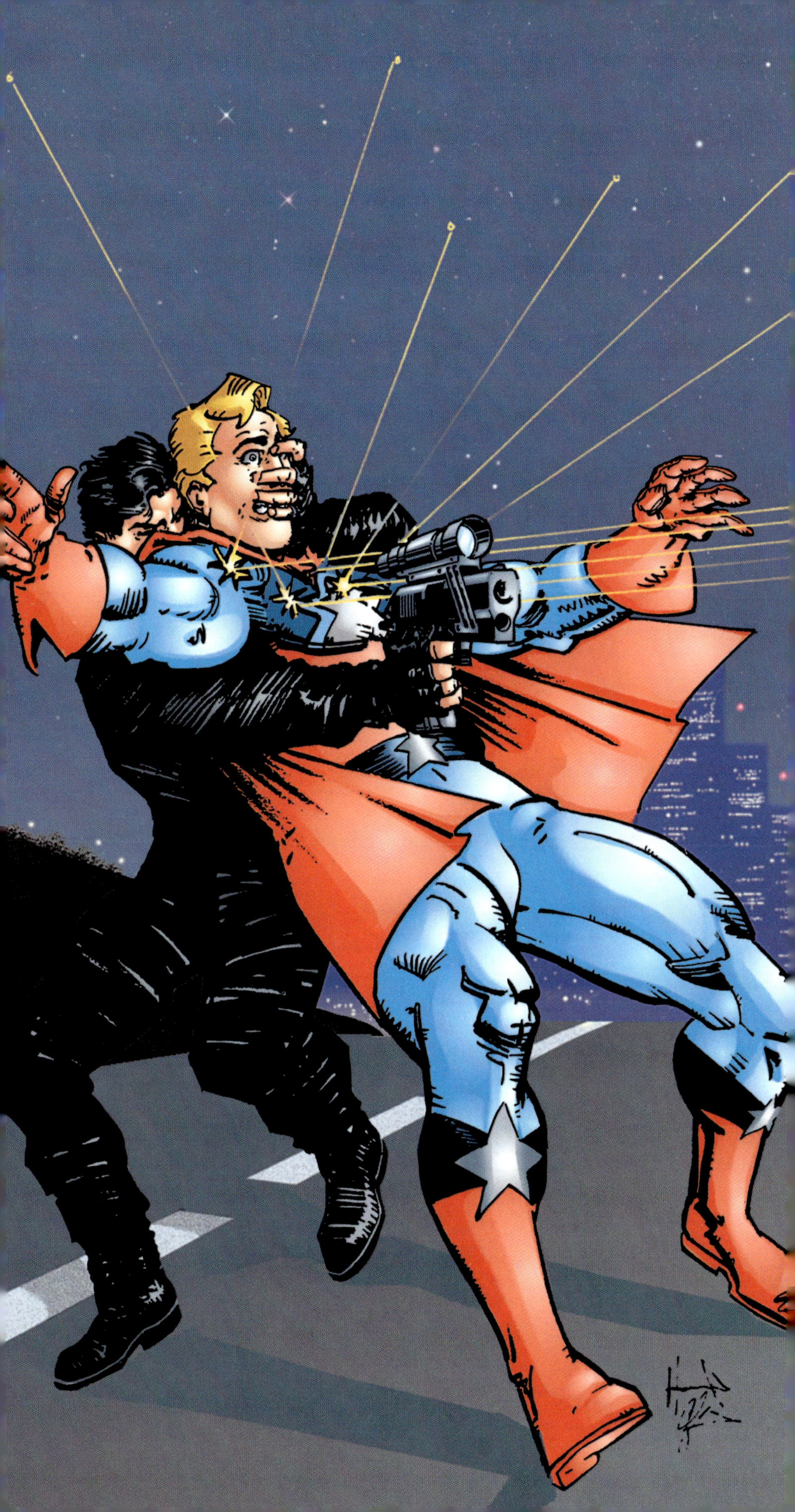

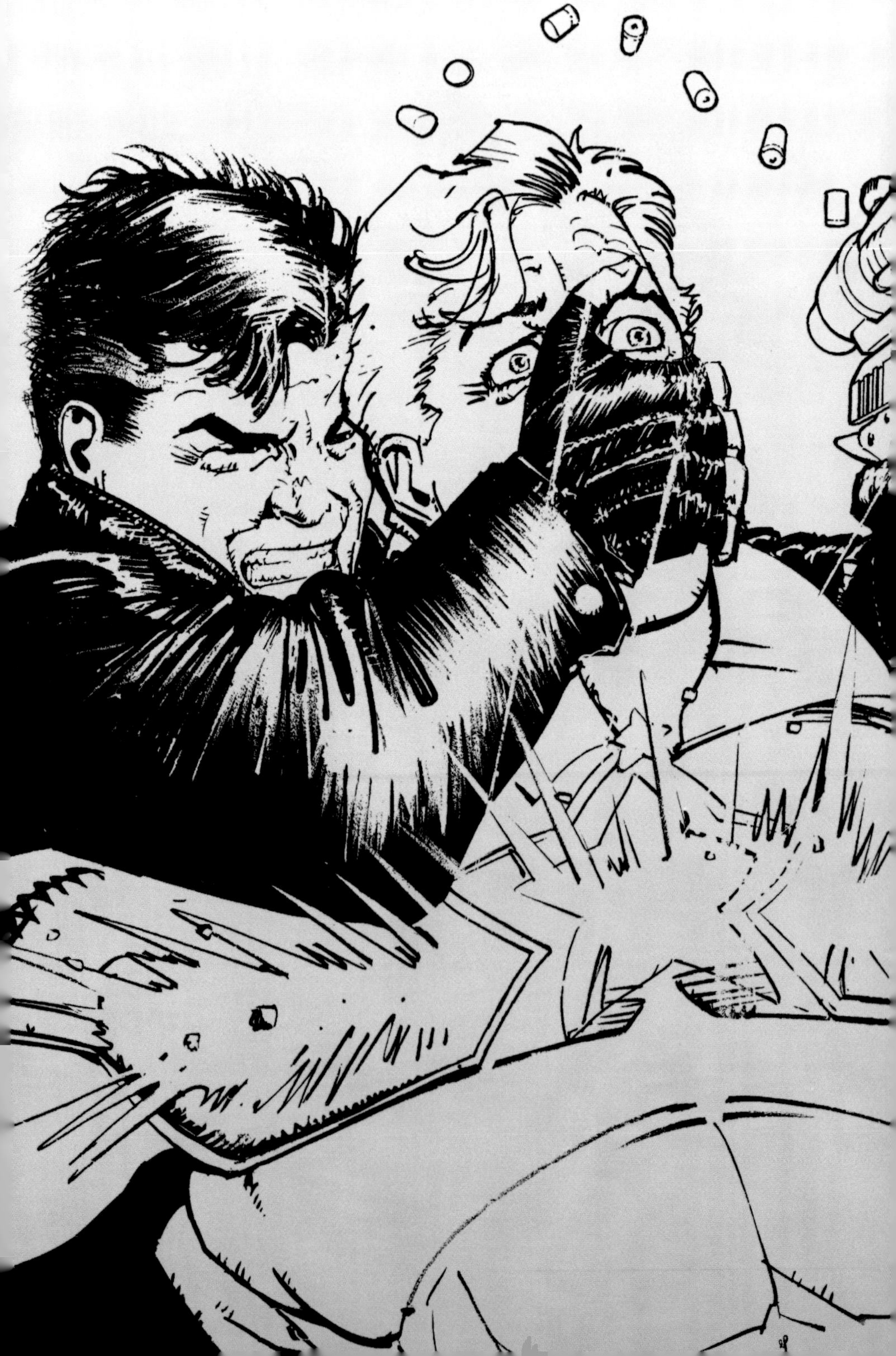

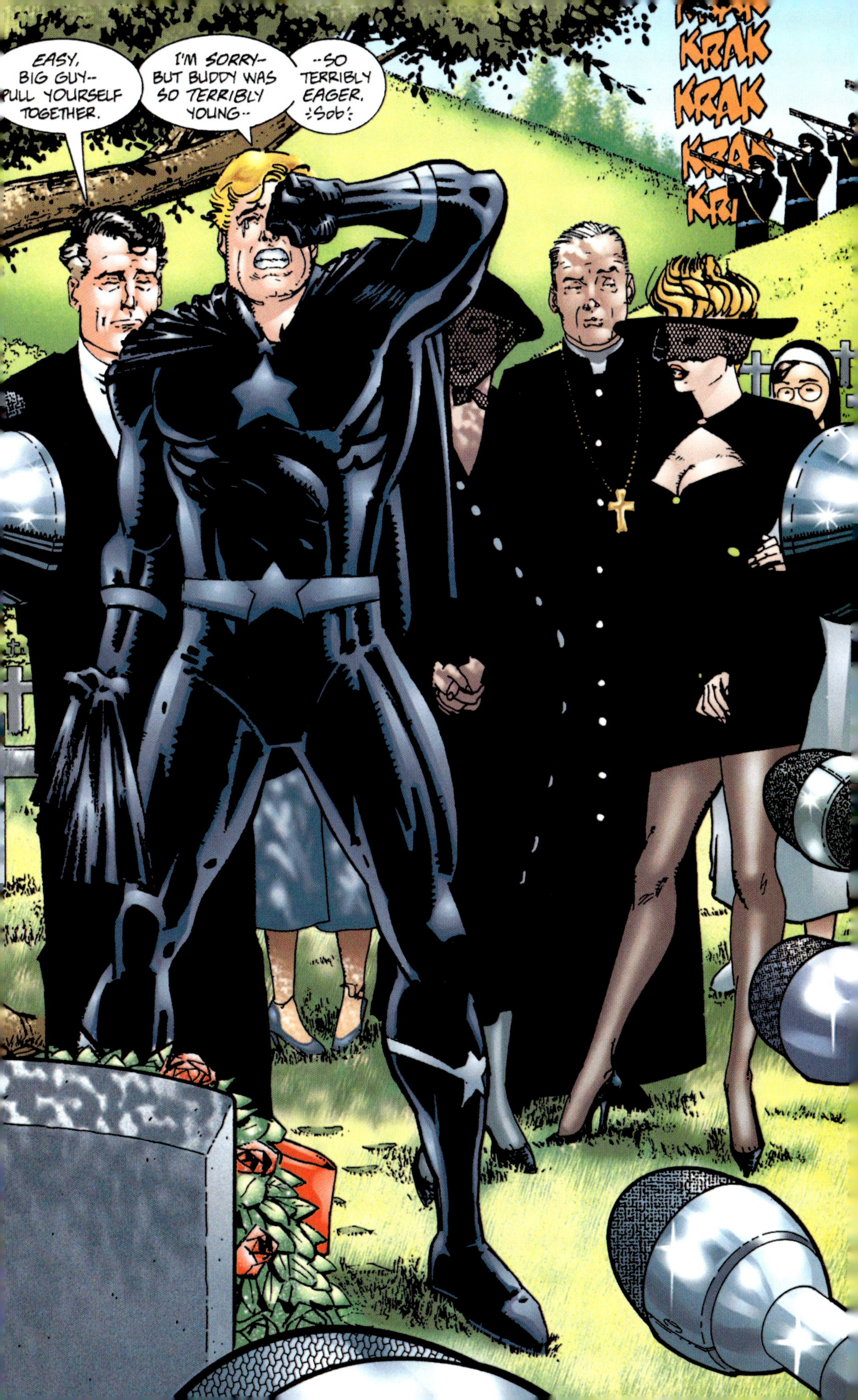
EASY, BIG GUY-- PULL YOURSELF TOGETHER.
I'M SORRY-- BUT BUDDY WAS SO TERRIBLY YOUNG--
--SO TERRIBLY EAGER. *SOB*
KRAK KRAK KRAK

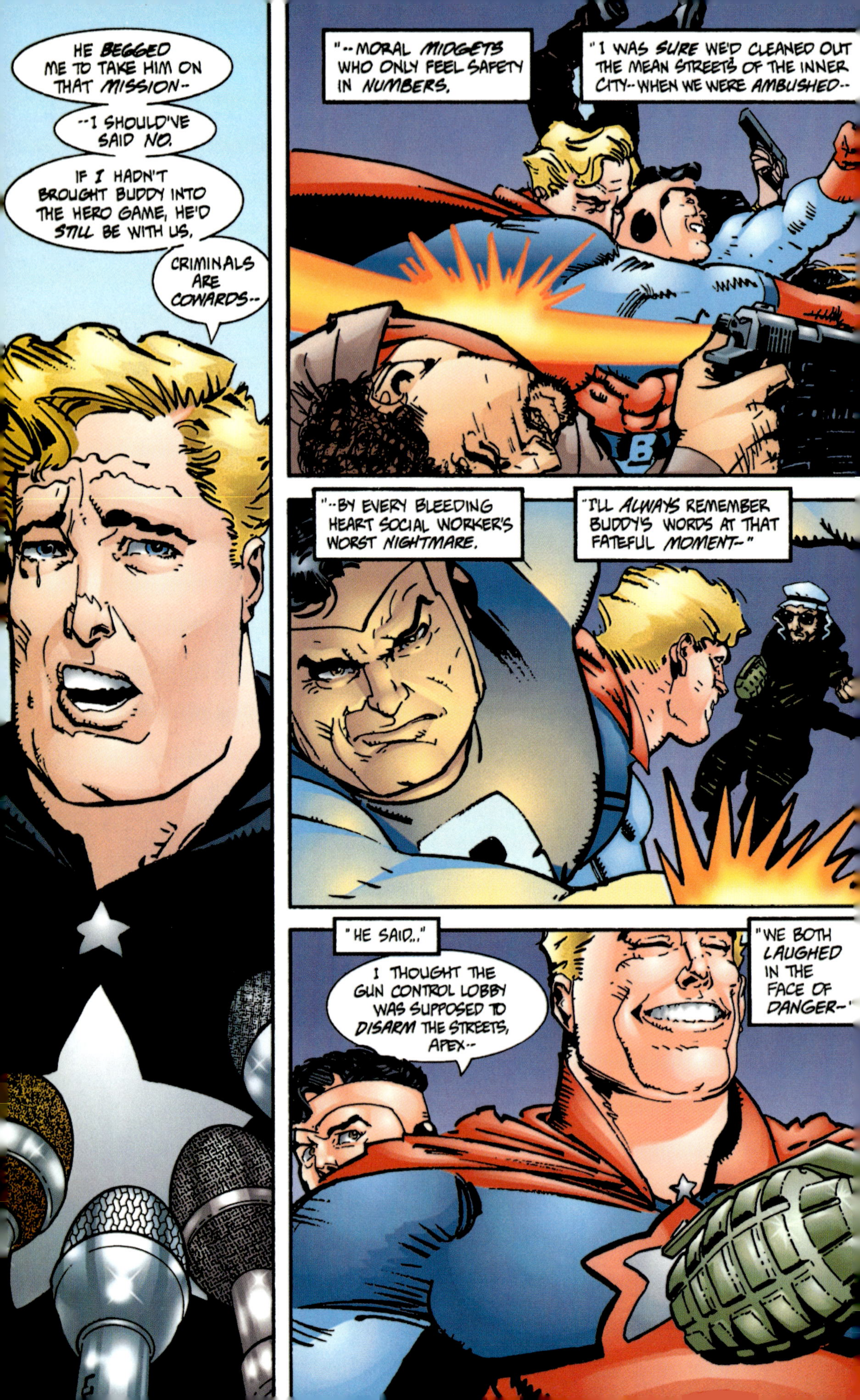
HE BEGGED ME TO TAKE HIM ON THAT MISSION--
--I SHOULD'VE SAID NO.
IF I HADN'T BROUGHT BUDDY INTO THE HERO GAME, HE'D STILL BE WITH US.
CRIMINALS ARE COWARDS--
"--MORAL MIDGETS WHO ONLY FEEL SAFETY IN NUMBERS.
"I WAS SURE WE'D CLEANED OUT THE MEAN STREETS OF THE INNER CITY--WHEN WE WERE AMBUSHED--
"--BY EVERY BLEEDING HEART SOCIAL WORKER'S WORST NIGHTMARE.
"I'LL ALWAYS REMEMBER BUDDY'S WORDS AT THAT FATEFUL MOMENT--"
"HE SAID..."
I THOUGHT THE GUN CONTROL LOBBY WAS SUPPOSED TO DISARM THE STREETS, APEX--
"WE BOTH LAUGHED IN THE FACE OF DANGER--"

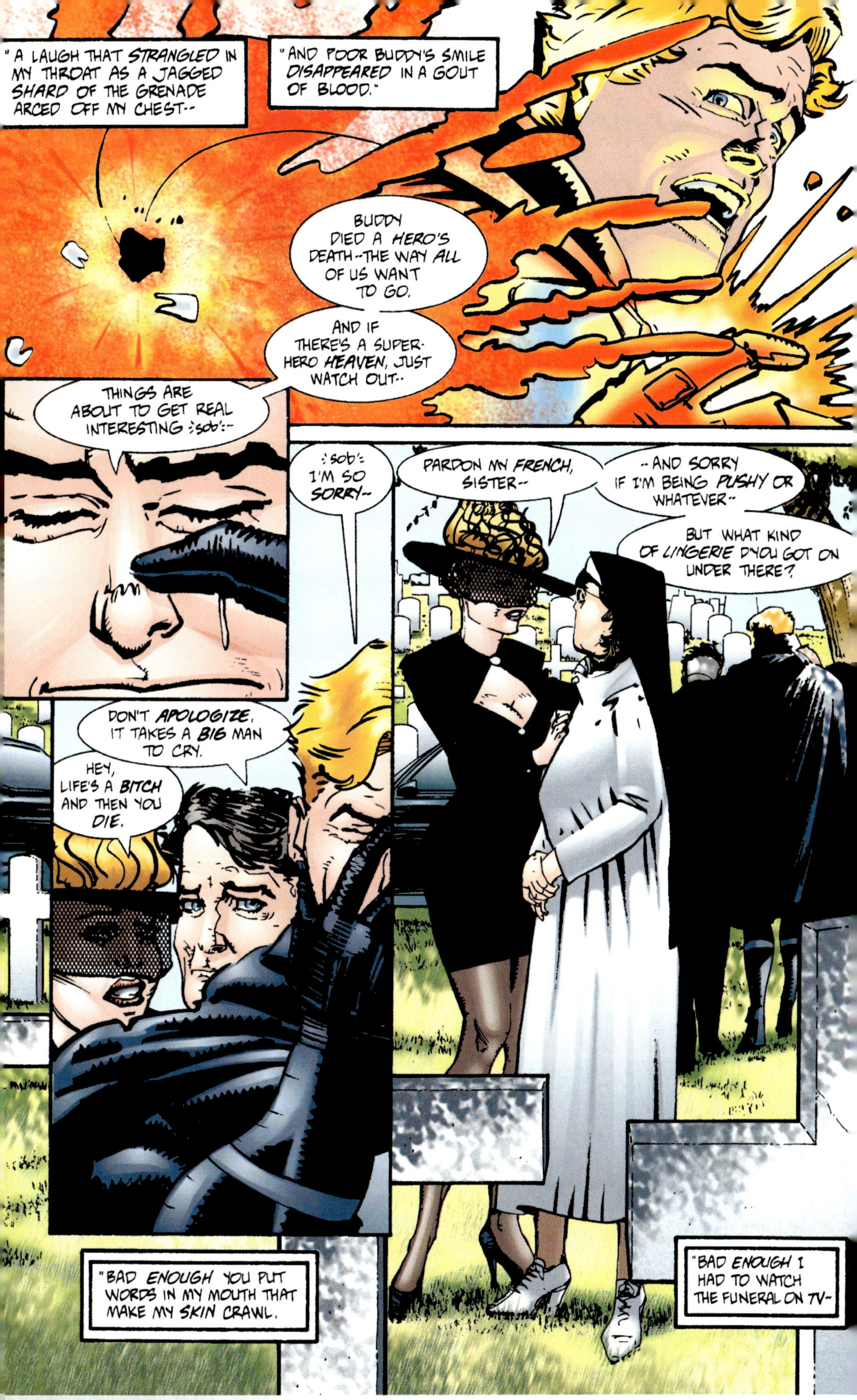
"A LAUGH THAT STRANGLED IN MY THROAT AS A JAGGED SHARD OF THE GRENADE ARCED OFF MY CHEST--
"AND POOR BUDDY'S SMILE DISAPPEARED IN A GOUT OF BLOOD."
BUDDY DIED A HERO'S DEATH--THE WAY ALL OF US WANT TO GO.
AND IF THERE'S A SUPER-HERO HEAVEN, JUST WATCH OUT--
THINGS ARE ABOUT TO GET REAL INTERESTING :sob:--
:sob: I'M SO SORRY--
PARDON MY FRENCH, SISTER--
--AND SORRY IF I'M BEING PUSHY OR WHATEVER--
BUT WHAT KIND OF LINGERIE D'YOU GOT ON UNDER THERE?
DON'T APOLOGIZE. IT TAKES A BIG MAN TO CRY.
HEY, LIFE'S A BITCH AND THEN YOU DIE.
"BAD ENOUGH YOU PUT WORDS IN MY MOUTH THAT MAKE MY SKIN CRAWL.
"BAD ENOUGH I HAD TO WATCH THE FUNERAL ON TV--

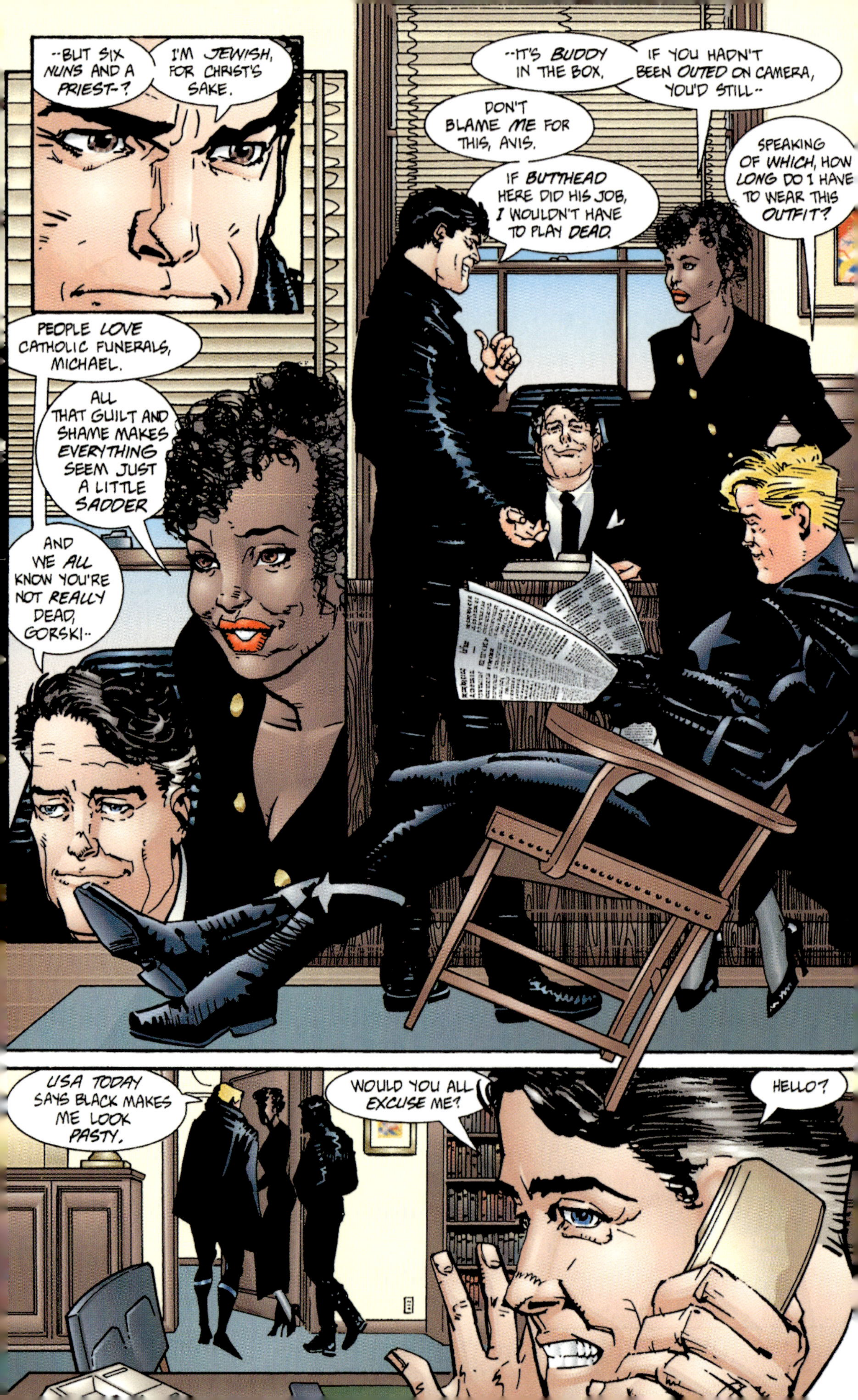
--BUT SIX NUNS AND A PRIEST-?
I'M JEWISH, FOR CHRIST'S SAKE.
--IT'S BUDDY IN THE BOX.
IF YOU HADN'T BEEN OUTED ON CAMERA, YOU'D STILL--
DON'T BLAME ME FOR THIS, AVIS.
IF BUTTHEAD HERE DID HIS JOB, I WOULDN'T HAVE TO PLAY DEAD.
SPEAKING OF WHICH, HOW LONG DO I HAVE TO WEAR THIS OUTFIT?
PEOPLE LOVE CATHOLIC FUNERALS, MICHAEL.
ALL THAT GUILT AND SHAME MAKES EVERYTHING SEEM JUST A LITTLE SADDER
AND WE ALL KNOW YOU'RE NOT REALLY DEAD, GORSKI--
USA TODAY SAYS BLACK MAKES ME LOOK PASTY.
WOULD YOU ALL EXCUSE ME?
HELLO?

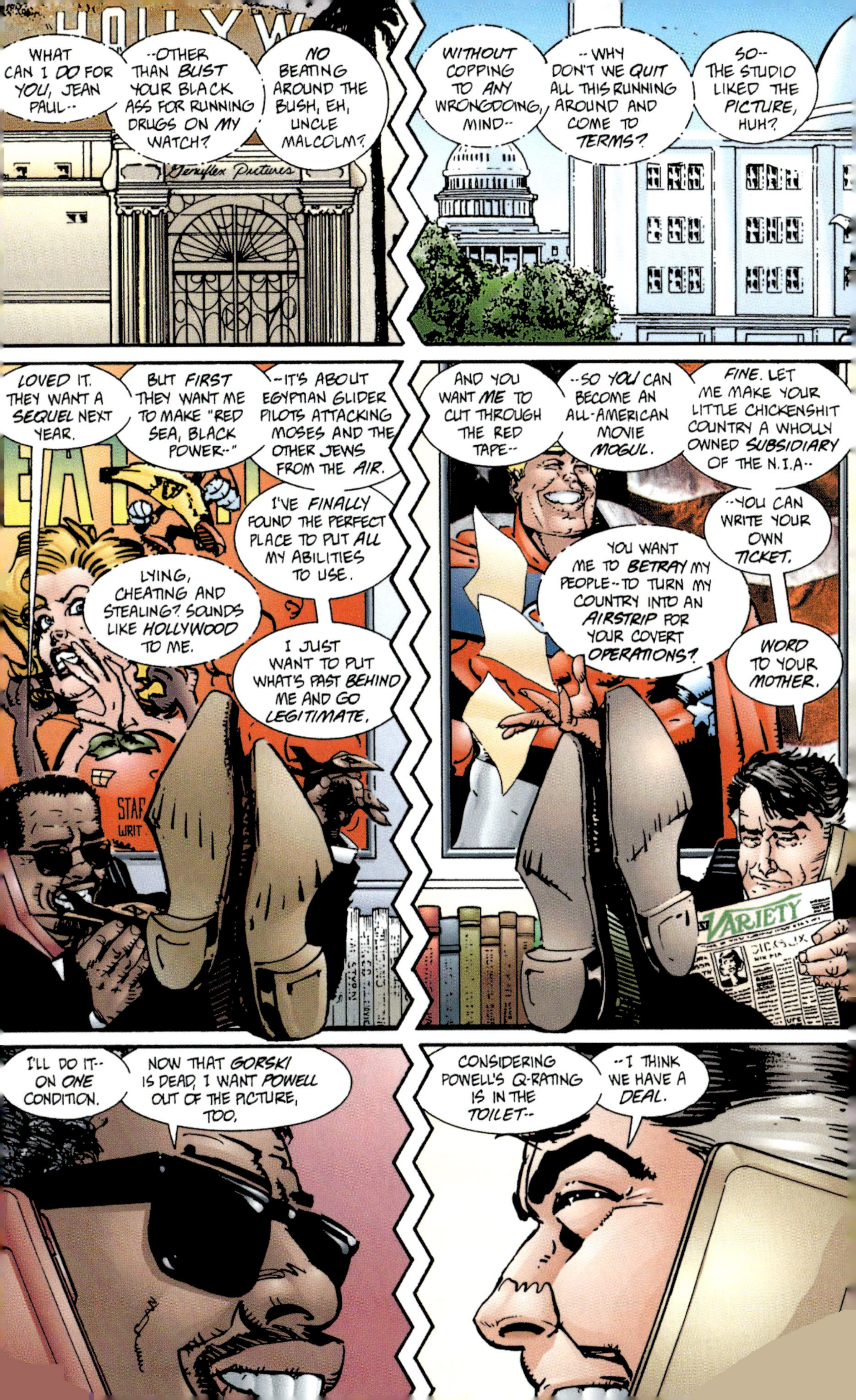
WHAT CAN I DO FOR YOU, JEAN PAUL--
--OTHER THAN BUST YOUR BLACK ASS FOR RUNNING DRUGS ON MY WATCH?
NO BEATING AROUND THE BUSH, EH, UNCLE MALCOLM?
Genuflex Pictures
WITHOUT COPPING TO ANY WRONGDOING, MIND--
--WHY DON'T WE QUIT ALL THIS RUNNING AROUND AND COME TO TERMS?
SO-- THE STUDIO LIKED THE PICTURE, HUH?
LOVED IT. THEY WANT A SEQUEL NEXT YEAR.
BUT FIRST THEY WANT ME TO MAKE "RED SEA, BLACK POWER--"
--IT'S ABOUT EGYPTIAN GLIDER PILOTS ATTACKING MOSES AND THE OTHER JEWS FROM THE AIR.
AND YOU WANT ME TO CUT THROUGH THE RED TAPE--
--SO YOU CAN BECOME AN ALL-AMERICAN MOVIE MOGUL.
FINE. LET ME MAKE YOUR LITTLE CHICKENSHIT COUNTRY A WHOLLY OWNED SUBSIDIARY OF THE N.I.A--
I'VE FINALLY FOUND THE PERFECT PLACE TO PUT ALL MY ABILITIES TO USE.
LYING, CHEATING AND STEALING? SOUNDS LIKE HOLLYWOOD TO ME.
I JUST WANT TO PUT WHAT'S PAST BEHIND ME AND GO LEGITIMATE.
--YOU CAN WRITE YOUR OWN TICKET.
YOU WANT ME TO BETRAY MY PEOPLE--TO TURN MY COUNTRY INTO AN AIRSTRIP FOR YOUR COVERT OPERATIONS?
WORD TO YOUR MOTHER.
VARIETY
I'LL DO IT-- ON ONE CONDITION.
NOW THAT GORSKI IS DEAD, I WANT POWELL OUT OF THE PICTURE, TOO.
CONSIDERING POWELL'S Q-RATING IS IN THE TOILET--
--I THINK WE HAVE A DEAL.

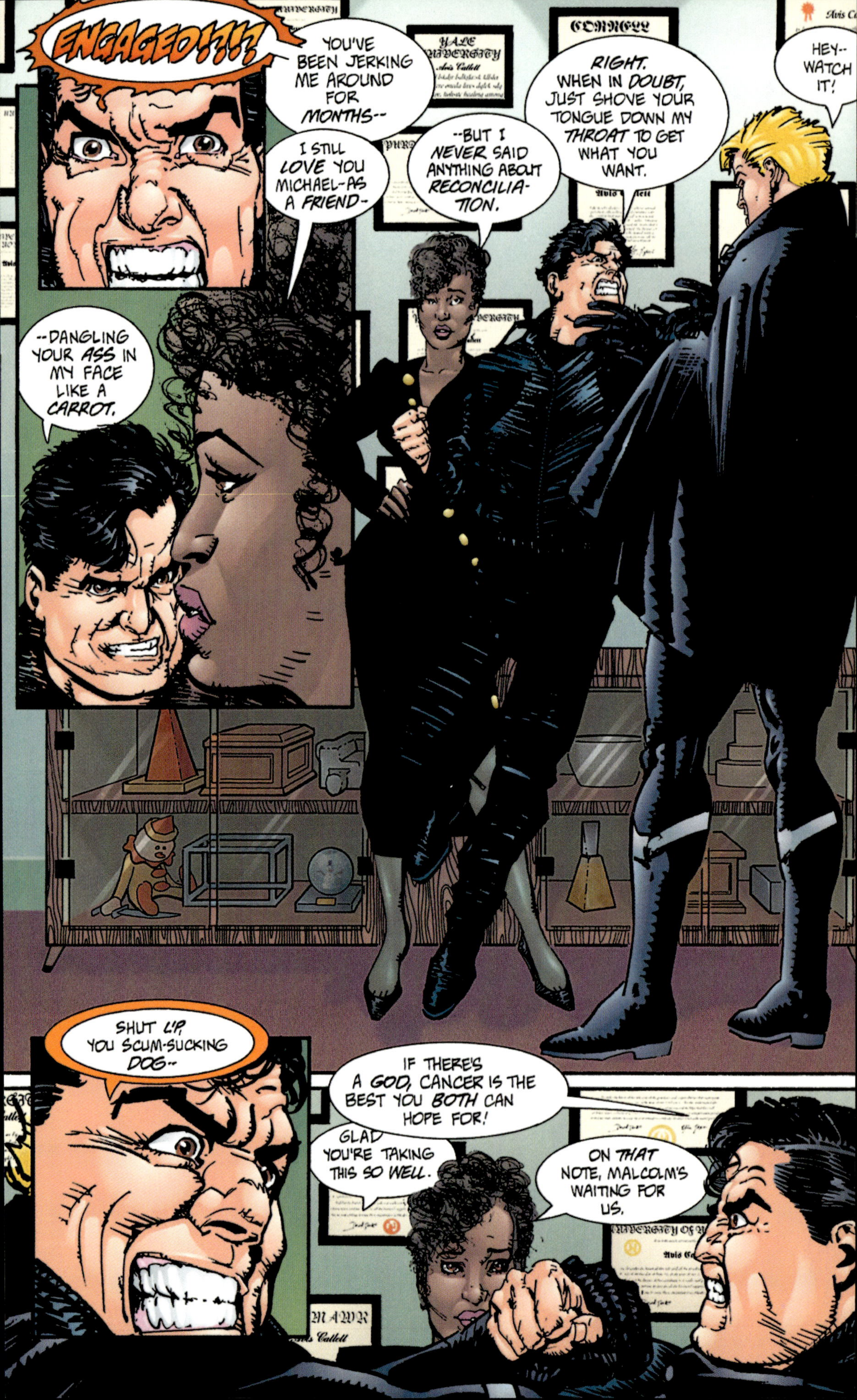
ENGAGED!?!?
YOU'VE BEEN JERKING ME AROUND FOR MONTHS--
I STILL LOVE YOU MICHAEL--AS A FRIEND--
--BUT I NEVER SAID ANYTHING ABOUT RECONCILIATION.
RIGHT. WHEN IN DOUBT, JUST SHOVE YOUR TONGUE DOWN MY THROAT TO GET WHAT YOU WANT.
HEY--WATCH IT!
--DANGLING YOUR ASS IN MY FACE LIKE A CARROT.
SHUT UP, YOU SCUM-SUCKING DOG--
IF THERE'S A GOD, CANCER IS THE BEST YOU BOTH CAN HOPE FOR!
GLAD YOU'RE TAKING THIS SO WELL.
ON THAT NOTE, MALCOLM'S WAITING FOR US.

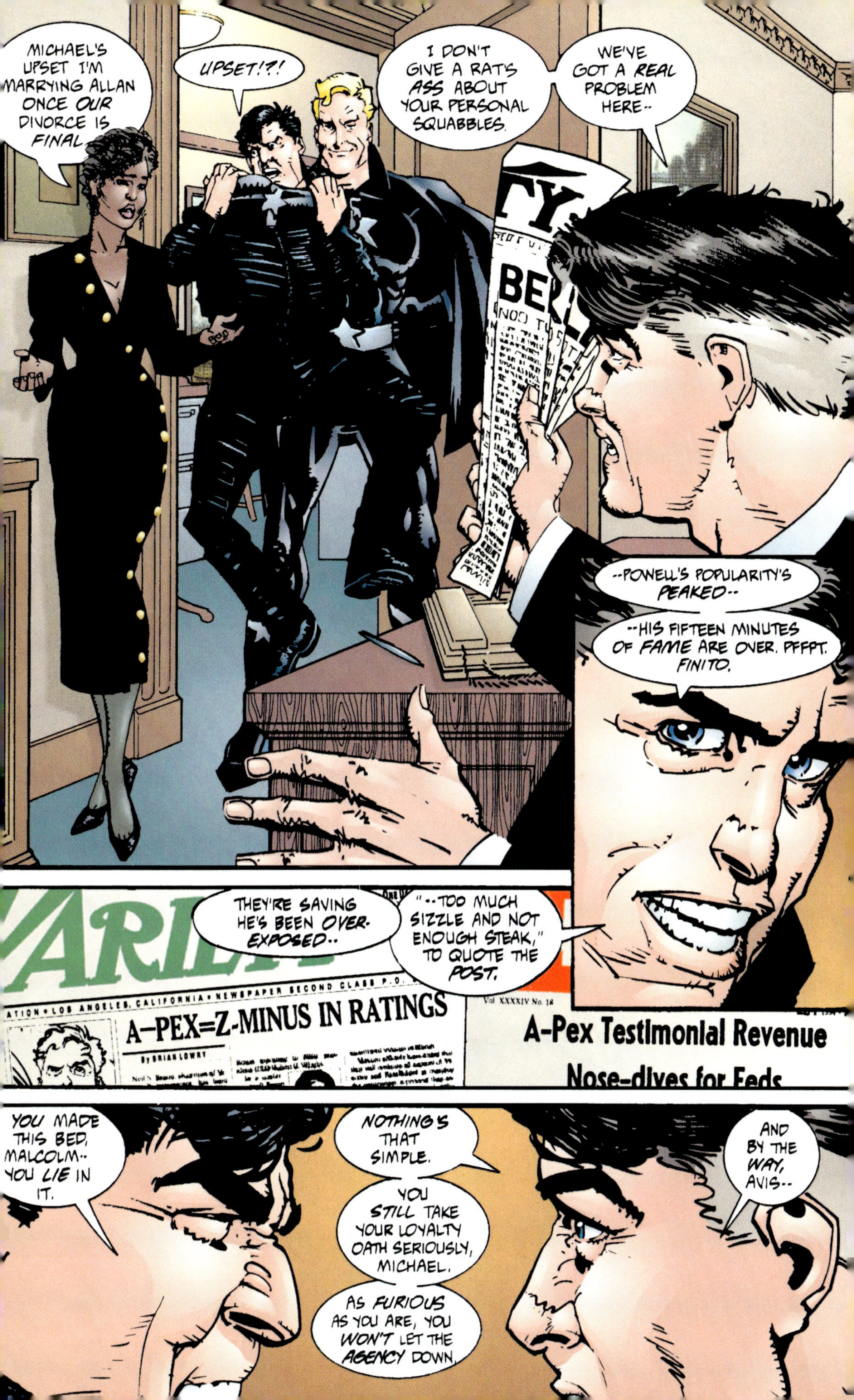
MICHAEL'S UPSET I'M MARRYING ALLAN ONCE OUR DIVORCE IS FINAL.
UPSET!?!
I DON'T GIVE A RAT'S ASS ABOUT YOUR PERSONAL SQUABBLES.
WE'VE GOT A REAL PROBLEM HERE--
--POWELL'S POPULARITY'S PEAKED--
--HIS FIFTEEN MINUTES OF FAME ARE OVER. PFFPT. FINITO.
THEY'RE SAYING HE'S BEEN OVER-EXPOSED--
"--TOO MUCH SIZZLE AND NOT ENOUGH STEAK," TO QUOTE THE POST.
A-PEX=Z-MINUS IN RATINGS
By BRIAN LOWRY
A-Pex Testimonial Revenue
Nose-dives for Feds
YOU MADE THIS BED, MALCOLM-- YOU LIE IN IT.
NOTHING'S THAT SIMPLE.
YOU STILL TAKE YOUR LOYALTY OATH SERIOUSLY, MICHAEL.
AS FURIOUS AS YOU ARE, YOU WON'T LET THE AGENCY DOWN.
AND BY THE WAY, AVIS--

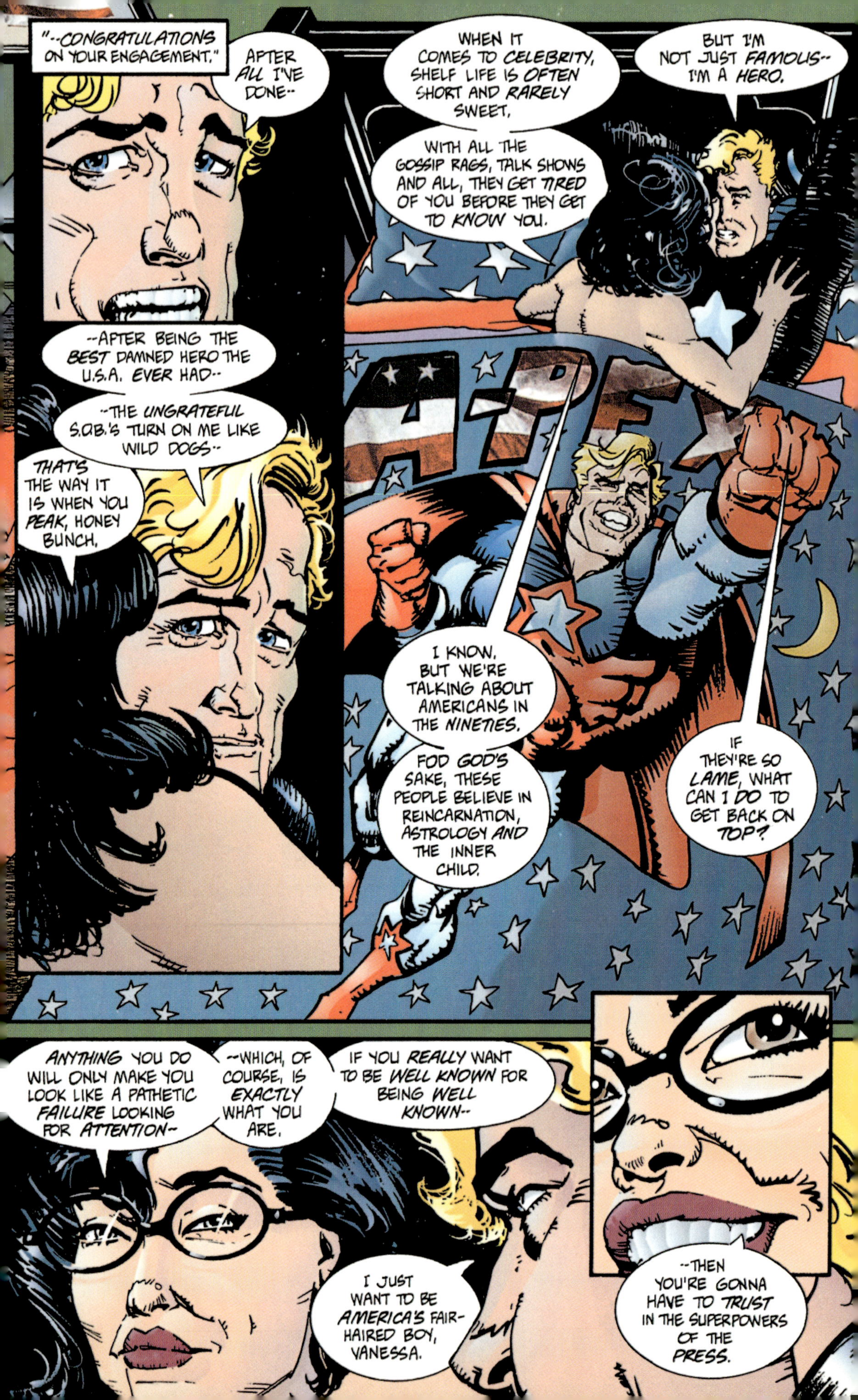
"--CONGRATULATIONS ON YOUR ENGAGEMENT."
AFTER ALL I'VE DONE--
WHEN IT COMES TO CELEBRITY, SHELF LIFE IS OFTEN SHORT AND RARELY SWEET.
WITH ALL THE GOSSIP RAGS, TALK SHOWS AND ALL, THEY GET TIRED OF YOU BEFORE THEY GET TO KNOW YOU.
BUT I'M NOT JUST FAMOUS-- I'M A HERO.
--AFTER BEING THE BEST DAMNED HERO THE U.S.A. EVER HAD--
--THE UNGRATEFUL S.O.B.'S TURN ON ME LIKE WILD DOGS--
THAT'S THE WAY IT IS WHEN YOU PEAK, HONEY BUNCH.
I KNOW. BUT WE'RE TALKING ABOUT AMERICANS IN THE NINETIES.
FOR GOD'S SAKE, THESE PEOPLE BELIEVE IN REINCARNATION, ASTROLOGY AND THE INNER CHILD.
IF THEY'RE SO LAME, WHAT CAN I DO TO GET BACK ON TOP?
ANYTHING YOU DO WILL ONLY MAKE YOU LOOK LIKE A PATHETIC FAILURE LOOKING FOR ATTENTION--
--WHICH, OF COURSE, IS EXACTLY WHAT YOU ARE.
IF YOU REALLY WANT TO BE WELL KNOWN FOR BEING WELL KNOWN--
I JUST WANT TO BE AMERICA'S FAIR-HAIRED BOY, VANESSA.
--THEN YOU'RE GONNA HAVE TO TRUST IN THE SUPERPOWERS OF THE PRESS.

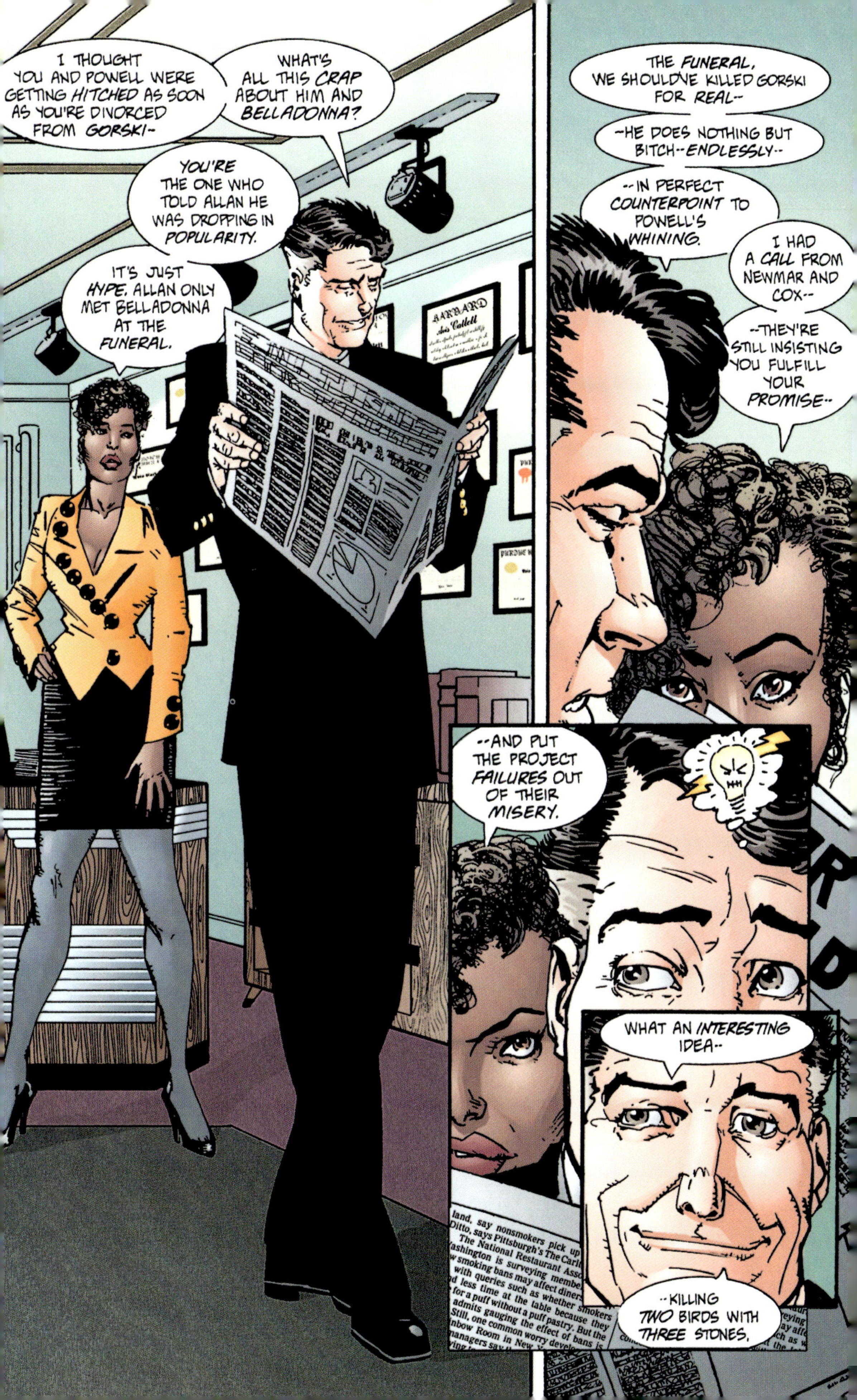
I THOUGHT YOU AND POWELL WERE GETTING *HITCHED* AS SOON AS YOU'RE DIVORCED FROM *GORSKI*-
WHAT'S ALL THIS *CRAP* ABOUT HIM AND *BELLADONNA?*
YOU'RE THE ONE WHO TOLD ALLAN HE WAS DROPPING IN *POPULARITY.*
IT'S JUST *HYPE.* ALLAN ONLY MET BELLADONNA AT THE *FUNERAL.*
THE *FUNERAL.* WE SHOULD'VE KILLED GORSKI FOR *REAL*--
--HE DOES NOTHING BUT BITCH--*ENDLESSLY*--
--IN PERFECT *COUNTERPOINT* TO POWELL'S *WHINING.*
I HAD A *CALL* FROM NEWMAR AND COX--
--THEY'RE STILL INSISTING YOU FULFILL YOUR *PROMISE*--
--AND PUT THE PROJECT *FAILURES* OUT OF THEIR *MISERY.*
WHAT AN *INTERESTING* IDEA--
--KILLING *TWO* BIRDS WITH *THREE* STONES.

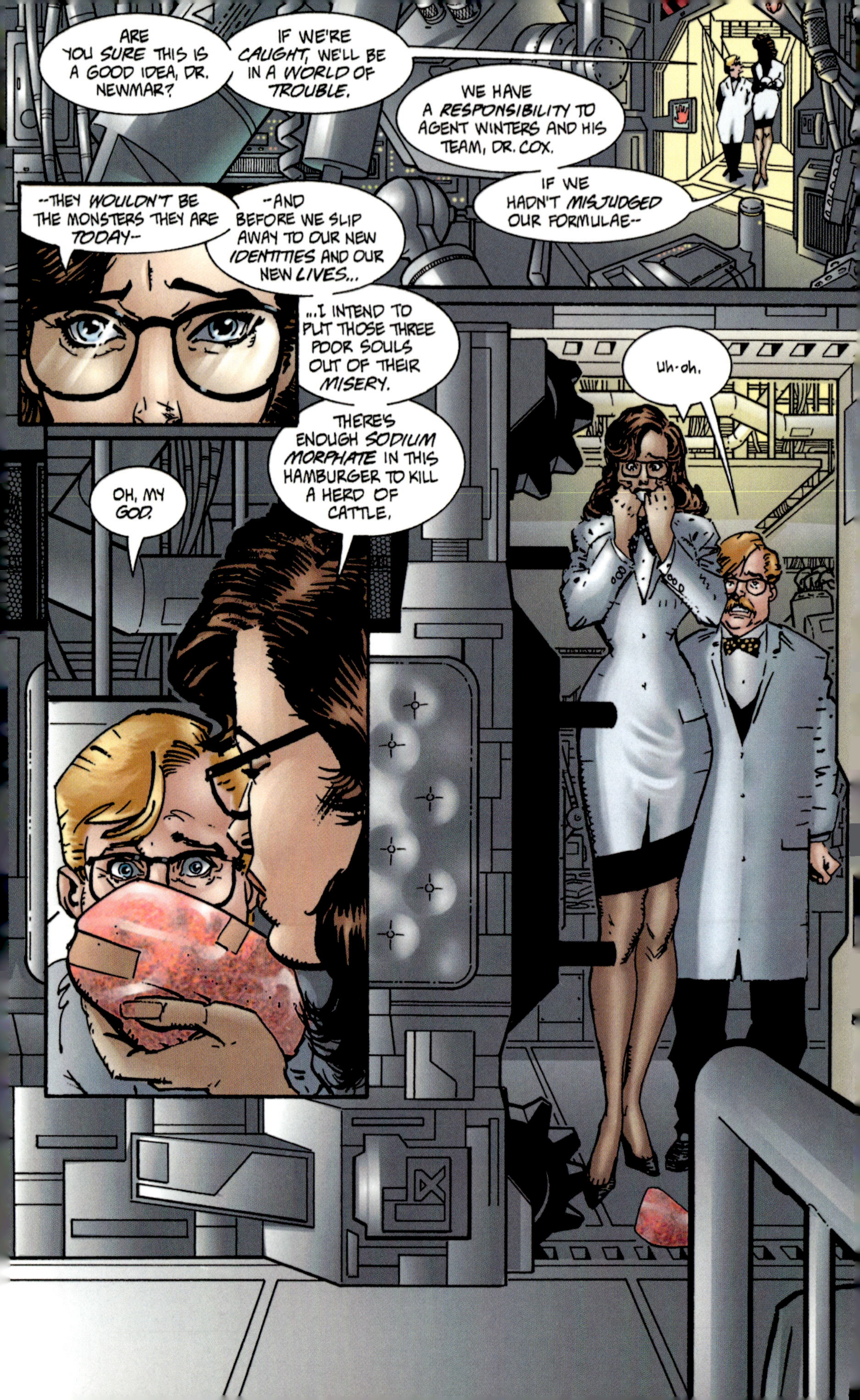
ARE YOU *SURE* THIS IS A GOOD IDEA, DR. NEWMAR?
IF WE'RE *CAUGHT*, WE'LL BE IN A *WORLD OF TROUBLE.*
WE HAVE A *RESPONSIBILITY* TO AGENT WINTERS AND HIS TEAM, DR. COX.
IF WE HADN'T *MISJUDGED* OUR FORMULAE--
--THEY *WOULDN'T* BE THE MONSTERS THEY ARE *TODAY*--
--AND BEFORE WE SLIP AWAY TO OUR NEW *IDENTITIES* AND OUR NEW *LIVES*...
...I INTEND TO PUT THOSE THREE POOR SOULS OUT OF THEIR *MISERY.*
THERE'S ENOUGH *SODIUM MORPHATE* IN THIS HAMBURGER TO KILL A HERD OF CATTLE.
OH, MY *GOD.*
uh-oh.

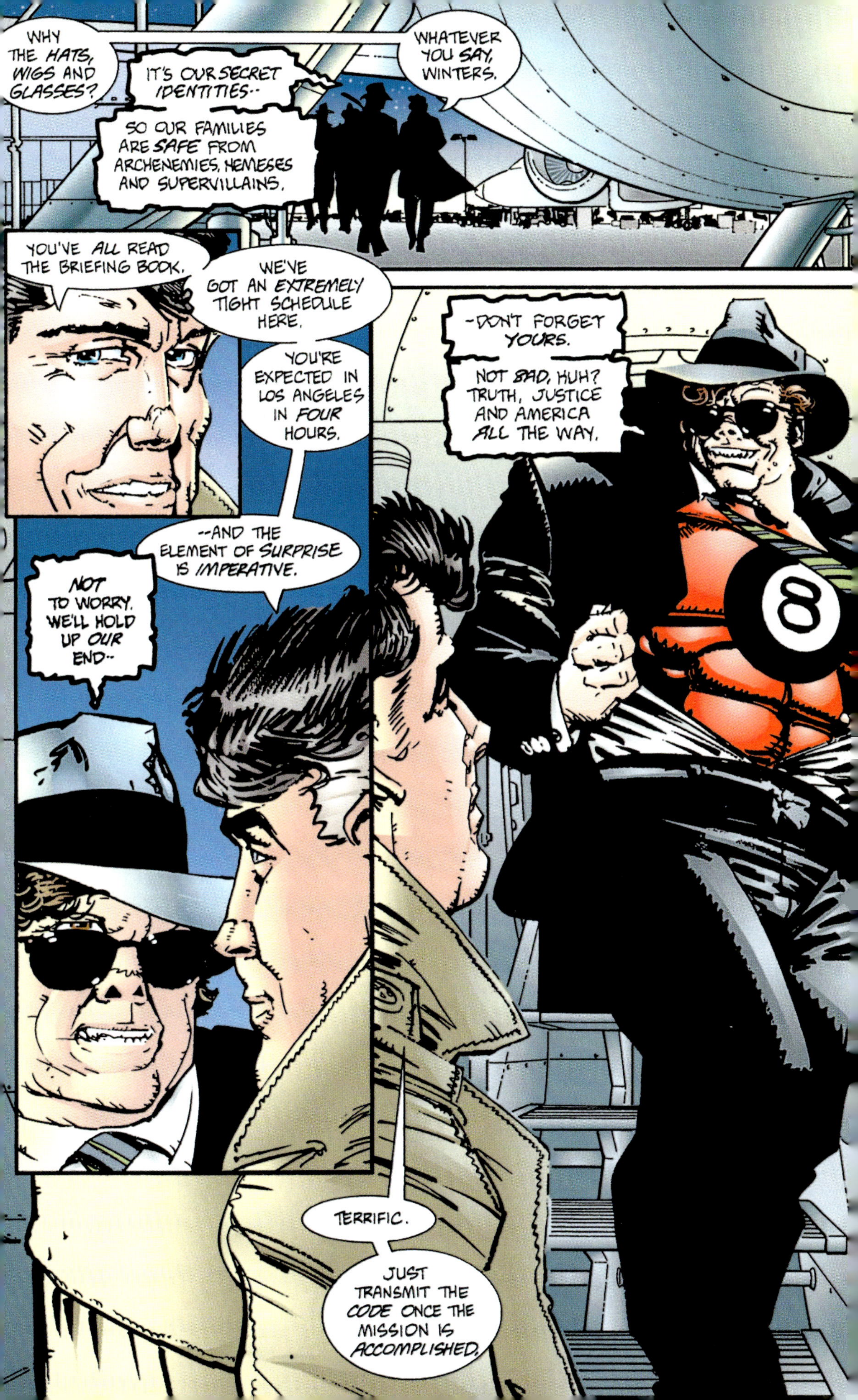
WHY THE HATS, WIGS AND GLASSES?
IT'S OUR SECRET IDENTITIES--
SO OUR FAMILIES ARE SAFE FROM ARCHENEMIES, NEMESES AND SUPERVILLAINS.
WHATEVER YOU SAY, WINTERS.
YOU'VE ALL READ THE BRIEFING BOOK.
WE'VE GOT AN EXTREMELY TIGHT SCHEDULE HERE.
YOU'RE EXPECTED IN LOS ANGELES IN FOUR HOURS.
--AND THE ELEMENT OF SURPRISE IS IMPERATIVE.
NOT TO WORRY. WE'LL HOLD UP OUR END--
-DON'T FORGET YOURS.
NOT BAD, HUH? TRUTH, JUSTICE AND AMERICA ALL THE WAY.
8
TERRIFIC.
JUST TRANSMIT THE CODE ONCE THE MISSION IS ACCOMPLISHED.

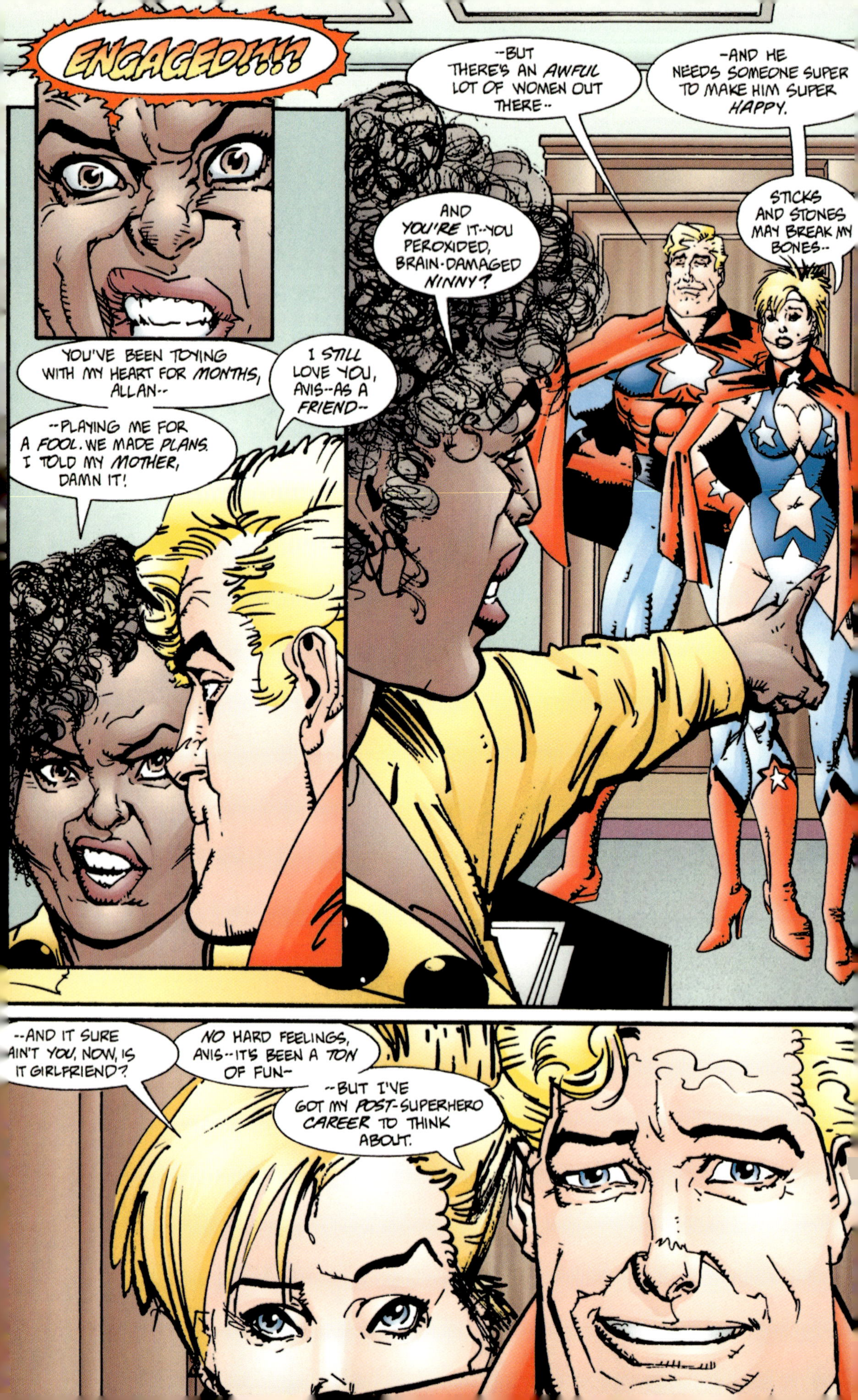
ENGAGED!?!?
--BUT THERE'S AN AWFUL LOT OF WOMEN OUT THERE--
--AND HE NEEDS SOMEONE SUPER TO MAKE HIM SUPER HAPPY.
AND YOU'RE IT--YOU PEROXIDED, BRAIN-DAMAGED NINNY?
STICKS AND STONES MAY BREAK MY BONES--
YOU'VE BEEN TOYING WITH MY HEART FOR MONTHS, ALLAN--
I STILL LOVE YOU, AVIS--AS A FRIEND--
--PLAYING ME FOR A FOOL. WE MADE PLANS. I TOLD MY MOTHER, DAMN IT!
--AND IT SURE AIN'T YOU, NOW, IS IT GIRLFRIEND?
NO HARD FEELINGS, AVIS--IT'S BEEN A TON OF FUN--
--BUT I'VE GOT MY POST-SUPERHERO CAREER TO THINK ABOUT.

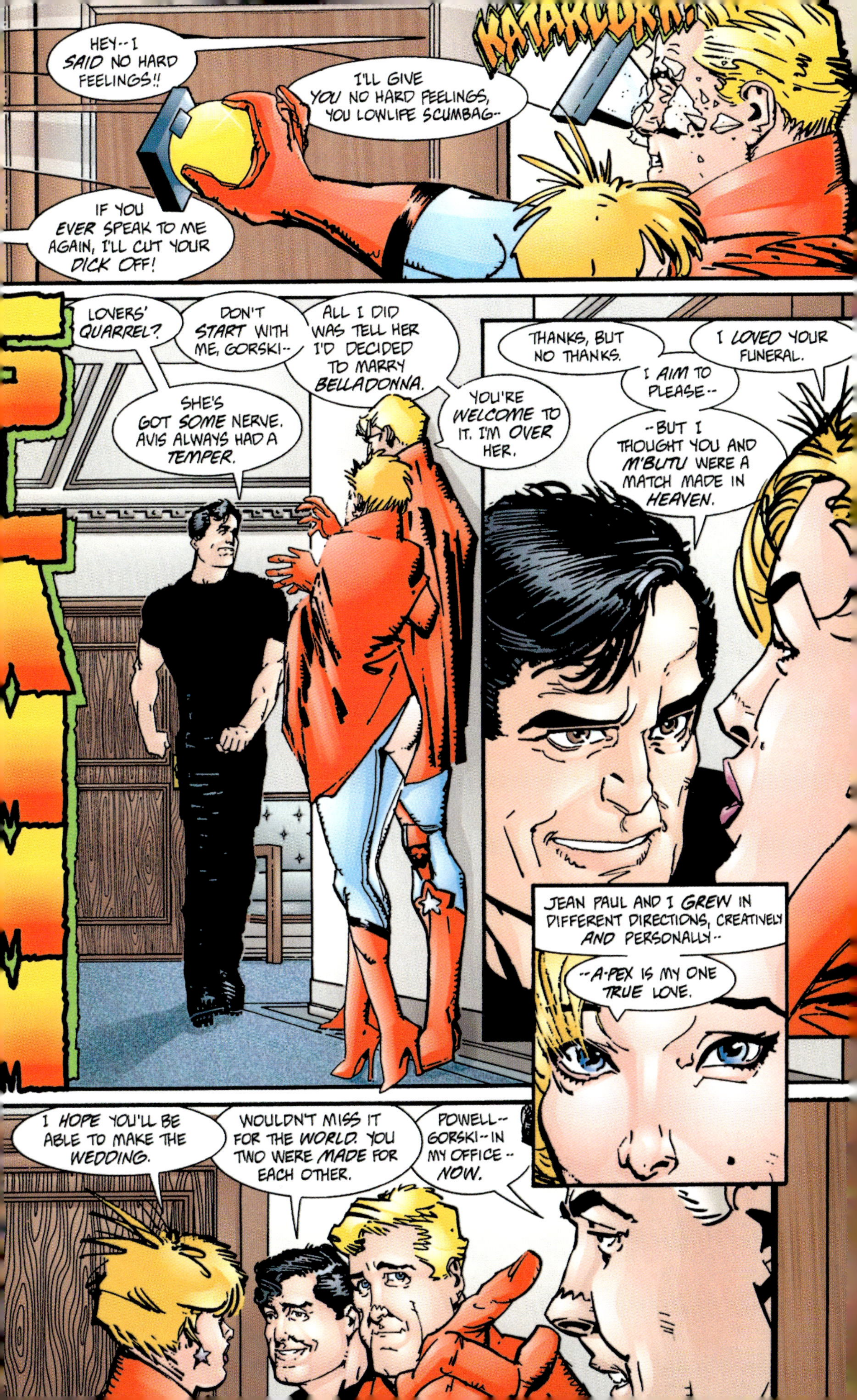

HEY--I SAID NO HARD FEELINGS!!
I'LL GIVE YOU NO HARD FEELINGS, YOU LOWLIFE SCUMBAG--
IF YOU EVER SPEAK TO ME AGAIN, I'LL CUT YOUR DICK OFF!
LOVERS' QUARREL?
SHE'S GOT SOME NERVE. AVIS ALWAYS HAD A TEMPER.
DON'T START WITH ME, GORSKI--
ALL I DID WAS TELL HER I'D DECIDED TO MARRY BELLADONNA.
YOU'RE WELCOME TO IT. I'M OVER HER.
THANKS, BUT NO THANKS.
I LOVED YOUR FUNERAL.
I AIM TO PLEASE--
--BUT I THOUGHT YOU AND M'BUTU WERE A MATCH MADE IN HEAVEN.
JEAN PAUL AND I GREW IN DIFFERENT DIRECTIONS, CREATIVELY AND PERSONALLY--
--A-PEX IS MY ONE TRUE LOVE.
I HOPE YOU'LL BE ABLE TO MAKE THE WEDDING.
WOULDN'T MISS IT FOR THE WORLD. YOU TWO WERE MADE FOR EACH OTHER.
POWELL--GORSKI--IN MY OFFICE--NOW.

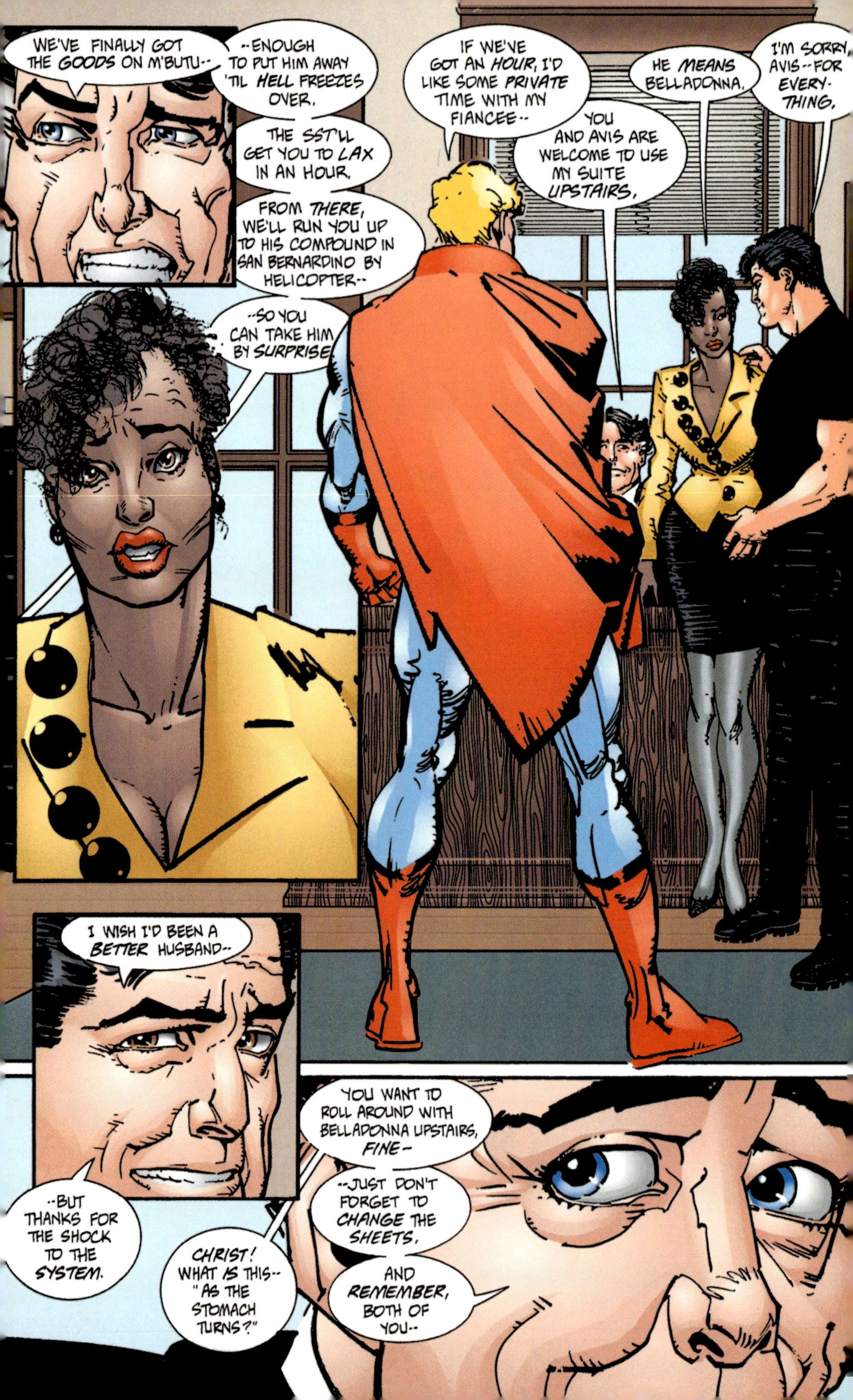
WE'VE FINALLY GOT THE GOODS ON M'BUTU--
--ENOUGH TO PUT HIM AWAY 'TIL HELL FREEZES OVER.
THE SST'LL GET YOU TO LAX IN AN HOUR.
FROM THERE, WE'LL RUN YOU UP TO HIS COMPOUND IN SAN BERNARDINO BY HELICOPTER--
--SO YOU CAN TAKE HIM BY SURPRISE.
IF WE'VE GOT AN HOUR, I'D LIKE SOME PRIVATE TIME WITH MY FIANCEE--
YOU AND AVIS ARE WELCOME TO USE MY SUITE UPSTAIRS.
HE MEANS BELLADONNA.
I'M SORRY, AVIS--FOR EVERY-THING.
I WISH I'D BEEN A BETTER HUSBAND--
--BUT THANKS FOR THE SHOCK TO THE SYSTEM.
YOU WANT TO ROLL AROUND WITH BELLADONNA UPSTAIRS, FINE--
--JUST DON'T FORGET TO CHANGE THE SHEETS.
CHRIST! WHAT IS THIS-- "AS THE STOMACH TURNS?"
AND REMEMBER, BOTH OF YOU--

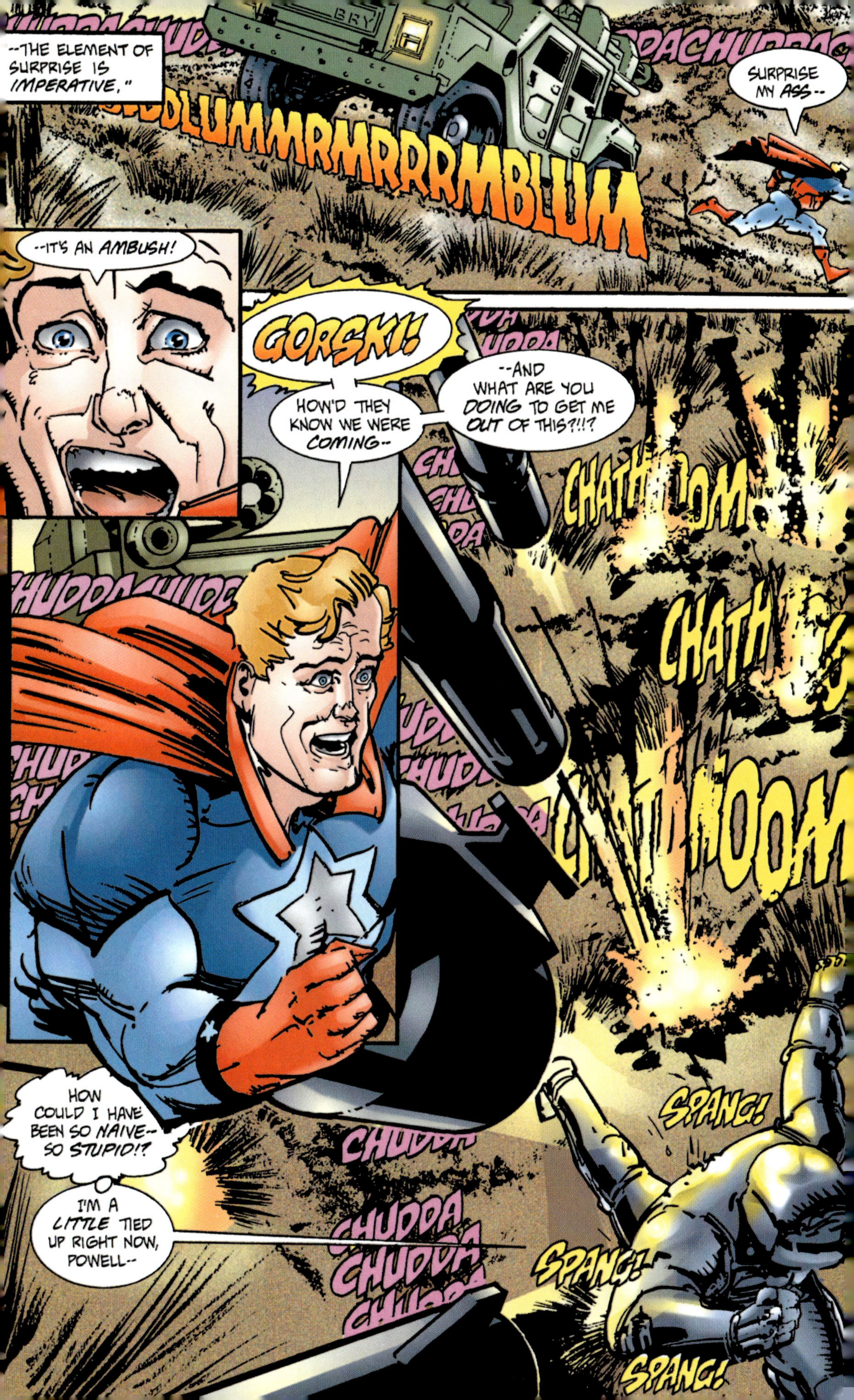
--THE ELEMENT OF SURPRISE IS IMPERATIVE."
SURPRISE MY ASS--
BLUMMRMRRRMBLUM
--IT'S AN AMBUSH!
GORSKI!
HOW'D THEY KNOW WE WERE COMING--
--AND WHAT ARE YOU DOING TO GET ME OUT OF THIS?!!?
CHATHOOM
CHATH
HOOM
HOW COULD I HAVE BEEN SO NAIVE-- SO STUPID!?
I'M A LITTLE TIED UP RIGHT NOW, POWELL--
CHUDDA CHUDDA
SPANG!
SPANG!
SPANG!

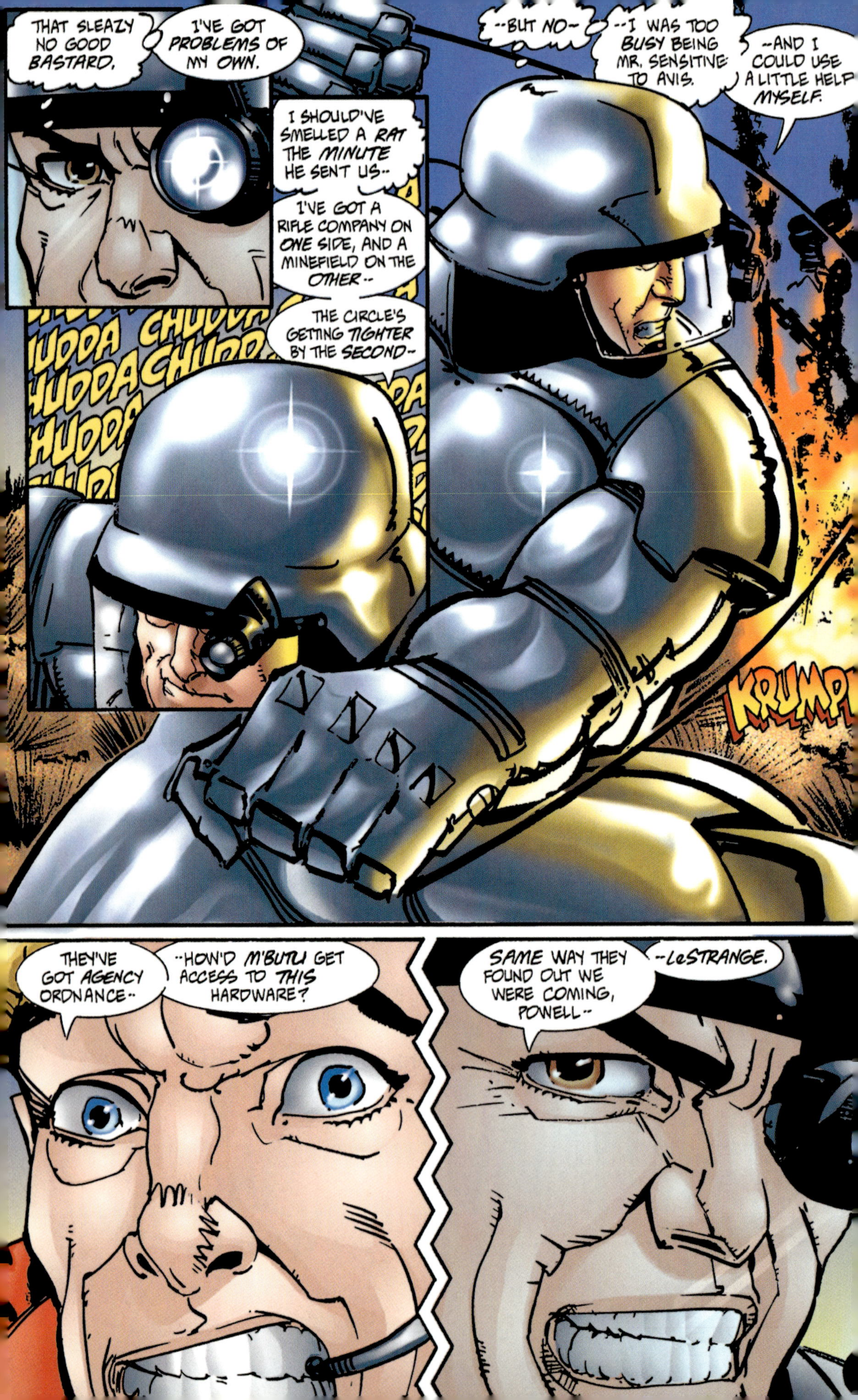
THAT SLEAZY NO GOOD BASTARD.
I'VE GOT PROBLEMS OF MY OWN.
--BUT NO--
--I WAS TOO BUSY BEING MR. SENSITIVE TO AVIS.
--AND I COULD USE A LITTLE HELP MYSELF.
I SHOULD'VE SMELLED A RAT THE MINUTE HE SENT US--
I'VE GOT A RIFLE COMPANY ON ONE SIDE, AND A MINEFIELD ON THE OTHER--
THE CIRCLE'S GETTING TIGHTER BY THE SECOND--
CHUDDA CHUDDA CHUDDA CHUDDA CHUDDA
KRUMP
THEY'VE GOT AGENCY ORDNANCE--
--HOW'D M'BUTU GET ACCESS TO THIS HARDWARE?
SAME WAY THEY FOUND OUT WE WERE COMING, POWELL--
--LeSTRANGE.

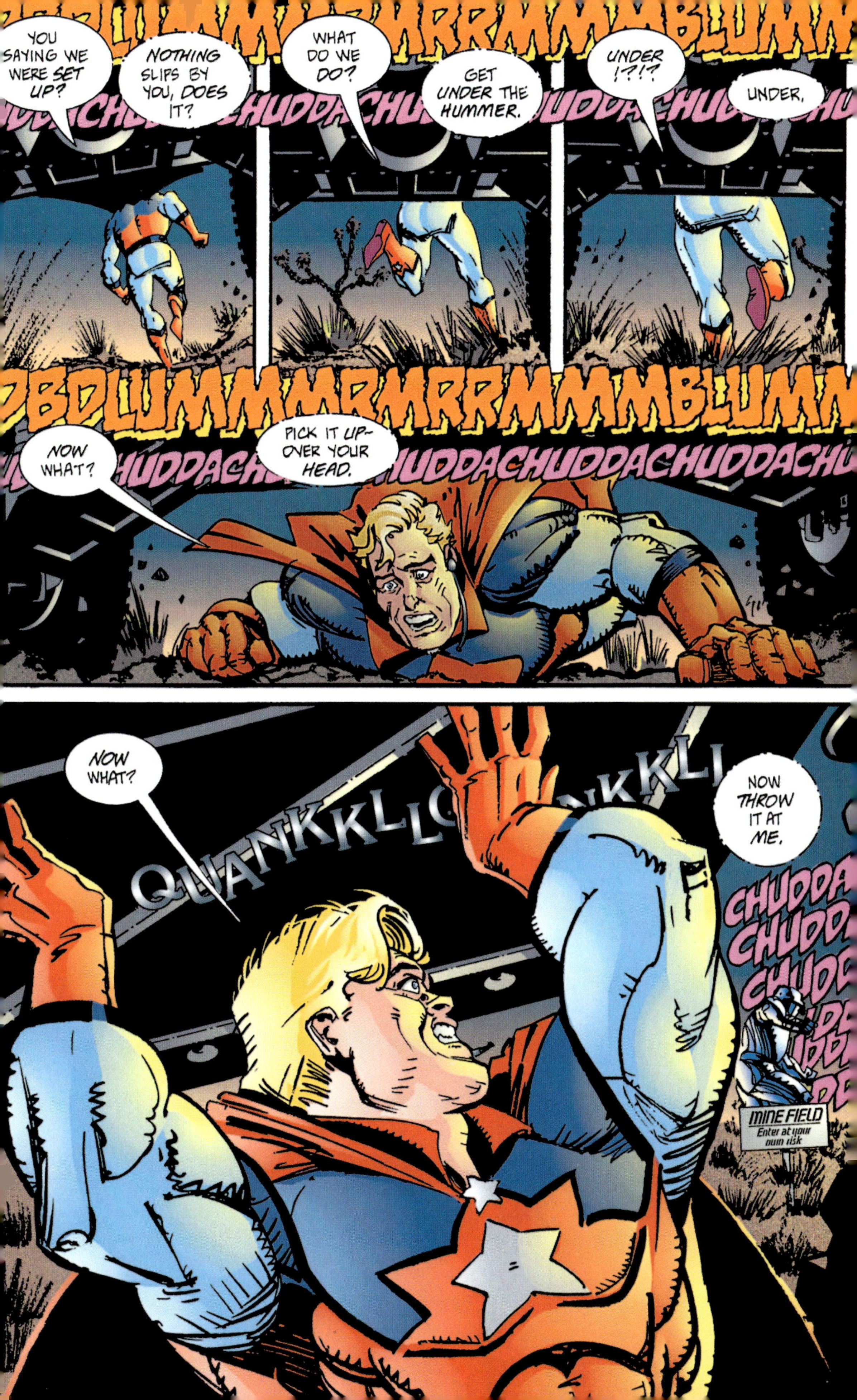

YOU SAYING WE WERE SET UP?
NOTHING SLIPS BY YOU, DOES IT?
WHAT DO WE DO?
GET UNDER THE HUMMER.
UNDER !?!?
UNDER.
NOW WHAT?
PICK IT UP-- OVER YOUR HEAD.
NOW WHAT?
NOW THROW IT AT ME.
MINE FIELD
Enter at your own risk

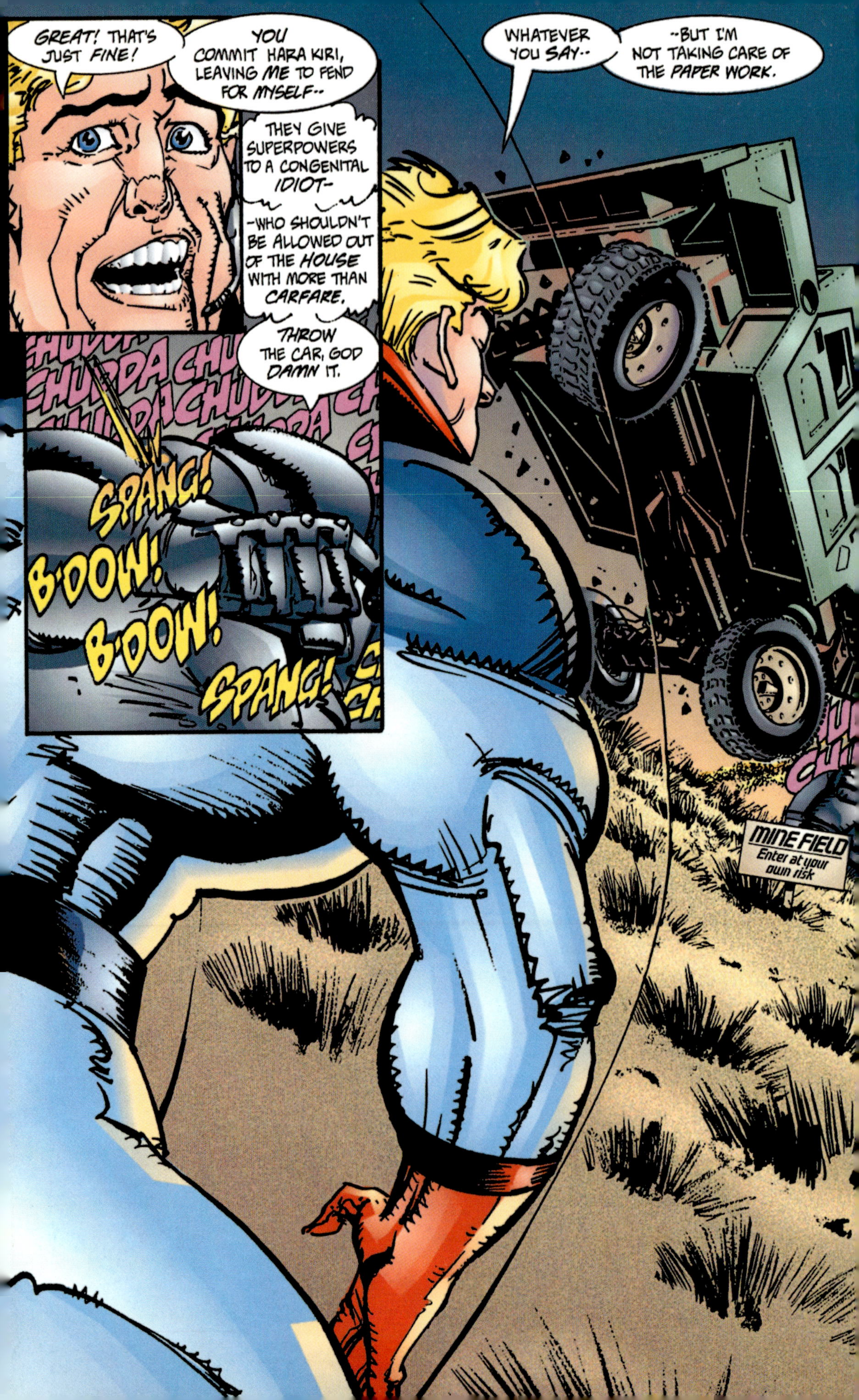
GREAT! THAT'S JUST FINE!
YOU COMMIT HARA KIRI, LEAVING ME TO FEND FOR MYSELF--
THEY GIVE SUPERPOWERS TO A CONGENITAL IDIOT--
--WHO SHOULDN'T BE ALLOWED OUT OF THE HOUSE WITH MORE THAN CARFARE.
THROW THE CAR, GOD DAMN IT.
CHUDDA CHUDDA CHUDDA
SPANG!
B-DOOW!
B-DOOW!
SPANG!
WHATEVER YOU SAY--
--BUT I'M NOT TAKING CARE OF THE PAPER WORK.
MINE FIELD
Enter at your own risk

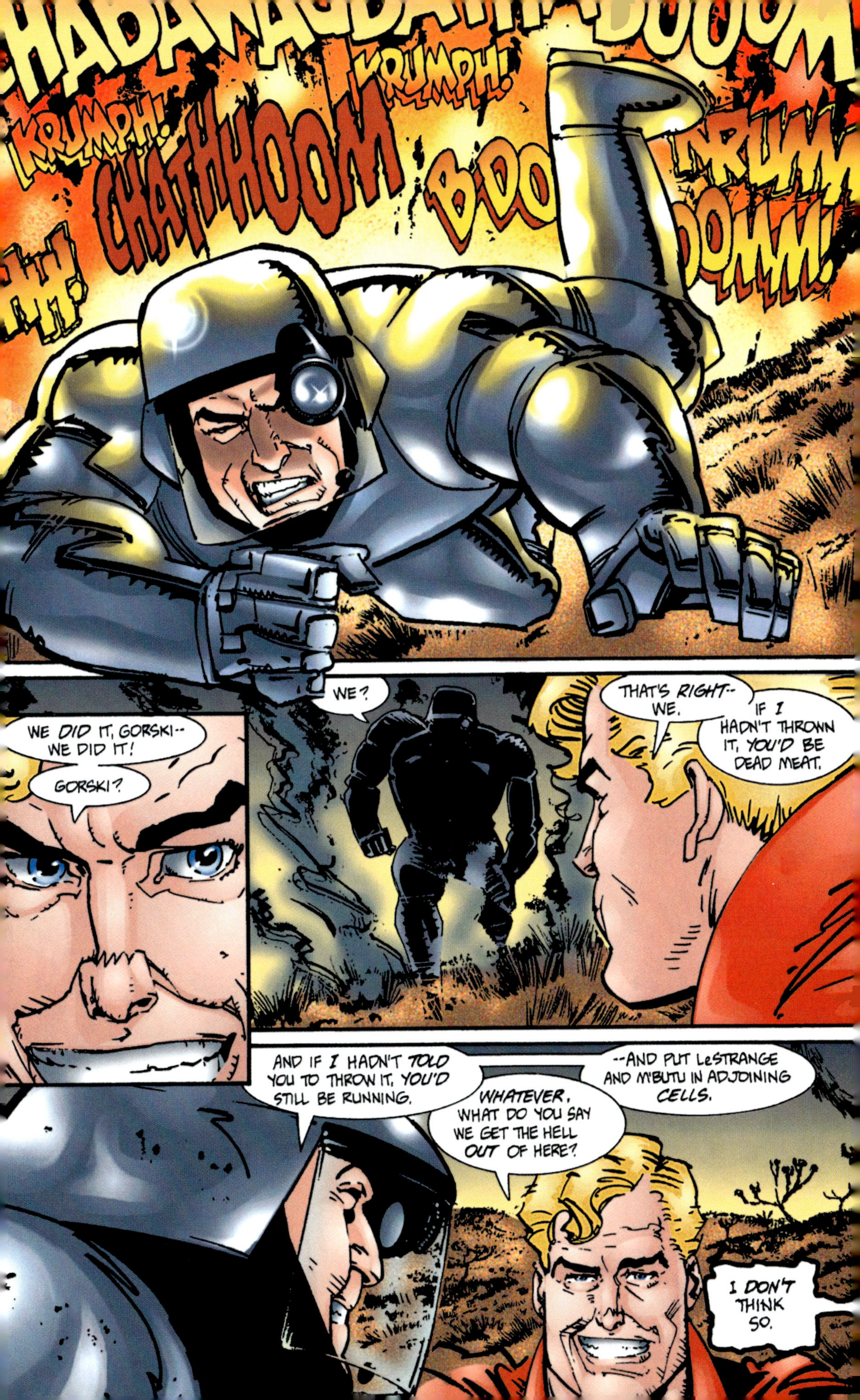
HABANAGDAH-DOOOM
KRUMPH!
KRUMPH!
CHATHOOM
BOO
TRUM
OOMM!
WE *DID* IT, GORSKI-- WE DID IT!
GORSKI?
WE?
THAT'S *RIGHT*-- WE.
IF *I* HADN'T THROWN IT, *YOU'D* BE DEAD MEAT.
AND IF *I* HADN'T *TOLD* YOU TO THROW IT, *YOU'D* STILL BE RUNNING.
WHATEVER. WHAT DO YOU SAY WE GET THE HELL *OUT* OF HERE?
--AND PUT LeSTRANGE AND M'BUTU IN ADJOINING CELLS.
I *DON'T* THINK SO.

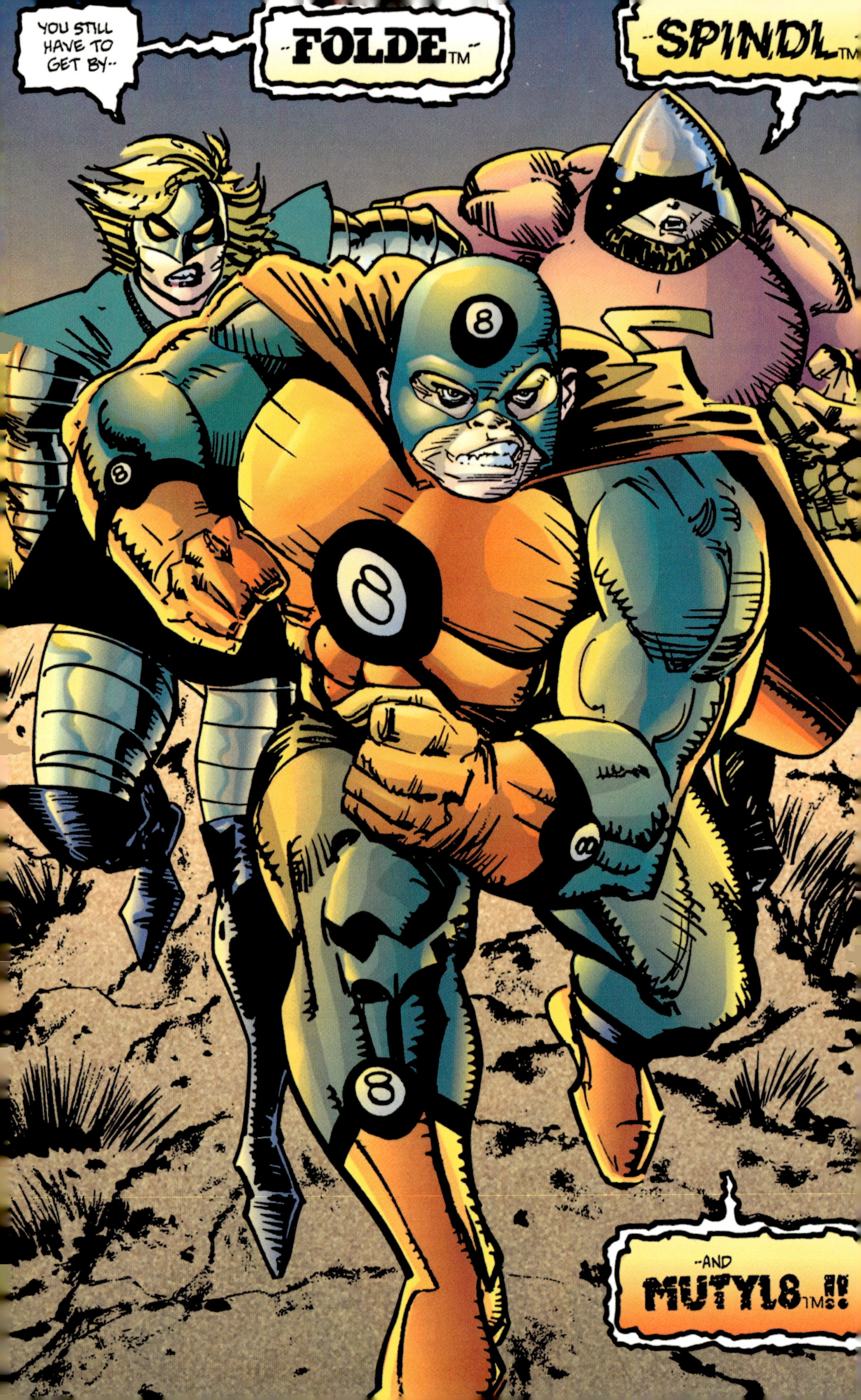
YOU STILL HAVE TO GET BY--
--FOLDE™--
--SPINDL™
--AND
MUTYL8™!!

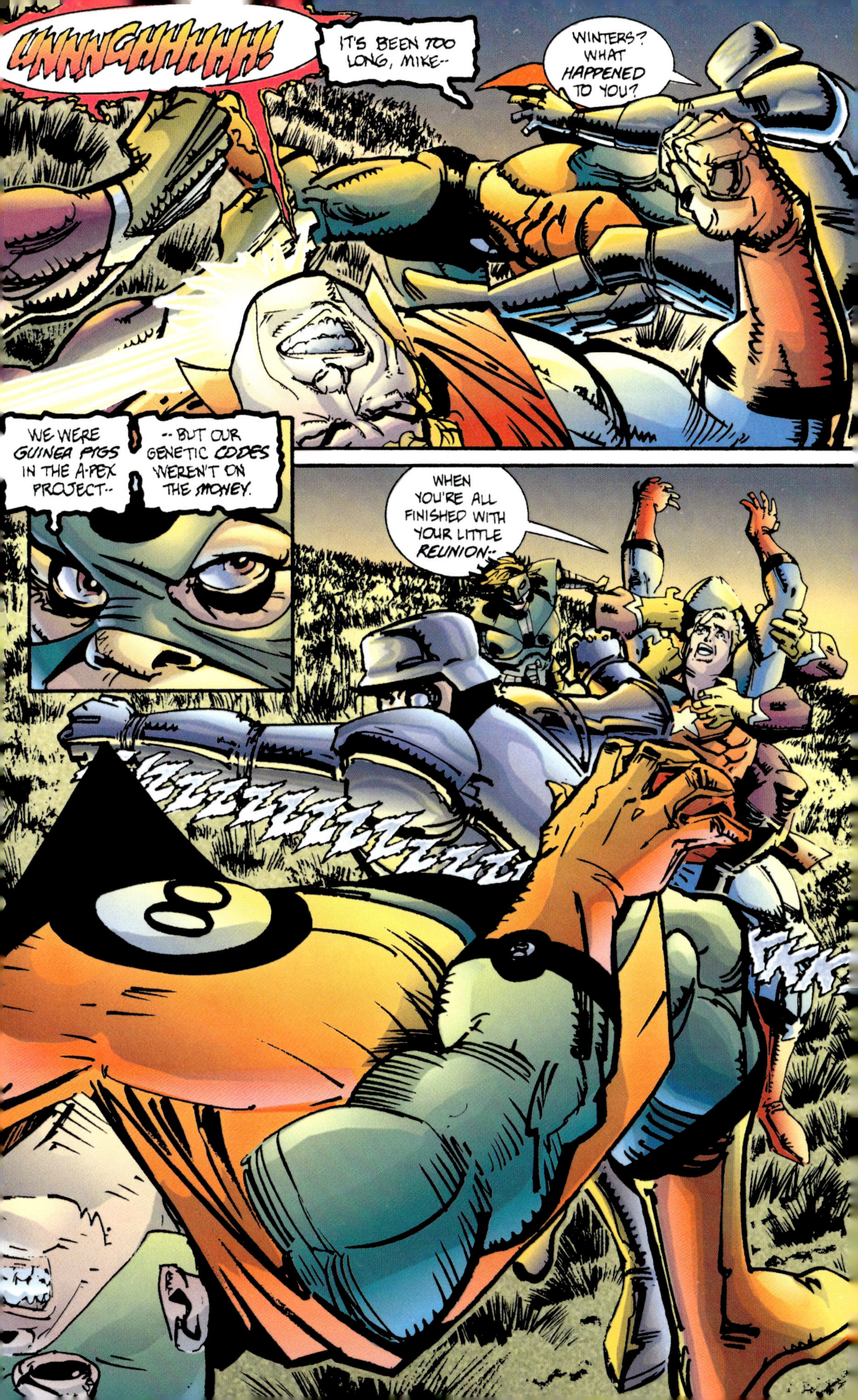
UNNNGHHHHH!
IT'S BEEN TOO LONG, MIKE--
WINTERS? WHAT HAPPENED TO YOU?
WE WERE GUINEA PIGS IN THE A-PEX PROJECT--
--BUT OUR GENETIC CODES WEREN'T ON THE MONEY.
WHEN YOU'RE ALL FINISHED WITH YOUR LITTLE REUNION--
ZZZZZZZZZZZZZZZZZZZZ
FKK

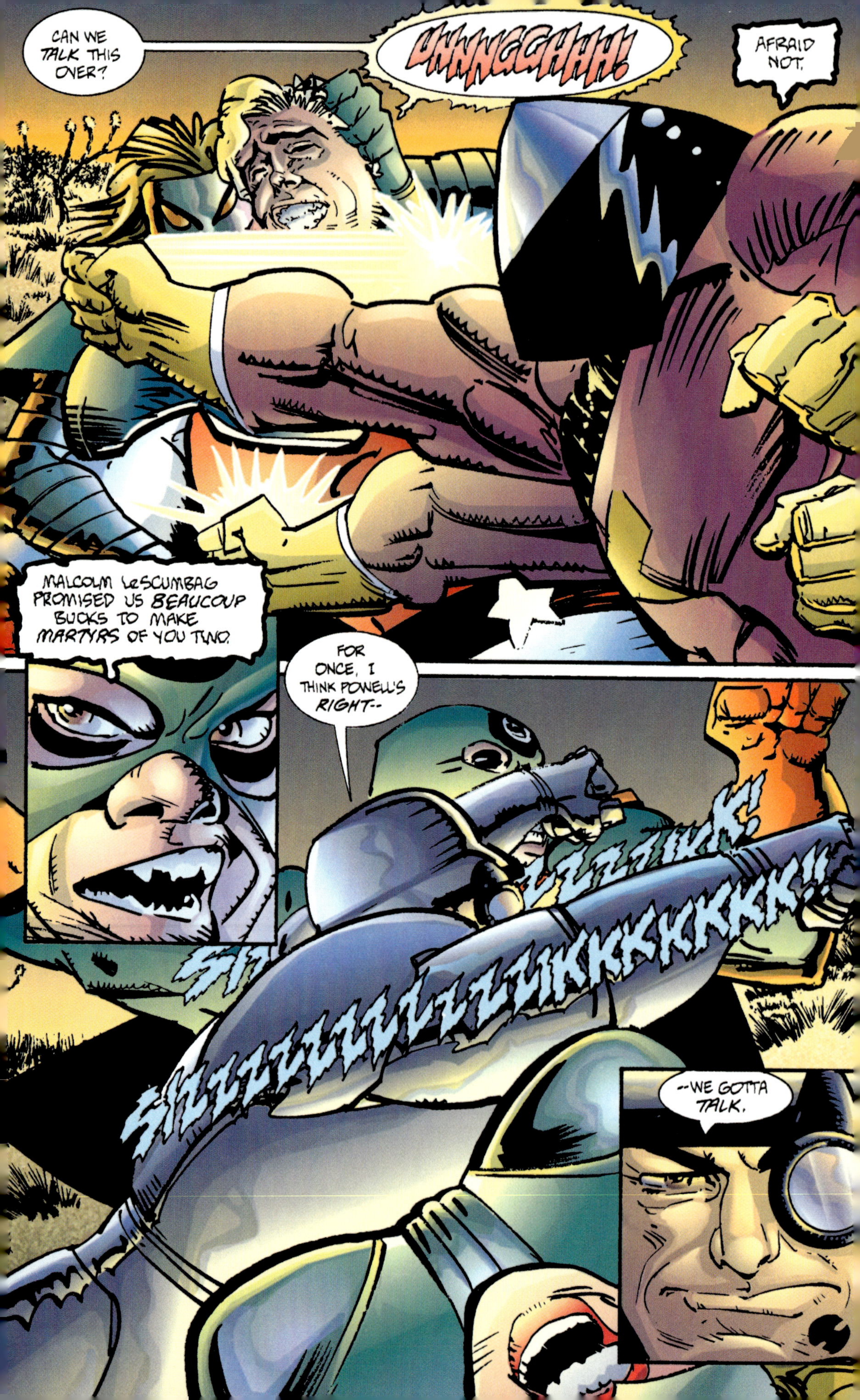
CAN WE TALK THIS OVER?
UNNNGGHHH!
AFRAID NOT.
MALCOLM LeSCUMBAG PROMISED US BEAUCOUP BUCKS TO MAKE MARTYRS OF YOU TWO.
FOR ONCE, I THINK POWELL'S RIGHT--
SIZZZZIKK!
SIZZZZZZZZZZZIKKKKKKKK!!
--WE GOTTA TALK.

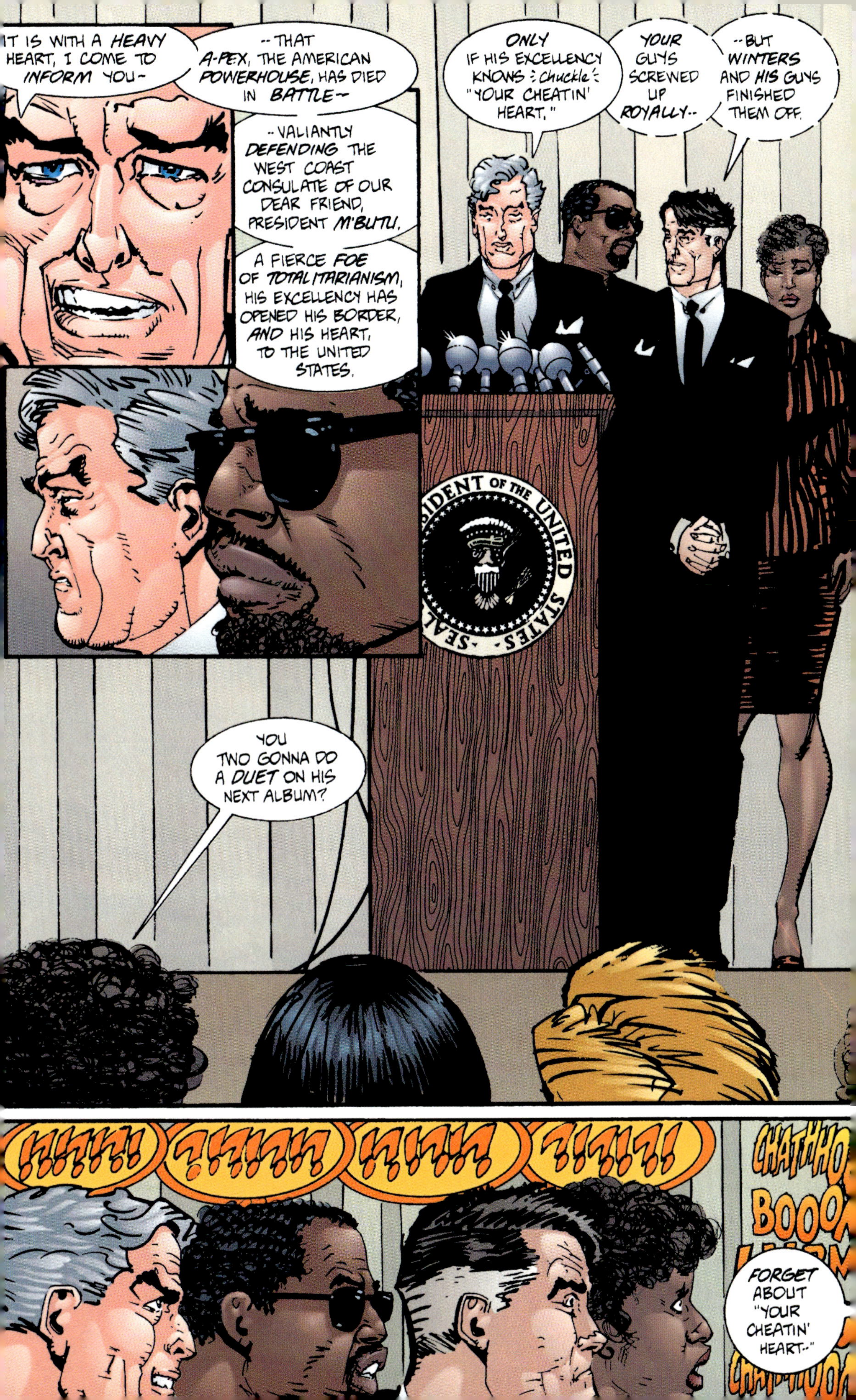
IT IS WITH A HEAVY HEART, I COME TO INFORM YOU-
--THAT A-PEX, THE AMERICAN POWERHOUSE, HAS DIED IN BATTLE--
--VALIANTLY DEFENDING THE WEST COAST CONSULATE OF OUR DEAR FRIEND, PRESIDENT M'BUTU.
A FIERCE FOE OF TOTALITARIANISM, HIS EXCELLENCY HAS OPENED HIS BORDER, AND HIS HEART, TO THE UNITED STATES.
ONLY IF HIS EXCELLENCY KNOWS :chuckle: "YOUR CHEATIN' HEART."
YOUR GUYS SCREWED UP ROYALLY--
--BUT WINTERS AND HIS GUYS FINISHED THEM OFF.
PRESIDENT OF THE UNITED STATES
YOU TWO GONNA DO A DUET ON HIS NEXT ALBUM?
FORGET ABOUT "YOUR CHEATIN' HEART--"

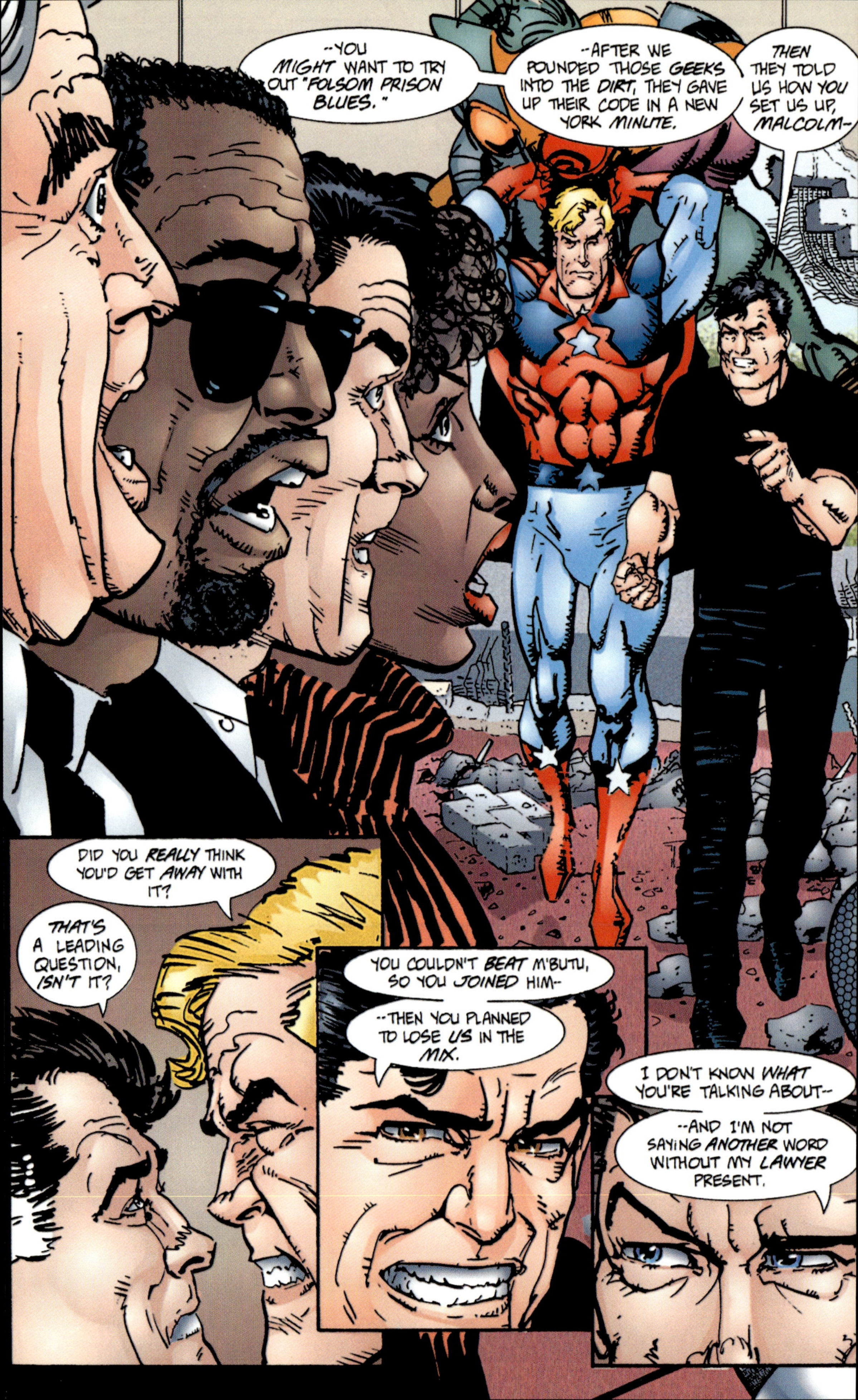
--YOU MIGHT WANT TO TRY OUT "FOLSOM PRISON BLUES."
--AFTER WE POUNDED THOSE GEEKS INTO THE DIRT, THEY GAVE UP THEIR CODE IN A NEW YORK MINUTE.
THEN THEY TOLD US HOW YOU SET US UP, MALCOLM--
DID YOU REALLY THINK YOU'D GET AWAY WITH IT?
THAT'S A LEADING QUESTION, ISN'T IT?
YOU COULDN'T BEAT M'BUTU, SO YOU JOINED HIM--
--THEN YOU PLANNED TO LOSE US IN THE MIX.
I DON'T KNOW WHAT YOU'RE TALKING ABOUT--
--AND I'M NOT SAYING ANOTHER WORD WITHOUT MY LAWYER PRESENT.

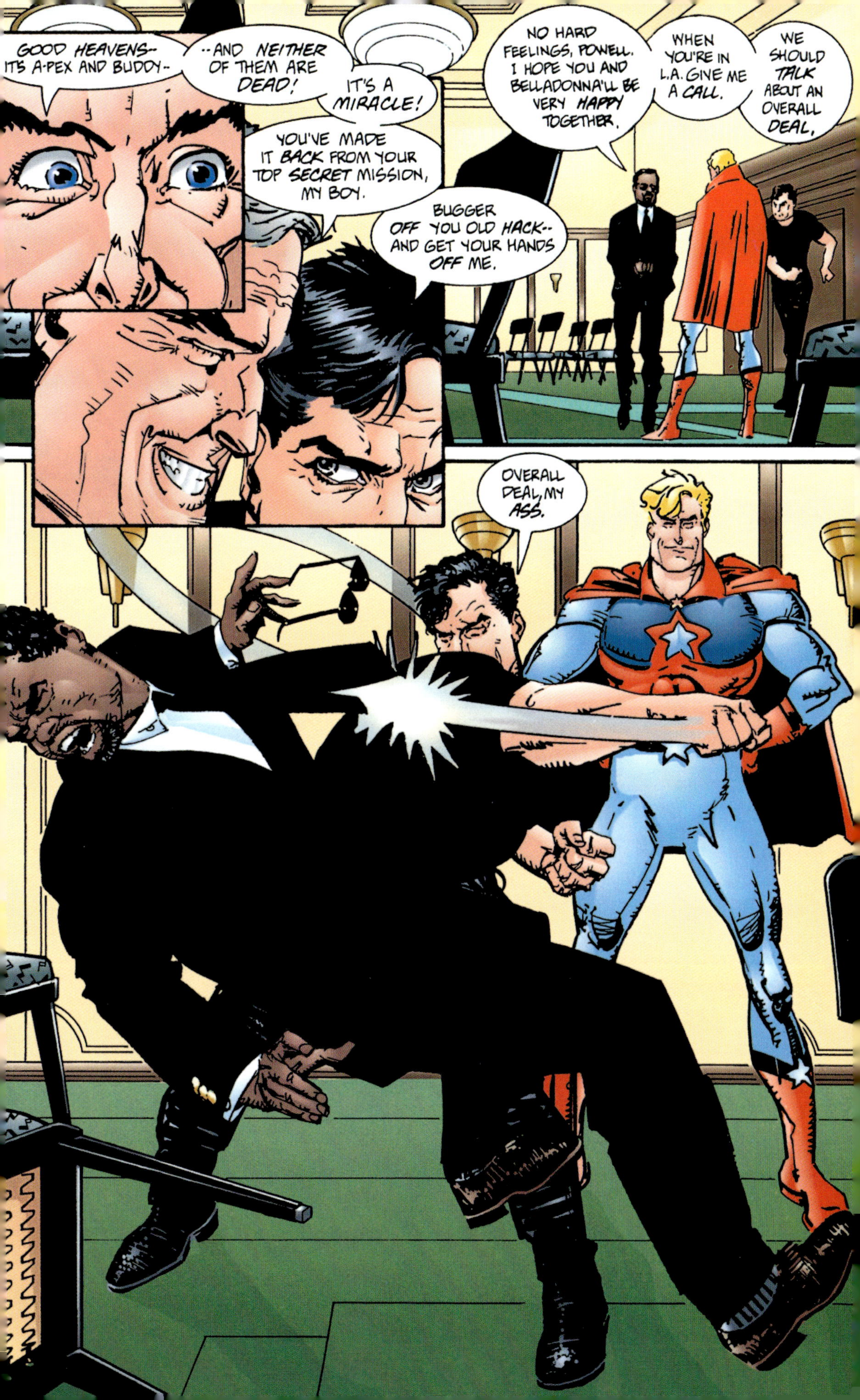
GOOD HEAVENS-- IT'S A-PEX AND BUDDY--
--AND NEITHER OF THEM ARE DEAD!
IT'S A MIRACLE!
YOU'VE MADE IT BACK FROM YOUR TOP SECRET MISSION, MY BOY.
BUGGER OFF YOU OLD HACK-- AND GET YOUR HANDS OFF ME.
NO HARD FEELINGS, POWELL. I HOPE YOU AND BELLADONNA'LL BE VERY HAPPY TOGETHER.
WHEN YOU'RE IN L.A. GIVE ME A CALL.
WE SHOULD TALK ABOUT AN OVERALL DEAL.
OVERALL DEAL, MY ASS.

Caught on video, superhero wannabe Michael "Buddy" Gorski, presumed dead, assaults President for life and former pop-star, now Hollywood producer Jean Paul M'Butu.
Both men declined comment.
Public PROSECUTOR
TODAY
NO. 1 IN THE USA . . . FIRST IN DAILY READERS
LeStrange indicted in Supergate
President dumps NIA h
Menudo
Reagan
A-PEX
People weekly
POWELL AND GORSKI
The downside of superpowers–the upside of not really being dead. Here's the full story of who they are, why they do it, and their secret workout tips.
Superpowered monstrosities, and the men and women who love them–next, on Oprah.
It's really "The Birds" with food, Roger.
I agree, Gene–but once you get past that, it's a sensational thriller.
Here's an opportunity to put something away for the kid's education–
That's right– it's an official American Powerhouse© certificate of genetic authorship, signed by us
Caveat Emptor Television

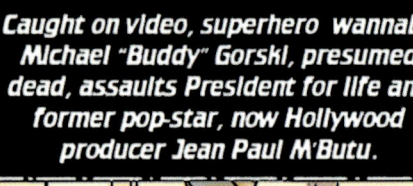

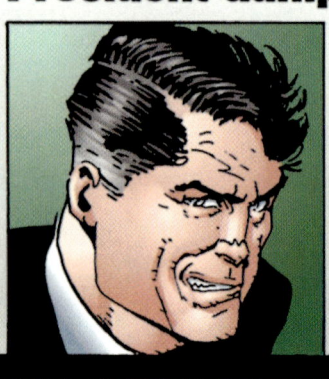

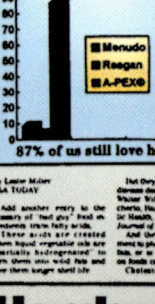

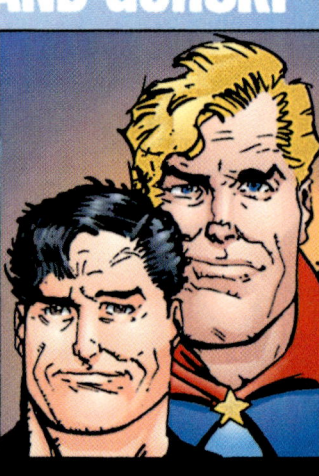

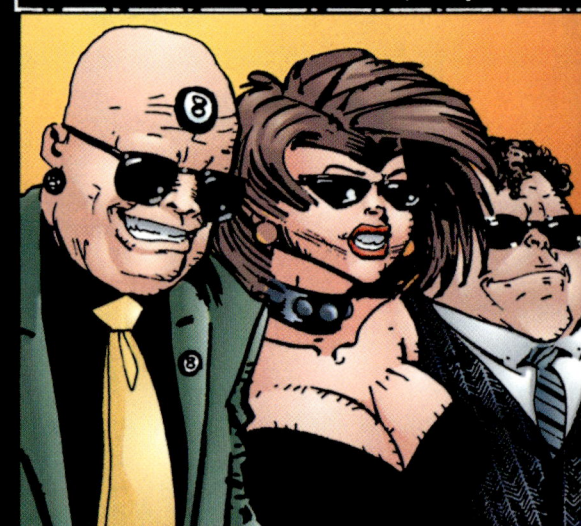

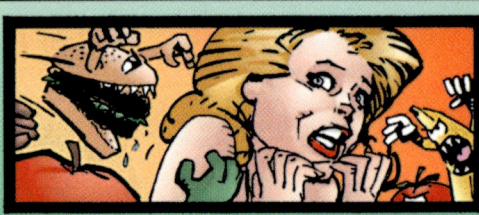

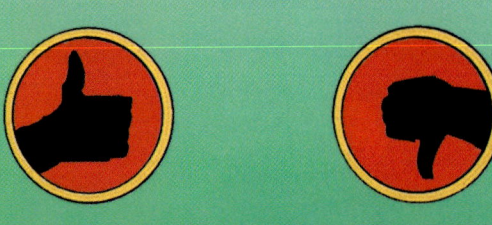

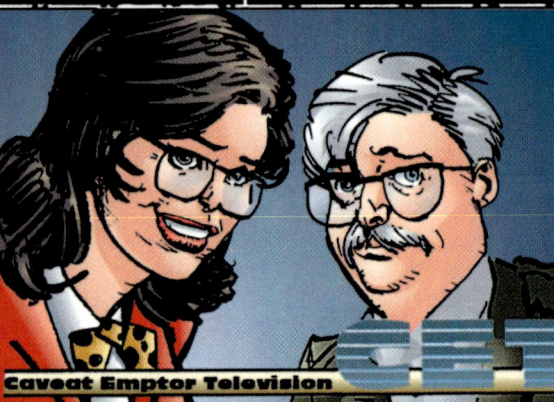

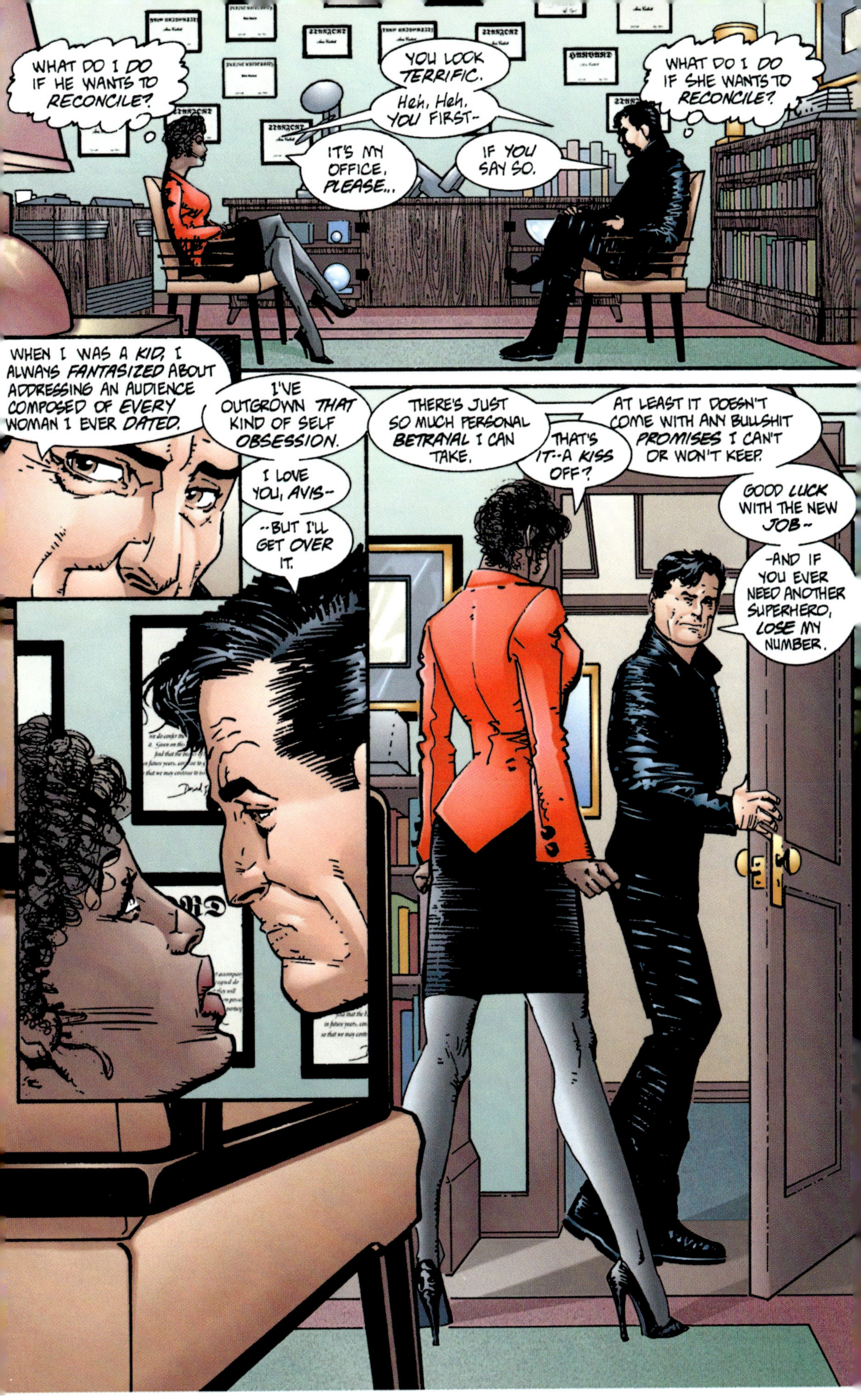
WHAT DO I DO IF HE WANTS TO RECONCILE?
YOU LOOK TERRIFIC.
Heh, Heh. YOU FIRST-
IT'S MY OFFICE. PLEASE...
IF YOU SAY SO.
WHAT DO I DO IF SHE WANTS TO RECONCILE?
WHEN I WAS A KID, I ALWAYS FANTASIZED ABOUT ADDRESSING AN AUDIENCE COMPOSED OF EVERY WOMAN I EVER DATED.
I'VE OUTGROWN THAT KIND OF SELF OBSESSION.
I LOVE YOU, AVIS--
--BUT I'LL GET OVER IT.
THERE'S JUST SO MUCH PERSONAL BETRAYAL I CAN TAKE.
THAT'S IT--A KISS OFF?
AT LEAST IT DOESN'T COME WITH ANY BULLSHIT PROMISES I CAN'T OR WON'T KEEP.
GOOD LUCK WITH THE NEW JOB--
-AND IF YOU EVER NEED ANOTHER SUPERHERO, LOSE MY NUMBER.

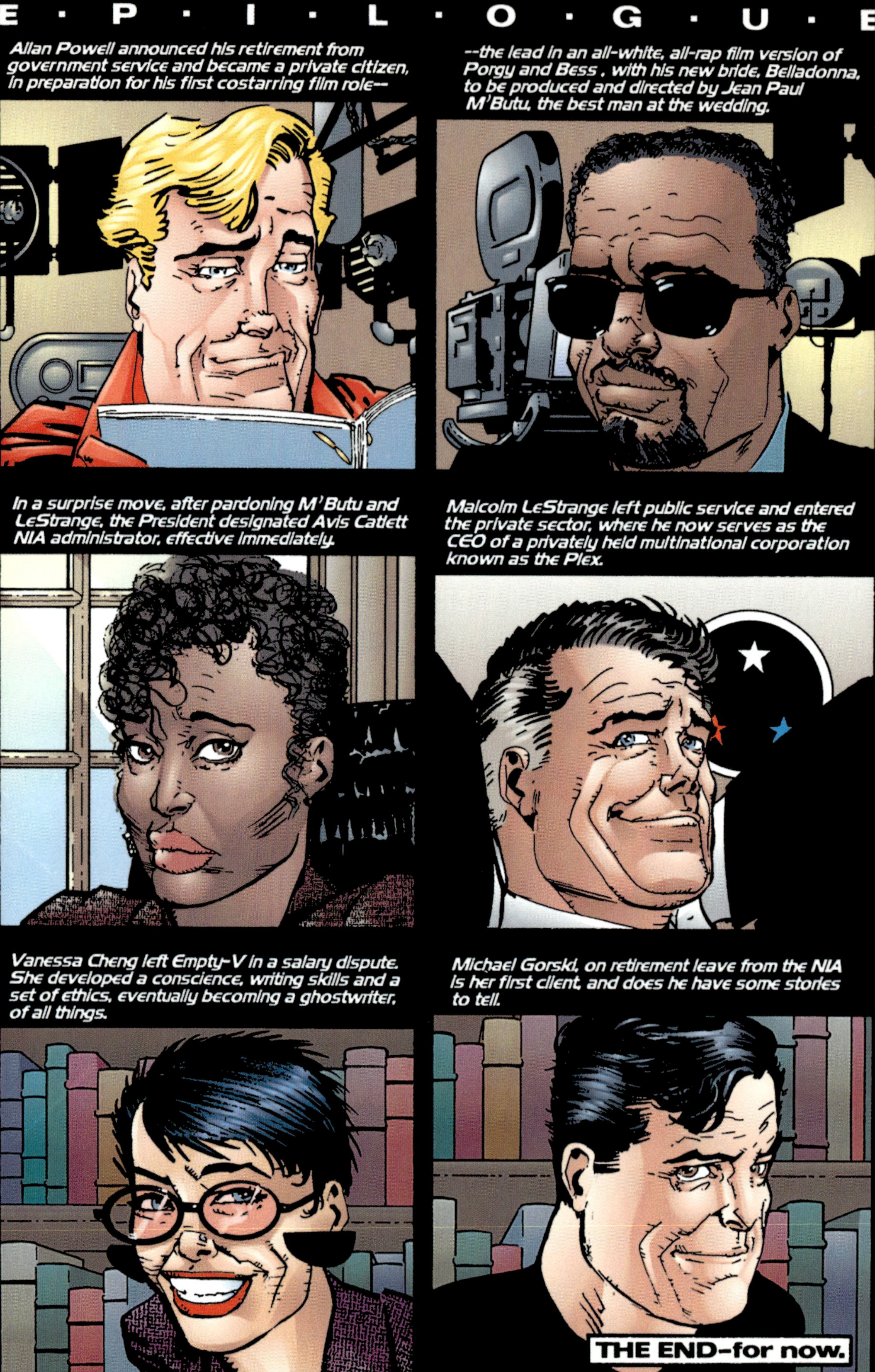
E · P · I · L · O · G · U · E
Allan Powell announced his retirement from government service and became a private citizen, in preparation for his first costarring film role--
--the lead in an all-white, all-rap film version of Porgy and Bess , with his new bride, Belladonna, to be produced and directed by Jean Paul M'Butu, the best man at the wedding.
In a surprise move, after pardoning M'Butu and LeStrange, the President designated Avis Catlett NIA administrator, effective immediately.
Malcolm LeStrange left public service and entered the private sector, where he now serves as the CEO of a privately held multinational corporation known as the Plex.
Vanessa Cheng left Empty-V in a salary dispute. She developed a conscience, writing skills and a set of ethics, eventually becoming a ghostwriter, of all things.
Michael Gorski, on retirement leave from the NIA is her first client, and does he have some stories to tell.
THE END–for now.

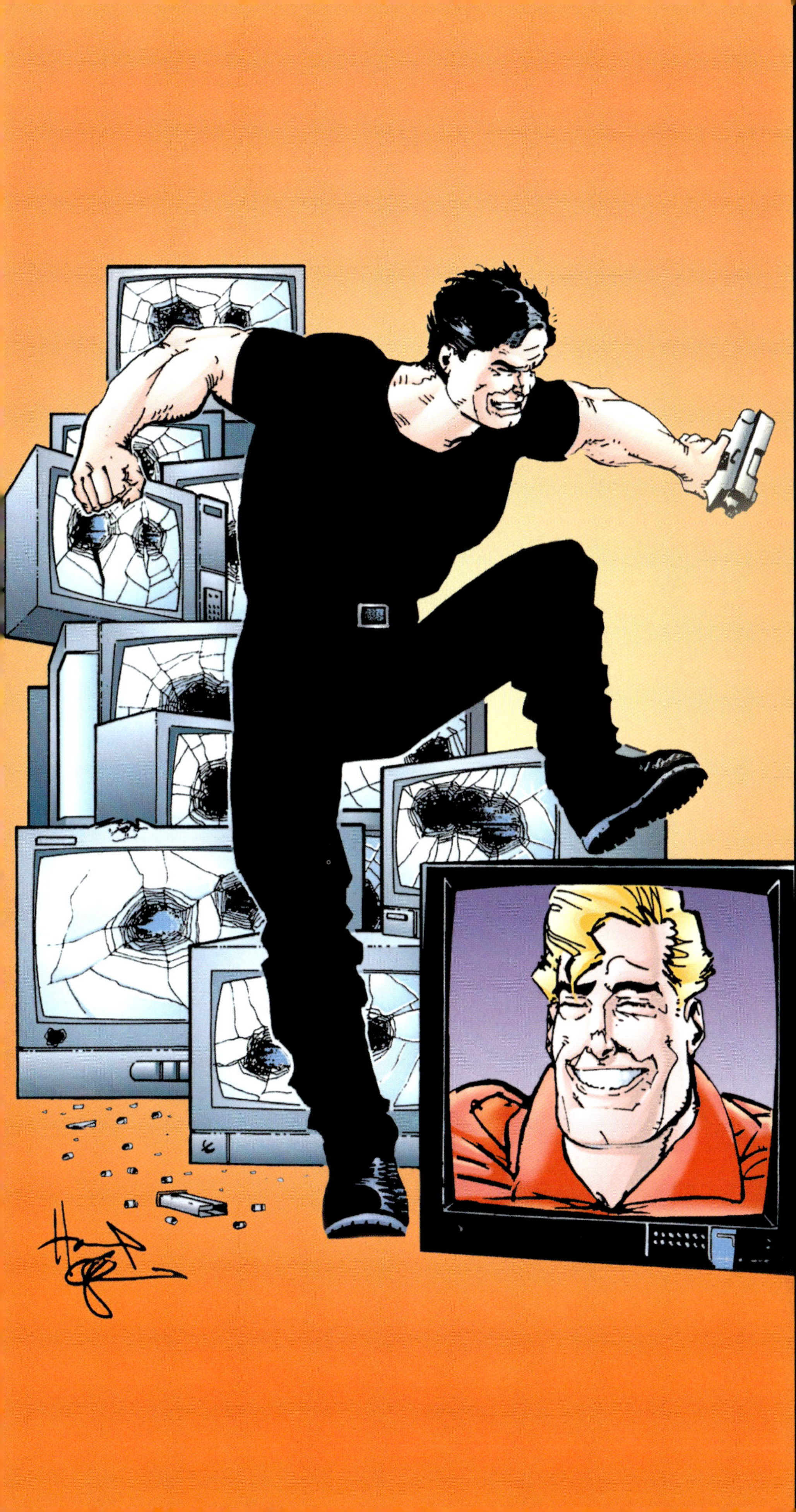

POWER & GLORY TRADE PAPERBACK ORIGINAL COVER

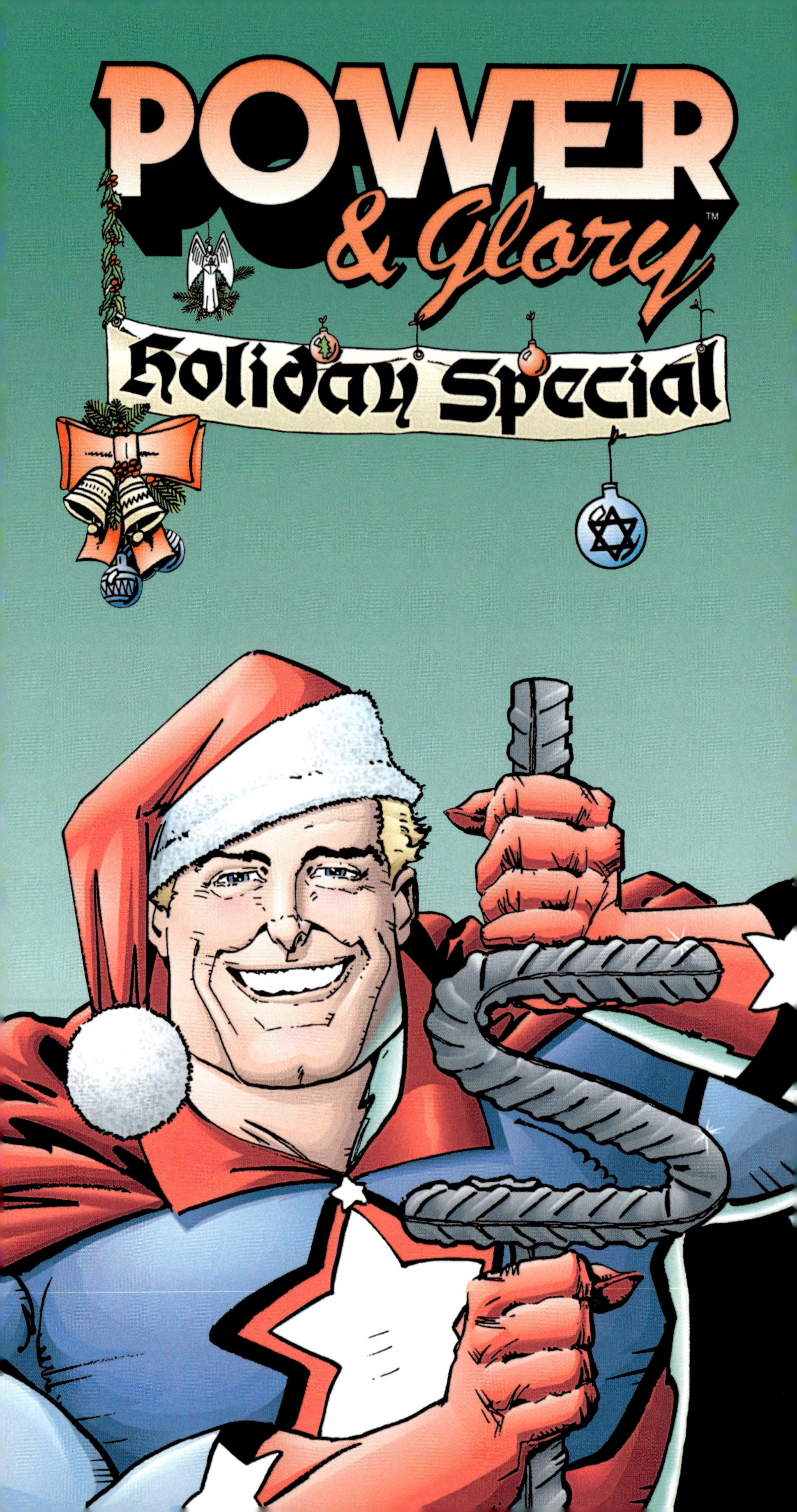
POWER
& Glory™
Holiday Special

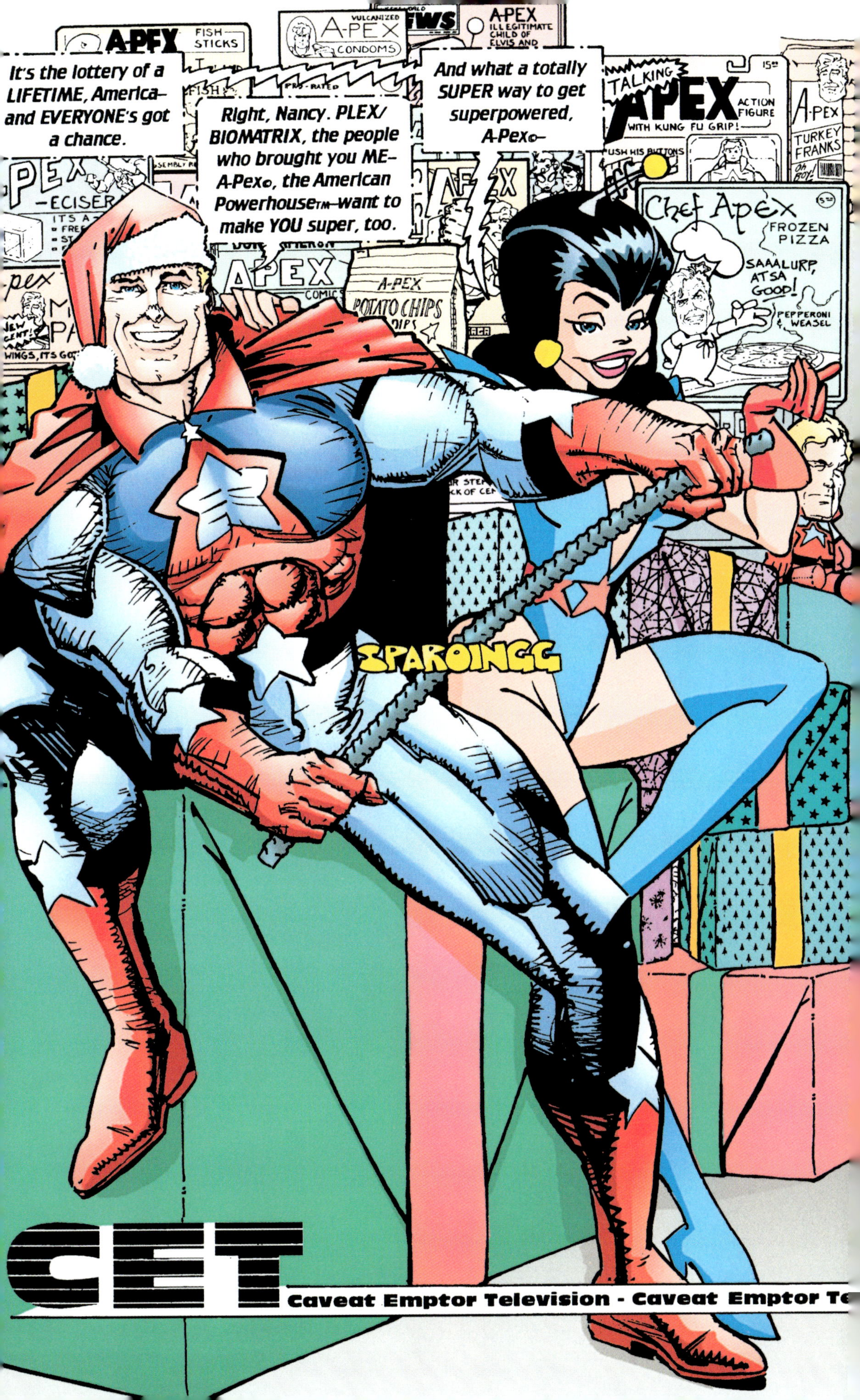
It's the lottery of a LIFETIME, America– and EVERYONE's got a chance.
Right, Nancy. PLEX/ BIOMATRIX, the people who brought you ME– A-Pex©, the American Powerhouse™–want to make YOU super, too.
And what a totally SUPER way to get superpowered, A-Pex©–
SPAROINGG
Chef Apex
FROZEN PIZZA
SAAALURP, ATSA GOOD!
PEPPERONI & WEASEL
TALKING APEX ACTION FIGURE
WITH KUNG FU GRIP!
A-Pex TURKEY FRANKS
A-PEX POTATO CHIPS
APEX FISH STICKS
VULCANIZED A-PEX CONDOMS
A-PEX ILLEGITIMATE CHILD OF ELVIS AND
CET
Caveat Emptor Television - Caveat Emptor Te

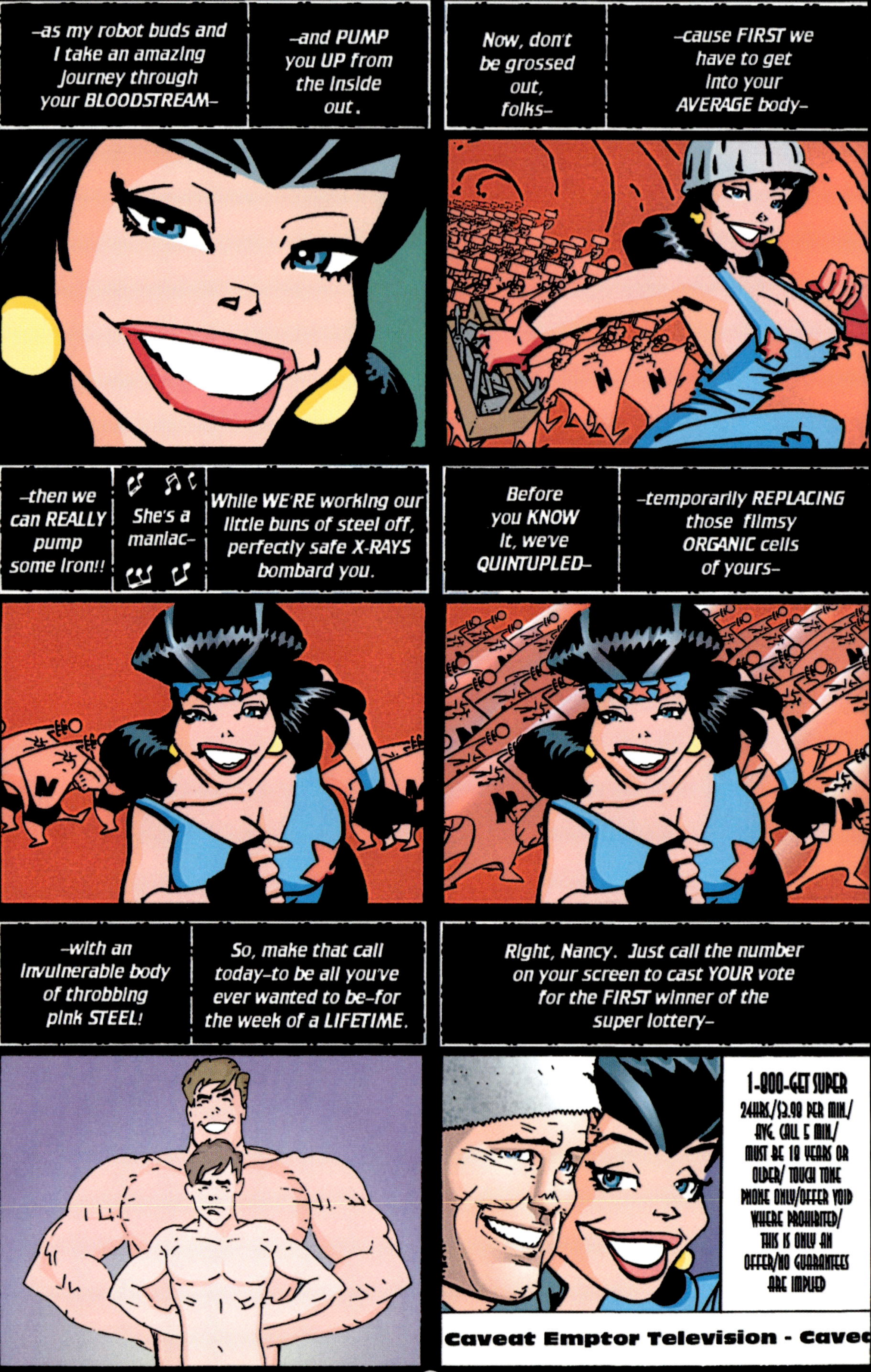

–as my robot buds and I take an amazing journey through your BLOODSTREAM–
–and PUMP you UP from the inside out.
Now, don't be grossed out, folks–
–cause FIRST we have to get into your AVERAGE body–
–then we can REALLY pump some iron!!
She's a maniac–
While WE'RE working our little buns of steel off, perfectly safe X-RAYS bombard you.
Before you KNOW it, we've QUINTUPLED–
–temporarily REPLACING those flimsy ORGANIC cells of yours–
–with an invulnerable body of throbbing pink STEEL!
So, make that call today–to be all you've ever wanted to be–for the week of a LIFETIME.
Right, Nancy. Just call the number on your screen to cast YOUR vote for the FIRST winner of the super lottery–
1-800-GET SUPER
24HRS/$3.98 PER MIN./ AVG. CALL 5 MIN./ MUST BE 18 YEARS OR OLDER/ TOUCH TONE PHONE ONLY/OFFER VOID WHERE PROHIBITED/ THIS IS ONLY AN OFFER/NO GUARANTEES ARE IMPLIED
Caveat Emptor Television - Cavea

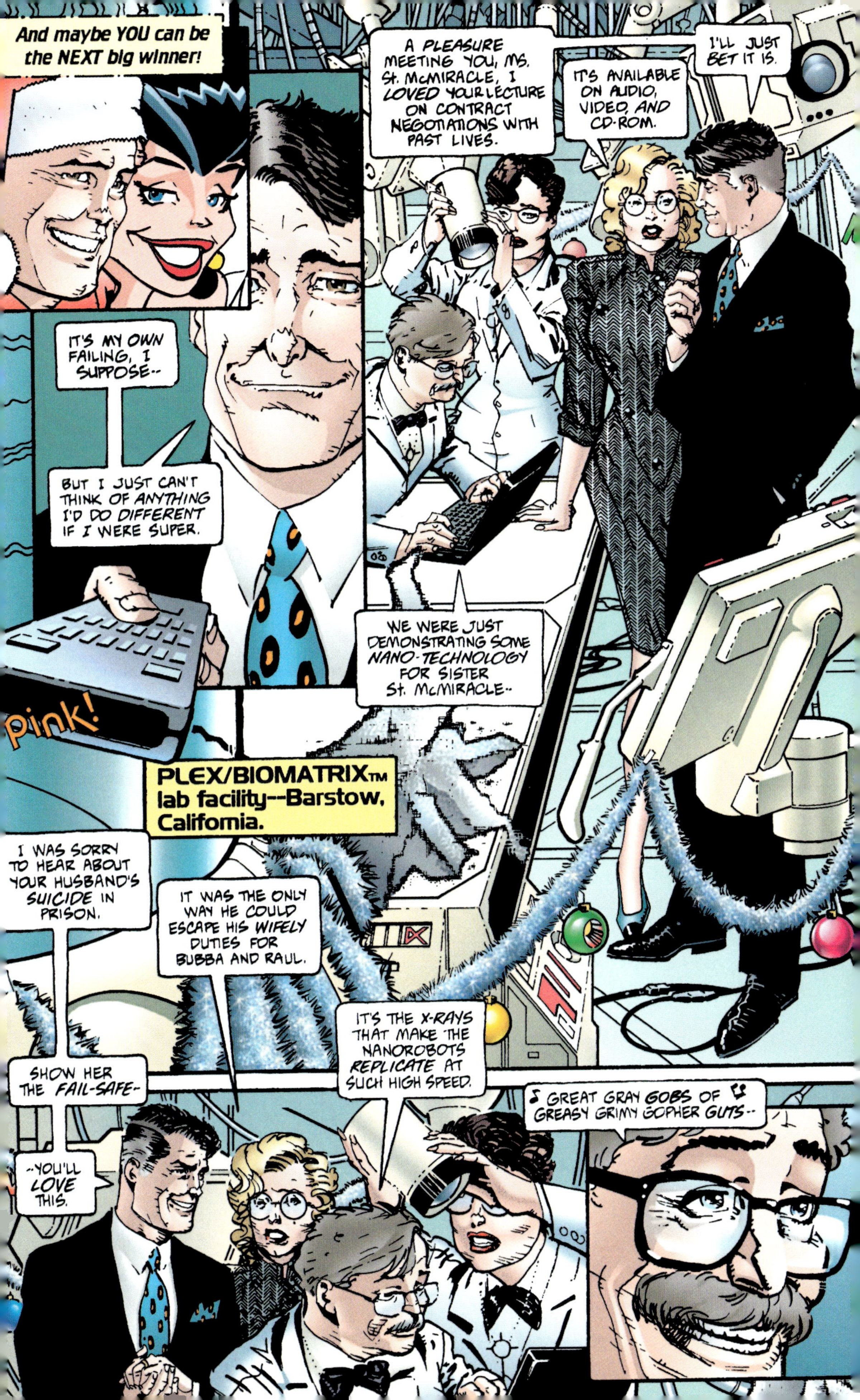

And maybe YOU can be the NEXT big winner!
IT'S MY OWN FAILING, I SUPPOSE--
BUT I JUST CAN'T THINK OF ANYTHING I'D DO DIFFERENT IF I WERE SUPER.
pink!
A PLEASURE MEETING YOU, MS. St. McMIRACLE. I LOVED YOUR LECTURE ON CONTRACT NEGOTIATIONS WITH PAST LIVES.
IT'S AVAILABLE ON AUDIO, VIDEO, AND CD-ROM.
I'LL JUST BET IT IS.
WE WERE JUST DEMONSTRATING SOME NANO-TECHNOLOGY FOR SISTER St. McMIRACLE--
PLEX/BIOMATRIX™ lab facility--Barstow, California.
I WAS SORRY TO HEAR ABOUT YOUR HUSBAND'S SUICIDE IN PRISON.
IT WAS THE ONLY WAY HE COULD ESCAPE HIS WIFELY DUTIES FOR BUBBA AND RAUL.
SHOW HER THE FAIL-SAFE--
--YOU'LL LOVE THIS.
IT'S THE X-RAYS THAT MAKE THE NANOROBOTS REPLICATE AT SUCH HIGH SPEED.
♪ GREAT GRAY GOBS OF GREASY GRIMY GOPHER GUTS--

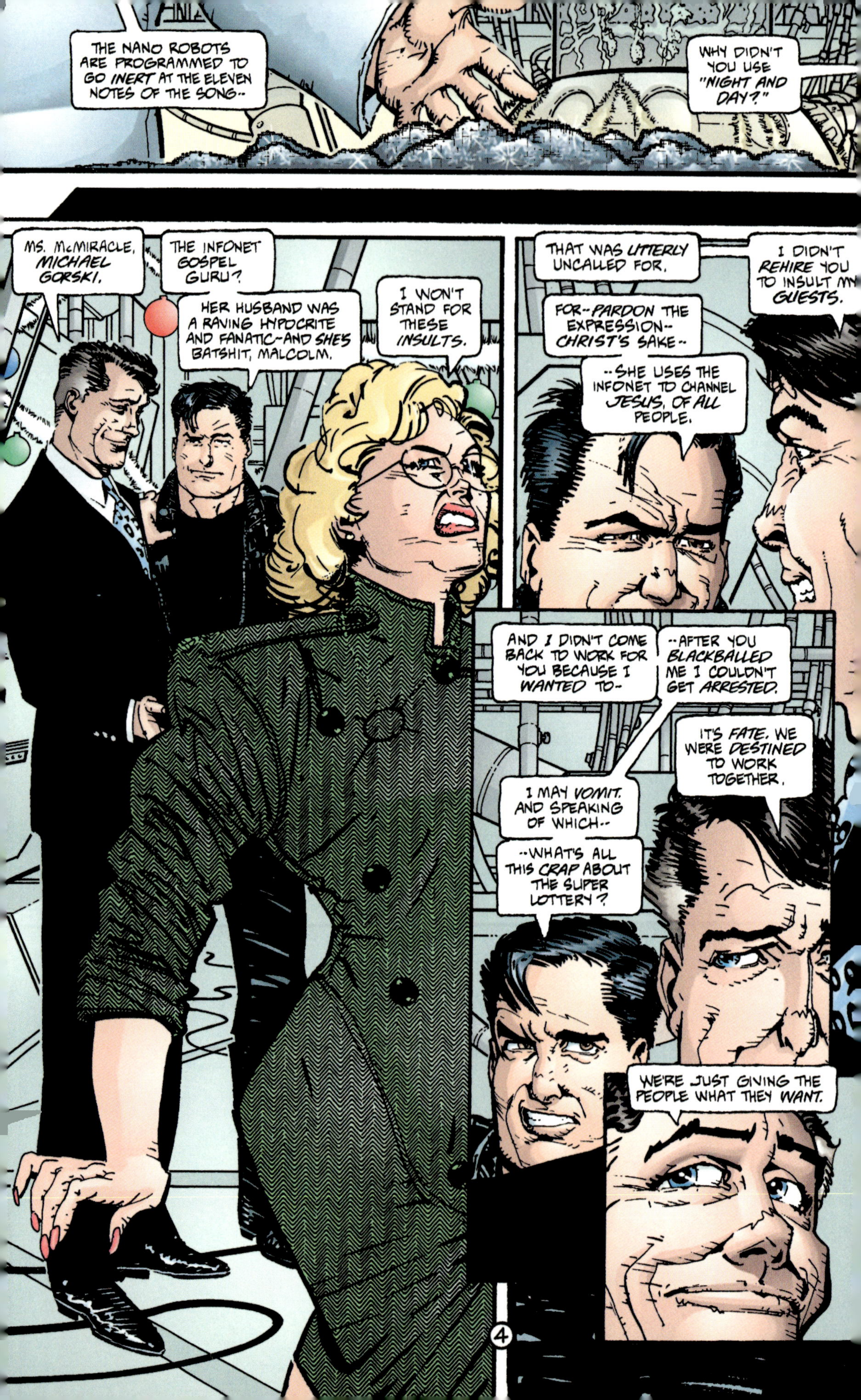
THE NANO ROBOTS ARE PROGRAMMED TO GO INERT AT THE ELEVEN NOTES OF THE SONG--
WHY DIDN'T YOU USE "NIGHT AND DAY?"
MS. McMIRACLE, MICHAEL GORSKI.
THE INFONET GOSPEL GURU?
HER HUSBAND WAS A RAVING HYPOCRITE AND FANATIC--AND SHE'S BATSHIT, MALCOLM.
I WON'T STAND FOR THESE INSULTS.
THAT WAS UTTERLY UNCALLED FOR.
I DIDN'T REHIRE YOU TO INSULT MY GUESTS.
FOR--PARDON THE EXPRESSION--CHRIST'S SAKE--
--SHE USES THE INFONET TO CHANNEL JESUS, OF ALL PEOPLE.
AND I DIDN'T COME BACK TO WORK FOR YOU BECAUSE I WANTED TO-
--AFTER YOU BLACKBALLED ME I COULDN'T GET ARRESTED.
IT'S FATE. WE WERE DESTINED TO WORK TOGETHER.
I MAY VOMIT. AND SPEAKING OF WHICH--
--WHAT'S ALL THIS CRAP ABOUT THE SUPER LOTTERY?
WE'RE JUST GIVING THE PEOPLE WHAT THEY WANT.

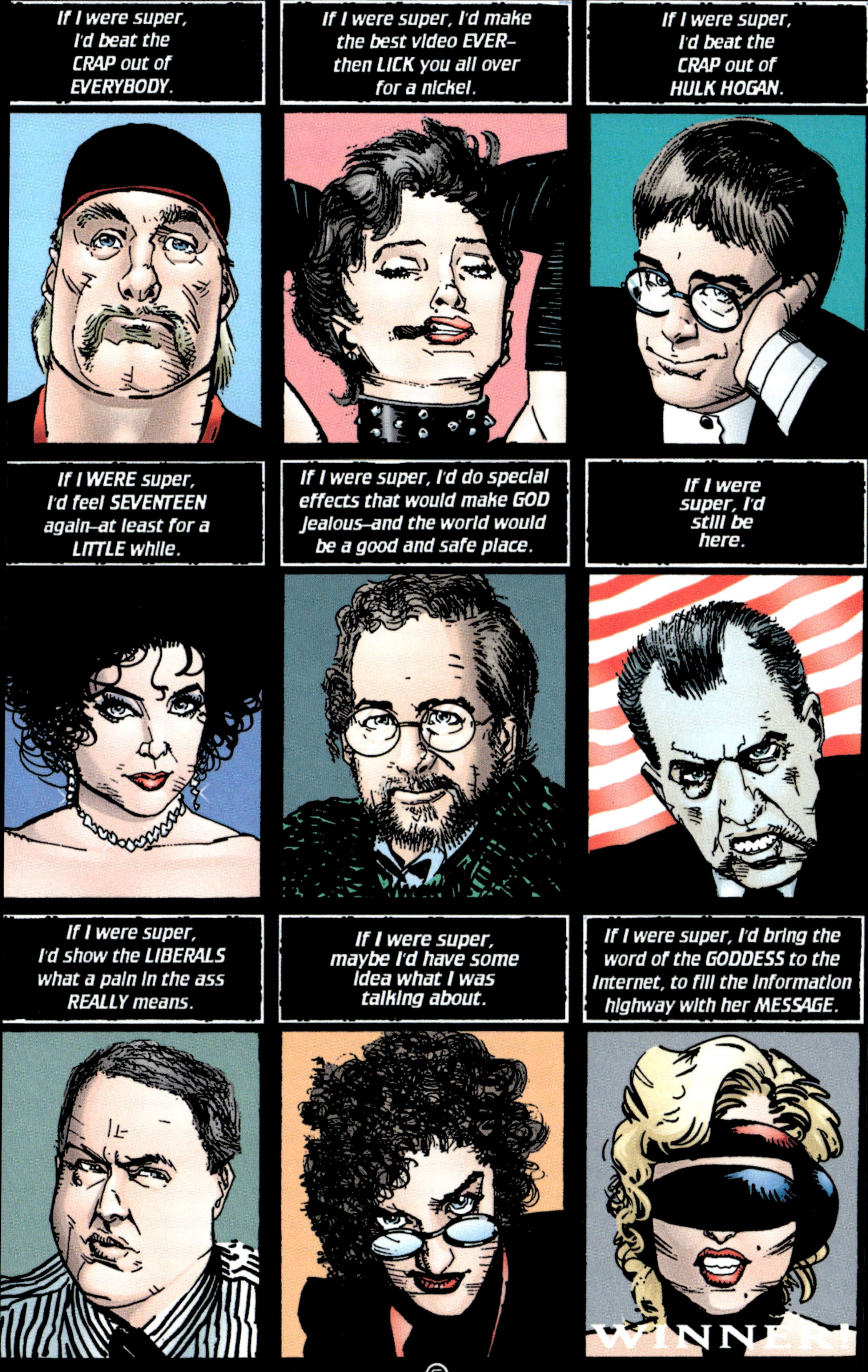
If I were super, I'd beat the CRAP out of EVERYBODY.
If I were super, I'd make the best video EVER– then LICK you all over for a nickel.
If I were super, I'd beat the CRAP out of HULK HOGAN.
If I WERE super, I'd feel SEVENTEEN again–at least for a LITTLE while.
If I were super, I'd do special effects that would make GOD jealous–and the world would be a good and safe place.
If I were super, I'd still be here.
If I were super, I'd show the LIBERALS what a pain in the ass REALLY means.
If I were super, maybe I'd have some idea what I was talking about.
If I were super, I'd bring the word of the GODDESS to the Internet, to fill the information highway with her MESSAGE.
WINNER!

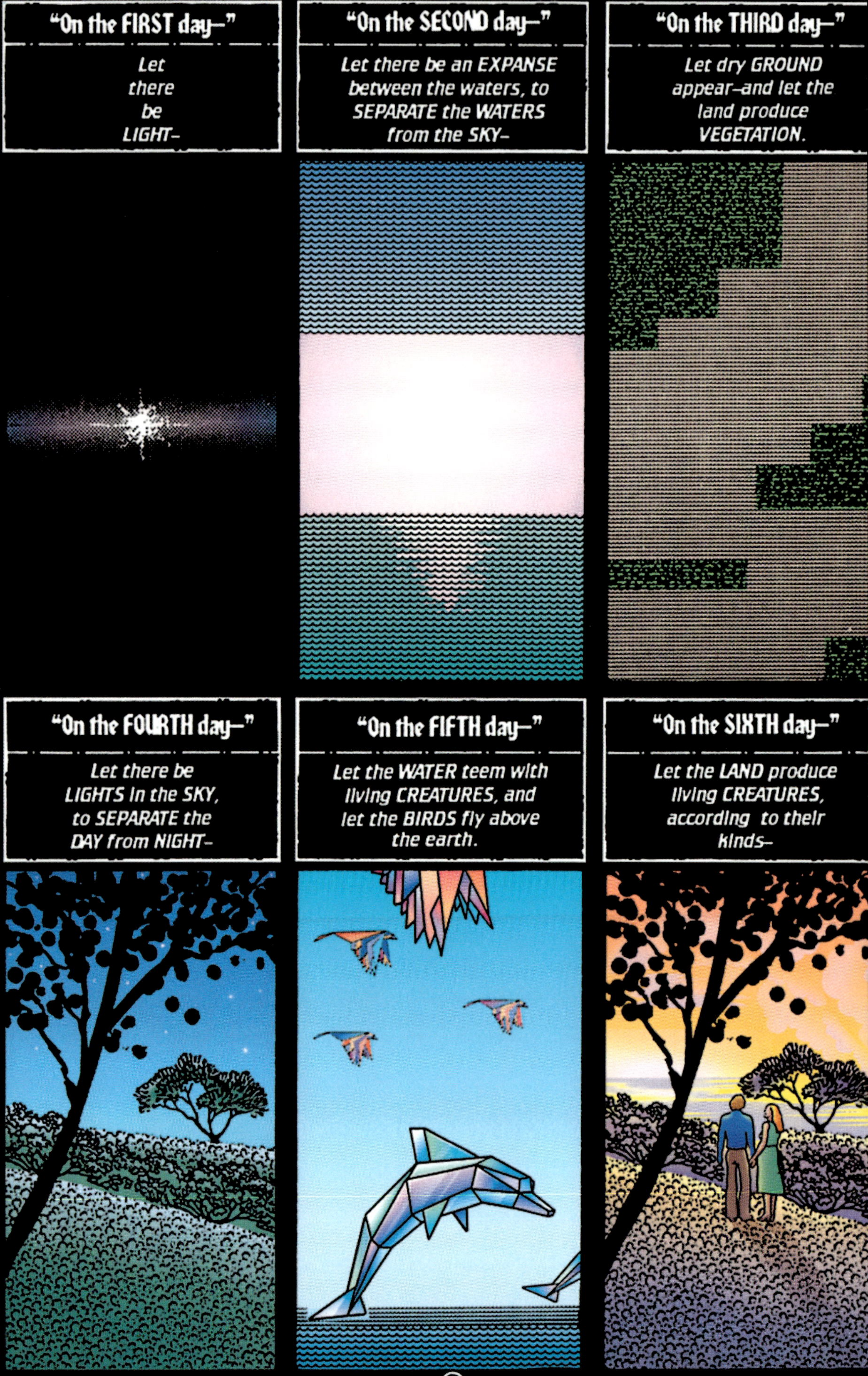
"On the FIRST day–"
Let there be LIGHT–
"On the SECOND day–"
Let there be an EXPANSE between the waters, to SEPARATE the WATERS from the SKY–
"On the THIRD day–"
Let dry GROUND appear–and let the land produce VEGETATION.
"On the FOURTH day–"
Let there be LIGHTS in the SKY, to SEPARATE the DAY from NIGHT–
"On the FIFTH day–"
Let the WATER teem with living CREATURES, and let the BIRDS fly above the earth.
"On the SIXTH day–"
Let the LAND produce living CREATURES, according to their kinds–

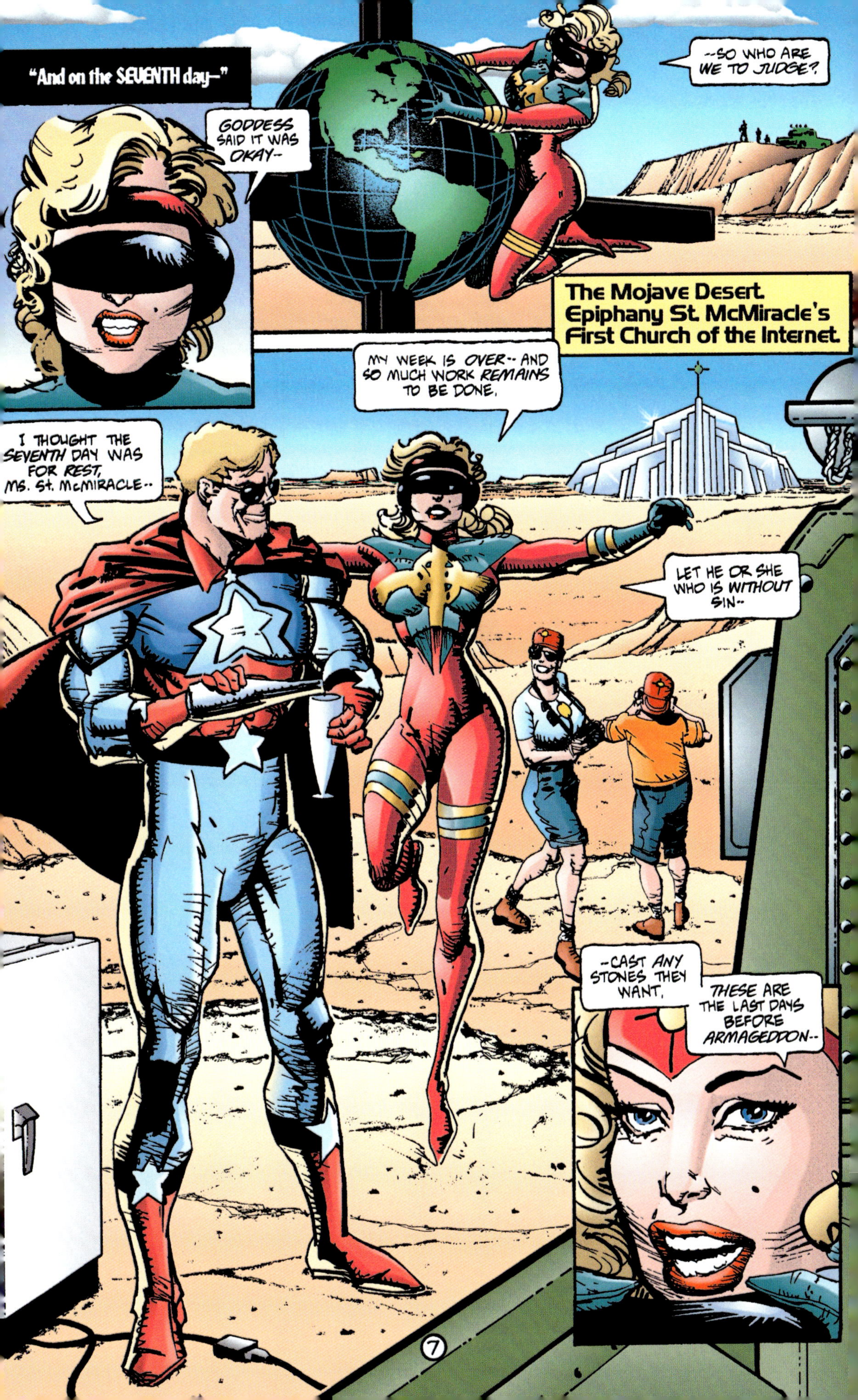
"And on the SEVENTH day—"
GODDESS SAID IT WAS OKAY--
--SO WHO ARE WE TO JUDGE?
The Mojave Desert.
Epiphany St. McMiracle's First Church of the Internet.
MY WEEK IS OVER-- AND SO MUCH WORK REMAINS TO BE DONE.
I THOUGHT THE SEVENTH DAY WAS FOR REST, MS. St. McMIRACLE--
LET HE OR SHE WHO IS WITHOUT SIN--
--CAST ANY STONES THEY WANT.
THESE ARE THE LAST DAYS BEFORE ARMAGEDDON--
7

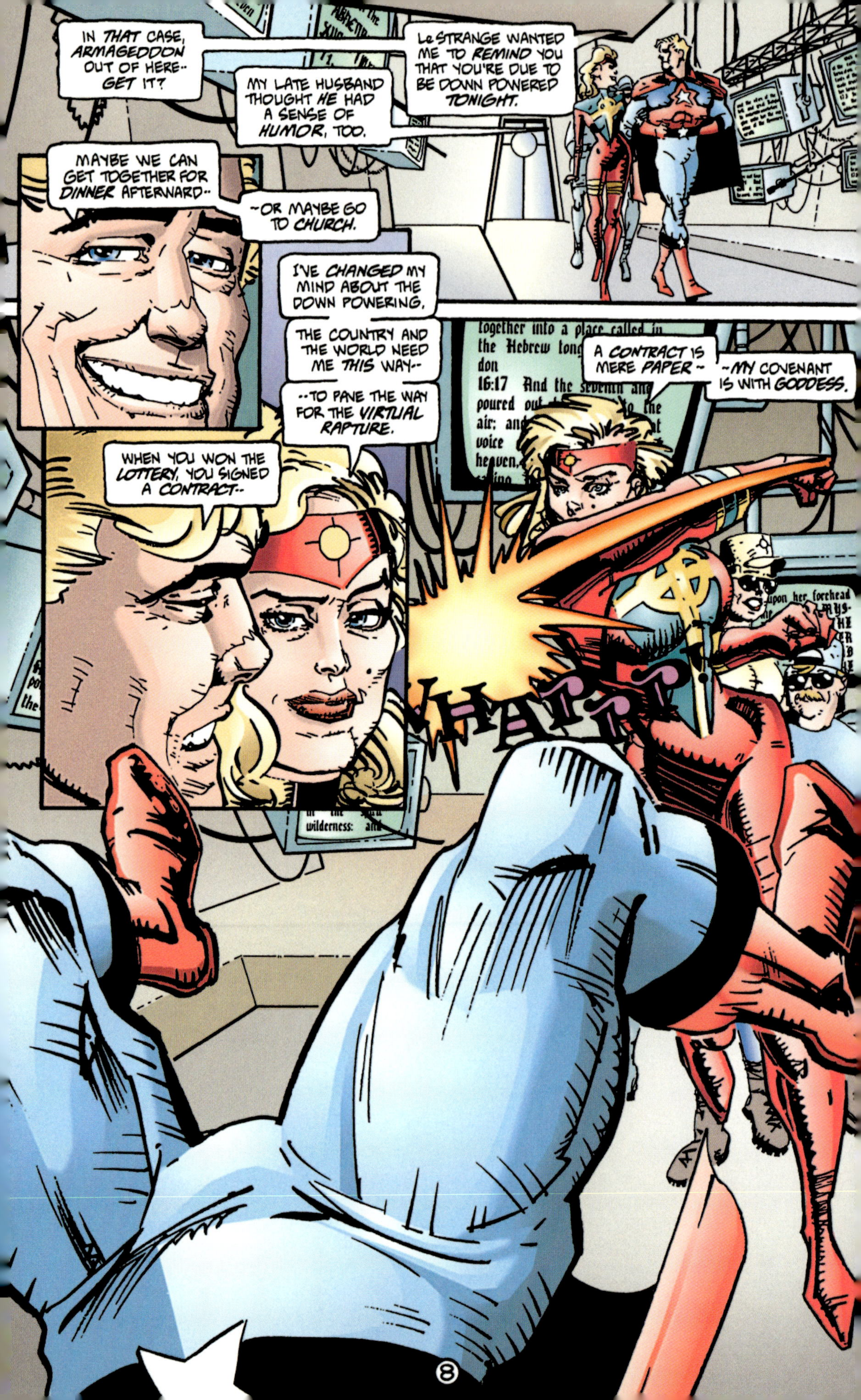

IN THAT CASE, ARMAGEDDON OUT OF HERE.. GET IT?
Le STRANGE WANTED ME TO REMIND YOU THAT YOU'RE DUE TO BE DOWN POWERED TONIGHT.
MY LATE HUSBAND THOUGHT HE HAD A SENSE OF HUMOR, TOO.
MAYBE WE CAN GET TOGETHER FOR DINNER AFTERWARD--
--OR MAYBE GO TO CHURCH.
I'VE CHANGED MY MIND ABOUT THE DOWN POWERING.
THE COUNTRY AND THE WORLD NEED ME THIS WAY--
--TO PAVE THE WAY FOR THE VIRTUAL RAPTURE.
WHEN YOU WON THE LOTTERY, YOU SIGNED A CONTRACT--
A CONTRACT IS MERE PAPER--
--MY COVENANT IS WITH GODDESS.
together into a place called in the Hebrew tong
don
16:17 And the seventh an
poured out
the air;
voice
heaven,
wilderness:

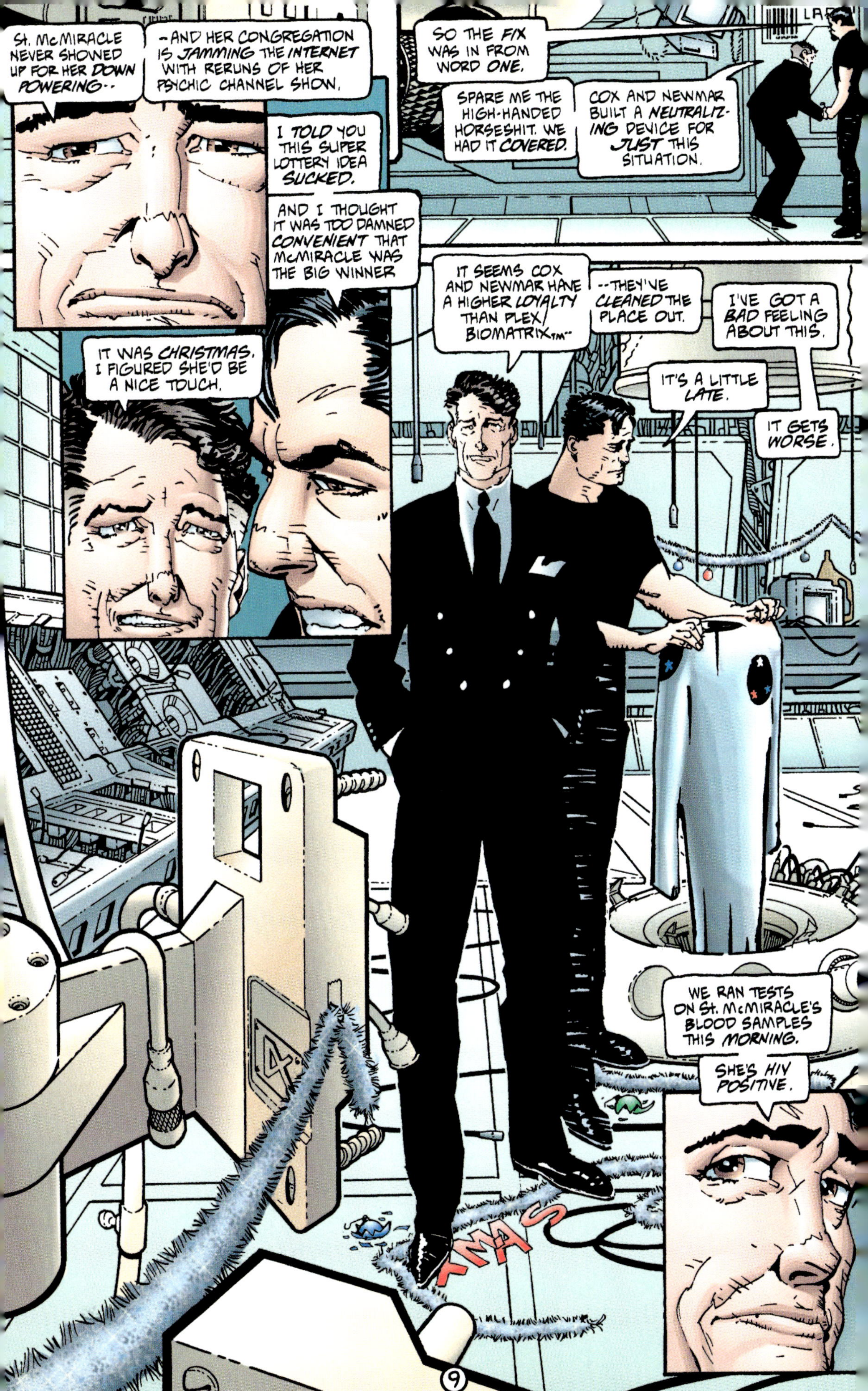

St. McMIRACLE NEVER SHOWED UP FOR HER DOWN POWERING--
--AND HER CONGREGATION IS JAMMING THE INTERNET WITH RERUNS OF HER PSYCHIC CHANNEL SHOW.
I TOLD YOU THIS SUPER LOTTERY IDEA SUCKED.
AND I THOUGHT IT WAS TOO DAMNED CONVENIENT THAT McMIRACLE WAS THE BIG WINNER
IT WAS CHRISTMAS. I FIGURED SHE'D BE A NICE TOUCH.
SO THE FIX WAS IN FROM WORD ONE.
SPARE ME THE HIGH-HANDED HORSESHIT. WE HAD IT COVERED.
COX AND NEWMAR BUILT A NEUTRALIZING DEVICE FOR JUST THIS SITUATION.
IT SEEMS COX AND NEWMAR HAVE A HIGHER LOYALTY THAN PLEX BIOMATRIX™--
--THEY'VE CLEANED THE PLACE OUT.
I'VE GOT A BAD FEELING ABOUT THIS.
IT'S A LITTLE LATE.
IT GETS WORSE.
WE RAN TESTS ON St. McMIRACLE'S BLOOD SAMPLES THIS MORNING.
SHE'S HIV POSITIVE.
XMAS

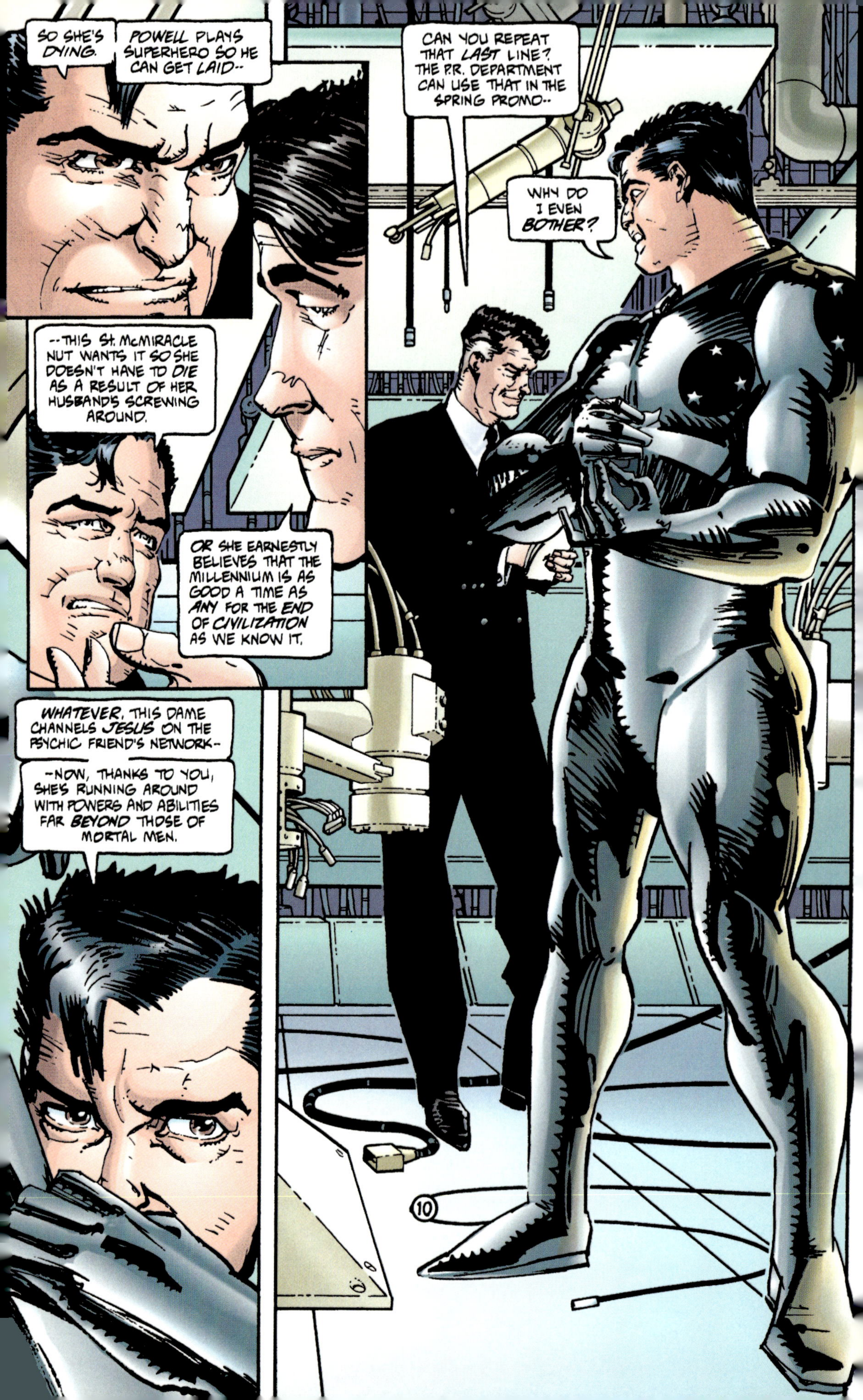
SO SHE'S DYING.
POWELL PLAYS SUPERHERO SO HE CAN GET LAID--
--THIS St. McMIRACLE NUT WANTS IT SO SHE DOESN'T HAVE TO DIE AS A RESULT OF HER HUSBAND'S SCREWING AROUND.
OR SHE EARNESTLY BELIEVES THAT THE MILLENNIUM IS AS GOOD A TIME AS ANY FOR THE END OF CIVILIZATION AS WE KNOW IT.
WHATEVER. THIS DAME CHANNELS JESUS ON THE PSYCHIC FRIEND'S NETWORK-
-NOW, THANKS TO YOU, SHE'S RUNNING AROUND WITH POWERS AND ABILITIES FAR BEYOND THOSE OF MORTAL MEN.
CAN YOU REPEAT THAT LAST LINE? THE P.R. DEPARTMENT CAN USE THAT IN THE SPRING PROMO--
WHY DO I EVEN BOTHER?
10

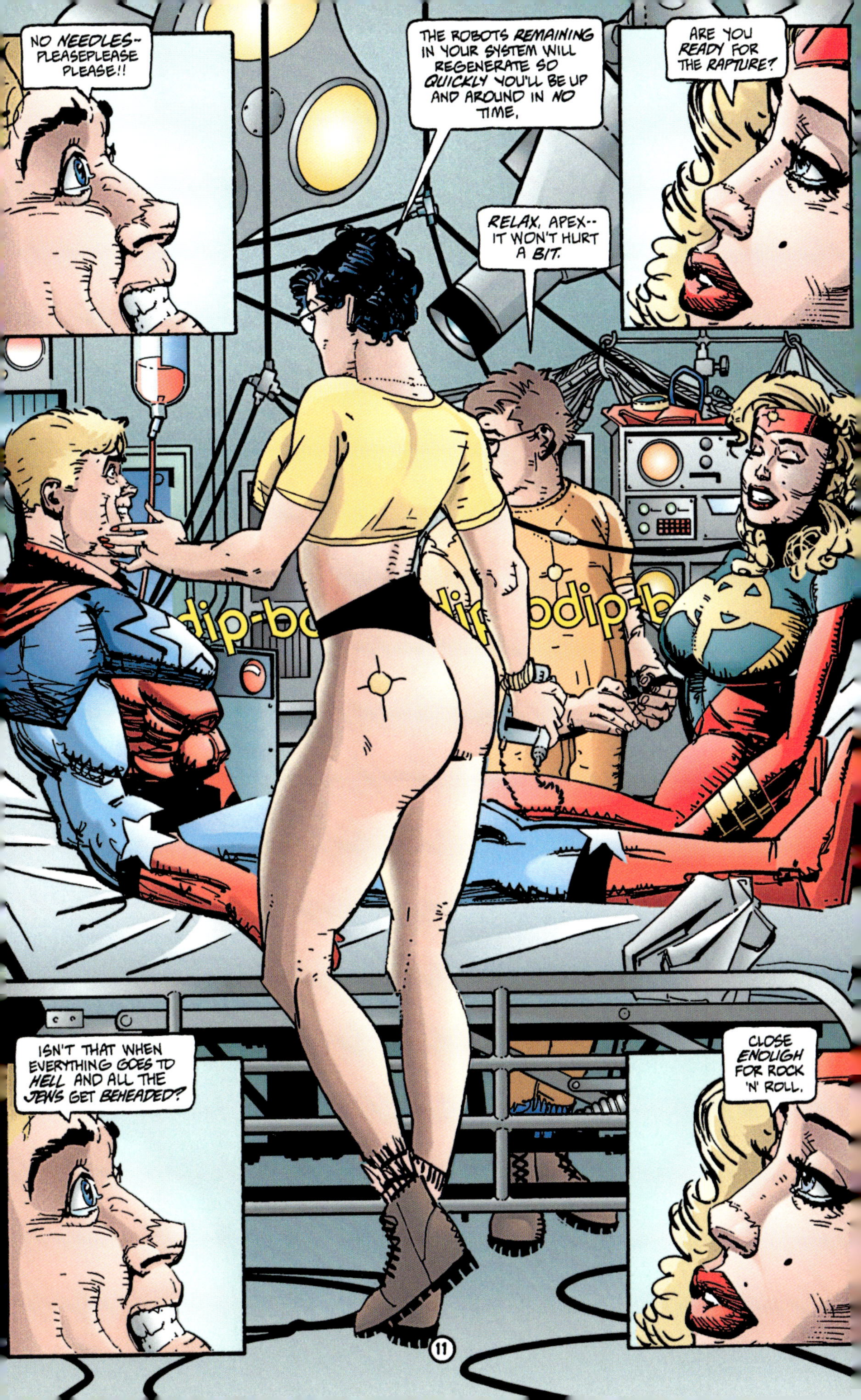

NO NEEDLES-- PLEASEPLEASE PLEASE!!
THE ROBOTS REMAINING IN YOUR SYSTEM WILL REGENERATE SO QUICKLY YOU'LL BE UP AND AROUND IN NO TIME.
ARE YOU READY FOR THE RAPTURE?
RELAX, APEX-- IT WON'T HURT A BIT.
dip-bodip-bodip-bodip-b
ISN'T THAT WHEN EVERYTHING GOES TO HELL AND ALL THE JEWS GET BEHEADED?
CLOSE ENOUGH FOR ROCK 'N' ROLL.

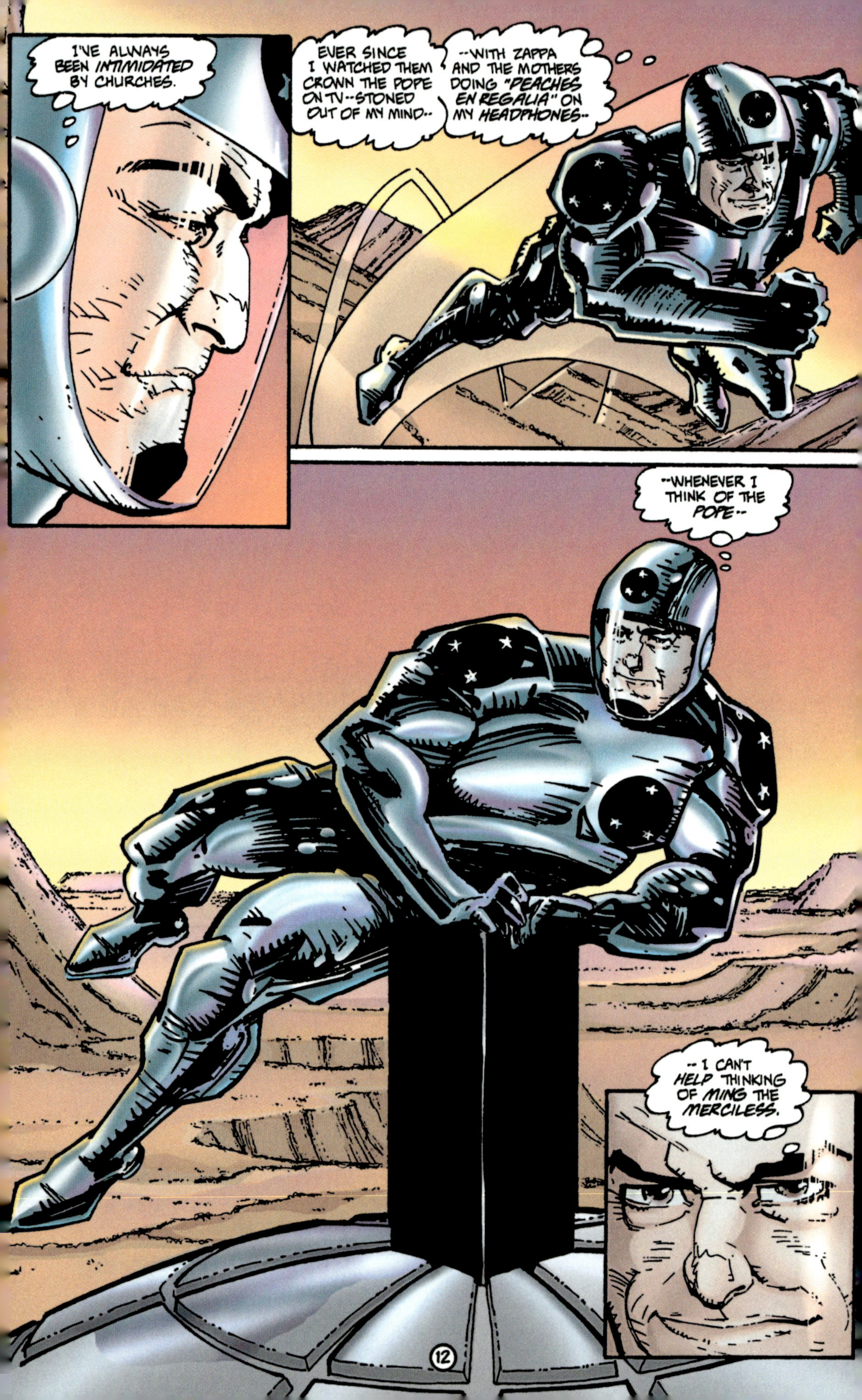
I'VE ALWAYS BEEN INTIMIDATED BY CHURCHES.
EVER SINCE I WATCHED THEM CROWN THE POPE ON TV--STONED OUT OF MY MIND--
--WITH ZAPPA AND THE MOTHERS DOING "PEACHES EN REGALIA" ON MY HEADPHONES--
--WHENEVER I THINK OF THE POPE--
--I CAN'T HELP THINKING OF MING THE MERCILESS.
12

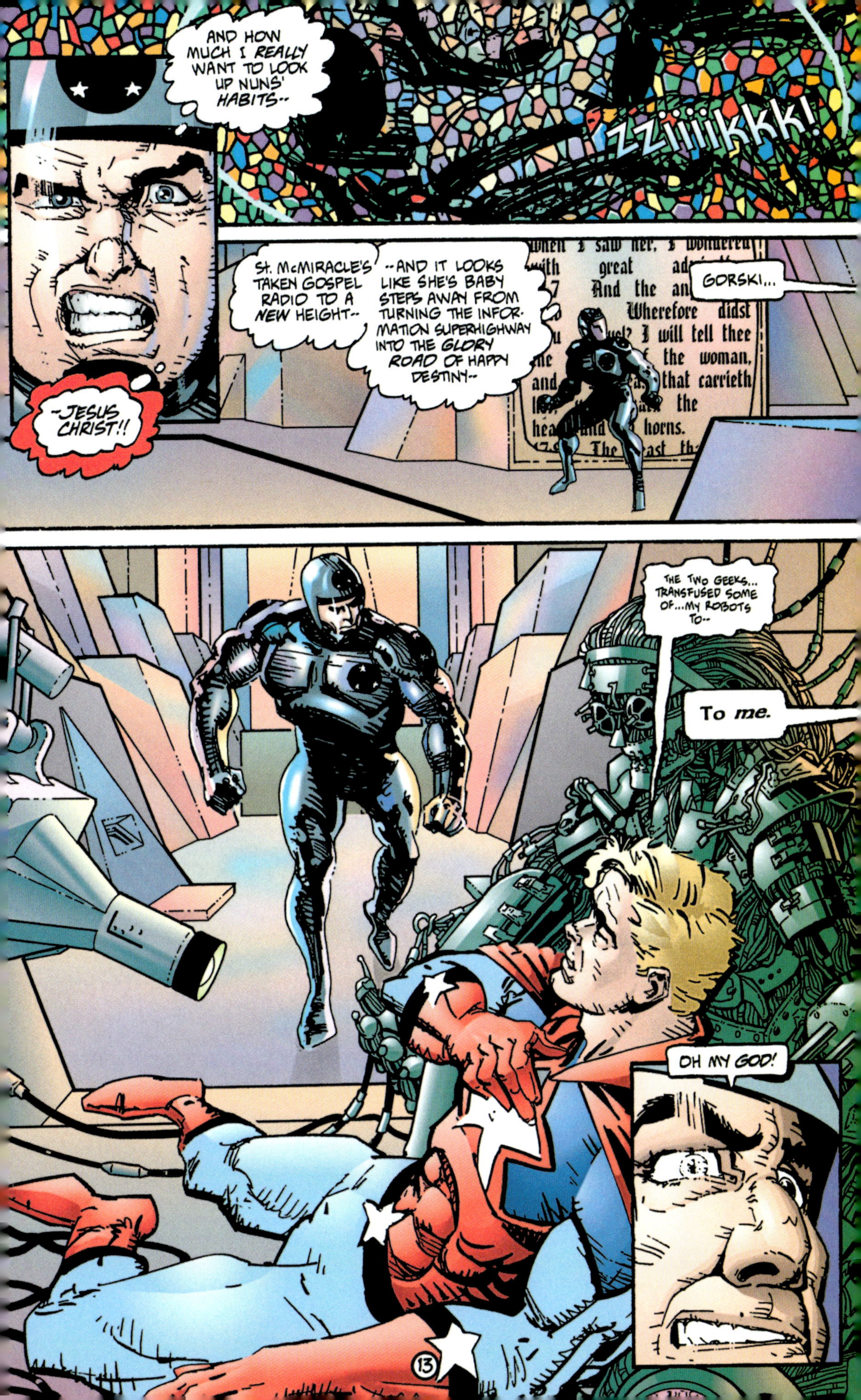
AND HOW MUCH I REALLY WANT TO LOOK UP NUNS' HABITS--
ZZIIIIIKKK!
--JESUS CHRIST!!
ST. MCMIRACLE'S TAKEN GOSPEL RADIO TO A NEW HEIGHT--
--AND IT LOOKS LIKE SHE'S BABY STEPS AWAY FROM TURNING THE INFORMATION SUPERHIGHWAY INTO THE GLORY ROAD OF HAPPY DESTINY--
GORSKI...
THE TWO GEEKS... TRANSFUSED SOME OF...MY ROBOTS TO--
To me.
OH MY GOD!

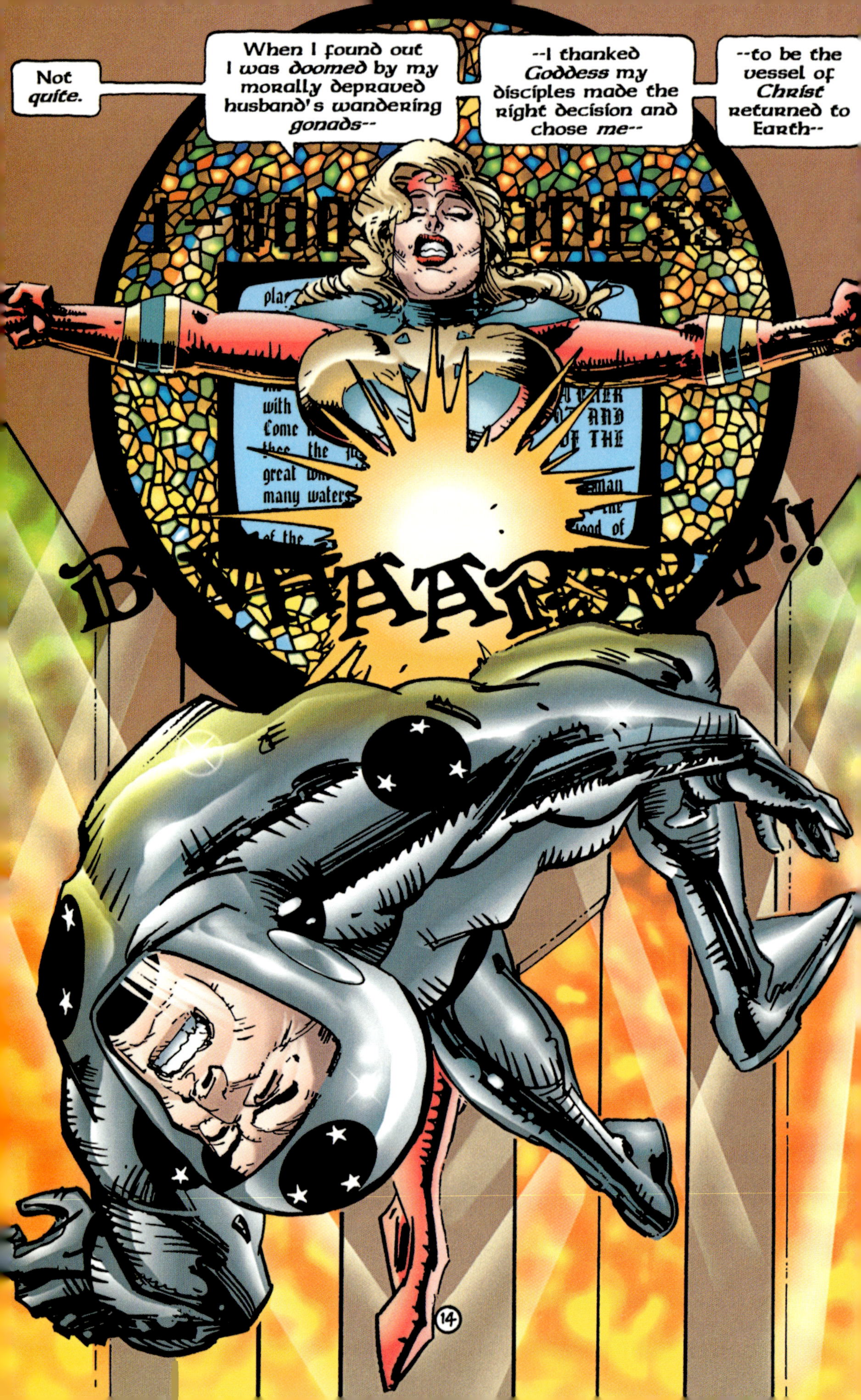
Not *quite.*
When I found out I was *doomed* by my morally depraved husband's wandering *gonads*--
--I thanked *Goddess* my disciples made the right decision and chose *me*--
--to be the vessel of *Christ* returned to Earth--
14

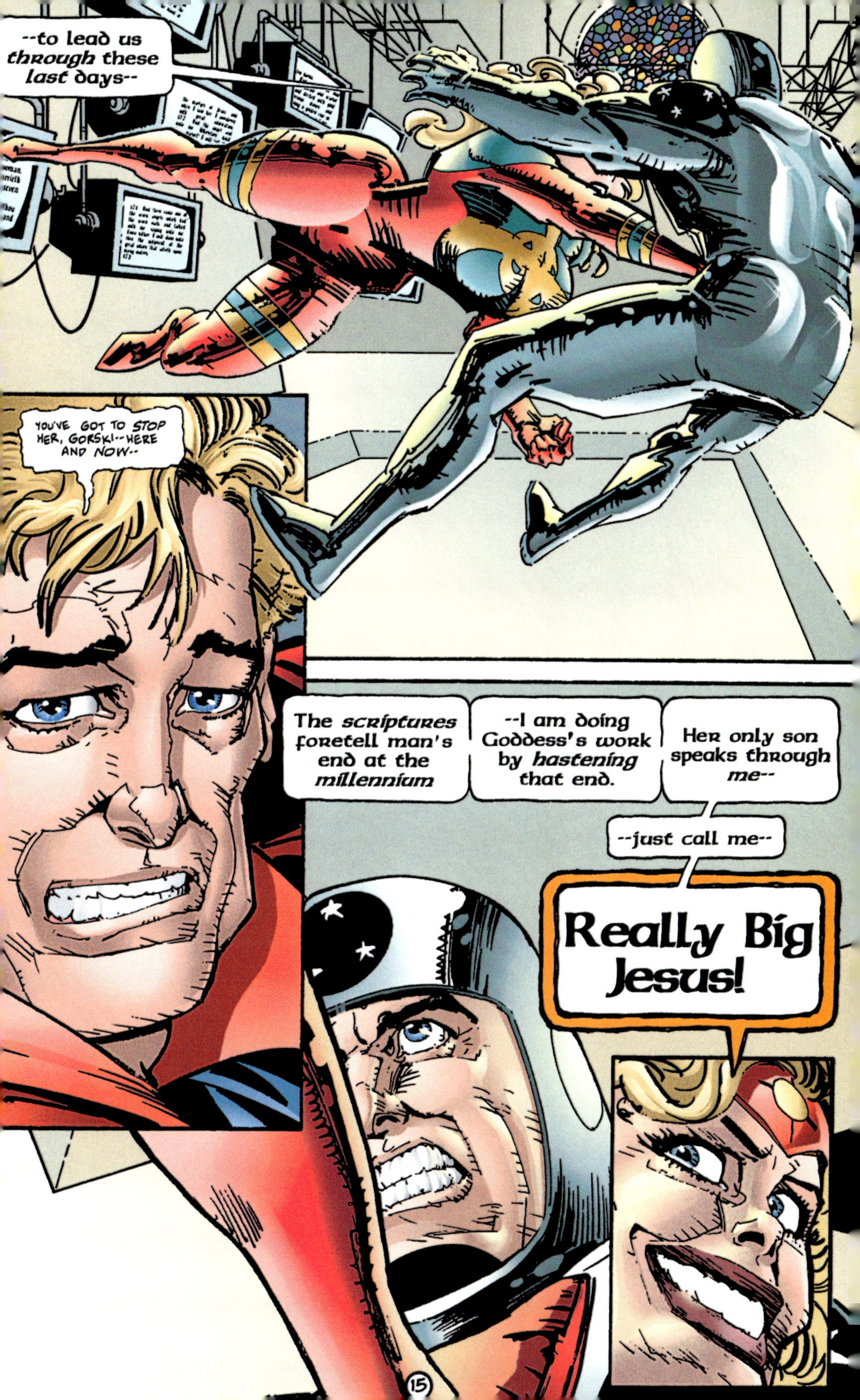
--to lead us through these last days--
YOU'VE GOT TO STOP HER, GORSKI--HERE AND NOW--
The scriptures foretell man's end at the millennium
--I am doing Goddess's work by hastening that end.
Her only son speaks through me--
--just call me--
Really Big Jesus!

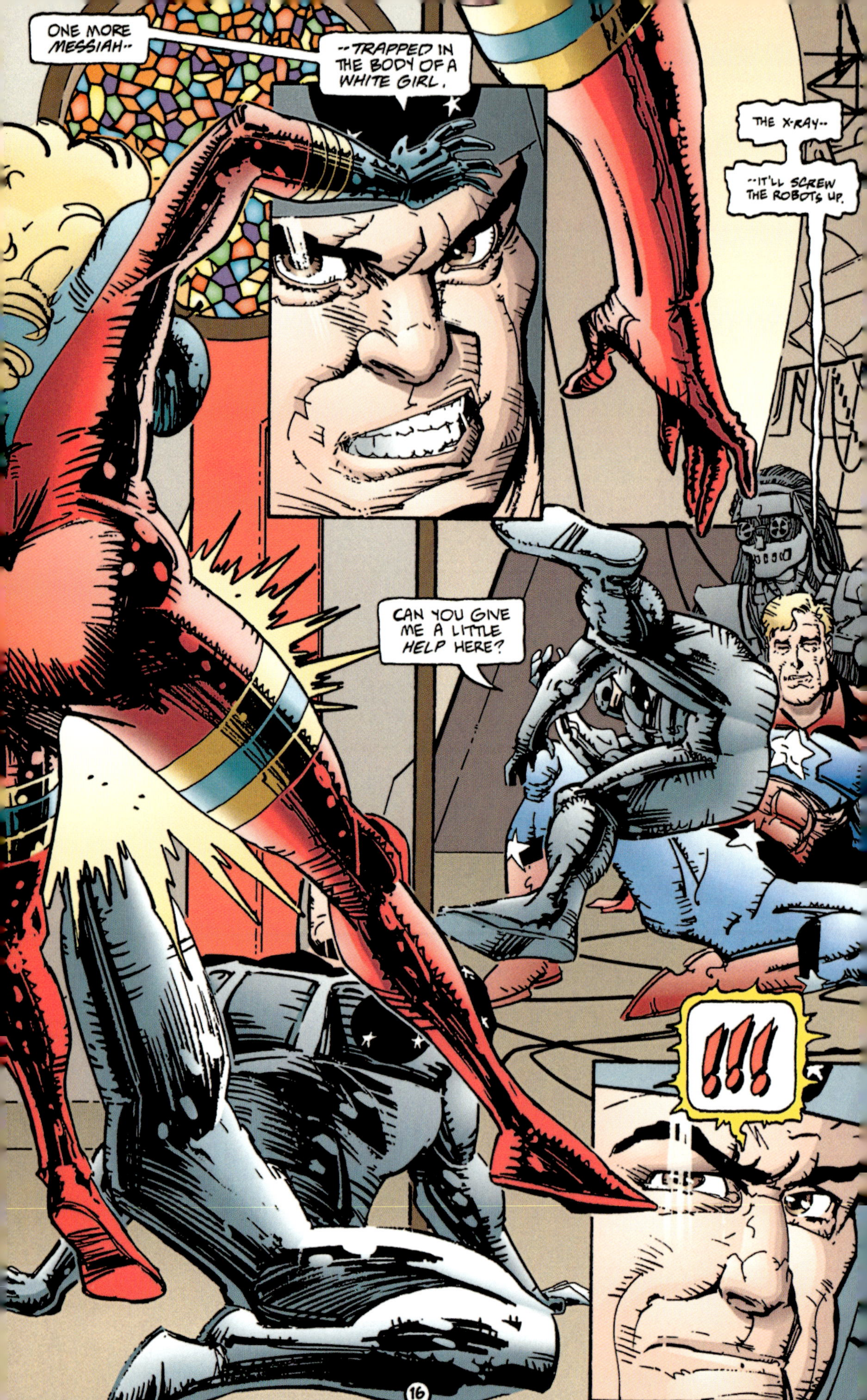
ONE MORE MESSIAH--
--TRAPPED IN THE BODY OF A WHITE GIRL.
THE X-RAY--
--IT'LL SCREW THE ROBOTS UP.
CAN YOU GIVE ME A LITTLE HELP HERE?
!!!

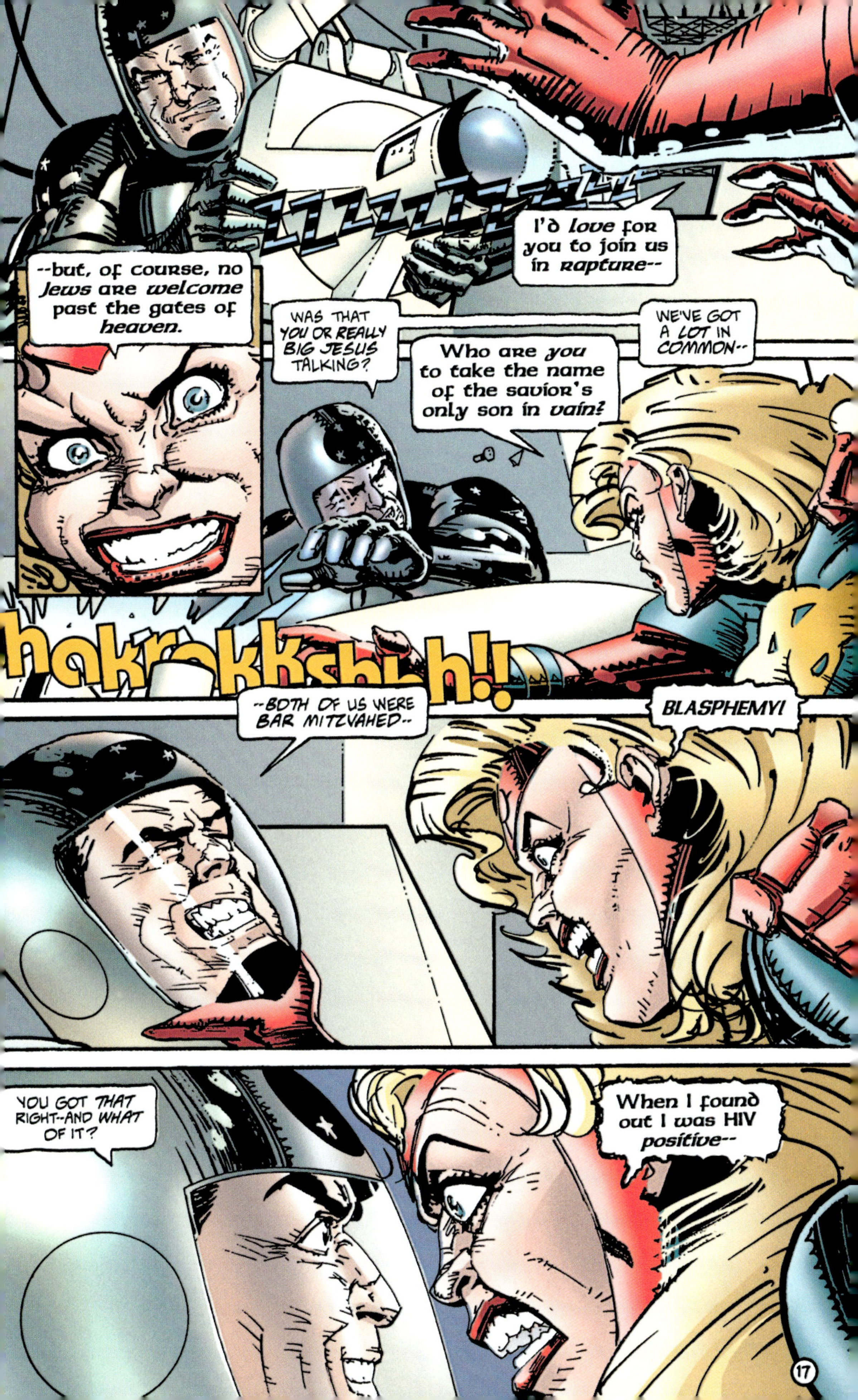
I'd love for you to join us in rapture--
--but, of course, no Jews are welcome past the gates of heaven.
WAS THAT YOU OR REALLY BIG JESUS TALKING?
Who are you to take the name of the savior's only son in vain?
WE'VE GOT A LOT IN COMMON--
hakrakkshhh!!
--BOTH OF US WERE BAR MITZVAHED--
BLASPHEMY!
YOU GOT THAT RIGHT--AND WHAT OF IT?
When I found out I was HIV positive--

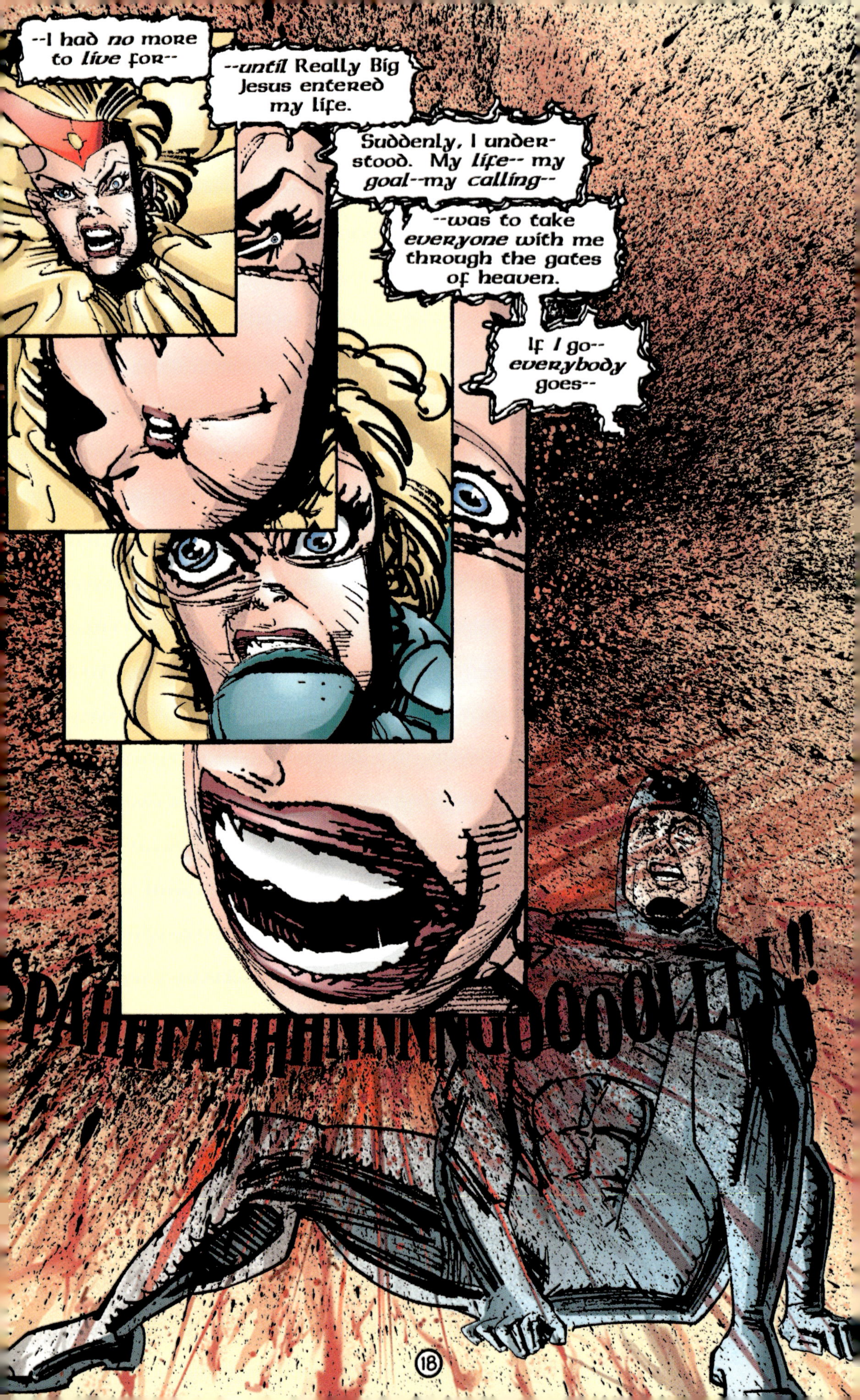
--I had *no* more to *live* for--
--*until* Really Big Jesus entered my life.
Suddenly, I understood. My *life*-- my *goal*--my *calling*--
--was to take *everyone* with me through the gates of heaven.
If *I* go-- *everybody* goes--

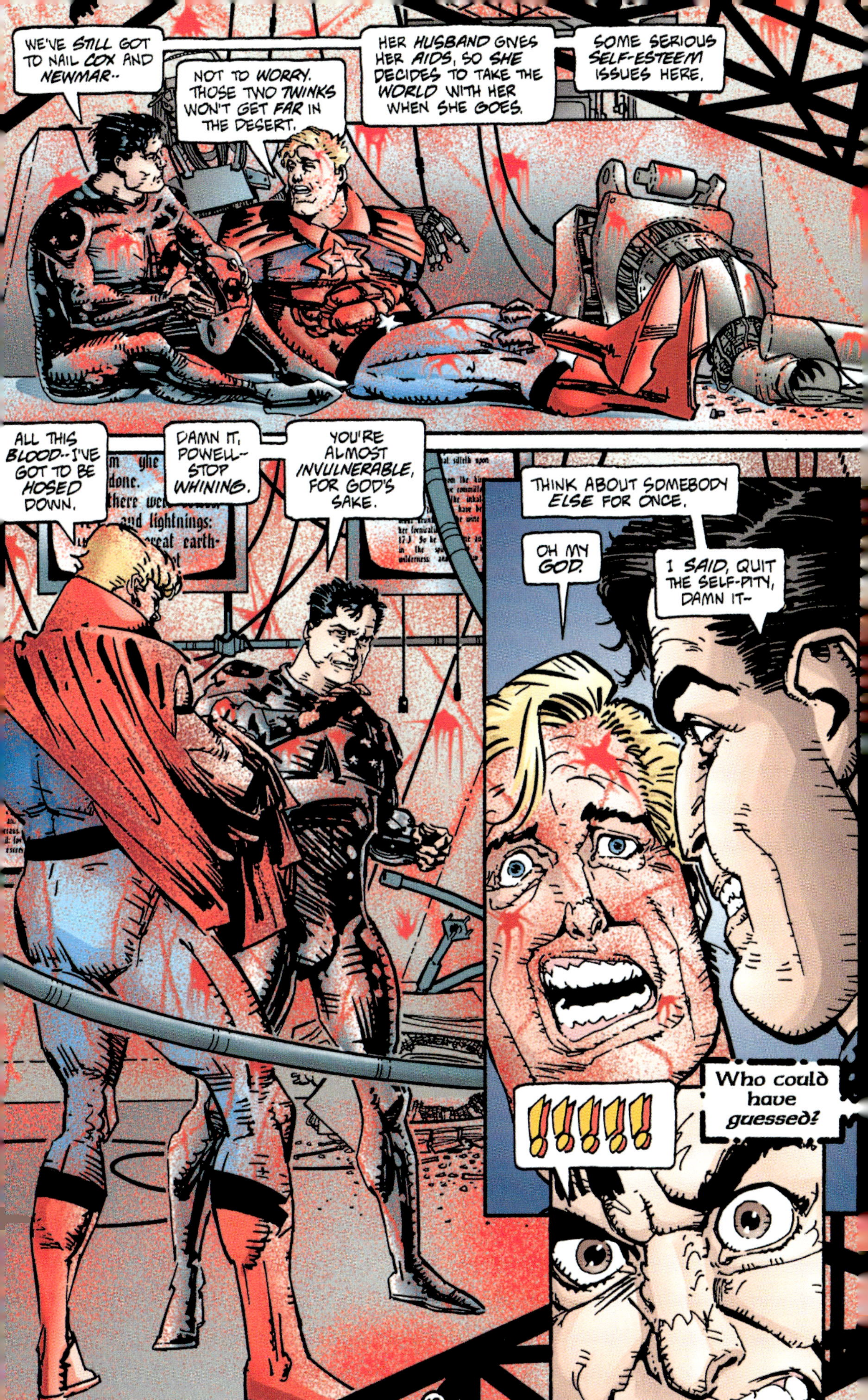
WE'VE STILL GOT TO NAIL COX AND NEWMAR--
NOT TO WORRY. THOSE TWO TWINKS WON'T GET FAR IN THE DESERT.
HER HUSBAND GIVES HER AIDS, SO SHE DECIDES TO TAKE THE WORLD WITH HER WHEN SHE GOES.
SOME SERIOUS SELF-ESTEEM ISSUES HERE.
ALL THIS BLOOD--I'VE GOT TO BE HOSED DOWN.
DAMN IT, POWELL-- STOP WHINING.
YOU'RE ALMOST INVULNERABLE, FOR GOD'S SAKE.
THINK ABOUT SOMEBODY ELSE FOR ONCE.
OH MY GOD.
I SAID, QUIT THE SELF-PITY, DAMN IT--
!!!!!
Who could have guessed?

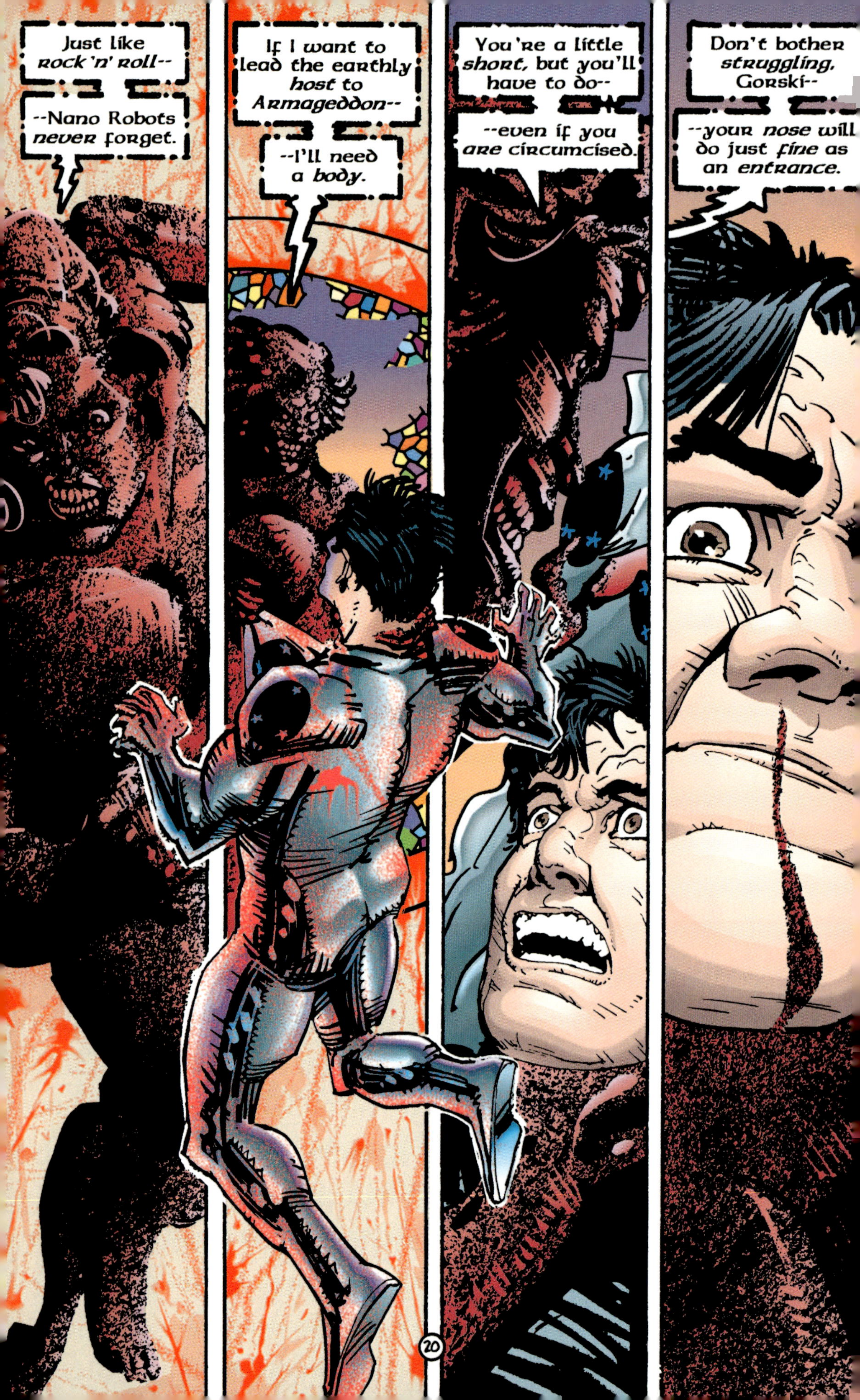
Just like rock 'n' roll--
--Nano Robots never forget.
If I want to lead the earthly host to Armageddon--
--I'll need a body.
You're a little short, but you'll have to do--
--even if you are circumcised.
Don't bother struggling, Gorski--
--your nose will do just fine as an entrance.
20

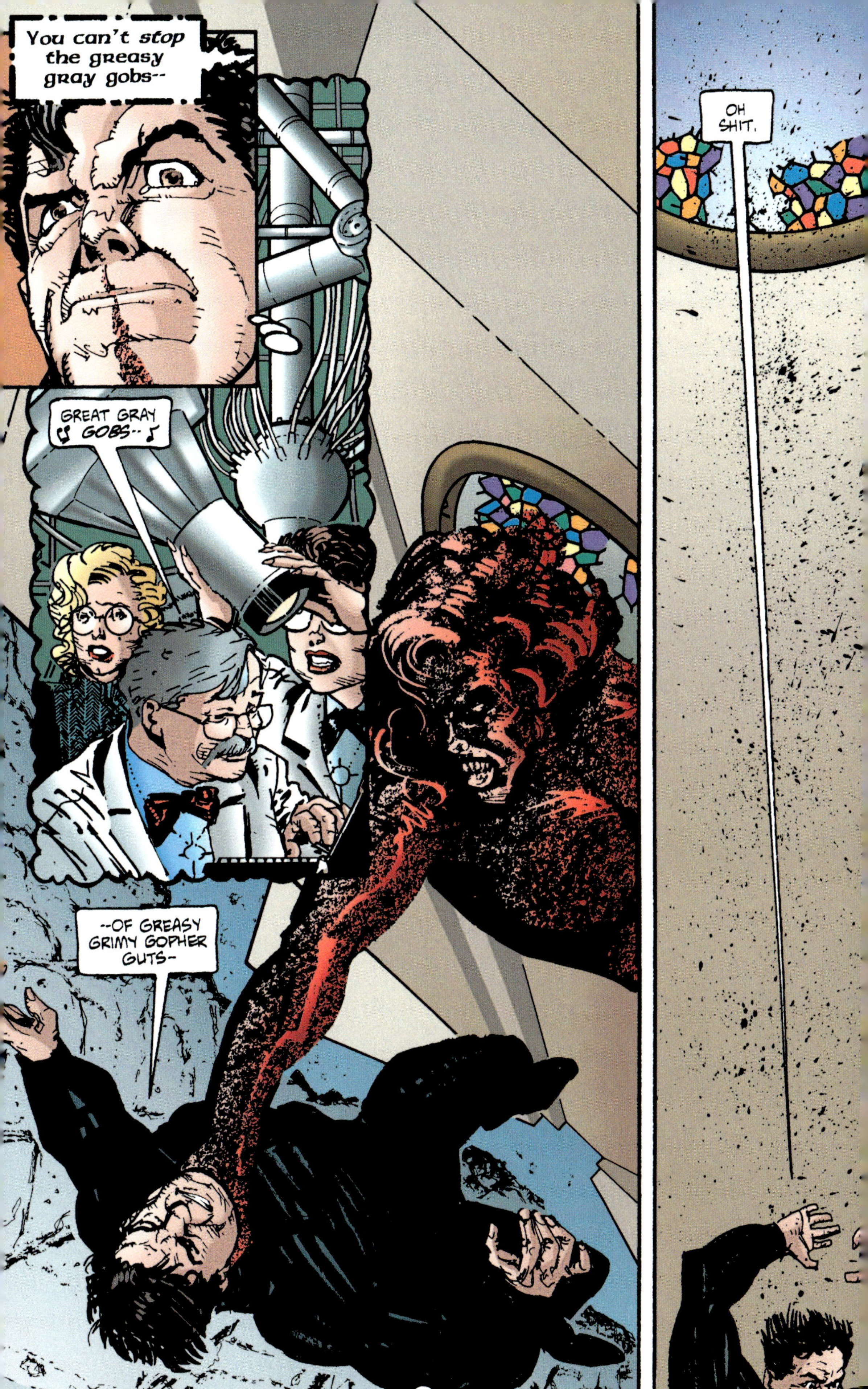

You can't stop the greasy gray gobs--
GREAT GRAY GOBS--
--OF GREASY GRIMY GOPHER GUTS-
OH SHIT.

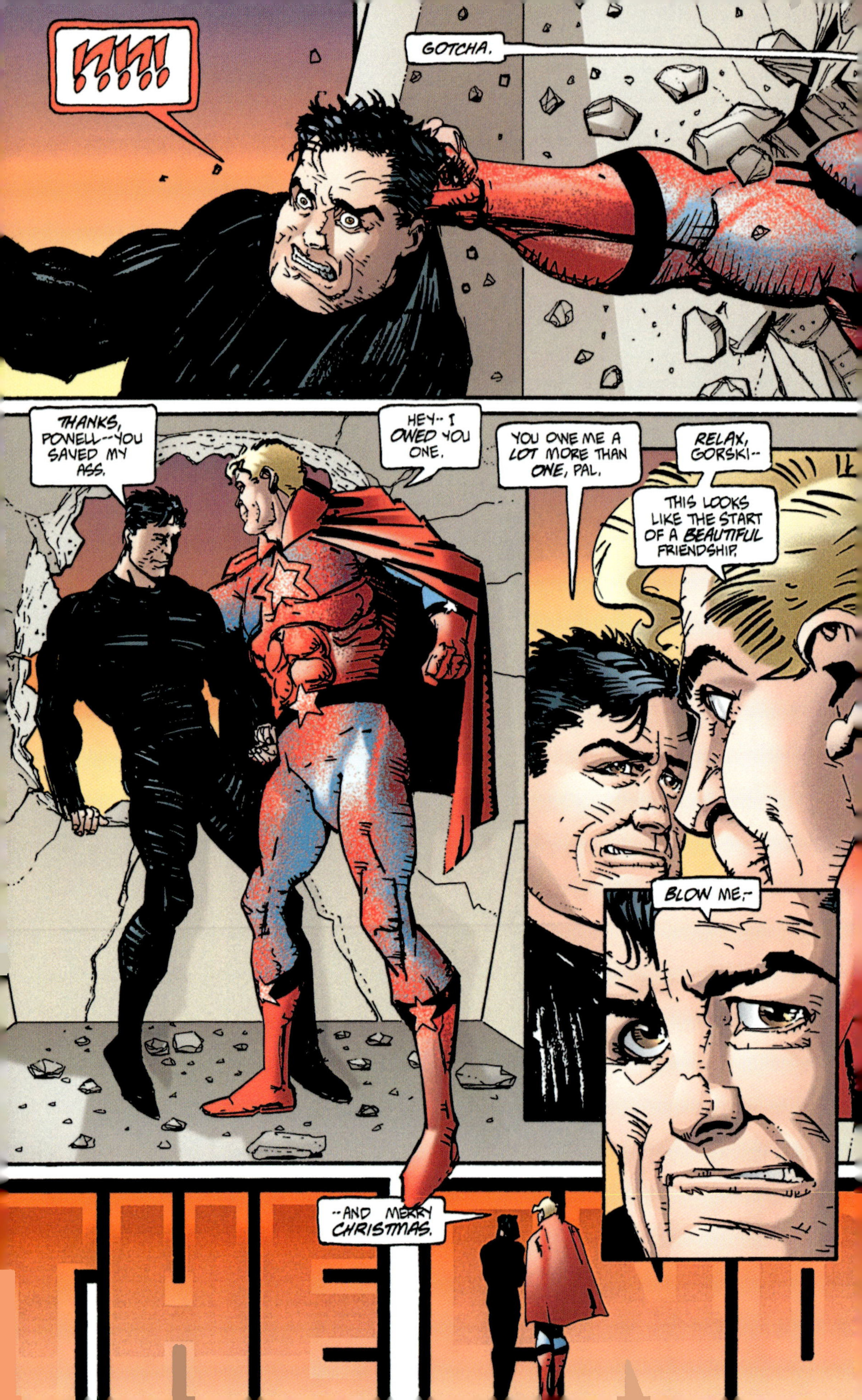
!?!?!
GOTCHA.
THANKS, POWELL--YOU SAVED MY ASS.
HEY-- I OWED YOU ONE.
YOU OWE ME A LOT MORE THAN ONE, PAL.
RELAX, GORSKI--
THIS LOOKS LIKE THE START OF A BEAUTIFUL FRIENDSHIP.
BLOW ME,-
--AND MERRY CHRISTMAS.
THE END

Sketchbook

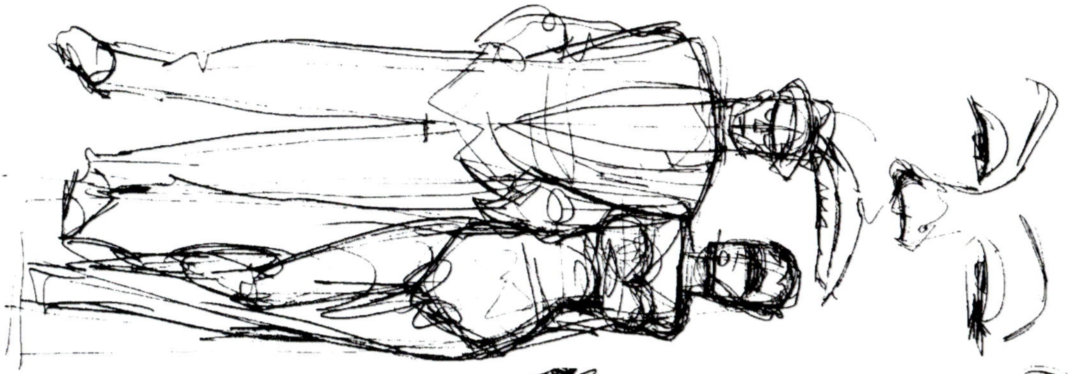

"Bad guys are not bad guys. Bad guys are heroes who lost."
—Howard Chaykin

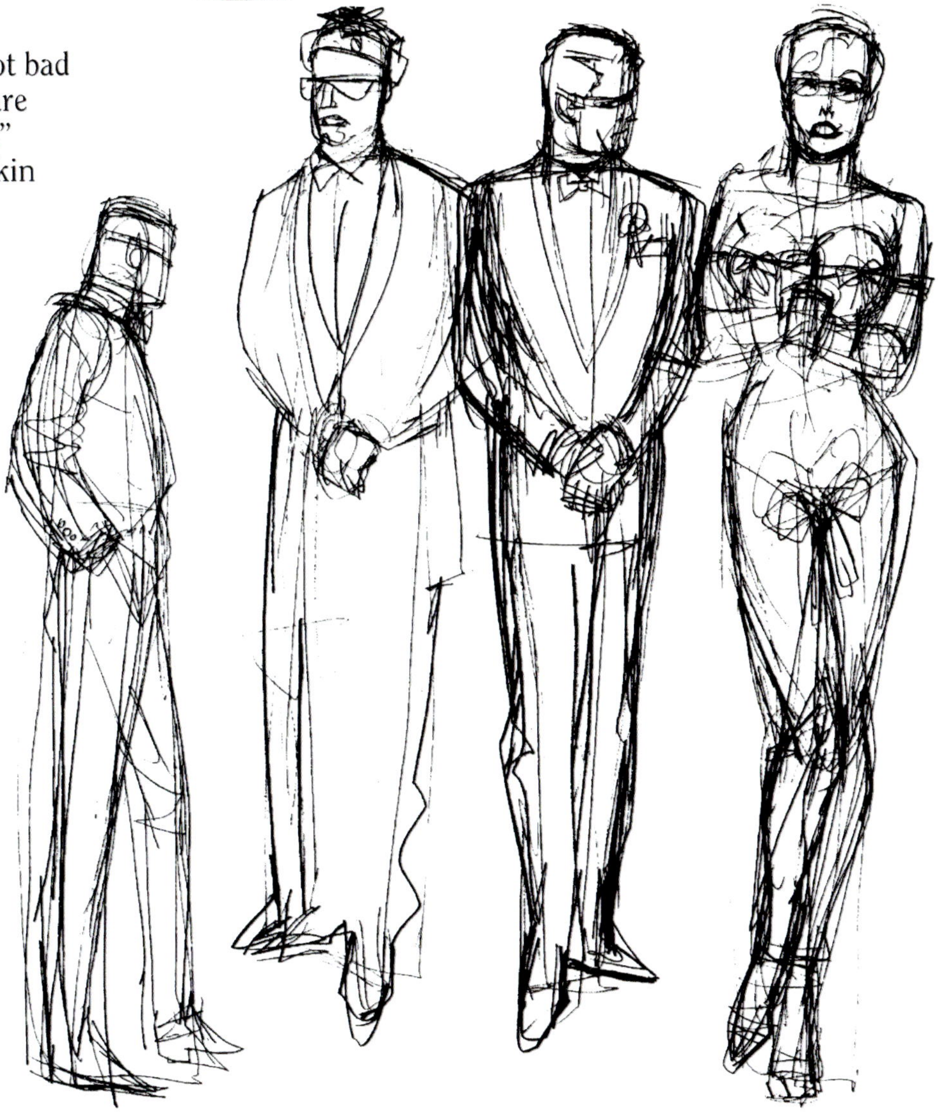

"I don't trust guys who think they're heroes. The guys who think they're heroes think they have our best interests at heart. What a bunch of psychos."
—Howard Chaykin

Sketchbook

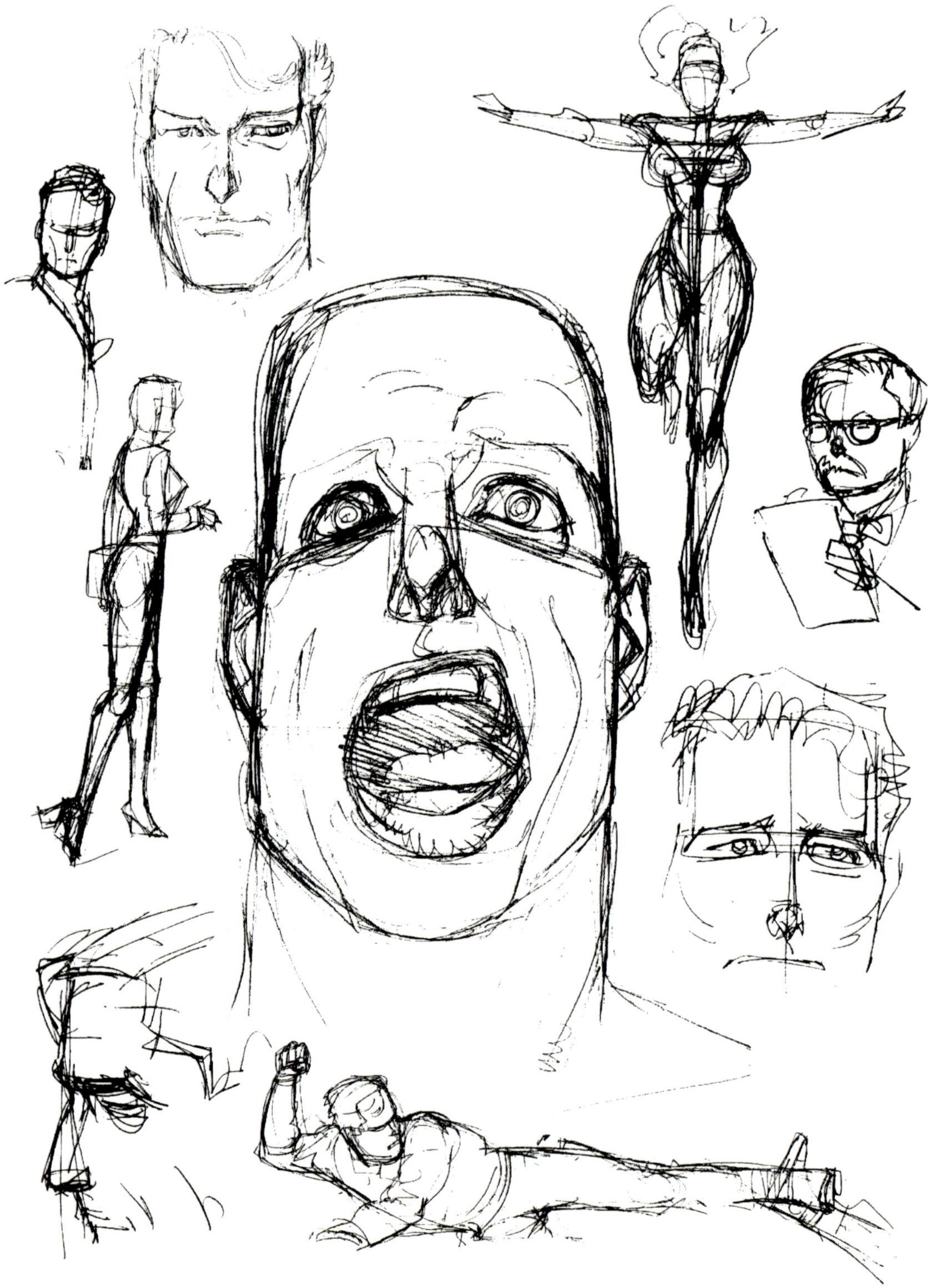

"The way comic book characters function is based on rules that have nothing to do with the way real people behave. I've always adjusted comic book reality to serve reality, as opposed to the other way around."
—Howard Chaykin

Sketchbook

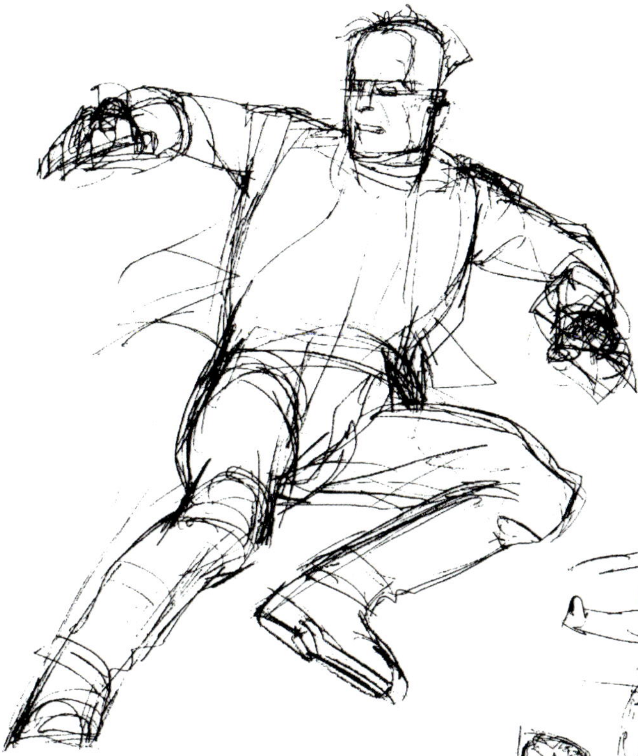

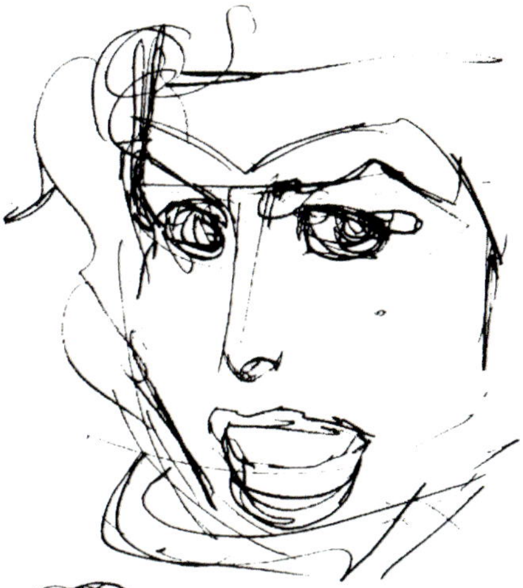

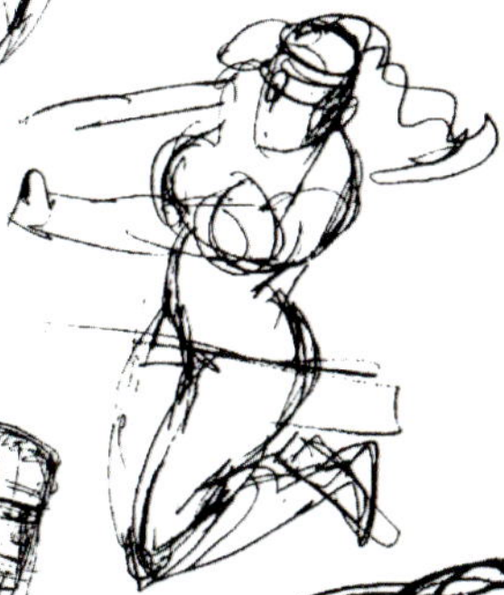

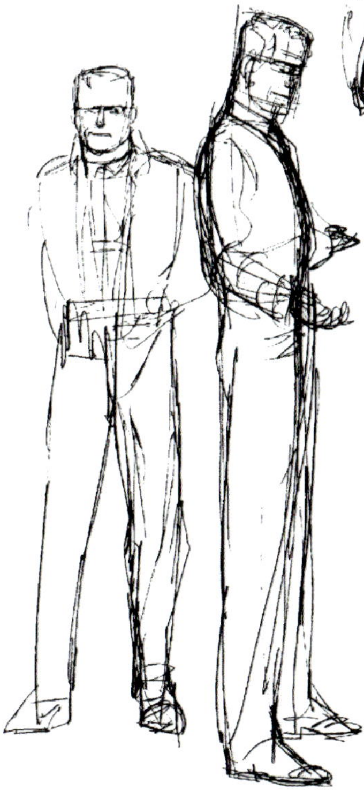

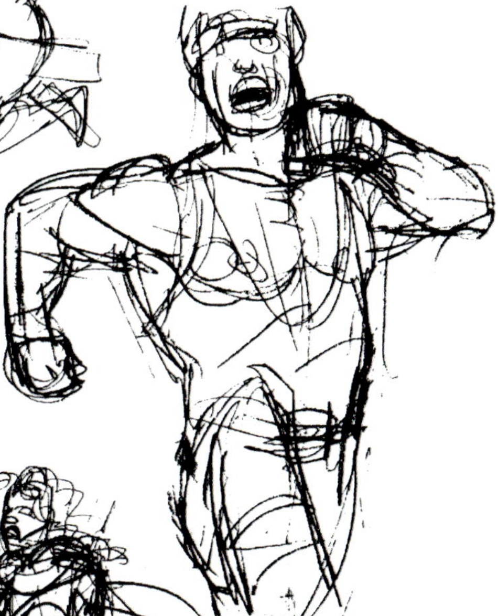

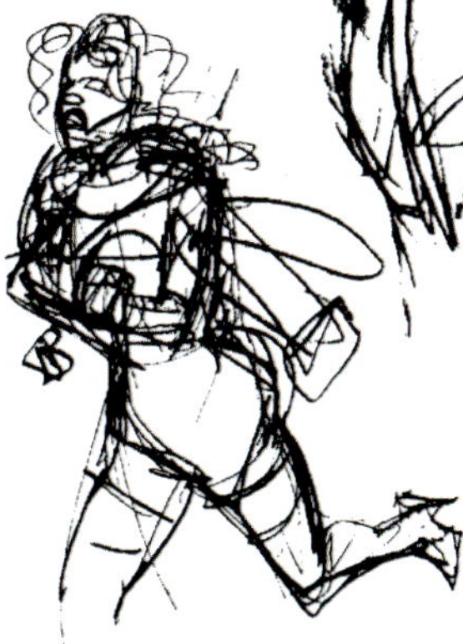

"*Power & Glory* is about looking like a hero, and being one. It's about how the guy who looks like a hero, and the guy who really is a hero learn from each other about how to be whole. Neither of them is really complete."

—Howard Chaykin

Sketchbook

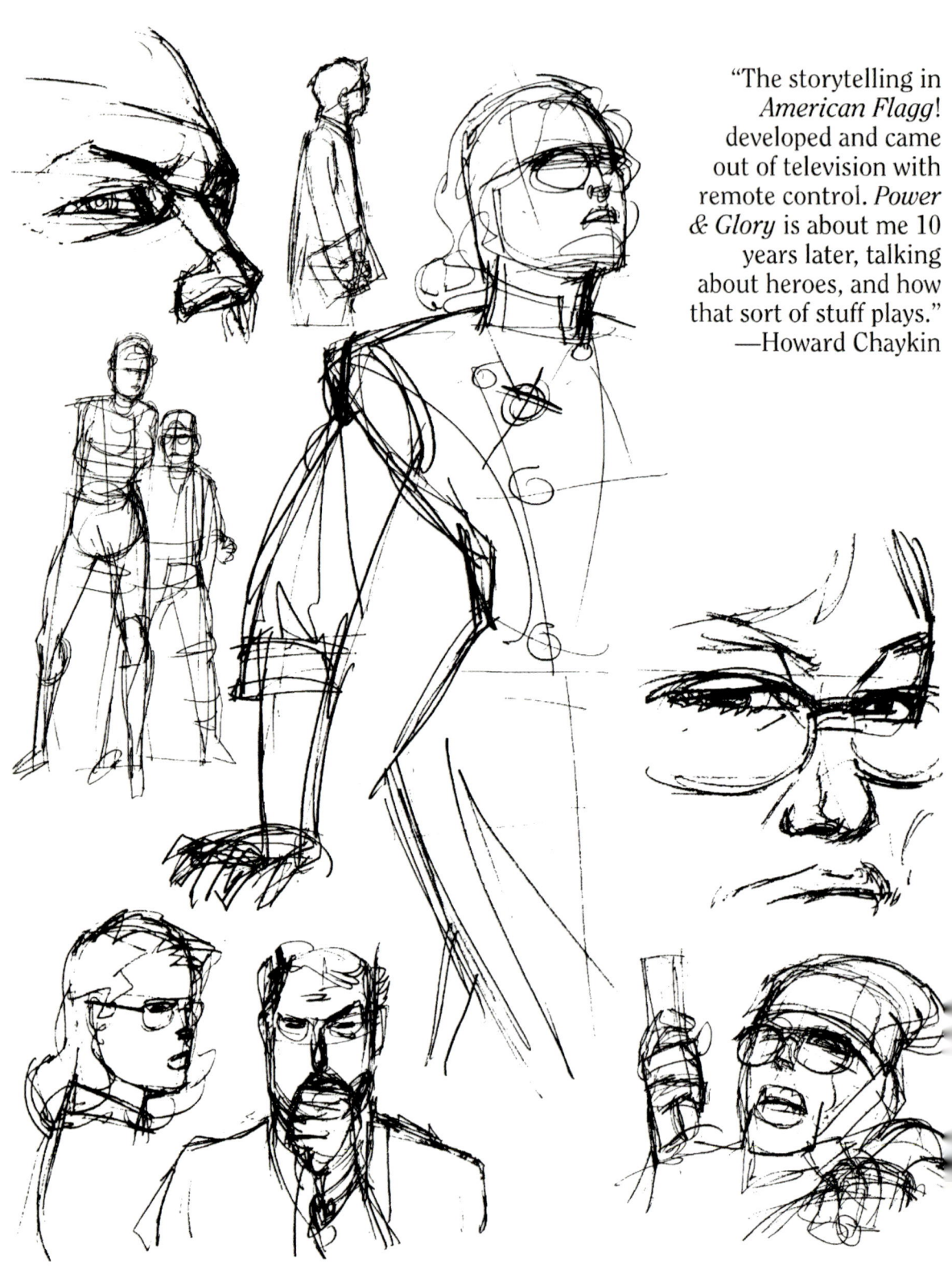

"The storytelling in *American Flagg!* developed and came out of television with remote control. *Power & Glory* is about me 10 years later, talking about heroes, and how that sort of stuff plays."
—Howard Chaykin

Sketchbook

"I believe in a higher moral state. For example, when I smoked cigarettes, my heroes smoked cigarettes. When I quit smoking, my heroes quit."
—Howard Chaykin

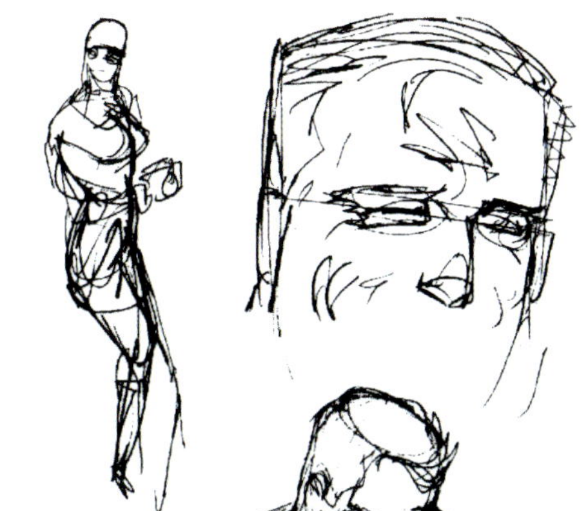

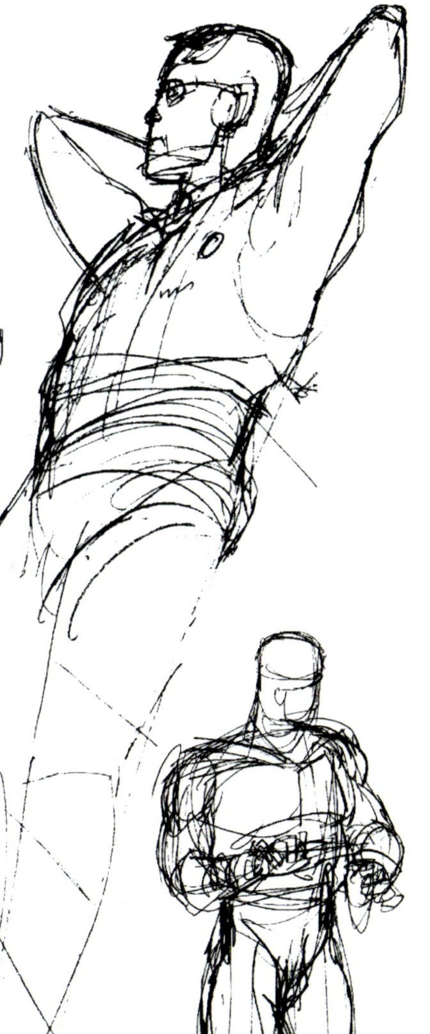

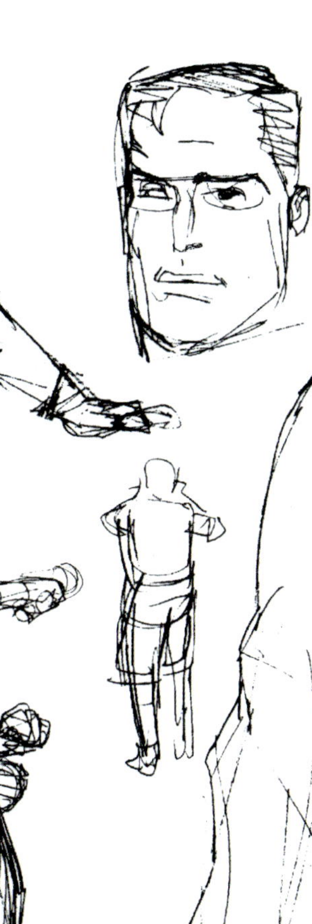

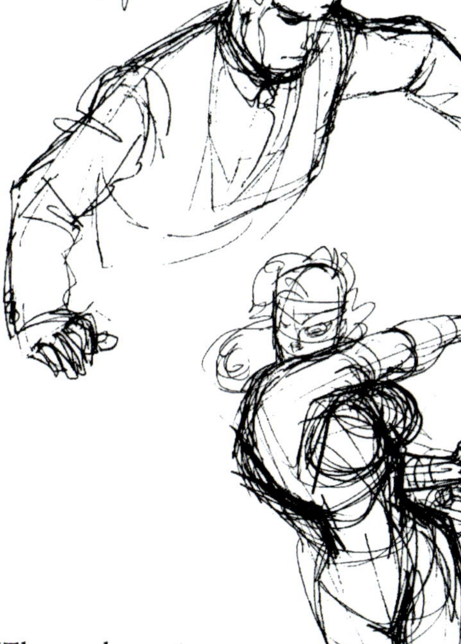

"These characters exist in the way I posit the real world. Malcolm LeStrange is in constant phone contact with M'Butu the villain of the book."
—Howard Chaykin

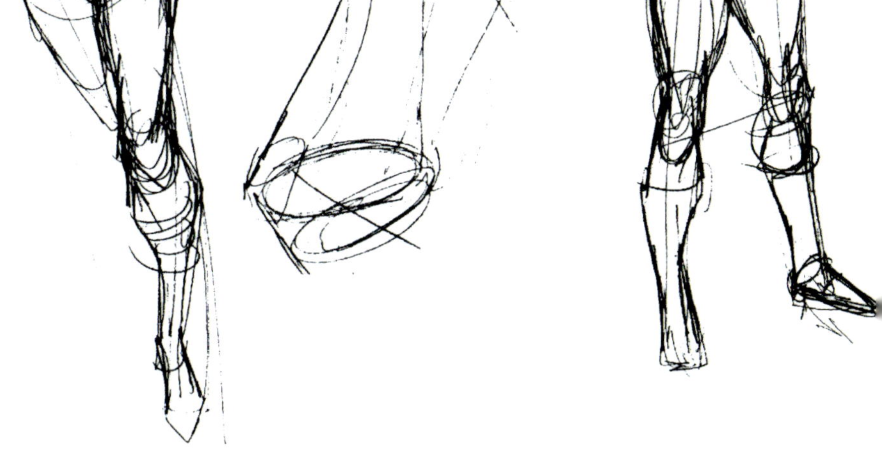

CURRENTLY AVAILABLE AND UPCOMING COLLECTIONS FROM DYNAMITE ENTERTAINMENT

Adventures of Red Sonja Vol. 1
Thomas, Thorne, More
SC ISBN: 1-933305-07-X

Adventures of Red Sonja Vol. 2
Thomas, Thorne, More
SC ISBN: 1-933305-12-6

Adventures of Red Sonja Vol. 3
Thomas, Thorne, More
SC ISBN: 1-933305-98-3

American Flagg! Definitive Collection Vol. 1
Chaykin
HC ISBN: 978-1-58240-983-2
SC part 1 ISBN: 978-1-5824-418-9
SC part 2 ISBN: 978-1-5824-419-6

Army of Darkness: Movie Adaptation
Raimi, Raimi, Bolton
SC ISBN: 1-933305-17-7

Army of Darkness: Ashes to Ashes
Hartnell, Bradshaw
SC ISBN: 0-9749638-9-5

Army of Darkness: Shop 'Till You Drop Dead
Kuhoric, Bradshaw, Greene
SC ISBN: 1-933305-26-6

Army of Darkness vs. Re-Animator
Kuhoric, Bradshaw, Greene
SC ISBN: 1-933305-13-4

Army of Darkness: Old School & More
Kuhoric, Sharpe
SC ISBN: 1-933305-18-5

Army of Darkness: Ash vs. The Classic Monsters
Kuhoric, Sharpe, Blanco
SC ISBN: 1-933305-41-X

Army of Darkness: From The Ashes
Kuhoric, Blanco
SC ISBN: 1-933305-77-0

Army of Darkness: The Long Road Home
Kuhoric, Raicht, Blanco
SC ISBN: 1-933305-86-X

Army of Darkness: Home Sweet Hell
Kuhoric, Raicht, Perez
SC ISBN: 1-60690-016-1

Army of Darkness: Hellbillies & Deadnecks
Kuhoric, Raicht, Cohn
SC ISBN: 1-60690-076-5

Army of Darkness vs. Xena Vol. 1: Why Not?
Layman, Jerwa, Montenegro
SC ISBN: 1-60690-008-0

Xena vs. Army of Darkness Vol. 2: What...Again?!
Jerwa, Serrano, Montenegro
SC ISBN: 1-60690-032-3

Bad Boy 10th Anniv. Edition
Miller, Bisley
HC ISBN: 1-933305-54-1

Borderline Vol. 1
Risso, Trillo
SC ISBN: 1-933305-05-3

Borderline Vol. 2
Risso, Trillo
SC ISBN: 1-933305-99-1

Borderline Vol. 3
Risso, Trillo
SC ISBN: 1-933305-22-3

The Boys Vol. 1: The Name of the Game
Ennis, Robertson
SC ISBN: 1-933305-73-8

The Boys Vol. 2: Get Some
Ennis, Robertson, Snejbjerg
SC ISBN: 1-933305-68-1

The Boys Vol. 3: Good For The Soul
Ennis, Robertson,
SC ISBN: 1-933305-92-4

The Boys Vol. 4: We Gotta Go Now
Ennis, Robertson,
SC ISBN: 1-606900-35-8

The Boys Definitive Edition Vol. 1
Ennis, Robertson,
HC ISBN: 1-933305-80-0

The Boys Definitive Edition Vol. 2
Ennis, Robertson,
HC ISBN: 1-606900-73-0

Classic Battlestar Galactica Vol. 1
Remender, Rafael
SC ISBN: 1-933305-45-2

Classic Battlestar Galactica Vol. 2: Cylon Apocalypse
Grillo-Marxuach, Rafael
SC ISBN: 1-933305-55-X

The Complete Dracula
Stoker, Moore, Reppion, Worley
SC ISBN: 1-60690-060-9

Dan Dare Omnibus
Ennis, Erskine
HC ISBN: 1-60690-027-7

Darkman vs. Army of Darkness
Busiek, Stern, Fry
SC ISBN: 1-933305-48-7

Darkness vs. Eva Vol. 1
Moore, Reppion, Salazar
SC ISBN: 1-933305-85-1

Dead Irons
Kuhoric, Alexander, Lee
HC ISBN: 1-606900-69-2

Dreadstar The Definitive Collection
Starlin
HC ISBN: 0-9749638-0-1
SC part 1 ISBN: 0-9749638-1-X
SC part 2 ISBN: 0-9749638-2-8

Dreadstar: The Beginning
Starlin
HC ISBN: 1-933305-10-X

Eduardo Risso's Tales of Terror
Risso, Trillo
SC ISBN: 1-933305-23-1

Garth Ennis' Battlefields Vol. 1: The Night Witches
Ennis, Braun
SC ISBN: 1-60690-028-5

Garth Ennis' Battlefields Vol. 2: Dear Billy
Ennis, Snejbjerg
SC ISBN: 1-60690-057-9

Garth Ennis' Battlefields Vol. 3: The Tankies
Ennis, Ezquerra
SC ISBN: 1-60690-075-7

Garth Ennis' The Complete Battlefields Vol. 1
Ennis, Braun, Snejbjerg, Ezquerra
HC ISBN: 1-60690-075-7

Hellshock
Lee, Chung
HC ISBN: 1-58240-505-0
SC ISBN: 1-58240-504-2

Highlander Vol. 1: The Coldest War
Oeming, Jerwa, Moder, Sharpe
HC ISBN: 1-933305-31-2
SC ISBN: 1-933305-34-7

Highlander Vol. 2: Dark Quickening
Jerwa, Laguna
SC ISBN: 1-933305-59-2

Highlander Vol. 3: Armageddon
Jerwa, Rafael
SC ISBN: 1-933305-67-3

Highlander Way Of The Sword
Krul, Rafael
SC ISBN: 1-933305-87-8

Jungle Girl Vol. 1
Cho, Murray, Batista
HC ISBN: 1-933305-78-9

Jungle Girl Vol. 2
Cho, Murray, Batista
HC ISBN: 1-60690-036-6

Just A Pilgrim
Ennis, Ezquerra
HC ISBN: 1-60690-003-X

Kid Kosmos: Cosmic Guard
Starlin
SC ISBN: 1-933305-02-9

Kid Kosmos: Kidnapped
Starlin
SC ISBN: 1-933305-29-0

The Lone Ranger Vol. 1: Now & Forever
Matthews, Cariello, Cassaday
HC ISBN: 1-933305-39-8
SC ISBN: 1-933305-40-1

The Lone Ranger Vol. 2: Lines Not Crossed
Matthews, Cariello, Cassaday, Pope
HC ISBN: 1-933305-66-5
SC ISBN: 1-933305-70-3

The Lone Ranger Vol. 3: Scorched Earth
Matthews, Cariello, Cassaday
HC ISBN: 1-60690-031-5
SC ISBN: 1-60690-041-2

The Man With No Name Vol. 1: Saints and Sinners
Gage, Dias
SC ISBN: 1-60690-012-9

Masquerade Vol. 1
Ross, Hester, Paul
SC ISBN: 1-60690-065-X

Mercenaries Vol. 1
Reed, Salazar
SC ISBN: 1-933305-71-1

Monster War
Golden, Chin, more
SC ISBN: 1-933305-30-4

New Battlestar Galactica Vol. 1
Pak, Raynor
HC ISBN: 1-933305-33-9
SC ISBN: 1-933305-34-7

New Battlestar Galactica Vol. 2
Pak, Raynor
HC ISBN: 1-933305-53-3
SC ISBN: 1-933305-49-5

New Battlestar Galactica Vol. 3
Pak, Raynor, Lau
HC ISBN: 1-933305-58-4
SC ISBN: 1-933305-57-6

New Battlestar Galactica Complete Omnibus V1
Pak, Raynor, Jerwa, Lau
SC ISBN: 1-606900-90-0

New Battlestar Galactica: Zarek
Jerwa, Batista
SC ISBN: 1-933305-50-9

New Battlestar Galactica: Season Zero Vol. 1
Jerwa, Herbert
SC ISBN: 1-933305-81-9

New Battlestar Galactica: Season Zero Vol. 2
Jerwa, Herbert
Mass SC ISBN: 1-606900-17-X
Direct SC ISBN: 1-606900-18-8

New Battlestar Galactica Origins: Baltar
Fahey, Lau
SC ISBN: 1-933305-88-6

New Battlestar Galactica Origins: Adama
Napton, Lau
SC ISBN: 1-606900-15-3

New Battlestar Galactica Origins: Starbuck & Helo
Fahey, Lau
SC ISBN: 1-606900-38-2

New Battlestar Galactica: Ghosts
Jerwa, Lau
SC ISBN: 1-606900-29-3

Essential Painkiller Jane Vol 1
Quesada, Palmiotti, Leonardi, more
SC ISBN: 1-933305-97-5

Painkiller Jane Vol. 1: The Return
Quesada, Palmiotti, Moder
SC ISBN: 1-933305-42-8

Painkiller Jane Vol. 2: Everything Explodes
Quesada, Palmiotti, Moder
SC ISBN: 1-933305-65-7

Painkiller Jane vs. Terminator
Palmiotti, Raynor
SC ISBN: 1-933305-84-3

Power & Glory
Chaykin
SC ISBN: 1-933305-06-1

Project Superpowers Chapter 1
Ross, Krueger, Paul, Sadowski
HC ISBN: 1-933305-91-6
TPB ISBN: 1-60690-014-5

Raise The Dead
Moore, Reppion, Petrus
HC ISBN: 1-933305-56-8

Red Sonja She-Devil With a Sword Vol. 1
Oeming, Carey, Rubi
HC ISBN: 1-933305-36-3
SC ISBN: 1-933305-11-8

Red Sonja She-Devil With a Sword Vol. 2: Arrowsmiths
Oeming, Rubi, more
HC ISBN: 1-933305-44-4
SC ISBN: 1-933305-43-6

Red Sonja She-Devil With a Sword Vol. 3: The Rise of Kulan Gath
Oeming, Rubi, more
HC ISBN: 1-933305-51-7
SC ISBN: 1-933305-52-5

Red Sonja She-Devil With a Sword Vol. 4: Animals & More
Oeming, Homs, more
HC ISBN: 1-933305-64-9
SC ISBN: 1-933305-63-0

Red Sonja She-Devil With a Sword Vol. 5: World On Fire
Oeming, Reed, Homs
HC ISBN: 1-933305-89-4
SC ISBN: 1-933305-90-8

Red Sonja She-Devil With a Sword Vol. 6: Death
Marz, Ortega, Reed, more
HC ISBN: 1-933305-89-4
SC ISBN: 1-933305-90-8

Red Sonja She-Devil With a Sword Vol. 7: Born Again
Marz, Ortega, Reed, more
HC ISBN: 1-60690-010-2
SC ISBN: 1-60690-011-0

Red Sonja vs. Thulsa Doom Vol. 1
David, Lieberman, Conrad
SC ISBN: 1-933305-96-7

Savage Red Sonja: Queen of the Frozen Wastes
Cho, Murray, Homs
HC ISBN: 1-933305-37-1
SC ISBN: 1-933305-38-X

Red Sonja: Travels
Marz, Ortega, Thomas, more
SC ISBN: 1-933305-20-7

Sword of Red Sonja: Doom of the Gods (Red Sonja vs. Thulsa Doom 2)
Lieberman, Antonio
SC ISBN: 1-933305-76-2

Savage Tales of Red Sonja
Marz, Gage, Ortega, more
SC ISBN: 1-60690-081-1

Scout Vol. 1
Truman
SC ISBN: 1-933305-95-9

Scout Vol. 2
Truman
SC ISBN: 1-933305-60-6

Sherlock Holmes Vol. 1: The Trial of Sherlock Holmes
Moore, Reppion, Campbell
HC ISBN: 1-606900-58-7

Six From Sirius
Moench, Gulacy
SC ISBN: 1-933305-03-7

Street Magik
Lieberman, McCarthy, Buchemi
SC ISBN: 1-933305-47-9

Super Zombies
Guggenheim, Gonzales, Rubi
HC ISBN: 1-60690-067-6

Terminator: Infinity
Furman, Raynor
SC ISBN: 1-933305-74-6

Terminator: Revolution
Furman, Antonio
SC ISBN: 1-606900-30-7

Witchblade: Shades of Gray
Moore, Reppion, Segovia, Geovani
SC ISBN: 1-933305-72-X

Xena Vol. 1: Contest of Pantheons
Layman, Neves
SC ISBN: 1-933305-35-5

Xena Vol. 2: Dark Xena
Layman, Champagne, Salonga
SC ISBN: 1-933305-61-4

Zorro Vol. 1: Year One Trail of the Fox
Wagner, Francavilla
HC ISBN: 1-60690-019-6
TPB ISBN: 1-606900-13-7